Who Is Shayla Hacker

EVAN KILGORE

✝

WHO IS SHAYLA HACKER

BLEAK HOUSE BOOKS
MADISON | WISCONSIN

Published by Bleak House Books
a division of Big Earth Publishing
923 Williamson St.
Madison, WI 53703
www.bleakhousebooks.com

©2007 by Evan Kilgore

This is a work of fiction. Any similarities to people or places, living or dead, is purely coincidental.

ISBN 13 (cloth): 978-1-932557-36-7

Library of Congress Cataloging-in-Publication Data has been applied for.

Printed in the United States of America

11 10 09 08 07   1 2 3 4 5 6 7 8 9 10

For my parents, Dave and Leigh,
and my brother, Chris.

Acknowledgements:

There are so many people without whom this book would never have been possible. My parents raised me on stories of all kinds and supported me in my every creative endeavor. For that, I owe them an entire lifetime of gratitude. My brother's prolific body of work and boundless creativity inspired and intimidated me into pressing on with my own projects even when I felt like shoving them in a drawer and forgetting all about them.

Julie Kuczynski at Bleak House Books was, I guess, the first to lift this particular story from the pile of manuscripts deposited at their door every day, and from there, the scarily-smart and end-lessly energetic Alison Janssen helped to shape it from the ramblings of a madman to something resembling a coherent story.

Both Alison and Bleak House's Benjamin LeRoy have been incredible in not only getting the book out there and holding a first-timer's hand through the Neverland of the publishing industry, but also in taking a chance on a 20-year-old with no credentials and little more than a shot-in-the-dark query letter to his name.

To them, to the gang of amazing friends at USC, and to my family—it is because of you that I wake up and write every day. The scary voices in my head are also involved.

Chapter 1

Gregory Klein watched the children fight over a rubber ball in the street. A Ford Explorer swerved to avoid them, and the driver leaned out the window to give them a piece of his mind. He was a short, pudgy man with a dirty rag wrapped around his head. Gregory thought he looked sad. Maybe he was coming from a funeral. Or maybe he had just spent the day alone.

Gregory could identify with that.

And so it was that he found himself picking up the phone. He had no idea who he was going to call. Most of his friends were out of town for the holiday weekend, and his family was so far away that the only thing on their minds would be how much he was spending to beam his voice to their ears.

He looked at the handset. It was dirty, smudged from a dozen different fingers at a party that shouldn't have happened. It had been Lupe's idea. Lupe the bane of his existence. The reason he was okay with being single for the rest of his life. He hadn't found out until the next morning that she'd gone home with not one, but two different men that night. The next morning, she'd interrupted him with a call at work. He'd thought something must be wrong, but she just wanted to know where he kept the maple syrup.

Gregory tried to wipe one of the keys off and heard a noise from the speaker; he had pressed a nine. The five was also looking particularly grubby, so he pressed it a few times as well, and a couple of other keys, just for good measure.

Before he knew it, the phone was ringing, and then somebody was picking up on the other end. He waited for the obligatory *Hello*, the annoyed silence, and then the *click* that would come when whoever it was realized he'd forgotten to check the caller ID.

There was no *Hello*.

"Where am I?" The voice sounded old but not senile.

Gregory blinked at the receiver. He tried to stammer something, but nothing came out of his mouth. There was some kind of music in the background, only it didn't sound quite like anything he had ever heard before. It was familiar, reminiscent of something in the way modern techno remixes conjured up in Gregory's mind wistful memories of the songs they were butchering.

"It's cold here," the voice said. "But I'm glad you called. You're scaring me, but at least there's a you." There was a bark, an almost animal scream from somewhere nearby, and then a sigh. "I have to go," the voice said. "It was nice talking to you."

Then came the *click*. After ten seconds, the receiver started beeping, and Gregory jumped and replaced it in its cradle.

He had no idea that his life had just changed forever.

Jackie Savage liked it when the teacher told them all to read, because then it got quiet and she could sit and listen to the wind. It gently toyed with the thicketed forests of cornstalks around the edges of the playground. All too often, the sigh of rustling husks fell away beneath the shouts and laughter of the younger kids on the swings and the merry-go-rounds, but today, the charcoal sky had opened up at lunchtime, and the slide stood empty and slick with buckets of rain.

Cradling her chin in her hands, Jackie propped her elbows on Charles Dickens and stared out at the warm, fat droplets splattering in the mud. *It was a day like this*, she thought, and then she sensed Ms. Breyer coming toward her and she turned and pretended to read.

"If you spent more time in your books and less in your thoughts, you might be better prepared for our class discussions, Miss Savage," Ms. Breyer told her.

Jackie looked up from her book and nodded. Her mind was everywhere but here.

That afternoon, five minutes after the bell had dismissed the final class of the day, Jackie got into her brother's car and waited for him to reappear. He did this sometimes. He would never tell anyone where he had been, but he was known to stay away for fifteen, twenty, sometimes forty minutes. Then he would just climb out from behind some bush and smile and nobody would dare say anything about it.

Today was different. Jackie waited an hour. The rain got a little lighter and then stopped altogether. She got out of the car and walked around the parking lot a few times. Ms. Breyer came out and dumped a stack of old books in the trunk of her bronze Tercel. She paused on her way back to the sidewalk for her purse and frowned at Jackie.

"Everything okay, Jackie?" she asked.

Jackie shrugged. "Just waiting for a ride." She saw the worry flash across the teacher's face, but it was gone almost as quickly as it had come. *She doesn't want to scare me*, Jackie thought.

"Well," Ms. Breyer said "you could probably use the time to catch up on your reading. Unless you're going to tell me that you finished the book already."

Jackie smiled and nodded, and after a few moments of hesitant silence, Ms. Breyer got in her car and drove away. Jackie watched it retreat down the road, kicking up sprays of rain behind its tires. The glow of the taillights disappeared, and then she began to feel cold and very alone. It was situations like these that she imagined when she read with a flashlight well into the night. Then, the fear felt good—exciting. Not like now.

There were no other cars in the parking lot. Jackie went back to her brother's '72 Nova and walked all around it one more time, wondering if he was playing some kind of joke. He had done that to her once, too—waited beneath the car for twenty minutes until she got bored and got out. Then he had snatched her ankles and made noises like a monster. She had squealed, but then, she had only been eight years old.

Walker was not under the car, and the gravel beneath the Nova was dry. It had been here since before the rain started, since just after lunchtime.

Don't panic, Jackie told herself. There was going to be a reasonable explanation for this.

By nightfall, Jackie was scared. She did not know why she had waited at the school the whole time. It was creepy after dark. There were only a few lights on here and there—one in the hallway, illuminating row upon row of deserted lockers; and one fluorescent bulb suspended over the office entrance. It flickered now and then as the wind shook it.

She was sitting on the hood. She had gotten inside a couple of times when the rain had started up again, but the windows always fogged up, and anyway, she felt like she couldn't hear anything from in there. If Walker called for her, she wanted to know.

Walker never called.

Her digital sports watch read ten fifteen. That meant it was close to nine. She had never learned how to set it, because to tell the truth, she had never liked it very much. But Mrs. Eubank had given it to her for her birthday, and the summer after that, Mrs. Eubank had suffered a violent death in a fire, and Jackie felt guilty for wanting to throw the watch away.

She was going to be late for Dad's nightly call. He would be worried. But if she were there, if she answered, what would she tell him when he asked to speak with Walker? He'd think she was imagining things again, and that would only make him mad.

She circled around the school one last time, but it was even worse behind, in the playground. There were no lights back there, and only the sound of water rolling down cornstalks. The nearest house was a half-mile away. She could see the lights across the field, but that didn't mean anything. That was Winton Keener's place, and he was gone more often than he was there. He always left the place lit up to scare off the burglars, so it was impossible to tell if anyone was home.

Still, she had to try.

Of course, if Walker came back, he would be mad that she had left the Nova unlocked. She went back and sat on the hood for another fifteen minutes, but it was clear now that he was not coming. Something was terribly wrong.

Terry Young put in a new coffee filter and started the water boiling. Then he sat on the kitchen counter and put his face in his hands and cried.

One of the guests walked in and gave a little start. Terry rubbed his eyes and tried to pretend as though he had only been tired, but he could see by his reflection in the windowpane that his eyes were far too red for that.

It was Mrs. Newell. She was halfway to the handbag she had left on the table that afternoon when she walked in and threw her arms around Vicki. Her lipstick had probably gone stale, or perhaps it was time for her medication again. Her eyes were riveted on Terry's face. When he cleared his throat, she awkwardly moved one hand to brush a silver strand of hair from her forehead.

She was flustered. She opened the bag, rooted through it, and muttered something about cough drops. Terry said nothing to her. They had been neighbors most of his life. She had regularly checked his family's mail while they were living in South America, yet to Terry, she had always felt like a stranger.

He poured more water in the coffee and then sat and tried to look past himself to the darkened backyard beyond the window over the sink.

Mrs. Newell extracted a hand mirror from her purse and made

it almost all the way to the door before she stopped and turned around.

"Terry," she said very delicately, "is something the matter?"

He shook his head. "Nerves, Mrs. Newell." He wasn't going to have this conversation now—not with her, not the night before.

"Are you certain, my dear?" she asked.

He nodded, and after another few moments, she left. He hopped off the counter, poured himself a cup of coffee and went up the back stairs to the guest bedroom. He could still hear the murmur of voices downstairs, the faint rise and fall of ballroom music.

A strange feeling overtook him. He could close his eyes and imagine it was fifteen years ago and he was still a teenager, already in bed while his parents partied on into the night with their friends from down south.

He passed three or four hours up there. The commotion began to die down, and as the evening wore on, he went to the window and watched the guests depart in their Suburbans and Lincoln Towncars. They were all the same, dolled up in flowing pink dresses and elaborate tuxedo jackets.

A braying laugh filtered up from the front path, and Terry's skin crawled. Who were these people? Mostly Vicki's friends. No, mostly her parents' friends. He had never felt like he truly knew anyone here, and all of his childhood buddies were too cheap or too far away to make the trip.

He was in bed by the time he heard Vicki's feet on the stairs. He listened to her pad softly around the second floor, searching for him, until at last, there was a tap on the guestroom door.

"Terry?" Her voice was muffled, hesitant. "Are you in there?"

It frightened him how much he didn't want to answer. This was the woman with whom he was going to spend the rest of his life, starting tomorrow, and the revulsion he felt was enough to bring the tears back. He blinked them away and got up from the bed.

Vicki looked haggard. Her dress was rumpled, and there were a few smudges of cake where she had been clumsy and dropped crumbs at the dinner table. She smiled up at him, then let it fade. "What's the matter, sweetie?"

Because he could think of no other way to answer, he told her, "Nerves." It was a lie.

They spent an hour in front of a dying fire, surrounded by dirty dishes and shreds of wrapping paper. It had been the party for the acquaintances, the party for the guests who weren't guests at the real party.

Terry could sense that she was disappointed in him. Their conversation was light and superficial, the same way she had been talking to strangers the entire night. He felt her disapproval growing, and with it, his own sense of helplessness. Was this what it was going to be like for the next seventy years of his life? She would urge him to open up to her, and he would look back at her with blank hopelessness? For her, he had no words.

After a while, she said that she was tired. He kissed her on the cheek and she went upstairs to the master bedroom. He listened to her footsteps on the old wooden beams overhead until they stopped altogether and it was silent again.

He sat and watched the last glowing embers of the fire smolder to ash, and then he rose and went into the bathroom to mutilate himself.

There was something beautiful about blood on white porcelain. He stopped, set the knife on the counter, and went to get a disposable camera one of the guests had left behind. The blood had dried by the time he got back, though, gone brown and sticky.

He cried again and then bandaged himself up, rinsed off the knife, and left it in the dish drainer next to the cake plate. It ached when he walked, and he clung to that like a rock. It was something solid, something he could focus and hold onto.

Terry climbed upstairs, but when he reached the second floor, he kept climbing. He could hear his father's feet in his own footsteps, and with them the echoed laughter of the brothers and sisters he would never see again. Tomorrow, he was signing his life away. He was pledging himself to another human being. Why was he lonelier than ever?

It was warm in the attic, the way it had always been, even in the winter. Only one of the lights worked, and there were spider webs everywhere. He eased the trap door shut and then he sat on it and vomited into a hatbox his mother had brought back with her from Tibet. He had done it in there before; it smelled like lima beans.

He was deathly tired, but he couldn't sleep. He began opening old boxes and picking through papers he had written for high school, junior high, grade school. His father's guns were there, too, muzzles crumpling the pictures of ten-year-old Terry with a hunting rifle and a grin wide enough to cover his entire face. Happier times. Before his parents had brought him home and trapped him in this tiny town with his tiny *perfect life* for good.

Under the guns he found a drawing he had made in kindergarten, and then, at the very bottom, an old photograph of someone he didn't recognize. The paper was thin, dusty. He turned it over and squinted at the hand-written inscription on the back: *Hacker 19-?*

That was strange. He thought he had been through every box in this attic at one point or another, but he had never seen the picture before.

He finished off a bottle of cheap champagne and had nightmares about the face in the photo for the rest of the night. And then it was supposed to be the happiest day of his life.

As soon as Detective Joseph Malloy put down the telephone, it rang again. He hadn't realized he knew that many people in the department, but every five minutes another voice he had forgotten would greet him on the other end of the line.

He ducked his head out into reception, where Claire was stuffing something in the file cabinet, the way she had been doing for the last two decades. "Can you take my calls for a little bit?" he asked her. "I need to grab lunch."

She smiled and nodded at him. "Phone's been ringing off the hook, huh?"

"Don't tell anyone, but the last day on the job is the busiest you'll ever have."

"Not all of us are as popular as you."

"Just you wait."

He grabbed his coat and was almost out the door when the phone rang again. Claire caught up with him at the end of the hallway.

"Now the point about you answering the phone," he told her, "was that I wouldn't have to worry about it for thirty minutes."

"It's your wife," she said. "I thought you might want to talk to her."

Malloy paused. The elevator was three steps away. His stomach growled, but then his conscience kicked in and he turned and followed Claire back to the office. Jean had always hated it when his work came between them, and today, he didn't have any excuses.

Tinny music was lilting through the receiver when he picked it up, and as soon as he answered, he could hear Jean and some of her friends burst into a resounding rendition of *For He's a Jolly Good Fellow*. Malloy cracked a thin smile. That was Jean in a nutshell. Call him three hours before he would see her anyway to make a little gesture that, in truth, was more annoying than anything else. But it was sweet. He supposed he should just appreciate that she felt like expending the energy on him.

When she was done, she came on the line, all out of breath. "How's work, sweetie?" she asked. She didn't sound a day older than when they had taken their first ride on the ferry together, forty-eight years ago.

"Busy," he said. "I was just on my way to lunch."

"Oh." Not disappointed—she was too excited to be disappointed, and that touched him even more. "Okay, well, I'll let you go. I just wanted to say hi and to tell you that the Mulligans are going to be over this afternoon for drinks whenever you can extract yourself from that cave of an office you work in."

"Okay."

"Oh, and the people from the dealership called, and they've got the piece the factory left out. We can snap it right in on the dashboard—there's no need to take it in. I was going to pick it up this morning, but I didn't know if you had any questions or if you wanted to go."

"No, that's okay."

She chatted several minutes longer than there was any call for, and then, at last, they agreed to hang up. He flashed another smile at Claire on the way out and told her this time, he didn't want to hear from anyone until he had cleared at least two or three bites of lunch.

The cafeteria was bustling with the usual noontime crowd, and so he did not notice the strange man by the coffee cart until they were practically standing on top of each other. The man nudged Malloy lightly with an elbow and stuck out a hand when Joseph turned.

"Detective Malloy?" he said.

Malloy looked him up and down. Too cheaply dressed to be from Internal Affairs, but too expensive for insurance or reception. Warily, he took the man's hand before grabbing a tray and diving into the lunch line. "What do you need, son?" He shuddered at the sound of his own voice. Some of the guys had told him he should try using expressions like that, because they made him sound more his age. But he hated his age, almost as much as he hated sounding it.

"Detective, I'm Kelsey Robins. They just brought me out here from the city. I guess I'm going to be inhabiting your office for a while."

Malloy blinked. This was his replacement? Somehow, it wasn't what he had expected. Kelsey was thin, tall, a little awkward, but muscular where it counted, and as tan as a potato. He was too good for a small-town assignment like this one. He belonged off in vice or busting the drug lords at the downtown precinct.

"Hi, Mr. Robins." Malloy scooped a shrink-wrapped turkey sandwich off of the pile. "Nice to meet you."

"Oh, please—*Kelsey*. Hell, it's my first day and your last. There's no need to be formal."

They made their way to a table—the two of them—and all the while, Malloy was wondering how long he was going to have to deal with this guy. It was his last afternoon here, just under three hours before he could clock out forever. How long would it take for those three hours to pass?

Robins had grabbed a small fruit cup from the cafeteria line, and when he had finished it off, he sat back in his chair and stared intensely at Malloy for a few moments. "Look," he said, "it's been great meeting you. I'd heard quite a bit, and I was curious what kind of person I'd be stepping in for."

Malloy expelled a silent sigh of relief. So this was over. No more awkward half-conversations about the weather, or past cases; no advice from the seasoned veteran. He could just go back to enjoying his lunch and—

"But the reason I came down here . . ."

Stop, Malloy thought. He didn't want to hear any reasons. He didn't want there to be any reasons. Couldn't someone just say hi and then retire in peace?

"They forwarded me all of your active files," Kelsey was saying. He had a Palm Pilot out and was clicking through some notes he must have taken in the morning. "Most of them seem pretty straightforward. I mean, hell, nobody solves everything, right? Our department back in the city had seventeen open cases, and that was just from the past two years. But there was this one that kind of had me scratching my head. I thought maybe you could shed a little light on it?"

"Why didn't you stop by my office?" Malloy asked. *This is my lunch hour, for God's sake.*

"Oh, I tried. Claire—your receptionist—Claire said that you weren't seeing anyone else, and that you'd been busy on the phone all morning."

"Claire was right."

"So if you could just look at this one file . . .?"

Malloy sighed. He shouldn't have left the protection of his office. He should have stayed right there on the phone and sent Claire out to pick something up from Subway or Wendy's.

"I really don't know . . ." Malloy said, but Kelsey was already getting out a few folded pieces of paper.

"I don't think it'll take any time at all. I just couldn't find any information on it, and I thought you could point me in the right direction."

Kelsey flattened out one of the documents, and Malloy saw that it was a Xerox of a photograph. It had originally been in color, so the details were grainy and smudged, but when Malloy turned it around, he could pick out a young woman's delicate features and some kind of foliage in the background—probably a portrait studio's props.

When he looked back up, Kelsey was staring at him. Malloy shrugged. "So? Where's the rest?"

"Oh, that's it."

"What do you mean, that's it?"

"That's all there was. See, that's why I'm confused. It was in your files under the name Hacker, so, I mean, it didn't just fall from someone's corkboard. And normally I wouldn't bother you about something like this, only they're all telling me you and Mrs. Malloy are taking off with your RV before the end of the week and you won't even have a phone, so I thought I'd just see if you knew what this was while I still had the chance."

Malloy sighed. "Sorry, Mr. Robins. I have no idea."

"Kelsey, please." He smiled and took the paper back. His eyes flitted over it. "Okay, Detective Malloy. Sorry to bother you during your lunch break, and it was truly an honor to meet you." He pushed back from the table and stood, sticking out a hand.

Numbly, Malloy took it. Kelsey dropped a card on the table next to his empty fruit cup. "If you happen to remember anything about her, I'd love to hear the details. Here—you can keep the picture. We've made copies. I'd really like it if you—I mean, I'm just curious. Stuff like this always bugged the shit out of me. I'm a details guy, I guess." He sniffed and then nodded. "Have a good trip, Mr. Malloy. See you around, maybe."

Prick, Malloy thought. *A details guy, unlike this old fart who keeps bad files and lets things slip through the cracks.* And what the hell was with the picture, anyway? He couldn't remember ever opening a file for a woman named Hacker, and her face had not looked remotely familiar.

All the way back up to the office, he couldn't stop thinking of her. It was stupid, because there was nothing to come up with— he wasn't going to recall who she was no matter how much he scoured his memory. Damn Kelsey Robins for bringing something like this up on the last day of his career. Why couldn't he just retire in peace like every other cop in the world?

There had been fifteen calls while he was at lunch, and all of them wanted to hear from him before he left the office. If he'd been this busy throughout his career, he would have burned out less than a month into the job.

Malloy plunked himself down behind the desk, picked up the phone, and started playing socialite, but his mind was no longer with the old friends and distant acquaintances who answered.

Hacker. There was something about her expression, something about the intensity in her eyes. He would see that stare when he left work that afternoon, and again when he tried to sleep that night. She plagued him. She wouldn't leave. It was almost as though he had known her without ever actually *knowing* her.

Who was she, and how had she gotten into his file cabinet?

They were supposed to have turned the water to this wing of the building off last summer. Debbie Wendell shook her head and mumbled obscenities to herself as she went for her cell phone and strode back down the corridor the way she had come. The crew men all looked at each other and then she heard their footsteps in her wake. Behind them, the little trickle was getting louder, larger, more insistent. If they didn't get this taken care of in the next five minutes, there was going to be a very big, very expensive mess, and she sure as hell wasn't going to be paying the bill when the corporate lackeys started looking for scapegoats.

"Wendell," she growled into the phone when the meek receptionist answered for Mr. Baines. "Tyler's office."

"May I say who's—"

"Wendell," she repeated. "You want me to write it down and fax it to you?"

There was a hesitant pause and then the soft jazz kicked in. On hold. On fucking hold. Debbie stopped abruptly and turned to stare out the floor-to-ceiling window at the planes as they taxied down the runway. Their tails were silhouetted against the early morning sky like shark fins circling in frigid water.

"Debbie?" Tyler sounded tired. He had probably been in a meeting of some sort, but both she and the receptionist had known that it wouldn't be pretty if she were made to wait. "Look, this isn't a good time," he said when she let him dangle for a few seconds too long.

"Then shut off the goddamn water to Concourse A like you were supposed to six months ago."

"The . . . the what?"

"We're taking a bath down here, Tyler. You want all of the international passengers to take it with us, or you want to do your fucking job and make it stop?"

"Hold on."

Jazz music.

Debbie sighed and sank into one of the chairs that had been cleared from the waiting area and stacked alongside the runway windows. Fifteen years and this job was starting to lose its appeal. Not that it had ever had too much in the first place.

Tyler was back. He fed her a line of bullshit and then said that the water would be off within ten minutes. *Great*, she thought.

That only meant one or two heated conversations with airport personnel instead of a dozen. She didn't know what the point was. They were demolishing the whole wing anyway. It was only because the airport was federally-managed that they gave a shit about all of the proper inspections and permits. They had to check three times for asbestos and then half a dozen other random chemicals and architectural treatments Debbie had never heard of.

She slapped the cell phone shut and jammed it back in her jeans pocket. The crew was watching her in rapt silence. "Okay," she said, rounding on them, "it's going to be ten minutes, which means we can get some of this other bullshit done in the meantime. You two," she pointed, because honestly, she'd never been compelled to learn anyone's name. "There's a bunch of old wiring behind that wall that we're supposed to untangle and remove before we lay in with the sledgehammers. Make it happen. The rest of you should start pulling floor and ceiling tiles. We've got to isolate the ventilation ducts, because apparently they might be able to use them in the new wing."

"But they're by the window," one of the men said.

Debbie scowled at him. "You got a problem with a view?"

"He's got a problem with the wife who forgot to wash his shorts this morning and left him with nothing but long pants," another man quipped. "Sun's pretty hot right about now."

"Hey, I got a cousin who has an allergic reaction to the sun," the first man whined.

Debbie made a fist. "You got an allergic reaction getting your ass kicked?"

The two men sniggered and split up, scattering in different directions. She stood for a few moments and just watched. It always amused people who happened to catch her crew at work that she could so effectively govern men who looked about as friendly and obedient as a pack of wolves. There were online courses you could take to build your confidence and try to achieve the kind of respect she had garnered, but in the end, she knew the secret formula—be pissed off, strong, and scary, and people would do what you wanted. A few thousand years after mankind's earliest days, and might very much still made right.

"Wendell!" one of the guys called.

She scanned the terminal and found him waving at her from the other end, away from the windows. He was Bruce, if she was remembering correctly—moustache, hair to his elbows, last runner-up in any beauty contest she'd ever judge.

She nodded, held up a finger. Let him wait. If she came right over when they snapped their fingers, they'd learn that they could make her do their bidding. She pulled out her cell phone and pretended to be on a call for a few minutes before finally sauntering over.

"What is it?" she asked. "I'm busy."

"We found some old stuff in one of the vents."

"I don't give a shit. Either give it to the Port Authority if you think they'd want it or throw it away, cause I sure don't."

"But it's antiques or something."

She gave him a look. "Who do you think I am? I don't care what century it's from. It's in my fucking construction site, and that means it's in the way."

Bruce shrugged. "Okay." He knelt and bustled around in a cloud of old plaster.

Debbie was just turning back to the center of the terminal when she caught a glimpse of the object he was removing. It was a box—a jewelry box, perhaps—wooden, ornately carved, genuinely beautiful.

She strode over to his side and took it from him. It was heavy in her hands. Probably worth a fortune. And it smelled strange—slightly burnt. What the hell was this doing in an airport ventilation duct?

Chapter 2

Gregory waited for her to call for six days. He didn't know what number he had dialed that evening, so any time the caller ID didn't look familiar, he would pick it up and pray to hear her voice on the other end. He had become fascinated with her. He longed to know who she was the same way he had longed for Christmas or his birthday every day of the year as a child.

On Wednesday, the police knocked down his door while he was in the shower.

When he came out of the bathroom, dripping, towel around his waist, they were sitting at his kitchen table. There were three of them, two uniformed cops and an urgent looking woman with red hair and a black overcoat that would have landed her a roll in a sci-fi movie if she'd ever bothered to audition. She had helped herself to coffee and one of the street officers was eating a cinnamon-raisin bagel from Gregory's pantry.

"Who are you?" the woman asked. "How do you know her?"

Gregory didn't like it when people talked directly to him. He mumbled something noncommittal while he pulled on some jeans and got out the orange juice.

As he made some toast, the woman told him her name was Detective Sergeant Linda Usher, but that was the only time he was ever going to hear her first name, and he'd better not try it out himself, if he knew what she meant. Then, as he was getting out the butter, she asked him again—who was he?

He told her, closing his eyes and imagining it was a job interview. He was good at those. He showed her the diploma from MIT and the ID card he had to flash at the scanners every morning when he went to work. "Systems analyst," he told her, and when she wrinkled up her brow, he explained that it meant he was a computer nerd who stared at code all day while everyone else caroused around the office coffee cart.

Gregory used her momentary silence to ask if, by any chance, she had a warrant for the door she had liberated from its hinges.

"Paperwork," she said with a derisive snort. Apparently that was the end of that. "You called someone last week," Detective Usher pressed on. "I want to know why, and how you know her."

That part was difficult. She was never going to believe that he just picked up the phone and punched in random numbers. After all, who would do a thing like that? Who would be that pathetically lonely?

"Wrong number," he told her. "I was meaning to call my mother."

"Yeah?" Usher pulled a folded piece of carbon paper out of her jacket pocket and smoothed it out on top of the toast crumbs. "What's her phone number?"

Gregory recited it before he realized why she was asking.

She arched an eyebrow at him. "You're going to tell me that by mistake, you dialed six out of the seven digits wrong?"

He could feel his cheeks coloring. "I'm clumsy."

"You're lying."

So he told her the truth. She didn't believe that at first either, but after she and the other officers insisted on looking around his apartment, she was willing to be more reasonable. It was the *Playboy* posters in the hall that won her over.

"You said you're thirty-six?" Usher asked. "And you still have wet dream, college boy fantasies pinned up?"

Now you're beginning to understand me, he thought, but aloud, he simply grunted. They stayed until lunchtime, quizzing him and going through his tax returns. He said several times that he was going to be late for work, but that didn't seem to make a difference to Detective Sergeant Linda Usher. She worked with unhurried, methodical ease, thumbing her way through his periodicals and his bank statements with equal, calm disinterest.

"Okay, Mr. Klein," she said when the bell at the church down the road had just chimed one o'clock, "I don't have enough evidence to take any kind of action right now, but I'm going to ask that you not travel anywhere for the next few weeks, until you hear differently from someone at my office. Can you promise me that?"

Gregory shrugged. "I guess so." He never went anywhere anyway. He and Lupe had planned a trip to Atlantic City once, but that had fizzled out when Lupe's new boyfriend asked her to marry him in Hawaii.

The next day, Gregory had an idea at breakfast. During his lunch break, sitting at the trendy little coffee bar next door to his office, he called AT&T and asked for a transcript of his recent calls. The customer service representative was very helpful, and he listened to the clatter of her fingernails on the keyboard as she entered his personal information. Then the clattering stopped.

"Klein, you said?" she asked. The pop of bubblegum.

"Gregory Klein. Yeah, that's right."

"I'm afraid I can't help you."

He looked at the phone. "What are you talking about? You said it would be easy to retrieve my file."

"There's a problem. It's restricted."

"I don't think you understand. This is my own account. I'm the only person who uses this account, so it's okay—it's just numbers I've called. You can tell me."

"I can't. There's a lock on your account."

"A what?" He was pissing off the other software engineers.

They were on their laptops, pretending to work while they ate. Gregory knew better; they were just browsing the internet or sending emails to their friends, but they liked to maintain the pretense of serious productivity.

"A lock, sir," the representative said. "Look, you can talk to my supervisor if you like, but I can't get you in."

"But I didn't order any lock on my account."

There was another pause, more chewing, more clattering on the keyboard. "Oh, no shit," the girl said. She sounded like she was about fourteen. "No, it's the police. They've confiscated all your records. It's a blank book here."

"The police?"

"Sorry, sir. I should probably get on to another call. They don't like it if we spend too long with any one customer. It's not fair to the people on hold."

He let her go. She was right anyway—what more could she do?

That night, Gregory was feeling sick, so he drew himself a bath and turned up the thermostat on the central air system. He was just slipping into the suds when the phone rang. Probably vinyl siding. That, or a mortgage company. But for some reason, he got out, wrapped a towel around his dripping legs, and went to the living room to pick up.

"Hey," he said.

"It's you."

The throbbing head, the aching limbs—everything was gone in an instant. She had his full attention. "Who is this?"

"Me."

"Who are you?"

"I'm lost. I'm glad you're talking this time. You scared me before."

"I thought you were in trouble. Last time there was that noise—it sounded like, I don't know, an animal or something."

"Yeah, that." She didn't elaborate.

"I'm glad you called." It was true. Somehow, he felt comfortable talking with her as he did no one else.

"Me, too. Could you come here?"

He was dripping on the carpet. The soap was going to stain. He sat down on the couch, knowing it, too, wouldn't take the water well. It didn't matter. "Where's *here*?"

"Do you think you could find out for me?"

"You don't know where you are?"

"I have to go. It's cold outside, and it snowed here the day before yesterday. You sound rational. Nobody else will be. Help."

She was off the line before he could say another word.

By midnight, he'd narrowed it down to three metropolitan areas—Boston; Portland, Maine; and Hartford. Gregory stared at the glowing list on the screen. Three cities. How could he find one woman in three cities when he didn't even have so much as a name or a physical description?

Gregory was at work when the police showed up again. Leo, the Managing Supervisor for the whole department, brought them to Gregory's cubicle and then told him to come for "a chat" after the authorities were done.

The two officers said it would be better if they could talk in private, and when they got to the conference room one floor up, Gregory wasn't entirely surprised to find Detective Usher waiting for him.

She smiled, did her lipstick, and told him that she wanted him in jail. Gregory shrugged. That would take time, he told her, and evidence. "Paperwork."

"You're trying to find her." Usher slapped down another piece of carbon paper—a log of all the web sites he had visited over the past few days, and in a second column, the calls he'd subsequently made. "We told you to stay away from this woman."

He blinked. "No, you didn't."

"No? Well, I'm telling you now. Stay away. She's none of your business. I'm warning you, Mr. Klein. We don't want to see this kind of activity anymore."

You won't, Gregory thought. He smiled and nodded, all the while working through the code in his mind. They could watch his house all they wanted after this, and all they'd see were a few visits to his internet email account and a telephone order for Pay-Per-View.

Afterward, Leo told him that he didn't like seeing the authorities in the office. "It makes everyone jumpy. If they visit you again, I'm going to have to let you go."

Gregory couldn't think of work right now. All he could think of was the voice.

Who was she?

She needed a name, and so he decided to call her Frida. It seemed appropriately exotic and mysterious.

For the rest of the week and well into the next, he did his best to forget about her. She never called, and he couldn't narrow down her location any more than he already had. At one point, he picked up the phone and dialed Boston information, but when the operator came on, he froze up and felt like a fool. What was he going to say? There was a woman somewhere, but he didn't know her name, and he wasn't even sure that she was in this city.

Then she called again.

This time she was frantic. Something was wrong.

He was at work, but the call had come in on his cell, so he locked his workstation and walked to the bathroom.

"God," she moaned, out of breath, frenzied. "God, what am I going to do? I can feel it—inside me. What they've done . . ."

"Slow down," he told her. "What's happening?"

"They're watching me. They're all over the place. I . . . there are lights. The walls are moving. Can't you help me? Where are you? I told you to come help me!"

"Where *are* you?"

She was breaking up. He could feel the static closing in on the call like the four walls of a shrinking room. "I've looked all over the place. Portland, Boston, Hartford—which is it?"

"I . . . Portland? Maybe? Bangor. No. I don't know. I don't know how much longer I can carry this on before . . . I don't know what I'll do. I feel like I'll tear my own eyes out. I'm trapped."

"Slow down. Talk to me. What's your name?"

There was a bark on the other end of the line. "They're here again!" A scuffling noise.

"Who?" Gregory demanded.

Someone coughed in the stall next to his, and that was the first time he became conscious of the fact that he wasn't alone. What if the police had someone in here, pretending to read a magazine and wipe their ass just so they could spy on him?

"I have to go. Please come! Please! Things are moving in the dark!"

"Frida—"

Click.

Gregory was almost back to his cubicle when he realized that she had called him on his cellular phone. That was impossible. He had called her from the landline at home before. There was no way for her to know this was his number.

Unless she knew who he was.

Chapter 3

That night, walking home alongside the highway, three different cars tried to pick up Jackie Savage. Two of them were just concerned motorists on their way from one place to another; the last was a creepy old man in a 1968 Ford Minibus that made her keep checking over her shoulder from then on.

The rain continued intermittently, slowly soaking her clothes. If only it weren't so cold, she would have enjoyed listening to the sound of the droplets on the swaying cornhusks.

It was dark at the house when she got there. The driveway was slick, the mail still waiting in the mailbox, the living room cold and deserted. There was a message on the answering machine.

She locked the door behind her and played the message, hoping it would be her father. It was just a recording from some local tire manufacturing plant that had just opened up an outlet somewhere nearby.

The answering machine beeped. *No more messages.*

She made dinner for herself, all the while half-expecting to hear Walker's car in the driveway. There wasn't much in the refrigerator, but she put together a burrito from some refried beans and a few old tortillas.

When she was done, she locked herself in her bedroom and stayed by the window until early into the morning, watching for headlights on the street and listening for the telephone. This wasn't supposed to be how true adventures started. At some point, her eyelids drooped, and she fell back onto the pillows.

~~#~~

Pale morning light filtered in through the crooked Venetian blinds. Jackie blinked. For a few moments, she was completely disoriented. She didn't usually wake up for school before her alarm, but the sky was still dotted with stars, and the sun had yet to appear above the horizon.

She stumbled out into the living room, and then she remembered everything. Somehow, some youthful, naïve part of her had been hoping, assuming that all would be okay when she woke up the next morning. Wasn't that how it was supposed to work? The transition from night to day was supposed to cleanse the world of all its problems.

She was too tired to think about it, and so, methodically, she showered and got ready for school.

Jackie got as far as the middle of the driveway before she stopped. Walker wasn't there. Her father hadn't called. Nobody was going to care if she went to school or not. It was both terrifying and the freest she had ever been in her life.

She left her backpack on the kitchen table and wrote on a piece of stationery she'd grabbed from her *Looney Tunes* notebook:

Walker —
Where are you? What happened yesterday? I'm leaving for a while.
I'll be back sometime. I think. Hope everything's okay. Later.
J

Then she went outside, locked the front door, and began walking down the highway. She had no idea where she was going. She was not quite sure what had come over her, whether she hoped to find Walker or if she was just looking for escape.

She must have walked for several hours, because all at once, she found herself a long way out of town, and the sun now hovered directly overhead. She paused to rest for a few moments and wipe her brow, and that was when the van came back.

She recognized it at once from the sound of the motor, before she even turned. There it was, lumbering down the road toward her. In the light of day, she saw that it was lime green, the paint long since faded and peeling. The windows were curved and grimy, masking whoever crouched behind the steering wheel.

For the second time in twenty-four hours, the van pulled to the side of the road and stopped a few feet ahead of her. The door did not open. After a few moments, the brake lights went off; the driver had put it in park.

Jackie waited, her breath caught in her throat. He was not going to come for her, she realized. He was going to let her come to him. She shivered and dove off the road into the weeds. She waited until the stalks had stopped rustling around her and then she stuck her head out so that she could see the road, but where she didn't think the driver of the van could see her.

They waited for each other for almost twenty minutes. Then, as though struck by a sudden, idle fancy, the brake lights came on again, and a few moments later, the van pulled back onto the highway and kept on going.

She didn't come out from her hiding place until it had vanished beneath a dip in the road several miles down. Then she began to shake all over.

Jackie picked her way back out to the road and sat on one of the larger rocks on the shoulder, her back to the road. She was lost, dazed, confused. What were they doing in school right now, she wondered? She checked her sports watch—it read 2:18, which meant it was around one. Trigonometry. Polynomials. She could picture her empty desk in the row by the window and the disapproving grimace Ms. Breyer would have made as she ticked her pencil down the attendance list and put an X next to the name, *Savage, Jaclyn M.*

She hadn't noticed the approaching car until the brakes squeaked a few inches from her head. It was white, a Chevy sedan several years old that had seen better days. Dents riddled its dusty side panels, and the front license plate, U.S. Government issue, hung from one screw.

The passenger door opened, and a large man with olive skin and a froth of black hair poked his head out.

"Are you okay, Miss?"

She let out a little noise that was half-cough, half-giggle. He hadn't asked why she wasn't in school. She must have looked like an adult. "I'll be alright," she told him.

"You sure? You need a ride somewhere?"

"I'm fine." She made up a story about how she was an artist doing research for some paintings. She could tell he wasn't buying it, but what could he do?

"If you need any help, call me." He slipped her a card, and she turned it over in her hands: *Jason Buckley, Deputy, Weylan County Sheriff's Office.*

"Thanks," she said, and tucked the card away. He looked reluctant to leave her. When he did pull away, he drove very slowly, as though expecting her to change her mind at any moment and come running after him on the highway. She watched until he, too, was gone.

If he were anyone else, she told herself, she would've gone with him. She had no reason to stay here. But he was a cop. He would ask questions. If someone else came along, though, she would climb into the passenger seat and never think twice about it. She wasn't going to pass up another opportunity.

The afternoon passed slowly. Her legs were getting tired, but she couldn't stand another night back at home, alone, so she kept walking. She came to a service station and a small diner as the sun was beginning to paint the sky with a smear of dying colors. It smelled like barbecuing meat. Suddenly, she was ravenous. Jackie walked into the diner and the plump little old hostess with the curly red hair had her seated at a booth in the corner before she realized that she didn't have enough money to eat anything. She had just over two dollars. She examined the menu. That would buy a half-order of French fries and nothing to drink, if there was no tax added.

The waitress brought them to her in a paper bag smeared with grease, and Jackie dropped the last of her coins on the table before sauntering back outside. It was dusk and oppressively moist. The air hung about her shoulders like a thick, wet shawl.

Jackie wandered over to the service station, hoping she might be able to get a free candy bar or a bottle of water out of one of the attendants, if he was nice. There was only one car there, a 1965 Lincoln Continental, black and shined up so that it looked brand new. The windows were tinted and rolled up, and there didn't appear to be anyone in or around the car.

Tony, the attendant with the beer gut, came out of the office when he saw her and looked her up and down. She could see from his expression that he didn't like kids. Place like this, they probably sped through every night, breaking bottles, making trouble. She was just another one of them to him.

"What can I do for you, ma'am?" he asked grudgingly. He had already scanned the lot and seen that she'd brought no car with her.

"Who owns that car?" she asked, pointing to the Lincoln.

"One of our customers. Do you need something?"

She shook her head, and under Tony's watchful eye, she went over to the Continental. She wasn't sure why she was doing it. Normally, she never would have approached strangers like this—at least, not in real life. Often, in class, she would sit and stare out the window and imagine that she was a pop star or a super spy, or just someone who had the good fortune to live somewhere else, where something happened. But she'd never done anything brazen outside her own imagination.

Until now.

The driver's window rolled down when she was a few feet away. A chauffeur in a suit and a black cap leered out at her. His skin was pale, his hair tangled and bleached white. It hung like knotted, albino curtains on his forehead. His eyes were sunken deep in shadowed troughs that dug into his bony face.

Jackie bent, trying to get a glimpse over his shoulder, into the back seat. A glass partition, also heavily tinted, stood between the driver and the rear compartment.

"Can I help you?" he asked.

"My name's Jackie Savage."

He blinked at her. "Okay."

"Who are you driving around back there?"

She felt a heavy hand on her shoulder. Tony gave her a little tug. "Leave the customers alone. They don't like being disturbed."

"Nobility," the chauffeur told her. He barely moved when he spoke, his face a marble statue, save for his thin lips. "I think you might belong in here, too."

She smiled self-consciously. She was used to adults talking to her like that, sending her quiet, underhanded little compliments, but somehow, coming from this man, it was strange and awkward. Perhaps it was in the way he kept staring at her, without wavering.

Then it hit her: he wasn't joking.

A chill gripped her heart. She took a step backward and found herself leaning against Tony's oil-smeared overalls. The smell of gasoline and sweat enveloped her. She wasn't sure which of the two men frightened her more. But there was a difference—Tony was sleazy. Given the chance, without the laws and the possible witnesses to stop him, he'd probably clap a hand over her mouth, take her in the back room, and force himself upon her.

The chauffeur was different. He was like something out of a children's fantasy book, or perhaps a horror novel. He was somehow fantastic, the product of a diseased mind. She looked the car over and then she went to the back door and placed a hand on the latch.

"Yes," she said. "I'll come with you, if you'll let me."

Tony shook his head. "I'm sorry about this, mister." He clomped toward her, blackened fingers outstretched. "I don't think she's even with anyone. I'll send her on her way, and she won't bother you anymore."

"It is unlocked," the chauffeur's eyes were still on Jackie. "Step inside."

And so she did. She pulled the door shut just as Tony reached it. The silver lock sank into its well. She heard him gripping the latch, then saw him lean in and cup his hands around his eyes. He was trying to see her.

She shivered and scooted away from the window, and then she had the chilling thought that she might be lifting herself straight into someone else's lap. She turned and looked and received another shock.

The back of the limousine was empty. The seats, covered in black velvet, looked as though they had not been sat upon for some considerable time. The only thing that betrayed any kind of recent occupation were the interior lights—switched on, as though they had been used to read something.

Jackie swallowed. It smelled musty in here, like dust and old clothing. She crawled across the expansive floor and tapped on the tinted glass partition. A silver speaker to her left crackled to life as the limousine pulled away from the gas pumps and out onto the narrow highway.

"Yes?" the chauffeur's voice asked.

"Why isn't there anyone back here? Who are you?"

"Nobility," the chauffeur repeated.

"But I'm alone."

She could hear the smile in his voice when he spoke. "Not for long."

Chapter 4

It was all a blur. He was still a little hung-over from the night before.

By the time the alarm went off on his wedding day, Terry felt like shit. He'd barely slept. Alcohol always did that to him. He envied the guys who would pass out in the middle of a party, before everything went sour, and wake up the next morning with nothing but the good memories.

His stomach churned when he rolled out of bed, and he almost fell asleep several times in the shower. Standing in front of the mirror, he scarcely recognized himself. Lines and blotches covered his face, and there were enough shadows to fill an abyss beneath each of his eyes.

Adrienne—Vicki's mother—had hired someone to do make-up, a little Southern girl with a slow drawl of an accent and sprigs of blonde hair that would've driven him wild back in college. When Adrienne saw him in his rumpled tuxedo, wilting on the front lawn, she rushed him back to the bathroom and ordered the girl over to go to work on him immediately. With some powder and a little rouge, they managed to make him look like a passable statue of himself.

The rest of the day slipped by like any other. He resented that. This was supposed to be special, but he couldn't take his mind off of the picture he'd found in the attic. For a while, he thought he must have invented it, because he couldn't find it anywhere, and it seemed like the sort of thing that materialized only in a drunken fantasy.

Then, while he was searching for his cufflinks, he found it wedged beneath his pillow. She looked so young and innocent, so helpless and so needy. It drove him wild. He shouldn't be having feelings for another woman like this on his wedding day. Especially not one who could very well be dead or married to someone his grandfather's age. What was coming over him? What kind of madness was this?

People bustled around, and he hardly noticed them. They were in the living room—the photographer, flashes of light—then in the back of a limousine, and people were smiling and telling him how sharp the two of them looked, how they were meant for each other and how they should appear on the cover of *People*.

He idly watched the countryside drift by outside the tinted windows. That was the one moment he remembered with any clarity from the entire morning—Wagner's mill. He'd always loved the mill as a child. He'd read his first novel there, over one of the few summers back from South America. He'd had his first kiss beneath the swaying turbines, a few years later. He caught a glimpse of it as the limo slid past on the highway, and his eyes locked upon the peeling paint, the splintered wood. This was the last time he'd see it, he thought. If he happened this way again, it wouldn't be the same. He'd be showing his children the town where he grew up or reminiscing, decades down the line.

Shit, this was goodbye. He wasn't ready. When had he stopped *living* and started merely *observing*?

He wanted to scratch his thigh. With something sharp.

They were almost late to the church. All of the guests were already there, most of the family, too. *Hacker*, he thought. And those eyes. Why couldn't it have said more than half a name?

"I do."

It was that simple. There was something warm on his mouth,

and he realized with a shock that it was his wife. He'd never been this numb before in his life. It was scaring him.

Hacker.

Vicki was smiling. She withdrew, but her fingers lingered on the back of his neck.

Damn her. Damn the picture. And at the same time, he knew he wasn't going to be able to forget it.

They were forty-five minutes early for their flight. Everyone in the airport knew who they were, even though they'd changed back into jeans, sneakers, and T-shirts. The clerk at the gift shop had a package of flowers and bath salts for them, and at McDonald's they each got a free small Oreo McFlurry with special pink ice cream. They sat in front of the windows that looked out onto the tarmac, and neither of them said a word.

Halfway through their dessert, Terry realized that she was waiting for him to start the conversation. "I can't wait to get to the beach," he said when the strain of staying quiet outweighed the strain of saying something meaningless.

She giggled like a little girl. "It's going to be fantastic. M'God, this is the first day of the rest of our lives! We can say, 'I can't wait to get to the beach tomorrow,' and then tomorrow, we can say the same thing. And again and again, as many times as we like."

What had been in the background of the picture? He couldn't remember now, which was foolish, because that was almost as important as what was in the foreground. Perhaps there was a landmark or some other identifiable shape. He might already have all he needed to find her.

Vicki snapped her fingers in front of Terry's eyes. "Sweetie?" she asked. "Sweetie, are you all right? You look . . . far away."

"I'm tired," he told her truthfully. "I didn't sleep much last night."

She giggled again. "Nervous?"

How could he have fallen in love with that laugh? He looked at her with a revulsion that astounded him. Once, he had loved her. He could dimly recall the times they had snuck away to the hills and shared picnics and passionate kisses as the orange sunset faded and gave way to twinkling stars. Somehow, between all of the loans and the checks and the plans for the future, he'd lost sight of all of that. He was dead. Desperately dead inside.

She grabbed the back of his head, pressed him into her lap. "Rest, sweetie," she said. "It's hard to sleep on the plane. Rest now."

Terry lay there, feeling miserable for ten full minutes before he sat up and went to the bathroom to mutilate himself again. He did it carefully with a plastic McDonald's fork, and when he was done, he stuck paper towels to his flesh so that the blood didn't seep through his jeans. It felt better. At least this way, there was something he could keep his mind on. The pain was like a physical object hovering in the air in front of him, a handle he could grasp and squeeze as hard as he needed.

He sat down next to Vicki, and she snaked an arm beneath his shirt.

"Vicki," he said, "I'm not going to Hawaii."

Silence. Icy silence.

"What do you mean?"

"I can't."

"Terry? Terry, we've got everything laid out. We have the reservations. We have tours and hotels and—"

"I'm just ... there are things I have to do . . ."

"Are you tired? We can see if we can push back some of the reservations." She was frantic, panicking.

Terry stood up. "I'm going now, Vicki. You can come with me, if you want, but I wouldn't blame you if you never wanted to see me again."

When he got back to the house, Terry went straight to his bedroom and pulled the photograph out from beneath the pillow. What was that in the background? A rope bridge. Banana plant leaves. Somewhere hot, tropical—there was a sheen on her skin. Sweat, the thick, jungle air. Or maybe it was just a studio. He squinted at the picture, but it was too old and too grainy to see if the foliage was real or if she was just standing in front of an elaborate painting on a roll-down screen. They could have misted her forehead with water; she might be in the middle of a city.

Back up in the attic, he ripped open four more cardboard boxes before footsteps sounded on the stairs. Mrs. Newell poked her head up through the trapdoor in the floor and caught him in an anguished glare.

"Terry?" She had probably come back to clean up for them, a present to the newlyweds from their dear old neighbor.

He didn't say anything. Instead, he pulled open a fifth box. This was just models—cars, fighter planes, warships—all of the plastic obsessions he'd wasted his time on as a child once they had come back to the States for good and he had figured out he would never fit in. He needed to find the old albums his mother had kept. What if the woman was a friend of the family? What if she had come to the house when he was a child? He would've remembered.

"I just got off the phone with Vicki," Mrs. Newell said, clambering up to sit on the side of the trap door. "I need you to talk to me, Terry. I need you to tell me what's going on in your head right now, because your *wife* is scared out of her mind that you think you made a mistake today."

He ignored her, and after a while, she went away. She probably said something more to him, but he wasn't listening. He went through most of the rest of the attic, but there were no other pictures of the woman. Again and again, he came back to the one photograph he had. It was driving him crazy.

Mother might know, he thought. If she was having a good day, she might be able to help him.

Five minutes after the idea had struck him, he was downstairs, leafing through the yellow pages. Greyhound. There was an 800 number. He dialed, listened, and in ten minutes, had booked a bus out after sundown that evening. He had no idea what he was doing, and somehow, he found that enormously appealing.

Fifteen minutes after he'd found a seat, they closed the doors, and the bus rolled out of the station. He leaned forward and watched the lights streak by into the night. It was all so familiar, yet strangely foreign from this perspective. There was the automotive repair shop, the antique store, all of the places he would walk by every day, now beneath him, moving away at forty miles-per-hour.

Then he was out of town.

Terry put his head in his hands. He was a pathetic human being. There was nothing he could say in his defense.

An hour later, when the driver stopped to stretch his legs and a few of the passengers got out to use the bathroom at a service station, Terry looked up at the clouds and saw the blinking lights of a jet flying overhead. He checked his watch—that might have been their flight to Hawaii. They had said something about storm delays, and how it might be evening before they were able to get off the runway.

Quietly, Terry snuck back on the bus before anyone else had emerged from the fluorescent pool of light surrounding the service pumps. *What am I doing?* Then he caught a glimpse of the picture and he knew.

Chapter 5

Jean and Joseph Malloy did not leave town on the eighth of March as they had been planning to for more than a year. It was all arranged—most of their furniture was in storage at a locker just down the street; the house-sitters were staying in a hotel. But the RV had suddenly developed a problem with the fuel line. Joseph had tried to talk the mechanic into saying that they'd be okay with it, but with a trip like they were taking on the horizon, the mechanic wasn't willing to let them take any chances. It would take at least a week to fix.

Jean was dreadfully disappointed. She'd arranged a going-away party three days ago; she'd said goodbye to all of her friends, and she felt like it would be awkward to see them again now. So she shut herself in the house, eating only what she could make out of what they had on-hand. Ham-and-cheese sandwiches became cheese sandwiches, then mayonnaise, as slowly their ingredients dwindled.

Secretly, though, Joseph was a little relieved. On the second day, when she had exhausted their meager collection of old VHS movies and gone on to network television, he announced that he was going out for a brief drive.

"Joseph, dear," Jean said, "what about the neighbors?"

He had to assure her that he would keep a low profile.

Over the last few years on the job, he'd been busier and busier, and he'd found himself spending more time at the office than he did at home. These last few days in the house with Jean, boring and uneventful as they were, had reminded him how much he still loved her. There were little things she did—the way she would carefully wipe all the toast crumbs from the blade of the knife before dipping it into the butter; the way she would sponge down the shower curtain after she'd gotten out, so that the droplets wouldn't leave a stain.

But that morning, when he was shaving, he found the picture. He'd wedged it in his briefcase on his way off the job on that last day, and it had somehow gotten folded and crumpled into a magazine he'd later dropped on the bathroom counter. He wouldn't have seen it had the magazine not been pressed up against the mirror; Jean again, organizing, keeping everything in tidy stacks.

"Where will you go, anyway?" she asked him.

"Need some air, is all. Get out of the house for a while. Get some sun on my face." But he knew exactly where he was going.

Adam Valenti's 1986 Camaro was parked at an angle across the grass next to the downtown office of the *Sun Times*. Joseph put his Jeep behind it and sniggered at the latest collection of charms Valenti had hanging from the mirror. It was a perpetually-rotating queue—sometimes there was religious paraphernalia, crosses and tiny Jesuses. Then, the next week, Valenti would disavow the church and put up a shrunken head or a voodoo doll.

"Joseph, baby!" he said when Joseph Malloy walked through the front door. Valenti strode around the corner of his chest-high desk and threw his arms around Joseph. He smelled of licorice, which Joseph knew was to mask the scent of tobacco and alcohol from Valenti's wife.

Joseph smiled. They'd known each other for almost twenty years. They'd met in a bar, when Joseph was investigating a brawl and Valenti was participating in some hands-on journalism.

From there on, Joseph Malloy and Adam Valenti collaborated on more than a few cases. Valenti had a way of mixing with the unsavory types, gaining their trust, learning things, and then exploiting them to sell newspapers. Joseph was fine with that, so long as he got to make the arrest before Adam got to make the morning headlines.

There was a time when Valenti had been over at the house for dinner five nights a week. Jean had put a stop to that after a while—after Adam had managed to scratch most of their glasses and break half of their silverware—but Joseph still met the guy for lunch almost every week.

"Shit, Joe," Valenti was saying now, "I thought you guys were supposed to be out of town by now. Weren't you going to go on some grand tour of the country? See all the places they don't tell you about in the guidebooks?"

"Car trouble," Joseph told him.

Valenti nodded. "Those RV's are finicky bastards." He brushed the greasy black hair from his face and slipped around the counter. "Margarita? Just got this new blender for the office . . ."

Malloy smiled and told Valenti that he'd come for a reason. He wanted some information about a young woman who might have been involved with a case a while back.

"You manipulative old bastard." Valenti grinned. "And here I thought you were just getting lonely without me. Why not ask the guys downtown? No heartbreak that way, not that you'd care."

"I'm retired."

"No friends who will step out onto a branch for you?"

"Well, there's you."

"Right. Not to put too fine a point on it or anything."

"This is a . . . a personal interest. I don't want people getting their feathers ruffled over nothing."

Valenti whistled. "I didn't know you had a personal life, Joe. Does the missus?"

"It's not like that. Just something from an old case that's been bugging me." He handed Valenti the picture.

They spent a few hours going through the records on the computer, but nothing came up. In the end, Valenti gave the snapshot to Brian Wexel, a mousy little assistant in his early-30s whom Joseph had never trusted.

"Wex'll search the archives for you."

"Eh, don't bother." Joseph reached for the picture, but Valenti shook his head and stepped between them.

"After all the shit you've gone through for me, Joe, this is the least I can do."

Joseph went home that afternoon and had a late lunch with his wife, and then the two of them sat in each other's arms and reminisced until dinnertime. He was happy, except for when he thought about the picture. Every five minutes or so, he would remember, and then he would squeeze Jean a little tighter. It was as though the strange woman in the photo was trying to muscle her way into their family, trying to exploit his own notorious curiosity and draw him away from what he truly cared about.

Tomorrow, when Valenti called, Joseph would tell him to keep the picture. Kelsey Robins could look into it on his own time, and if it were truly important, he could reopen the case and run a formal investigation.

In fact, Joseph told himself, *I won't even answer the phone.*

"Joseph Malloy."

"Joe, baby! I got some interesting results for you. I want to show you—drinks?"

Joseph met Valenti at the pub, a few doors down from the newspaper.

It wasn't until he was halfway through his vodka martini that Joseph realized he had picked up the phone when he'd decided yesterday to let the matter rest. It was a natural reaction. Jean had been in the shower; she couldn't have screened it for him.

"So, Joe." Valenti hauled out a grubby manila file folder. "It's real interesting, like I said. This woman you've turned up, this Hacker—you know who she is at all?"

Joseph shook his head. "That's why I wanted you to look into her."

"Yeah, okay. Well, see the funny thing is, nobody seems to know."

Joseph shrugged. Okay, he told Valenti—that wasn't that funny. It just meant she was an outsider, some random lead they'd probably picked up for a case that never ended up going anywhere. No need to blow this out of proportion. Right?

"That's not quite what I mean. I mean, yeah, sure, there's plenty of people nobody's heard of around here. There's probably about five billion of 'em, right?" He wheezed a laugh to himself and didn't hear Joseph correct him—*Six*. "But that's not quite what I mean, like I said. People know the girl; they just don't *know* the girl."

"What's that mean?"

"Well, first, Wexel didn't find anything in archives, which I mean, that kind of goes without saying. He's a few drawers short of a fucking ... a fucking armoire or whatever. But I believe him anyway, 'cause you know, why'd her picture be in the archives if it wasn't in the computer, you know? So I asked around a little, just the prominent people, business owners, a few of my friends."

"Oh, Adam, I didn't want to make a big deal out of all of this . . ."

"Nah, nah, you know, just casual-like. And you know what I found out? Most of 'em said they'd seen this girl sometime, probably a long while ago. But you know what else? Not one of 'em could tell me who she was."

Joseph frowned. "That's strange."

"Yeah. You've got my attention, Joe. You want to tell me who she is?"

"Honestly, Adam, I have no idea." After several more denials, Valenti actually seemed convinced.

"Well," Valenti said, "you just tell me if you find anything out, okay? Anything at all, because now Adam Valenti's curious, and that means the *Sun Times* is curious, and when the *Sun Times* is curious about something, that means the truth itself is desperate to get out!"

Joseph rolled his eyes and asked Valenti to please not make a big deal out of it. Reluctantly, Valenti agreed.

〜━〜

Joseph and Jean spent the next few days peacefully going about their lives, waiting to hear from the mechanic and filling their idle hours with television, cooking, and gardening—Jean had finally agreed to be seen outside, despite what the neighbors might think. Retirement. People in their prime dreamed of this. It should have been the happiest he'd ever been.

The house-sitters had begun breathing down their necks, and Joseph had had to offer to pay their hotel bill until the RV was fixed. They weren't happy. Their children were starting summer school in a few weeks, and they wanted a stable place for them to come back to, for them to make friends to bring for lunch or dinner. Joseph told them he understood, and that he and Jean would be out of town as soon as possible. The couple seemed impossibly young. Full of energy. Full of purpose. The father was a teacher, the mother an architect. They would do great things in their lives.

And Joseph—all Joseph had was a career of closed manila folders in a file cabinet.

He and Valenti got drinks a couple more times, and each time, Valenti brought up the picture. Joseph had broken down and told Jean about it a day after his first meeting with Valenti, and she'd been as skeptical as he'd thought she would.

"A picture?" she had asked. "From work? Why do you care, honey? Aren't you done with that? Let the kids in their snappy little uniforms handle it."

She's right, he told himself, and resolved never to think about it again.

Three days later, he and Jean went to the grocery store for some bread and tomatoes, and when they came back, their house had been knocked down.

Chapter 6

Debbie Wendell clutched the box to her chest. She didn't even stow it under the seat when the flight attendants came through with drinks and peanuts. From the corner of her eye, she saw the man in the seat next to her pretending not to notice at first, but after the first few jolts of turbulence, when she squeezed it so tightly that her knuckles turned white, he started to stare. The box was the most beautiful, most expensive thing Debbie had ever seen in her life, and it was hers. Nobody was going to get it away from her.

It was for her mother, of course, that she told herself she was doing this. Laura Wendell was eighty years old. She was dying—alone—in a home in Florida because Debbie was still trying to scare up the cash for her treatments. That was what she told herself.

The longer she massaged the smooth wooden surface with her fingers, the longer she let the oils sink into her skin, the more certain she became that there was something special about the box. It was going to set her free.

It was the man next to her who made her start to sweat. They had just started showing some old movie about lovers in Manhattan on drop-down television screens, and the children were all getting quiet with headphones wrapped around their heads. Debbie could feel the man's eyes on her, roving her body, caressing the box with their cold, fixed attention.

She turned. He had a gray moustache waxed into a curve that accentuated the mirthless straight line of his lips. His eyes hid behind glasses so large they were like hovering dinner plates strung together with wire. He did not smile when she looked at him, and when he brushed away a strand of his coarse, salt-and-pepper hair, she saw a scar on the top of his hand that looked as though it had been caused by a cigarette burn.

"Can I help you?" she asked.

"That is a nice piece you have there."

Debbie shivered and brought it even closer to her. "Thanks." There was a pregnant silence. "Could you stop looking at me?"

"Where did you get it?"

"It's a family heirloom." She scanned the cabin, searching for a flight attendant who could bail her out.

"May I look at it?"

"No."

Bracing his hands on the armrest that divided their two seats, he leaned closer. His breath came wafting across her in foul waves. It was rank, thick enough to taste. She recoiled.

"What is your name, young lady?" A burst of the ghastly odor.

She put a hand on his shoulder and firmly pushed him back. "I believe you're in my seat," she said, and quickly returned her hand to the box as his eyes jumped to the opening her hand had left.

He removed his glasses, wiped them down with a corner of his red sweater, and smiled at her. His teeth were straight but green-yellow. "Where are my manners?" he muttered. "I've neglected to introduce myself. My name is Kelson. Lloyd Kelson." He stuck out a hand and she took it coldly. Their handshake was brief and joyless. Any trace of pleasantry dropped from his mouth. "The box—it reminds me of someone."

"Great. Close your eyes, dream about them, and leave me alone."

"Someone whom I've been searching for. For a long time, Ms. Wendell."

He knew her name. A wave of claustrophobia overtook her. There were no exits from an airplane in mid-flight. "So, what, you're a private detective? My boss hire you to track me down or something?"

He took a sheet of paper from the pocket on the back of the seat in front of her and pulled it into the light, so that she could see. It was her boarding pass, and her name was printed across the top, right next to *Coach Class, Seat 23A*.

A tiny sigh of relief. He wasn't after her. Perhaps.

"The box, then," he prompted. "Where did it come from?"

"It's personal."

"I don't think it belongs to you. Does it?"

Still no flight attendants. "Who are you?" she asked.

"I think that answers my question."

"I found it. It's mine." There was no reason Lloyd Kelson should be getting to her the way he was. He wasn't a police officer. He was an old windbag who liked the look of her jewelry box and thought he could talk it out of her hands and into his pocket. Then she figured it out. He reminded her of her father.

"I'm going to ask to be reseated," she told him. She reached up to press the *Call* button, but he grabbed her arm before she touched the switch.

"You don't want to do that."

"Let go of me!" she snapped, a little too loudly. The little girl in the row in front of them took off her headphones and shot a questioning look over the aisle.

Kelson reached over and touched the box. She yanked it away from him, but the minor tactile contact he had made seemed enough to satisfy him. He squeezed his eyes shut and inhaled deeply, as though in the throes of passion.

"What is wrong with you?" she hissed.

"Thank you, Ms. Wendell. It is the box I thought it was."

Then he unbuckled his seatbelt and got up. She watched him as he climbed out to the aisle and filtered toward the lavatory at the front of the plane. He disappeared inside, and her shoulders dropped. She looked from side to side and caught the eye of the little girl in the next row.

Debbie picked a napkin out of the pouch in front of her and wiped down the smooth wood where Kelson had touched the box. His fingerprints melted away into the lacquer. She leaned out into the aisle and glared up toward the front of the plane, waiting for him to pop back out of the lavatory. He wasn't her father. She would give him a piece of her mind when he returned.

But Lloyd Kelson never came back from the lavatory.

Debbie checked her watch. It had been almost half an hour. Had she missed him? Of course not, that was foolish—where else would he go?

Forty-five minutes. This was getting ludicrous. What was he doing? He was counting on her coming to find him, she realized. He would corner her in the flight attendants' alcove while they were off serving coffee, and he would demand that she give him the box.

An hour. Debbie strode up the aisle and pounded on the lavatory door. "Lloyd! I know you're in there. I don't know what you're playing at, but it's got to stop. You can't harass me like this!"

A blonde twenty-something in a snappy blue uniform with a Delta Airlines nametag that read, *Sandy* tapped her on the shoulder. "Ma'am," she said, "it's not locked. If you want to go inside, push on the left-hand panel, and the door will fold."

Not locked? Absurdly, Sandy was right. Debbie pushed the door open. There was no Lloyd Kelson inside. There was nobody at all in the cramped little space. The droplets of water spattered across the stack of paper towels by the sink had dried. There was no sign that anyone had been there in the last half-hour.

Sandy was watching with a confused frown. Debbie rounded on her. "What happened to the man that went in here about an hour ago?"

"Ma'am, I haven't been watching the lavatory. Is it your husband? There's a first-class cabin upstairs, too. Are you sure he's not up there? Stretch his legs?"

"He sits next to me." She pointed back down the aisle. "23B, on the aisle." The seat was still empty.

Sandy shrugged. "Well, sometimes on flights that aren't so crowded, we allow certain passengers to upgrade to first class. I'd check the upstairs cabin before I got too worried."

He wasn't upstairs. The deck shook beneath her feet, and with a melodic chime, the *Fasten Seatbelts* sign came on. Sandy looked relieved. "Ma'am," she said, when she saw Debbie coming, "you're going to have to return to your seat. The captain—"

Debbie went for one of the other attendants. He was a little older, somewhat less easily-fazed. "Look," she told him, "I know this is an odd request, but could you page him? Please?"

A few minutes later, George, the older attendant, came onto the intercom and said that there was a message for a Mr. Lloyd Kelson. It was urgent.

Lloyd Kelson didn't show up.

They told her that she had probably gotten the name wrong, so she had them check the passenger manifest. At first, they were reluctant to help her, but she made it clear that she wasn't going anywhere until they did, and eventually they caved. It was then that she had at least George's attention. She was right; the passenger listed for 23B was Lloyd Kelson, and suddenly, now, there was no Lloyd Kelson on the airplane.

Chapter 7

"I'm sorry sir, we really don't know any more than that." She was pretty, the airline receptionist—not quite Gregory's type, but certainly someone he didn't mind looking at for a while. Not this long, though.

"Can you at least tell me if there are any other flights I might be able to get onto that will get me out there sooner?"

She shook her head, blonde hair dancing over her blue eyes. "Sorry, sir, I told you already—we have no more flights going out this afternoon. They cancelled the evening ones because of the weather, but I honestly couldn't tell you why this one's been held up."

"What about with other airlines?"

"You'd have to talk to a manager."

He finally talked a free meal voucher out of her. She told him not to go telling the other passengers, though. The airline didn't like to spring for anything it didn't have to. He got a bad Chinese chicken salad from one of the overpriced little restaurants farther down the terminal. He needed the walk, and anyway, Burger King didn't accept the voucher.

When he came back, the departure time had been pushed again. He looked at the line to the desk. It was at least a dozen people long. There had been eight in front of him when he started, and it had taken him forty-five minutes to get to the blonde girl at the counter. His feet hurt.

He wandered over to the bank of windows that looked out on the runway and bent to rest his chin on the handrail. People bustled about on the tarmac, rushing to unload luggage, to pull a plane back from one gate or the other, to ensure that thousands of people got from Point A to Point B as fast as they possibly could. The world was cooking along at breakneck speed for everyone but the passengers of Flight 333.

He was so tired that he almost didn't realize what he was looking at. Planes drifted back and forth with such regularity that when one stopped at the edge of the runway, it stuck out like a sore thumb. Gregory blinked.

Flashing lights. Blue and red ones. Not an ambulance—not an elderly passenger with a faulty Pacemaker. A squad car shot out from the garage beneath the airport toward the stopped jet. Gregory watched it with growing interest. .

He stood up and craned his neck, pacing down the length of the window as the aircraft taxied toward a hangar under full police escort. There weren't that many terminals in this airport. He wasn't sure where he was, but it was small. They'd said it would just be a thirty-minute layover, just long enough to switch the planes out. That was three hours ago.

The plane disappeared from view.

Gregory checked his cell phone reception. It was bad. If Frida called, would she be able to reach him? He'd run a reverse lookup on her number, but she'd never picked up. The last time, he got a recording from the phone company that said it had been disconnected.

That frightened him. She'd sounded like she was in trouble, and the more time that passed, the more he began to fear that he was never going to hear from her again.

He wasn't even sure his connection would land him in the right place. He'd chosen Bangor. For some reason, it had sounded promising. Small. Safe.

He would book another flight with one of the other airlines, he told himself. The agents at the front desk were hedging. Something was going on. They didn't want to issue any new tickets.

"Call your travel agent," a dickhead in a red suit told him over at Continental. "See if you can book something for tomorrow."

Gregory went back through security, back to the gate. A pair of men in expensive suits stayed behind him the whole way. "Stay away from her," Detective Usher had warned him. Could these be her people?

Passengers were now hiking across the tarmac from the hangar where they'd hidden the 727. Several more police cars had arrived, and officers were directing them toward the main building.

Gregory approached a bulging businessman in a suit who he had tracked from the runway. "What's the deal?" Gregory asked. "What is all this?"

The man grimaced. "Some lady went apeshit up there, and now they're doing this whole investigation."

A cop—a woman, brown hair trailing behind her in braids—stepped between them. "Sir," she said, "were you on Flight 5656?" Gregory shook his head. "Then you shouldn't be talking to these passengers." She directed him to one of the seats by the desk and told him that she was sure the airline would compensate him for the time he'd lost today.

He went to the window and watched them drag the 727 out of the hangar. It wasn't coming to the terminal. He was going to be here all night.

It was another half-hour before the woman came out. He recognized her without asking any of the weary passengers from Flight 5656, who now sat in a cordoned off waiting area on the other side of the gate. She had a police escort, several plain-clothes officers who looked pissed. And worried.

They left her by the desk while they went to consult with the airline attendants and the other blue-shirts. Gregory waited until he was sure they weren't looking, and then he walked up to her.

"What's going on?"

She looked at him. She was vulnerable, he thought, weak and tired and scared. And then her face became a steel wall. "Leave me alone," she snapped, and hugged herself tightly.

That was when he saw the box. She'd been holding it so close that he hadn't noticed it beneath her sleeves. It was wooden, smooth, glistening in the fluorescent airport light. It was beautiful, probably worth a fortune.

"I mean, if you . . ." he trailed off. He hated it when women looked at him. Lupe always told him that that was his problem—he was never going to find his soul mate if he couldn't make himself look her in the eyes. He told her he'd tried to overcome it once or twice, because he honestly had. Then he stopped caring. That was the part of him she'd seen.

"Ask the police," she told him and turned the other way.

He opened his mouth and closed it a couple of times. *Lupe*, he thought. *What would Lupe say if she saw me now?* Steeling himself, he tapped her on the shoulder. She was back around facing him again so fast that he thought she was going to karate-chop him on the neck.

"Don't ever touch me again," she hissed. "Who the hell do you think you are?"

"Gregory Klein!"

She looked at him. "Is that supposed to mean something to me?"

"No! That's just . . . that's who the hell I think I am."

She kept staring at him, and it was with such intensity that he almost didn't notice the tiny smile that drew at the corners of her mouth. Then one of the police radios squawked, and she looked, and when she was watching him again, the smile was gone. "The guy in the seat next to me disappeared," she told him. "He was creepy and then he went to the bathroom and never came back."

Gregory frowned. "Huh?"

"Yeah, I know how it sounds. Believe me, they're not happy about it. People aren't supposed to disappear on an airplane. They're not supposed to disappear in an airport either. This day and age, if everything doesn't go like oiled machinery in the airline industry, the shit never stops hitting the fan."

"Do they know what happened to him?"

She shook her head. "Ran dogs through everyone's stuff. We

all had to sit on the plane while they did it. They can't find him. They're detaining everyone until they figure out what they're going to do."

The policewoman with the brown braids, who had been standing at the counter filling out paperwork, turned and caught sight of him. She whipped around and was across the terminal in a few seconds. "Sir," she said sternly, "I told you not to talk to these people."

"I only wanted to know what's going on."

"We're not releasing any details." She took him by the shoulders and pulled him away from the woman.

"Debbie Wendell," the woman called after him.

"I beg your pardon?"

"Sir!" The policewoman tugged harder.

"My name," Debbie mouthed.

Lupe would've been ashamed. He hadn't even tried to get her name.

Whatever. He would never see her again, anyway. But he was wrong. He saw her again that very same night.

He had to wait in the terminal a further four hours before the airline confessed that it was not planning on running Flight 333. Gregory was devastated. When, another two hours later, his turn at the counter came up, he tried to argue himself a free ticket with another airline.

"They've grounded all flights out of this airport tonight," the attendant said with a shrug of her burly shoulders. "There's nothing we can do."

"Are there cars?" he asked the attendant. "Buses? Anything?"

"We don't handle those kinds of transactions." She didn't bother consulting her colleagues. "You'd have to call your travel agent or our manager…or both. I'm really not sure. In the meantime, we're offering complimentary hotel rooms to passengers from Flight 333. We can try to rebook you on another flight tomorrow morning."

"Are they going to allow flights going out tomorrow?" Gregory asked.

She shrugged. "We really can't say right now, Mr. Klein."

So it was that he ended up on an airport shuttle bus to the hotel a few blocks away. He had not been expecting the Ritz, but he'd figured the airline would probably be partners with a decent chain.

He was wrong. Or perhaps they were, but they didn't utilize their partnership when it came to the overflow on a delayed flight. The hotel was a demilitarized zone, nestled amongst suburban sprawl from four decades ago that had slowly, quietly melted into piles of bricks and mold. The front was a cracked façade, covered in scaffolding and painters' tarps, though there was no sign of any recent work.

It was dark by the time they dropped him in the lobby with nothing but a slip of paper from the airline. The neighborhood was sketchy at best. He was just approaching the reception desk when a sports car peeled out through a red light at an intersection half a block down. Someone screamed, and that started the dogs barking.

The line for rooms was almost as long as the line at the airline desk, and that was probably just because the next busload of passengers hadn't arrived yet. By the time he got to the front, the hotel clerks were looking as harried as their customers.

"We're running low on rooms," the moustached man behind the counter told him. "You're going to have to take what you can get."

Gregory shrugged. "Okay. What does that mean?"

Smoking. Overlooking the indoor pool. No TV. He slipped the key across the desk and flashed a tired smile at the person in line behind Gregory. "Next, please."

The ice machine sat directly outside Gregory's door, and every fifteen minutes, the motor would whir to life, stir the half-frozen water inside, and deposit a load of ice cubes into the giant metal container that sat on the rear half of the machine.

The room reeked of mildew, and he kept hearing Frida's voice, the terrified scream, the scuffle. He got out of bed and began pacing the room. He drew himself a bath and then let it out when he got a good look at the tub. He poured himself a glass of water, tasted it, watched it swirl down the drain.

At last, tired and in desperate need of a change of scenery, Gregory shrugged back into his wrinkled, sweaty clothes and walked back down to the hotel lobby.

That was when he saw her. Debbie Wendell was sitting on a mangy sofa near the front of the lobby, typing on a laptop computer that appeared to be connected to one of the nearby phone jacks. He couldn't believe the luck.

He cut through the dwindling line of displaced passengers and approached her from behind. She looked up and stuck out a hand. "Klein, right?"

"Gregory, actually."

There was an awkward moment when he hadn't realized he was still holding her hand. He let go, coughed, and looked away.

They shared an interminable silence, at the end of which Debbie gave a grunting little laugh and motioned to the couch next to her. "You want to take a seat there, Mr. Gregory Klein, or were you just passing through on the breeze?"

With some considerable relief, he lowered himself onto the sofa by her side. He could feel her watching him, and when he stole a glance at her face, he saw that there was a funny little smile lifting the corners of her mouth. That made him nervous. Usually women who smiled at him were only thinking of ways they could mock or take advantage of him. Lupe had been the worst. When she smiled, it meant she needed a couple hundred bucks. She would bring him dinner or propose a romantic evening together just so she could avoid her landlord or get him to pay for the morning-after pills she used on the three other boyfriends she'd never mentioned.

"So tell me," Debbie said into the silence, "where you were going."

"Huh?"

"At the airport."

"Oh." How to explain? "I was just doing something . . . stupid. Obsessive."

"No shit? I was doing something stupid, too." She reached over and patted the little wooden box she had been holding earlier. Gregory hadn't seen it sitting on the cushion next to her.

Another long silence fell over them.

"I like you, Gregory Klein," she said out of nowhere. "You're the first guy I've met in a good few years who hasn't been a total asshole from the get-go." Gregory sputtered something incoherent, and Debbie stifled a laugh. "Yeah, that's what kills me," she said.

So she *was* making fun of him. The hurt must have shown on his face, because she reached out and put a hand on his arm.

"I'm sorry," she said, "I didn't mean that the way it sounded. It's just, all the – when I run into a man who doesn't already think he knows who I am and what I should be doing with my life, it's refreshing, that's all. It's a good thing. Trust me, the women of the world will love you for it."

She was bullshitting him – right? He tried to work up the courage to look her in the eye.

Just as the silence was getting unbearable, there was a squeal of tires from the street. Someone shouted, and a moment later, there was the *bang* of a quick collision followed by the awful grinding of metal on metal. A second or two passed—something suspended in mid-air—and then a second *crash* as it landed. Then two more. The tinkle of shattered glass danced lightly atop the blare of a stuck horn.

Debbie and Gregory looked at each other, and then out the lobby window at the street. A few pedestrians scurried toward the intersection, and several people had come out of the decaying tenement buildings on the opposite side. A dozen sets of eyes peered out from behind curtains.

"Jesus." Debbie rose, setting the laptop computer on the coffee table, and went to the window.

Gregory felt awful for it, but the thing that commanded his interest was the computer screen. He sat forward, squinting at the tiny text. She was on the internet, looking up something in a search engine. There were photographs, names, phone numbers. *Lloyd Kelson*, the title of the page read. She had been searching for someone named Lloyd Kelson.

"Hey," she said. He looked up, guilty, but she wasn't watching him. "Come here."

A car rested on its side just off the intersection. Its nose was pressed up onto the sidewalk; it had demolished several parking meters and had taken half of a bus stop with it. Someone was sitting on the curb nearby, a young woman, her head in her hands. A small crowd had assembled around her, around the car, and around something else in the middle of the intersection that Gregory couldn't see.

"Let's go out there," Debbie said.

"We shouldn't." Gregory caught her as she started to slip past him. "It's voyeuristic. It's vulgar."

"They might need help." She pulled free from his grasp with surprising ease and speed and pushed out the lobby door.

The desk clerk looked from the place where she had just been standing to Gregory, as though to say, "What are you, a pussy? Go after her!"

He drew in a breath, bracing himself for the worst, and then dove out onto the street.

Chapter 8

The driver of the limousine pulled to the side of the road when it seemed they were farthest from civilization. Jackie waited, breathless. The partition rolled down a few inches.

"Are you hungry?" the chauffeur asked.

Nervously, Jackie shook her head. "Where are we going?"

The partition rolled back up, and the limousine pulled onto the highway again.

Jackie watched the scenery go by in blurs of slow-motion color. Every now and then, she would fix on a farmhouse or a pair of abandoned silos in the outskirts of a small town, and she would think of home. What if Walker had come back? What if something had happened to Dad? It wasn't as though the company ever gave him that much protection when they sent him contract-hunting in the most dangerous countries on Earth. She should've stayed, born out the loneliness and tried to understand what had been happening.

She watched the sun track across the sky. They drove for most of the day, farther than she had ever gone in her entire life. She had never been out of Weylan County before. She'd never been very far out of the village, for that matter. Walker had always told her they had everything they needed right where they were; there was no point in looking for trouble and corruption when you could be so happy without lifting a finger.

She resented that. She'd read so much, had seen art and photography from so many places that at times, while the other children were out playing under the summer sun, she would sit beneath the old tree in the backyard and visit faraway places in her imagination. She would pretend that she was sitting at a café in Florence, or that she was perched atop one of the great Egyptian pyramids.

It was funny; as a young girl, she'd had boundless respect for Walker. He was older, he knew better, he was the successful one. She had assumed that emulating him would bring her happiness and success as well, but there was one problem. As she grew up and saw him through more mature eyes, she realized that he wasn't happy, that he made mistakes, that he wasn't even particularly smart. That had even been before he started getting so distant. Before he woke up and realized his life was trickling away without him.

The limousine shuddered and started to pull to the side of the road again. The partition dropped an inch. "We have to stop for gas," the chauffeur said. "Then we drive another five minutes and we are there."

They had been on the road for hours—most of the day. They were stopping for a break *now?* "Where?" she asked. "Where's *there?*"

The partition closed again.

Jackie debated whether she should get out and try to make a break for it when they stopped at the service station another few miles down the road. The pump attendant was just a boy, maybe a year or two older than her, and kind of cute. She could sneak out and throw her arms around him while the chauffeur was in the restroom, and then he would have to protect her, because that was what young almost-men did when damsels in distress appealed to their masculinity.

But the chauffeur never got out of the car.

They pulled out of the station, and she twisted around in her seat to watch the attendant through the rear windshield. He was leaning against the pump, staring after them.

The driver didn't get back on the highway. Instead, the limousine bounced onto a small dirt road that wound along parallel to it for a while before curving up over a large, rocky hill. On the other side, they descended into a depression in the ground filled with dry grass and dead trees. It looked like an oasis that had dried up back in the '50s.

Up ahead, she glimpsed the roof of a magnificent house protruding from a stand of dead wood and shriveled foliage. The limousine wove toward it, slipping between the carcasses of abandoned luxury cars that had long since rusted and begun to sink into the earth.

She couldn't see the house anymore, and then the car stopped. The front door opened, and the limousine shifted on its shocks as the chauffeur got out. He approached a large iron gate and removed the lock that was hanging by a thick chain about its latch. With a groan like a whale, it swung open, and then they drove through it.

Jackie felt like she was entering another world in another time. Beyond the gate, dead branches clamored to touch the roof of the car. She heard their dry little fingertips scraping across the black paint. Between them here and there, a cobblestone path connected a dried-up fountain, a crumbling Roman statue, and a few small outbuildings that looked like they hadn't been opened since before she was born.

And then the car came to a halt. She gazed about, and then she realized that she'd been looking out the wrong window. She climbed across the black velvet seat and her jaw fell open.

She'd read about houses like this and even seen a few pictures from a dusty old history book at the library. It was enormous, a relic from a southern plantation, resplendent in its faded glory. Giant white columns supported a roof that came to a point over the curving driveway. Torches were mounted in sconces across the front of the façade, and when they were lit, she imagined, the place would look like a palace.

The limousine rocked again, and then the chauffeur was opening her door.

"We are here," he whispered to her when she didn't move. "Well, come on." He started for the front door. "We can't keep them waiting. I'm already almost half an hour late. I wasn't planning on stopping for gas, but the extra weight in the passenger compartment must have worn down on the fuel efficiency . . ."

She followed him, picking her way numbly up the front steps. From here, she couldn't even see the gate or the hills beyond. Crisscrossing branches obstructed her view. Where was she? But deep down inside, she didn't care—where didn't matter. She was in a fantasy. She couldn't have been happier.

Then the front door opened.

He didn't look human. That was the first thought that entered her head when she saw Thomas Marlowe's stooped form in the doorway. His face was too small, too pinched around the nose. His hair was too thin and spindly, his shoulders too bent and uneven. He was just over half her height, but his eyes burned with an intensity that frightened her.

Jackie took a step back, but the chauffeur took her shoulder in a firm grip. "Sir, I've brought a guest."

Marlowe's eyes widened. She shied away when he approached her. "Is this her?" He reached with fingers that looked as though they had been broken a hundred times in a hundred different places. "You've brought her already?"

The chauffeur shook his head. "Not her. But I thought you might enjoy her company along the way."

Marlowe's face registered mild disappointment. "No, of course." He looked her up and down again most disagreeably. "She's too imperfect. Too empty. I should have known." The old man turned and hobbled inside. "I want some tea," he said over his shoulder.

They remained on the porch. When he was halfway into the corridor beyond, he paused and turned back. "Oh, for heaven's sake, bring her in."

It was even more stunning inside than it was out. The walls

were papered with magnificent designs, each room decorated in a different theme. Jackie's favorite was the dining room, done up to feel like an African safari. Most of it was a mystic green with hints of jungle and foliage painted in at just the right places. A herd of elephants charged out from the footboards by one door, and near the ceiling, the green faded to bright yellow acacia trees and rolling, sun-drenched plains.

The furniture matched, carved wood and crumbling stone relics on every surface.

It was like a dozen different time warps built into a single secluded house.

By the time she and the chauffeur met up with the man in the sunroom at the back of the house, she saw him in a new light. She wanted to pick the brain that had developed a place like this.

But he was surly. On the table was a silver platter of cucumber sandwiches, and beside them, frosted sweet pastries that smelled delightful. He gobbled them up without meeting her eye. Then, when there was only one sandwich and nothing but crumbs left of the pastries, he slammed his fist down on the table and bellowed:

"Why do you insult me like this?"

It took her a few startled seconds to realize he was talking to her. "I . . . I'm sorry?"

"You do not like my cooking? Why do you not eat?" He shoved the platter at her so fast that she didn't have time to get her hands out of the way. It smashed her fingers, and she let out a yelp.

Not wanting to make him any angrier, she took the sandwich and shoved it in her mouth.

"Well. That's not very ladylike."

It was ghastly. It had looked wonderful on the platter, but there was something wrong with the mayonnaise. She wondered how long it had been sitting in his refrigerator, or if it had been refrigerated at all.

The chauffeur cleared the table while the old man stared at her. Jackie peered out through the arching windows, but there was little to see. The view was filled with dense, dry foliage.

"Yes," he said suddenly, out of nowhere. "You will do." He reached inside the flowing gold-leafed bathrobe he had donned for the meal and pulled out a small rectangular piece of paper. "You want to see your sister, my dear?"

Jackie frowned at him. *He must be mad*, she thought. Nevertheless, her curiosity was piqued. She nodded earnestly at him and leaned forward as he put the paper on the table and slid it across to her. It was a photograph, she saw, an old black-and-white one.

She picked it up and froze. It was a girl, maybe a few years older than she. She looked young, vital, but slightly uncomfortable. And there was something about her eyes—they seemed to fix Jackie in their stare and refused to release her.

She had seen it somewhere before.

She tried to think where. It had been at school. Perhaps in an old history book. That would seem appropriate, given the quality of the image. Or maybe in the attic, maybe looking through old things with Walker?

Smiling uneasily, Jackie slid it back across the table to him. "She's pretty," she said, because he seemed to be expecting some kind of response and she had no idea what to say.

"She's going to be my daughter," he said with no small measure of glee.

Going to be?

The chauffeur came back from the kitchen, wiping his hands on his trousers, and announced that they had better be on their way if they were going to keep any semblance of the schedule they had originally outlined. The old man sighed and rose, and after preparing himself for a further twenty minutes in one of the upstairs rooms, he was finally ready.

"Who is this man?" she asked the chauffeur while Marlowe was still occupied. Even though she could hear him moving about through the ceiling, she did not trust him not to have some way of listening to them while he dressed.

"Nobility," the chauffeur answered. "His name is Thomas Marlowe, but you are never to address him as such."

"What do I call him?"

The chauffeur gave her an odd look. "Father," he said, and then Marlowe was standing on the stairs, urging them to go.

The limousine ambled through the dead forest to the iron gate and paused again as the chauffeur got out to lock it behind them.

"Wave to the house," Marlowe commanded.

She looked at him and saw that he was turned around in his seat so that he could look out the back window. To her astonishment, there were tears on his wrinkled cheeks. "Say goodbye to it!" he barked.

She turned, gave a little wave, and muttered a goodbye. "Aren't you coming back?" she asked as the car pulled away and he slumped into his seat.

"Of course," he said, "but the house will miss us, and we will miss the house."

Jackie was frightened. Marlowe was genuinely unbalanced and completely in control. She shivered and crammed herself as far away from the old man as she possibly could. A strange smell hung about him. Trapped in a confined space, it became overpowering. It was fishy, with hints of other things. Like he hadn't washed in weeks. She started to open a window, but he turned and fixed her with such a venomous glare that she immediately put it back up.

"I will read you a story," Marlowe declared, and for the next several hours, well into the night, he read to her from old picture books that he kept stowed in a small compartment beneath the seat.

Whenever he finished one and went for another, she craned her neck and got a little longer of a glimpse at the contents of the box. There were other children's toys in there, too: a rainbow-striped rubber ball, a pile of Halloween masks, a few other odds and ends she couldn't quite make out. She thought again of the picture, of the girl with the piercing eyes.

⌐⫯⌐

Thomas had fallen asleep in the midst of a Dr. Seuss book, when the car shuddered beneath her feet. After another few miles, they pulled off at a small service station. It stood alone in the middle of the rolling plains, a single droplet of harsh white light in an ocean of blackness.

She started to get out of the car, but the chauffeur quickly came around and pushed her door shut again. "You shouldn't get out here," he said. "A place like this in the middle of the night can be dangerous."

Yeah, Jackie thought, *because of people like you.*

Tall but stocky, the attendant here was older than the kid at the last station, but he had been handsome once. He nodded and pointed down the road a little way. He couldn't take his eyes off of the limousine.

She'd give anything to be out and free again. She'd wanted an adventure, but all she wanted now was to be out of this car.

The limousine rocked. The engine started. They pulled away from the gas station. She crawled back to the back seat and watched out the rear window as the man and his pool of light receded into the darkness. *Goodbye*, she thought. *He* was worth waving to.

Thomas awoke and saw her just as she was turning back around. "Who was that?" he demanded.

"Just some station attendant. He looked lonely."

"Did he see you?"

Jackie shrugged. "It was dark. I don't think so."

"You don't think so?"

She gave a noncommittal grunt. She wasn't sure where Thomas was going with all of this, why he cared so deeply. He threw down the Dr. Seuss book and clambered to the front of the compartment. With twisted knuckles, he rapped on the partition. It lowered a few inches.

"We have to go back," he hissed to the chauffeur. "He saw her."

"I don't understand," Jackie said as Marlowe slumped back into the seat beside her.

"Stupid, stupid girl," he grumbled to himself.

A few moments later, the pool of fluorescent light reappeared ahead of them. The attendant, who was just walking back inside, heard the limousine on the highway and turned. His face lit up. He made his way back to the pump as the car came to a halt.

"Well howdy again," Jackie heard him say as the chauffeur stepped out of the driver's seat. "What can I do ya for?"

The chauffeur went around to the back of the car and opened the trunk. The attendant followed him like a lost puppy, bubbling puzzled remarks. Something *thumped* against the frame of the car. She could feel it through her shoes.

She twisted around in her seat so she could see out the back window just as the trunk slammed shut. There was the chauffeur, impeccably dressed, holding a crowbar.

"No!" Jackie shouted.

Thomas Marlowe started throwing things at her when she wouldn't stop bawling. Finally, he clapped a hand over her mouth. Each breath she inhaled brought stale drafts of something awful from his flesh. She got dizzy and lowered her voice.

When the chauffeur returned to the driver's seat, Marlowe tapped on the partition again. "There's still some blood on the back window," he scolded.

The chauffeur took care of it.

"And you." Marlowe rounded on Jackie as they pulled away for the second time. "See what you've done? See what a careless fool you've been? Don't ever do that again, do you hear me?"

She nodded. She wasn't even sure what she was agreeing to, but she knew she didn't want to make him mad.

Then, crassly, lewdly, he burst into dry laughter. "Don't you fear," he said. "You're my daughter, and I'll never hurt you. You can do no wrong. But if you do, you're not my daughter anymore." He went serious. "Then you'd better fear for your fucking life."

Jackie already did.

She didn't remember much from the rest of the drive. They went on, the sun rising, peaking, beginning to set again, her mind racing the entire time. She kept seeing it happen again and again. She closed her eyes and watched the stack of hubcaps topple, the lone tire rolling away onto the highway.

You're my daughter. She felt sick.

She was going to ask that they pull over, but then they were racing off the highway, deserted, rolling hills becoming dingy shops and burnt-out factories. They'd made it, wherever they were going. They would have to get out of the car at last, and when they did she'd have a prayer of getting away.

Something out the back window caught her eye. Her chest seized up. Two black cars, identical, prowling in the shadows behind them. She didn't think she'd seen them before, but somehow, instinctively, she knew they were following the limousine. She twisted back around to say something to the chauffeur.

Then they had the accident.

Chapter 9

A day into his trip, Terry knew why he and Vicki had decided not to take a bus ride on their honeymoon. After only a few hours, he felt like he was living in some strange half-alive, half-dead state. He could never grab enough sleep. The seats were shamefully uncomfortable, and whenever he managed to find a position that would afford him a little rest, the bus would begin to slow, the lights would come on, and the driver would announce that they were going to have another fifteen-minute stretch break.

Terry asked if they were really necessary at one stop, when they were pulled to the side of the road at around eleven at night. The driver just looked at him and shrugged. "Regulations," he said. "We've got a schedule. They have rules. I think it's so I don't doze off at the wheel."

He began to get a sore throat around two in the morning. He reached the point where he was too tired to sleep. He would close his eyes and his head would swim, and then they would stop and the lights would come on.

At around four, they pulled into a rest area. He hadn't been looking out the windows for some time. This time of night, the roads weren't lit very well, and the windows were glossed over with reflections of the passengers.

They were in a forest. Terry could see his breath when he

stepped off the bus into the parking lot. The other passengers milled around, some escaping to the restrooms, others heading to small patches of grass beside the empty parking spaces to stretch their legs and mingle with newly-formed friends.

Terry removed himself from the crowd and was about to skulk back onto the bus when he caught sight of someone hunched over a picnic table in the meadow a little way from the restrooms. It was a secluded place, surrounded on all sides by stands of tall trees and thick foliage. Terry tramped out across the grass until he was twenty or thirty feet from the table. Then, he slowed and looked more closely.

It was a woman—long brown hair in need of a good wash. She was wearing combat fatigues that would've been scraggly and repulsive on a man, but which somehow enhanced her image. He liked her already. She seemed rebellious, dangerous, mysterious, tucked away out here in a clearing among a remote stand of trees.

He brushed aside one of the low-hanging branches. A twig broke beneath his shoe, and suddenly, she straightened, looked around, fixed on him. Her face was still concealed in shadows, but there was something strange about her. Her body was heavily built, muscular in ways he would not have expected.

Oh. It hit him when he was ten feet away. It wasn't a woman. "Who are you?" the man asked.

"Hi," Terry stammered. "Sorry to bother you. I thought . . . I thought you were a woman . . ." He flinched.

The man straightened, squared his shoulders, challenged. "What the fuck is that supposed to mean?"

Terry glanced back at the tour bus, and suddenly it seemed very, very far away. "I didn't mean that the way it sounded." He took a few steps back. The man was on the offensive now, approaching with a steady, grim determination that frightened Terry. "I only meant . . . I'm looking for someone, a woman."

"Who? Who are you looking for? And why'd you think she was out here? Ain't you from the bus?" The light played upon his crooked teeth and the sizable gap between them.

"Can I show you her picture?" Terry pulled the photograph from his pocket. She caught his eye again, and his heart jumped. He didn't want to let her go.

He held it up, but when the man reached for it, Terry shook his head and pulled it away. "Just look," Terry said.

The man squinted, shrugged, and was about to shake his head when something caught his eye. He leaned a little closer. He smelled like pee. Terry tried not to show the disgust on his face.

"No shit." The man snorted to himself.

"What is it?" Terry started to put the picture away, but the man reached out and caught it with a dirty thumb and forefinger.

"Let me see that just a second," he said.

Terry tried to protest, but just then, the bus honked its horn. The driver was loading all of the passengers back onboard. They'd been here fourteen minutes. They were going to drive off, and then Terry would be alone here with this man.

"I have to go," Terry said with a hurried glance over his shoulder. "Please, do you know her? Do you know where she lives?"

"I've seen her," the man said. "No shit, no shit." He tugged a little harder on the picture. "Hey, man, let me see it."

"No . . ." Terry pulled back. Over in the parking lot, the passengers had almost all disappeared onto the bus. The driver, standing up by the grille, was looking around like the parent of a young child. Terry could see his mouth moving and knew just what he was saying—"Are we missing anyone? Everyone on the bus?"

He had to leave. Now.

The man sighed. "Look, I'll show you." He released his grasp on the photograph, and Terry stuffed it in his pocket. The man went for something tucked away in his waistband—a crumpled piece of paper—a picture.

It wasn't possible. Terry could see it before he even had it out in the light. By now, the slope of her shoulders and the look in her eyes were emblazoned in his mind. But how could it be true? The man held it up, and there she was. Hacker. Her name was Hacker.

"Does it have a date on it?"

The man squinted at him. "A what?"

"Turn it over. Let me see the back."

"Let me see yours first."

A second honk. The driver only ever honked twice. The engine started. The doors slid shut. Terry looked back. "Hey!" he shouted. "Just a minute!" There was no way the driver could hear him, nestled into his air-conditioned throne, submerged beneath the rattling, whirring of the diesel engine.

"Let me see it, kiddo. Your ride's going to take off without you."

Reluctantly, Terry surrendered his picture. He snatched the man's copy from his grimy fingers and turned it over. On the back, there was a penciled inscription. *The same thing*, Terry thought. No help at all. He was going to be late, perhaps going to be left behind, and he hadn't learned anything.

Except the inscription was different.

He blinked.

"Hey, who the hell is Hacker?" the man said.

Terry tipped the photograph so that the light spilled across the penciled letters: *Shayla*. Her first name was Shayla. Shayla Hacker. *19—?* The year wasn't on there, but he had a full name. He could search for someone if he had a name and a picture.

The bus shifted into gear and the engine kicked in. Terry glanced back just as the headlights came on and it started to rumble toward the edge of the parking lot. "Shit!" Terry said. "Give me my picture back."

"Hey, I've been looking for her, too, you know. Let's talk about it. I live in a cabin out here." Suddenly, he seemed very large, imposing, muscular.

Terry turned and ran. His heart thumped in his chest. His legs were weak from the lack of exercise over the last few days, and a stitch tied itself into a knot in his side.

The bus was almost out of the parking lot, and he could hear footsteps in the dry grass behind him.

"Wait!" Terry shouted at the top of his lungs.

The bus did not wait.

His shoes hit pavement. He was getting weaker. A couple of hundred feet and he would collapse. It was pathetic—but then, he hadn't eaten anything in hours, almost two days—and most of the time he'd been sitting down, inert, woozy.

When he glanced over his shoulder, the man was right there, five, maybe ten feet behind him. "Don't run!" the man called. "Let's talk. Let's go to the cabin!" He wasn't even winded.

Terry shivered. "Wait!" he called one more time.

The bus bounced up over the curb, into the street. Terry deflated. He started to fall to his knees, and then he saw red— brake lights. Someone had noticed him.

"Hey," the driver said.

Terry pounded up to him, wheezing, embarrassed. "I'm . . . I'm sorry. I just . . . there was this . . ." He turned, squinting into the pool of yellow light by the cinderblock restroom building. No sign of the man. No sign of anyone at all.

"Are you okay?" the driver asked. "You don't look okay. You look pale. You're sweating. Where did you go?" He tugged at Terry's arm, and the two of them started back inside the bus. "Don't you know that we have a strict schedule? Fifteen minutes at each stop. I told you to check your watch. I told everyone to check their watches."

Inside the bus, the air was warm, moist. Everyone was staring at him. It smelled like sweat, body odor. *This is my family*, he thought. How repulsive an idea it was.

Terry muttered a hasty apology to the driver and shuffled to one of the empty seats a few rows away from the Japanese tourists.

"Hi." It was a little girl, twelve, maybe thirteen, too young to be traveling on a Greyhound bus by herself, but obviously unattached to anyone in the compartment. "I'm the one who saw you. I thought I heard someone shouting."

"Thanks," Terry said. He reached out to shake her hand, and that was when he realized that he was still holding the man's copy of the photograph. He unfolded it and searched the back for the penciled inscription: *Shayla*. Not just Hacker. Shayla Hacker.

Out the window, he caught a brief glimpse of the man's shadow between two trees.

Later, he would be unsure whether he'd actually seen it, or if it had been another figment of his imagination. But it was in the right place, out there in the meadow beneath the yellow light. That was all he needed.

Terry tapped the girl on the shoulder. "Hey, tell me something." He held up the picture. "Do you know this woman?"

The girl looked it over, shrugged. "I don't think so."

He wasn't sure whether that was good or bad, but it was something. Not everyone in the world was creepy and crazy. He was about to fold it back up and put it away.

"But you know . . ." She bit her lip. "I don't know, I think I may have seen her, actually."

"You what?"

The girl squinted at the picture. "Yeah, she looks sorta like . . . I dunno, like maybe I've seen her is all."

"Who is she?"

"I don't know."

"Who is she? Who is Shayla Hacker?"

The girl got up and, giving him a funny look, walked to another seat at the back of the bus. This was going to kill him, he thought. This obsession was going to be the end of him. He needed something solid to hang onto, some island of reason in his life right now.

If only he could get an hour or two of undisturbed sleep, he might be able to think more clearly, but the question kept him up the rest of the night: *Who is Shayla Hacker?*

Chapter 10

The police came, but there was little for them to do. Joseph sympathized with them. Though he had never been to a crime scene quite as bizarre as this one before, there had been other instances when, upon arrival, his presence had seemed perfectly useless.

He and Jean were made to retell their side of the story, such as it was, several times, while different uniformed officers took down every word they spoke and nodded encouragingly whenever they paused for breath.

Jean was having trouble breathing. He put an arm around her shoulders and took her to the back of the pickup truck the officers had arrived in. "The furniture," she kept saying. "Thank god most of it was already in storage. But what about the loom? And the sofas?" She looked at him. "Joe, what about the dining room?"

He approached the pathetic remains of their house just as the whoop of a siren heralded the arrival of the cavalry. He climbed the cracked, brick steps and knelt by what once had been the front porch, the same porch to which he had come home every night for more years than he felt like counting.

"Joe!"

He looked back. Kelsey Robins. Christ, why was he here? This was small-time; he shouldn't have been out of the office for something like this, where it was unlikely there would be any developments in the case in the next few hours.

He nodded to Kelsey and then turned back. Joseph could distantly remember it from his own days at the academy—always give the victim room to mourn, unless circumstances prohibit such leeway. But perhaps Kelsey didn't have the real-world experience to realize that not all losses were human.

Crouching, Joseph perched atop a pile of splintered wood that had been a hanging bench swing. He and Jean had always said that they would rock their children to sleep on that swing. He remembered hot summer days, lying across it, eyes closed, imagining he could hear boys playing in the sprinkler on the front lawn, girls sharing secrets through the bedroom window.

Somewhere along the way, they'd stopped saying that to each other, and then he'd stopped coming outside altogether. It was only just beginning to dawn on him how much they had lost.

"Detective Malloy!" Kelsey crunched across the brown lawn, waving at him in his cheap brown suit. "I'm so sorry. I came as soon as I heard."

"I'm not sure there's much you can do."

"I trust the guys have already taken down all the information?" Joseph nodded.

"So I'm sure you've been over it a hundred times, but just so I'm up to speed—you have no idea why this might have happened? Who might have done it?"

Joseph shook his head.

"Well, shit." Kelsey shaded his eyes and peered across the rubble like a slaveholder surveying his plantation. "I'll get the team on this right away, of course. Bad business." An awkward pause. He came over and squatted beside Joseph. "Hey," he said, giving him a little nudge on the shoulder. "You okay? I mean, you going to be okay with this?"

"Can I ask you a favor?" Joseph said.

"Of course, Detective. That's what I'm here for."

"Jean was feeling a little light-headed. Could you go look after her?"

The young cop seemed confused. He glanced over his shoulder and squinted at the pickup truck, where Jean was now sprawled out in the flatbed. "Are you sure you'd rather not . . . I mean . . ."

"Thanks, Mr. Robins. It's a load off my mind." Joseph rose and made his way around to the back of the house before Kelsey could finish his sentence.

Joseph didn't have a chance to look over the grounds very thoroughly. Kelsey was back at his side five minutes later.

"She says she wants to talk to you," he said, and then there was no turning him down.

Jean and Joseph spent the rest of the afternoon filling out paperwork down at headquarters and talking on the phone to the insurance company. It was strange to be back at the police station. All of the receptionists smiled and said hi; everyone waved. Nothing had changed. This could have been any one of the times he had taken a week-long vacation and returned the Monday afterward.

He caught sight of his former office, the door hanging open, the walls white. A computer sat on a barren desk in the middle, and there were a few paper bags full of personal items on the floor near the far wall—Kelsey's things, probably. That was when he knew he didn't belong here anymore.

They stayed at a hotel that night, furnished by the police department in their sympathy for the Malloys' plight. The following morning, Joseph took a taxi over to the service center and picked up the RV. The mechanics hadn't quite finished with everything yet, but Joseph felt guilty using the taxpayers' money for a room at the Travelodge, and Kelsey wouldn't hear of him paying for it himself.

"It smells like paint," Jean said, wrinkling her nose. She set her bag gingerly on the carpet and climbed inside, looking around.

"They didn't finish with the trim."

"It'll be fine," he told her.

They checked into a local RV park and Joseph spent the rest of the afternoon hooking up all the hoses and building a campfire. He had just finished barbecuing a burger and a dog for himself and a Portobello mushroom for Jean when Kelsey stopped by. It was only a matter of time, he supposed. He hadn't realized how much he should have been appreciating the peace until now.

"Detective Malloy!" Kelsey called with his usual enthusiasm, before he'd even shut off the engine of the unmarked police cruiser. He climbed out and jogged across the leaf-strewn road. "You're quite the cook, if I may say so myself. I could smell your dinner from across the whole campground."

Jean gave Joseph the same dirty look she'd given him a hundred times when he'd brought home a colleague from work.

"What can I do for you, Kelsey?" Joseph asked.

"I just came by to see how you were settling in."

"Well, we're pretty good. Best as can be expected. Just sitting down to an old-fashioned camping meal . . ."

"You could've stayed in the hotel."

"We're planning on shipping out pretty soon," Jean spoke up.

Kelsey raised an eyebrow. "Not going to stick around for the rest of the case?"

"Jean wants to put it behind us. We've lived here since before you were born, Kelsey. We have mostly good memories. We're on our way out before we forget what it was like when all was right here. So if you need us, you can call . . ."

Kelsey snapped and drew a slow, guilty breath through his teeth. "See, that's the thing," he said. "I kind of have to ask you to stick around for a little bit. We're still going through all the motions right now, and there's just some . . . there are a few business points in all of this that we might . . . need your help on."

It was Joseph's turn to stare. "What business points?"

"Oh, just, you know, bureaucratic stuff." Kelsey was shifting his weight from foot to foot. He was nervous, suddenly ill-at-ease.

"I do know," Joseph said coldly. "Don't forget, Detective Robins, I've been right where you're standing more times than you've unzipped your fly."

Jean looked from Joseph to Kelsey. "What's going on?" she demanded.

"I just need you guys to be reachable . . ." Kelsey floundered.

"By phone? We just got a cell," Jean offered.

"By handcuffs," Joseph said, never removing his gaze from Kelsey's face. "He wants to be sure he can catch us and haul us off to the pen if it turns out we were behind all of this."

Genuine shock registered on Jean's face. "Behind it? Why on Earth would we knock down our own house?"

"You want to tell her, Detective?"

"Uh, well, Mrs. Malloy . . . I . . . uh . . ."

"Insurance money," Joseph interrupted. "He thinks we bulldozed our own house so we could collect on the cash before we split town in our RV. Isn't that right, Detective Robins?"

"Please, Joe, you know it's all just a formality."

"It is," Joseph said. "And we don't discuss formalities over dinner. I'll be by your office in the morning to sort all of this out."

"Well, I'm not sure how much sorting . . ."

"I'll see you tomorrow, Detective," Joseph barked.

Four minutes later, the sound of Kelsey's engine had faded on the evening air. They finished their dinner in silence. Joseph knew how it would turn out. They would never find the perpetrator. They would find no evidence of foul play either. The case would eventually be closed, and the official word would be that the house had somehow collapsed on itself. But suspicion would abound. Everyone in town would assume that they'd done it for the payoff. Their names would be sullied forever.

But the case was far from closed.

⌒◦⫘◦

That night, unable to sleep, Joseph called a cab and had the driver take him to 117 West Carver Street. He couldn't help it; being inert—useless—was killing him.

The gap between the houses was visible from the end of the block. All of the rubble was still there; Kelsey had ordered everything left as it was until they'd done a thorough once-over of the whole lot. Joseph's stomach gave a little turn. He wasn't used to seeing it this way; how could he be?

Broken pieces of wood and chipped bricks protruded at obscene angles from the rubble. The taxi driver glanced back through the wire screen partition and gave him a questioning look. "This the place?" he said. "Yeah?"

Joseph didn't say anything. He just paid him and told him he could go. He was going to be here a while.

Jean would kill him if she knew he was out here. He knelt and started sifting through the wreckage. There were shattered frames, a few intact photos or videocassettes here and there. Some of Jean's old statuettes and a silver cigarette tray had somehow escaped the giant wooden beam that had crushed the armoire and splintered the frame of the guest bed as it fell from the second floor.

It wasn't until he got to the back of the house, to the tool shed, that he found it. The shed had been left intact, though bulldozer tracks surrounded it in deep furrows through the wet earth. The police had roped off the structure, separating it from the crime scene, but they had evidently neglected to search it themselves.

There was a note pinned to the workbench inside. Anyone could have seen it if they'd bothered to look.

Let her be, it said. Beneath it was another Xerox of the Hacker girl. Joseph shivered. Was that what this was all about? A fragment of an investigation he hadn't even wanted? A trace piece, a clue of a case that wasn't even his?

Damn you, Kelsey Robins, Joseph thought.

As though on cue, he heard the sound of a car engine in front of the house. He didn't have to ask who it was. There were two people who might possibly be driving here in the middle of the night, and one of them was asleep in an RV.

Joseph picked his way back out through the remnants of the leveled house just in time to meet up with Kelsey on the front lawn. He recognized him from the slight imbalance in his shoulders, the tilt of his head. The old police cruiser was idling at the curb, but there was nobody else inside.

"Detective Malloy?" Not quite as enthusiastic as usual.

"Hello, Kelsey."

"I got a call from one of the neighbors, said she saw a suspicious person looking through the wreckage over here. I thought I knew who it would be, but you can never be too careful." He showed Joseph the gun he'd brought, and then quickly flipped the safety back on and jammed it into his pocket.

"So are you going to tell me what you're doing out here?" Joseph fixed him with a hard stare. "Uh, I mean, Detective Malloy . . . "

"It's my house, Robins. It's my property, and it's my right to be here."

Kelsey sighed. "Look, Joe, I'm going to be straightforward with you, because I can see we're never going to hit it off if we keep dancing around the issue like this. Yes, you're a suspect. We don't know what happened out here. I believe you, Joe, but I'm not the only one whose opinion counts, and legally, we've got to check all the options."

"You want to know why I don't have patience for any of your bullshit? You want to know why I hate you? Because I do hate you, Kelsey, I do. Here's why." He pulled out the note and jammed it into Kelsey's hand.

He was halfway down the block before it sank in and Kelsey came jogging to catch up with him. "Joe, I don't understand," Kelsey called. "What does this mean? Where did you get this? This is a joke, right?"

Joseph spun around. "This, Kelsey," he said, snatching the letter back, "is why my wife and I are living in an RV park."

"Where, Detective Malloy?"

"In the tool shed. Next time, tell your bloodhounds to do

their jobs. They should still know how from when someone competent was in the command chair." He left Kelsey standing in the middle of the sidewalk, staring brokenly after him.

He almost felt bad for the kid.

Fuck him, Joseph thought. He wanted nothing but to get out of this damn town and leave it all behind.

Except that wasn't quite true.

It was almost morning by the time he got back to the RV park. Jean was standing outside, holding a Styrofoam cup of coffee.

Neither of them said anything to each other. They made breakfast—bacon, eggs, pancakes, the works. Joseph recognized the pattern; they'd done it a hundred times. When they couldn't talk, they busied themselves with little meaningless chores until one of them finally cracked.

But this time, neither of them did. Joseph couldn't stop thinking about the girl. Who the hell was she? Why was she worth knocking down a goddamn house?

By the afternoon, he had resolved to go back into the office. He told Jean that he was going to run some errands. She still didn't talk to him. He wondered if she thought he was having an affair, or if he'd run off and done something awful; if so, she was beyond help right now. She should know better.

Kelsey wasn't happy to see him when he came in. The young detective had a haunted look about him; Joseph guessed that he'd been up the rest of the night, too. Probably even in the office.

"I don't know what to tell you right now, Joe," Kelsey said, when Claire had finally let him in. "If this is because of me, I'm sorry. If it's some kind of sick joke because you think I've been harassing you, I swear . . ."

"I want to find her," Joseph heard himself say. "I want to know who she is, and I want to know who cares so much that they'd knock down my house."

Kelsey stared at him for a long time, then got up and closed the door. He turned off the TV news, which was saying something about a possible sex scandal with the Pope. *Sensationalism*, Joseph thought, *all of it.*

"Officially, Joe, the investigation hasn't gone anywhere."

Joseph's eyes narrowed. "But there's a reason you closed that door."

"Yes." Kelsey nodded. "Yes, there is."

When Joseph walked out of the office that afternoon, he had with him a map and a list of names and addresses. And he had a new respect for Kelsey Robins. Whatever he thought of the man's personality, he had to admit that as a policeman, Kelsey was in the top of his class.

Joseph returned to the RV park in the evening to find Jean sitting inside, reading a book. She didn't look up when he came inside. He started the grill, chopped up a few onions and a couple of steaks, and started them cooking. Then he took Jean's book from her and told her he was leaving.

She watched him with eyes whose lifeless dispassion frightened him. Forty-eight years he had spent looking into those eyes, and never had he seen what he was seeing right now. He said that there was something he had to do, and she was welcome to come along if she liked, but it wasn't going to be a vacation, and he wasn't going to stop and explain everything that happened along the way. When he was done, he grabbed the steaks and put them on a plate and then he sat across from her and waited for an answer.

"I never liked steak," she said, and picked at one of the onions.

"You don't have to answer me now."

"Joe, I love you. We've never been apart. We're not going to start now. I just wish you'd be here."

"I'm here."

She shook her head. "Chase your demon, drag me along. Let's just find it and get rid of it."

After dinner, he started packing everything up. The RV was ready to go by midnight. He hiked to the building at the edge of the park, where the manager had his home in a small hut that had probably been built by some of the original homesteaders. He knocked on the door, handed the manager the balance of what they owed, then turned and went back to his stall.

They left about the same time he had left the night before. He knew he shouldn't drive like this, emotionally drained, physically weary, but he also knew that he couldn't sleep, and the longer he laid awake in bed, the less energy he would have to begin the journey the next morning. It gnawed at him, a driving purpose, a question that demanded an answer.

He handed Jean the paper Kelsey had given him and pointed to the address at the top of the list. "Where's it say?"

She read it off to him. It was in a small village about forty miles outside of town. He had been there once or twice about five years ago when an investigation into a smuggling ring had led them to all of the surrounding dots on the map. It had been a charming little place at the time, rising fast, full of energy, but now, either because of the late hour or the decay of small-town America, it looked as though it had fallen on severely hard times.

Most of the shops were closed as the RV rumbled onto Main Street, over half of them permanently. The houses all appeared deserted, the children's park empty, in disrepair.

He parked in an empty lot a few blocks away from the address and told Jean to wait in the camper. It was bitterly cold here, even more so than back in town. Joseph jogged down the sidewalk, past a couple of boarded-up antique shops and a wax museum from the 1940s.

Across the street, a lone light twinkled from the office of the

Sheriff's station. It was the one building Joseph still recognized from the time he'd been here before; everything else had deteriorated so drastically that it was almost like visiting a foreign country.

A couple of rows of houses crisscrossed each other just beyond Main Street. They were secluded from what had once been the bustling commercial center of the village. Most of them were regal, old estates, probably pretty nice around the turn of the century. Many had large, sweeping verandas, yards the size of open fields, circular towers and balconies that overlooked long, stretching driveways.

When he came to the street corner, his breath caught in his throat. Seconds later, he realized that he should have expected this, or at least have been prepared for it, but for that moment, he was petrified.

He didn't have to look at the address a second time. He knew that the gap in the middle of the street fell at 181st Street. With a sick feeling in his stomach, he traversed the remaining several hundred yards.

The same smell was there—dust, rotting wood, stirred up chemicals. The house was gone.

It was dark on either side of the rubble. No chance of finding a witness anywhere. He'd lay even money no one even lived on this side of town anymore. It was exactly the same—a few framed portraits here and there that had miraculously survived the disaster.

A garage still stood at the end of the backyard. Joseph didn't want to go inside, but a part of him knew he had to. Ducking beneath a clothesline tied to two rusty poles, he pulled open the sagging door. It gave too easily—opened not long ago.

There were footprints in the dust inside, flanked by other marks that might have been made by a long overcoat. Joseph stopped himself short of trampling over them. *Would Kelsey have thought of that?* he wondered. Like it or not, they still needed Malloy.

He knelt. Squinting, he pressed his head against the floor. It was a nonstandard tread, not something you'd buy at JC Penny or

Nordstrom or even at Men's Warehouse. He wished he'd thought
to bring a camera.

He looked around and alighted on a couple of spray bottles on
the shelf near the door. Tiptoeing around the edges of the room,
he grabbed one with a little water left in it, colored a ghastly yellow from all of the mold and chemicals and bizarre particulate
matter that had collected over the years it had spent on the shelf.
He had no idea what it had originally been—perhaps insecticide.
It could be swimming with carcinogens, but at the moment,
Joseph didn't have time to worry about it.

Treading as lightly as he could, he stretched himself back over
to the doorway and got to his knees. He pumped the sprayer until
a few droplets spattered out onto the dusty floor and then he pressed
the back of the map against the imprint. The moistened grime stuck
to the paper. It wasn't a perfect copy, but it was something.

Then he went to the workbench. The note was in the same
handwriting as the one Joseph had picked from his own tool shed
not twenty-four hours ago. There was another Xerox of Hacker's
picture beneath the words, *Faster than you can find them, they will
disappear. Leave her be.*

Halfway across the yard, a thought occurred to him. He didn't
know where Kelsey had gotten the addresses. He didn't know what
kind of work Kelsey had been doing over the last few days. He was
a fast worker, but was he also a sloppy one?

"Robins," Kelsey's tired voice said.

"How'd you get the address, Kelsey?"

"Joe?"

"The first address on the list—how'd you get it?"

"I called. I asked around about anyone who knew a Hacker.
On the internet, too. I scanned her picture. Got about half a
dozen answers."

"Jesus, Kelsey."

"Joe, where are you? What's going on?"

Joseph hung up and walked back to the RV as fast as he could. Jean started to ask what was going on, but he gave her a look—she'd promised: no questions. She shut her mouth, let out a deep sigh, and went to the back of the RV. He heard her rustling around there for a while, and then, the next time he looked back, she was asleep.

Focusing on the road, he allowed his foot to drop a little harder on the accelerator. The highway zipped past around them, and night slowly became day. And they drew that much closer.

They stopped four times along the way—three for gas, once at a rest area in the mountains. It had been a long time since Joseph had been over a thousand feet above sea level. The air felt thin in his lungs, and even walking the short distance up the hill to the restroom and back left him spent.

He wandered to the edge of the woods while he waited for Jean. The sun seemed different up here, too—paler, harsher. It was like early morning all day long. He shielded his eyes and gazed up through the arching pine trees and oaks. The sun played between the leaves and branches.

Joseph frowned. There was something blocking it, something thicker, more solid than the branches that high up. He took a few steps closer to the trunk and tried to see the thing from a different angle.

It was larger than he'd first thought, the size of a bear or a hefty safe. A thought struck him. Suddenly, ideas began pouring into his head, but the one he couldn't dash away was that Jean was going to hate him for this. But what could he do? His conscience would not leave him alone if he turned his back on this now.

She touched him on the shoulder. Joseph jumped and rounded on her with a suddenness that must have startled her. Taken aback, she retreated a few steps. "I was only going to tell you I was done," she said. "What's gotten into you?" Slowly, he watched her gaze rise, her head tip back as she looked where he was looking. "What is it? What do you see?"

So Joseph showed her. He could tell by the souring of her face that she knew what it was, too. Anyone else might have had a doubt—that size, that shape, it could've been a number of things. Not to Joseph. He was sure.

It was a body.

Lieutenant Isaac Keeler seemed uncomfortable with the fact that Joseph was a detective. When he confirmed that he was retired, Keeler's demeanor eased slightly, but he still seemed distant, protective.

"Show it to me." He was gruff, stroking a thick, brown moustache and a stubble of a beard that was somewhere between a five o'clock shadow and seven the next morning.

They tramped out to the edge of the woods, and Joseph pointed it out to him. They were there until nightfall, waiting for the forensics team to come up from the village and get the body down. He was a scruffy, middle-aged man, skin smudged with dirt and mildew, clothing distinctly odd—ruffled pants of a strange color, a button-down shirt that didn't quite match. It was nothing glaring, but it gave off the impression of foreign worldliness.

Jean stayed in the RV the entire time. Joseph joined her once or twice, made her a pot of coffee, asked if she at least wanted to come out and stretch her legs. He knew she did, and he knew with equal certainty that she would never give him such a concession. He was the enemy now, and she was going to freeze his balls off with clipped, frosty replies and a cold shoulder whenever she could. He knew she'd refuse any kindness he offered her and deny any suggestion he made.

The sad thing was, a part of him agreed with her. They were retired, on vacation. They shouldn't be worrying about all of this now. He should've turned his back, gotten behind the wheel, ripped up the map with the footprint and driven them to a ski resort.

But if he left it, a murder would go unpunished. It would be one more unanswered question. He couldn't tolerate that.

Keeler knocked on the door to the RV about a half hour after the sun had gone down. It was all the same questions, a second time—how had he seen it? Had anyone else seen it? Had he seen anyone suspicious in the area? Did he know the man? What did he know?

"How about this?" Isaac pulled out a piece of paper, unfolded it, and slid it across the table to Jean, who happened to be sitting closer to him.

She shook her head. He passed it over to Joseph. "How about you?"

Joseph's heart stopped. He sat forward, suddenly awake enough to ignore a thousand sunsets. It was *her*. It had to be her. The Hacker girl. He'd know that face, the shape of the shoulders anywhere.

"You recognize him?" Isaac said.

Joseph blinked. *Him?* He pulled the picture closer and studied it more carefully. The gooseflesh dissipated, and the adrenaline began to ebb from his veins. Not her. A man with semi-long hair, very young. The picture was much older than his, too. The quality was so poor that he hadn't been able to make out the features from where he had been sitting. *Jesus*, he thought. He was seeing the girl everywhere.

"Sorry," Joseph said. He slid the picture back toward the Lieutenant. "I don't."

"You're sure?" Isaac sounded suspicious.

"Thought it was someone else. It looked like this girl from work."

Jean was watching him. She didn't say anything, and she didn't have to. He knew without looking at her that she'd gotten the wrong idea, but there was nothing he could do about that. She would just have to suspect him of whatever she was concocting in her mind.

Isaac looked from their two faces to those of his assistants. He wasn't buying it. "I'm going to have to ask you two to come with us," he said.

"What?" Jean said. "We haven't done anything."

Joseph reached over and took her hand in his, and she shot him a murderous glare.

"Quiet, sweetie," he said. "It's just procedure."

To Isaac, she said, "We're supposed to be retired. We're supposed to be on vacation."

"You should listen to your husband, ma'am," Isaac said, standing. "It's just procedure. We'll have you in and out of there in an hour or two, and then you can be on your way."

Joseph squeezed Jean's hand a little tighter and willed her to be patient. *Just this once*, he prayed, *let her keep her mouth shut.*

One of the troopers drove the RV while Jean and Joseph road in the back of Isaac's police car. The lights from the town ahead had appeared shortly after they'd left the woods, and Joseph had watched them approach with placid resignation. This way, he thought, he could at least confer with the locals about what he'd found. Perhaps he could even get a little help with his search.

Jean wouldn't meet his eye the whole way. In a moment of tenderness, he longed to have her support back. He wanted to lean over and tell her everything, but he couldn't do that, not with Isaac in the front seat. So he just watched her with a longing he hadn't felt in their marriage for a very long time.

He thought she might have noticed, and she almost wanted to give in to him. She half-glanced in his direction a couple of times, but she was too proud. Besides, he didn't blame her. He'd been a dick to her for the last twenty-five years of their marriage. It had taken something like this for him to admit that to himself. Now, if only he could admit it to her, they might be getting somewhere.

He had just resolved to do that as soon as they had a moment alone when the light turned green, and Isaac pressed the accelerator. The cruiser edged out into the intersection. Joseph looked sideways. Before his gaze had come even halfway around, he saw the headlights.

"Keeler!" he shouted.

Isaac looked, and then, with lightning reflexes, he grabbed the wheel and hit the gas. The cruiser leapt forward and skidded around out of the way of the oncoming car. They bounced up onto the sidewalk as the crash came from behind.

It was so loud that for a few moments, Joseph thought they hadn't escaped it. Metal ground and glass shattered, and then it was all over. He twisted himself around in the seat to peer out the rear windshield at the battered limousine on the other side of the intersection.

"My lord in heaven!" Jean breathed. "What just happened?"

Chapter 11

She'd forgotten the box. Debbie turned and almost ran into Gregory Klein on her way back into the hotel. She headed to the sofa, invisible from the door—the reason she'd chosen to sit there in the first place.

It wasn't there. Dread turned to fear, fear to outrage. She'd left it right there. She'd been gone for thirty seconds, and someone had taken the box.

Debbie spun around, eyes roving across the lobby. The receptionist, clear across the room, was engrossed in a magazine. There was no way anyone could get from there to here and back again in that amount of time. And there was nobody else here.

The door came open and Gregory stepped back inside. "Debbie?" he called. "Weren't you coming? Don't you want to see if we can help?"

Of course. He'd been sitting right beside her. He'd seen the box.

"Turn out your pockets!" she snapped.

Gregory stopped short. "What?"

The box was far too large to fit in any pocket, but she didn't see it anywhere else on him, and he hadn't had time to get rid of it—unless he'd given it to someone outside just now. But that couldn't be right; it would take an enormous amount of coordination. The accident, her running out, him after her, her realization, the timing, the coincidences—it was all too much.

"What's gotten into you?" He let the door close behind him.

"Something's missing. Where is it?"

"Debbie, I have no idea what you're talking about." He looked from her to the sofa, and then there was a flash of realization in his eyes. "Oh, the box, right?"

"Yes. The box."

He shook his head. "It didn't look like anything in the world could get it away from you."

She stormed out through the door and looked up and down the street. There was a police car up on the curb just a few feet away from the hotel window they'd been behind. There were two people in back, an old couple, and a uniformed officer, presumably the driver, was gazing in through the window of the limousine on the other side of the street.

Debbie sprinted across the intersection, pushing her way through the gathering crowd until she'd reached him. "Sir!" she called. He looked back, but he was distracted.

"Give me a hand," he said over his shoulder. "Hold down the window; it wants to roll up for some reason. Short-circuit, I think. There's something wrong with the driver."

She started to shake her head, but then he grabbed her and yanked her in, so that she had no choice but to shove herself between the window and the bent metal at the top of the car while he reached inside and tried to pull the driver free.

She looked around, helpless, and again found herself staring at Gregory. He was lingering by the edge of the crowd, shoulders sagging, face confused. He was so useless and pathetic.

Then the officer was struggling to get the driver out on the pavement, and Debbie's attention was suddenly riveted on him. He was pale, bony, dressed in a suit, like a character out of some gothic horror novel.

"Gimme a hand?" the officer grunted.

It took Debbie a minute to realize he was talking to her. Together, they wrestled the man through the smashed window and out onto the pavement. Debbie was still panting from the exertion when the policeman took off running toward the other car, which sat in a mess of twisted steel and shattered glass at the center of the intersection.

"What do I do?" she called, but he just waved her away.

She looked down at the man. Blood trickled down his nose in a thin stream. Apart from that, he appeared as stiff and lifeless as a wax statue. She didn't want to touch him again. Something about his face, about the texture of his skin, made her hair stand on end.

There was a rustle from the back seat, and that was when Debbie Wendell, the woman whom men across the planet feared for her ferocity, turned and ran. She wasn't sure what it was that got to her at such a deep, visceral level. All she knew was that she couldn't stay there in the street any longer.

She could hear Gregory calling after her. There were a couple of other guests in the lobby of the hotel, standing by the reception desk. They all turned to stare as she collapsed on the dusty couch. She didn't care. She could be the spectacle of the century, and it wouldn't make a difference to her.

That face was burned into her brain. She couldn't make it go away. He had been so thin, so pale—it wasn't natural.

There was an odd sensation beneath her chin. She withdrew from the pillow and something crackled. Her skin crawled.

Steeling herself, she plunged one hand into the cushions. Paper—it was paper, that was all. She pulled it out, flattening it where the cushions and her own weight had turned it into a ball.

There was an image on the paper and a scrawled note beneath it. She blinked a few times, clearing the blurred half-tears from her eyes. A woman. Slender shoulders, light skin, eyes. *Eyes.* Debbie shuddered. What was it about those eyes? She looked dead— somehow more than dead. Dead *inside.*

Beneath it, in the handwriting of a hasty man, was the message, *You had my box. I took it back. Come to your room. I will show you.*

The bedroom was dark, colder than she'd left it. The faucet in the bathroom was dripping. Immediately, a hundred voices inside her head told her to leave. As a teenager, she'd been too macho, too strong-willed to listen to them. After growing up—she could face anything.

There was the box. *Call security*, she thought.

She took a few tiny steps inside and let the door slide shut behind her.

It wasn't completely dark. There was a dim, flickering light coming from just beyond the threshold of the bathroom. She stuck her head around the corner of the doorway and swallowed the startled yelp that threatened to leap from her mouth.

A single candle sat at the foot of a full bath. That was all. No flowers. No pool of blood. No creepy notes from strangers. Just a steaming bath and a single candlestick. She wanted to scream.

"Someone's been in my room," she told the receptionist. She was already out the door before he could say a word.

The intersection was filled with pulsing lights: reds, blues, whites. An ambulance had pulled up beside the limousine, and the driver was gone. Gregory stood on the sidewalk, talking to a young girl who had a bloody gash on her cheek. When he saw Debbie, his eyes brightened just a little, and he gave her a subtle wave to come over.

"Jackie," Gregory said, "this is Debbie. Debbie, Jackie Savage. She was in the limousine."

Debbie extended a shaking hand. Jackie looked at her.

"Are you okay?" the girl asked.

"Hey, yeah," Gregory chimed in. "Debbie, what happened? You look awful."

"Just tired," Debbie said. She frowned at the girl. There was something about her face, her expression—she looked as though she'd seen a ghost.

Despite everything she had just been through, Debbie realized, she was the most stable, most together one of all three of them. She tried to collect her thoughts. "Gregory, can I talk to you for just a second?"

Gregory gave Jackie an uncomfortable look. "Well, I told Jackie . . ."

"Now," she said, and it gave her a small thrill to hear the old assertiveness jump back into her voice. Gregory gave a slight start, then nodded and accompanied her to the lamppost a few feet away from the girl.

She pulled out the paper from her hotel room and showed it to him.

"Wow . . . I mean . . . Maybe you should call the police."

Very Gregory Klein. She looked at him, then shook her head and took the paper back. Her gaze wandered over his shoulder to the girl standing behind him. She still bore that teenaged awkwardness on her bony shoulders, but there was something even stranger about her. What had happened to her? Debbie caught the girl looking back in her direction and quickly averted her eyes.

"What's her deal?" she asked Gregory.

Gregory glanced over his shoulder. "Well, she was in the accident . . ."

"I mean before that. What was she doing in the limo with that . . . man?"

"She says her father was taking her somewhere."

"Her father? Where is he now?"

"On the way to the hospital."

She pushed past him. The girl looked up. "Hey," Debbie said, "what did you say your name was?"

"Jackie. Jackie Savage."

"How about a piece of pie or something?"

Jackie blinked at her. "A piece of pie?"

The paramedics didn't want to let Jackie go just yet, but Debbie could handle them. "What're you gonna do, make her starve?" she barked when the lead EMT tried to stop her. "She needs a bite to eat, all right? Put the goddamn badge away already."

They found a twenty-four hour diner a few blocks away. They were the only customers, and the place smelled like an attic, but a little privacy was just what they needed right now.

There was a glass case of pies on a rotating wheel. Debbie pointed to three different kinds and asked for a piece of each, and then she led the way to a booth in a dining room at the back, while the flustered waitress tried to keep up. When they were settled and there was coffee on the way, she looked the girl in the eye and asked her to repeat exactly what had happened.

This time, it wasn't her father; it was her uncle who had been in the back of the limousine. He was *taking* her to see her father. On a ranch somewhere. She wasn't sure where, because she hadn't been there since she was a little child.

Debbie fixed her with a piercing stare, and the words ran out. Jackie's lower lip began to tremble. Just then, the waitress arrived with the pies. She gave them all the strangest look, two adults and a crying teenager in the middle of the night. Debbie shifted the glare to her, and after a momentary pause, she shrugged to herself and scurried off to the kitchen.

"Now why don't you tell me what really happened." Debbie said—not a question; a command.

Jackie nodded, and then they got the real story. The girl told them everything: how her brother had disappeared, how her father couldn't be reached, how she had taken off on her own. Then the details got a little fuzzier, and Debbie again began to suspect that something was missing from the story.

But try as she might, she couldn't coax anything else out of the girl. The only thing she gained from the rest of the conversation was a certainty that there was still much to be told.

She ate her dessert, which was awful, and drank her coffee, which was worse, and then the three of them left and walked back to the hotel. When they got there, the intersection had been cleared. Only a smattering of glass across the pavement remained to show that anything had happened at all.

The receptionist looked up when they walked back inside, locking eyes with Debbie. "You. The police want to talk to you."

Debbie blinked. "What?" Beside her, she felt Jackie stiffen.

"I should go," the girl whispered. "I don't have a reservation here."

"Hold on," Debbie told her. "What's this about?"

"One of the maids was murdered in your room about an hour ago," the receptionist said. "That would be right about when I saw you leave here in a hurry."

Behind her, Gregory and Jackie shuffled a few steps away. "Hey, uh, Debbie?" Gregory mumbled. "We're going to, uh, head up to the room."

"Stay there," Debbie barked over her shoulder. "You're witnesses. You saw I wasn't here. I'm not having any bullshit pinned on me."

The receptionist pulled free of her and picked up the phone. "We'll see."

It was funny—of all the things that should have been on her mind, the one thing Debbie noticed the most while the police interrogated her was Jackie's discomfort. The girl kept shifting her weight from foot to foot and looking longingly at the door.

After they'd asked her the same questions a dozen times, the man in charge, some Lieutenant with a moustache who needed to shave more often, shook his head and closed the notebook he'd been scrawling in. "I think you should all come down to the station with me. We'll need to compare notes, run all of this by a few other people."

"I want a lawyer," Debbie said.

The Lieutenant took off his glasses and fixed her with a baleful look. "You're not under arrest yet."

"It's the 'yet' part that's holding me up."

Chapter 12

"So what are you doing out here?" Jackie asked him.

Gregory looked at her through the steam of his third cup of cheap coffee. They were waiting in the holding room at the police station downtown. Debbie Wendell had been talking to the authorities for almost three hours. Morning light was beginning to filter through the Venetian blinds from the offices outside.

"Uh…" He wasn't sure what to tell her. It was the first time she'd spoken since she asked him if he knew where the restroom was when they'd first walked in. He'd made lame attempts to start up a conversation with her a couple of times, but he was never certain what to say to children. He wasn't very comfortable talking to adults either, for that matter.

It just seemed like so much of what everyone said was bullshit. *Nice jacket. Where'd you get the scarf? It's supposed to rain tomorrow.* Sharing common knowledge with each other, repeating what they already knew. Gregory never saw the point. If he was going to say something, it might as well be something worthwhile. There was never anything wrong with silence. Except that it seemed to make other people uncomfortable.

"My flight got delayed at the airport. Some kind of mix-up. Something to do with a passenger on Debbie's flight, actually. They couldn't send us out tonight, so they put everyone up in the hotel."

She had been pacing in front of the window. Now she sat
down in one of the red plastic chairs and looked at him directly.
"Where were you going?" He didn't like this new version of her.
She'd been jumpy all night, but with the morning, there seemed
to be arriving in her countenance a new self-assurance. It made
him nervous. He didn't like it when other people found their
social footing and left him in the sand.

"Visiting someone."

"Where?"

"Maine. Bangor."

"Who were you visiting?"

"What were you doing in the back of a limousine with a
stranger?" he snapped back.

She blinked, gave him a hurt look, and turned away. He knew
he had been too harsh, but it was an automatic defense mecha-
nism. He tried to force himself to relax. They probably had cam-
eras in here, tape recorders. If he came across as too much of a
freak, they might start asking questions about him, too.

"Sorry," he said at length. "Long day . . . I . . . I'm very tired."

She nodded, but didn't look at him.

He drained his cup down to the coffee grounds at the bottom.
Silence for a while.

"She's just a . . . a friend of mine. Her name's Frida. I think
she might be in trouble, okay? That's why I was so nervous. I . . .
it's a long story. But I'm worried about her, okay?"

Jackie looked at him a little more softly, and he saw that he'd
made a mistake. She wasn't any surer of herself; she'd just spent the
night figuring out how to hide her insecurity. There was still fear
in those eyes, still the burden of concealed truth. *What are your
secrets?* he wondered. *What aren't you telling us?*

Another half-hour passed, and then the door opened and one
of the uniformed cops came in and pointed to Gregory. "What'd
you say your name was?" he asked, without any kind of introduction or apology for intruding. Gregory told him, and he nodded.
"Come this way."

Gregory frowned at Jackie, who was watching him now with some curiosity. "Wait," he said, "why do you need me? I thought this was about Debbie and the whole . . ."

The cop didn't wait for Gregory to finish, taking him by the arm and pulling him out the door. They went down a long hallway to an office behind a labyrinth of cubicles. It was small, cramped with a dozen different bookcases and framed awards. The door held a window of fogged glass on which was stenciled the name, *Captain Joel Hernandez.*

Inside, a big brick wall of a man sat planted behind the desk. He looked up through thick glasses as Gregory entered. He was the sort of guy who would have been a geek in elementary school, but had the muscles to make sure nobody teased him for it. Gregory had wished for those muscles more than once.

"Klein?" Hernandez barked. Gregory nodded meekly. "Siddown."

He did as he was told.

"Your name is Gregory Klein? You live alone in Los Angeles, California?" Again, Gregory nodded. Hernandez leaned back in his chair and formed a steeple with his fingers. "Is there anything at all you'd wanna tell me about yourself? About your recent history?"

Gregory was taken aback by the question. "About the accident? I tried to help the driver guy. Is he okay? Did he make it?"

Hernandez shook his head. "That's not what I'm talking about. That's a whole different ballgame, and your friend in there, by the way, the cute one with the whole schoolgirl thing going on, she's going to hear from us about that just as soon as we have a little more information. But I'm talking about you, Gregory."

Gregory thought for a moment, then shrugged. "I can't think of—"

"Really?" Hernandez brought his palm down hard on the desktop. "Maybe, then, you'd like to explain to Detective Sergeant Linda Usher why you're out here and why you've made a couple of calls you weren't supposed to make?"

Gregory's shoulders sank. What did they do, check the profile of everyone who walked through their doors? Captain Hernandez told him that he was going to be held here for the night, at least, until someone could fly out from Los Angeles and sort things out. "Get comfortable," Hernandez told him as several more uniforms ushered him out.

He felt dazed. They tugged him back through the cubicles toward the holding room. Dimly, other people's conversations filtered into his brain. Something about the Pope and a scandal. A body in a rest area. An elderly couple sat before a policeman at one of the desks—the woman tired, pissed off, the man wide awake, talking a mile a minute. He had handcuffs on.

An officer stayed with him in the waiting room while they waited for the paperwork. He wasn't supposed to talk about his case to anyone, least of all to Jackie Savage. The poor little girl watched him with ever-increasing distress. Every time she tried to ask him something, the officer intervened. "Sorry, kid, official police business."

"But he's my friend!" Jackie protested.

It made Gregory feel ludicrously good. How long had it been since someone had stood up for him?

"Your 'friend' is some kind of sick stalker pervert from Los Angeles," the officer sneered.

The blood drained from Gregory's face. He started to protest, but the cop smiled cruelly and slapped a hand over his mouth. No discussing the details of his case with anyone. It was slander. It was mistreatment. If he were back in LA, he could probably find a lawyer who would make him rich over something like this, but out here, he'd count himself lucky if he could just get one to defend him.

They took Jackie away, too. Her eyes stayed on him—burning, accusing. Just like that, a *friend* no more.

He couldn't help feeling a little indignant—who was she to judge him when she was clearly guilty of something, too.

Gregory just wished he knew what.

◦───✳───◦

So it was that Gregory Klein, an upstanding citizen who always paid his taxes and never exceeded the speed limit, spent the night in jail. It was a little place, and once the guards had gone to bed—which they did without any pretense of keeping watch on their prisoners—he could talk to Debbie and Jackie, who had been placed in the cells right across from him. They were only separated by two layers of bars, the old-fashioned kind they had in all the spaghetti Westerns of the '60s and '70s.

Debbie was the first one to speak, of course. She'd been watching the officers as they packed up their things and then bustled out of the room. "We'll be just outside," the last one warned them. "Don't try anything funny. Breakfast is at 7:30. Sleep tight." He snickered and then doused the lights.

"Fuckers," Debbie breathed. "You can see it on their faces. They're having the times of their lives putting us through all this shit."

"Us?" Gregory said.

"Big city people. Strangers. Out-of-towners."

"I'm not from a big city," Jackie whispered.

Gregory looked toward her cell. "Why'd they keep you here, Jackie?" he asked.

She fixed him with a glare and said nothing. When Debbie asked her, she answered that she'd been logged as truant from school, and someone was supposed to come in the morning to drag her back, unless she could prove that the man in the limousine was related to her and had some kind of claim to her freedom as a legal guardian.

Eventually, Debbie found her way to asking the increasingly-obvious question: why was Jackie avoiding Gregory? Jackie said that he was a sex fiend and he'd been deceiving them both. Even behind bars, Gregory cowered toward the back of his cell. Debbie would flay him. She would break all of his bones and staple his skin to the wall if she ever thought he'd abuse a child. Very calmly, quietly, she asked him if it was true.

He told her it wasn't what she thought. The police had misconstrued an effort to help a friend of his—Frida. She wasn't buying it.

He could feel all of the bonds they'd formed throughout the evening melting like paper in water. Just like that, he was back down to no friends again. This time, though, it was worse, because he had seen, however briefly, what it had been like not to be alone.

Debbie was gone the next morning. They'd taken her away before they even turned on the lights and brought out the dry toast and eggs. Jackie was the next to go. They said that the man from the limousine was awake in the hospital, and that he was asking for his daughter. They took her away in a squad car. Gregory listened to the sound of the wheels on the gravel parking lot, to the engine as it roared away down the road.

It was going to be a hot day. The cells were already warming up, and it wasn't even nine in the morning yet. He began pacing back and forth, pausing every few minutes to get a sip of water from the tap installed in the cinderblock wall. It tasted awful, full of minerals and flakes of rust and god knew what else, but he needed it. He had begun to sweat as soon as the first guard came in. Now there was one stationed by the door, watching his every move, and Gregory couldn't stand it.

They were going to cart him back to Los Angeles, and then what? Put him in jail out there? Prison in South Central was not going to be like the Sheriff's office out here. He knew he couldn't make it in a place like that. He'd be skinned alive. Especially if they tagged him as some kind of pervert.

By lunchtime, he had no appetite at all. He scarcely noticed the other prisoners; they'd been quiet the night before, either playing silent observers or asleep already by the time he'd been brought in. The couple was there, he saw, though they'd been accommodated with pillows and several other amenities that led him to believe they weren't so much suspects as valued witnesses. Perhaps they needed more protection than the hotel could offer. He didn't remember seeing them in the group of other displaced passengers.

Fuck Debbie for not trusting him, he thought—what if she *had* killed the maid? She had no reason to be all high and mighty about this. He knew less about her than she did about him. By mid-afternoon, he was a total wreck. The elderly couple was gone, off to be interrogated or shipped away, or god knew what. They'd been muttering something about a pressing situation, about arson or vandalism, and there had been a body. Gregory didn't care. All he could think of were scenes from all the prison movies he'd ever seen. He didn't want to go that way. He'd kill himself before he was stabbed by a prisoner or strangled by a cellmate.

But when the detective from Los Angeles finally showed up, it was nothing like Gregory had imagined. It wasn't Detective Sergeant Linda Usher and her eye-patched retinue. It was a little man in a tan overcoat and glasses who had a cold and kept complaining that it was too breezy out here. He filled out some paperwork with the guards and then he came to meet Gregory.

"Klein?" he asked. Gregory nodded. "My name is Neil Neville. I won't shake your hand; I've got this awful bug, and the weather here isn't making it any better. Look, I need you to sign this." He thrust a piece of carbon paper toward Gregory.

"What is it?" Gregory asked.

"A restraining order. The Los Angeles Police Department has issued an order that you shall no longer call or associate with the young lady you have been harassing." He wiped his nose and passed a pen through the bars of the jail cell.

Gregory wanted to whoop for joy. He could scarcely stop himself from bursting into laughter. "That's all? You're not going to take me back to LA and put me in prison?"

Neville gave him a strange look. "Should we be?"

"No, of course not." Gregory signed the paper almost without reading it. He was about to pass it back through the bars when he caught sight of something near the top. It was all a bunch of official information, typed out codes, names, addresses, phone numbers. And there, printed near the *List of Offenses* was Frida's address.

He couldn't believe his luck; it must be a mistake, he thought. Surely this was just the place where the form was manufactured or something, some other random list of digits and locations that had made it onto the sheet by mistake. He read it over three times: *9567 W. Haverford St., Trenton, ME*. Maine. Near Bangor. He had been right all along.

He looked up and found Neville watching him.

"Something wrong?" Neville asked, suspicious, probing. "What are you looking at? It's a simple form."

He repeated the address to himself several times and kept on mentally saying the numbers, the street name, as he handed the clipboard back through the bars.

Neville skimmed the form. "What was it you were looking at?"

Gregory shrugged. "I like to read everything I sign. Can I go now?"

He was fixed with another glare, and then Neville got up and turned to the guard behind him. "Keys," Neville said. To Gregory, he added, "You're free, Mr. Klein, but now everything's official, on paper. Don't violate this, or you'll be in serious trouble."

"No, of course."

Ninety-five sixty-seven. Ninety-five sixty-seven.

Chapter 13

Thomas Marlowe looked so frail and helpless in the hospital bed that Jackie could hardly believe he was the same man. His arms were covered in tubes and bandages, and a roll of gauze was wrapped about his head. Blood dotted it here and there. His eyelids moved when she came into the room, but he did not open them. His lips muttered something unintelligible.

The nurse, a young woman, little older than Jackie, ran to the side of his bed and put her ear to his mouth. "What is it?" she asked in the gentle voice of a governess. Marlowe repeated himself. The nurse looked over at Jackie. "Yes, your daughter's here." More mumbling. She looked uncertain. "I'm not supposed to let you alone yet," she said. "You're still very weak. If you were to have any problems…" More mumbling. She sighed. "Okay. But just for a few minutes."

When she was gone, Jackie fixed her attention on the old man. He lay there, silent, motionless. Jackie shuffled a little closer.

"Nurse?" Marlowe asked in a quavering voice.

"I'll get her." Jackie started to turn toward the door, but he halted her a moment later with a sharp:

"No!"

When she looked back, he was sitting up in bed, his eyes once again afire with a voracious intensity. He threw back the covers and ripped the tubes from his flesh. His skin was pockmarked with tiny little dots of red—blood and bruises—where they had slashed him up to start his intravenous drugs.

"Mr. Marlowe?" Jackie said.

He was out of bed, on his feet, gathering his things together. One of the machines beside the pile of sheets the nurse had left began to beep. Jackie glanced at it and caught a severe look from Marlowe.

"We're leaving," he said as he pulled on his shoes.

"But . . . but are you okay?"

He flapped his hands in a dismissive wave. "Fine. What difference does it make?"

"But if it's unhealthy . . ."

"Can you drive?" Marlowe was standing by the window now. "Never mind. It's not your worry. Just hurry, or we'll be caught. That ghastly nurse said she was coming back in five minutes." A smile twisted one corner of his mouth. "She smells like refried beans." He threw open the window and motioned for Jackie to join him. "You first." He gave her a nudge. "I want someone to catch me if I slip."

When she hesitated, he picked her up by the waist and, before she could grasp at anything, he shoved her out the window. Everything happened too fast for a proper scream. The wind rushing, the churning in her stomach, and then the branches of the tree scratching her face; the shrubs embracing her body.

She hit the dirt hard. It was loose earth, and with the foliage, she didn't think she'd broken anything, but it was still a painful landing. She got to her feet and looked around, shaking. Ironically, her first concern was whether anyone had seen her. A part of her knew she should be going for the authorities, but what if they found out about the murder at the gas station? They'd want to know why she hadn't told anyone about it when she had the chance, and she wouldn't be able to give them a reason.

She wasn't sure why she'd kept her mouth shut. It was something about Thomas Marlowe, something about his hungry but

earnest search for the mysterious girl that made Jackie long to
uncover her identity. And then there had been the black cars following them into town.

"Hey!" Marlowe hissed. He was halfway out the window, waving to her. "You catch me now!"

They snuck across the parking lot. Marlowe stopped when they
reached the middle and told Vicki to pick a car—whatever she felt
like driving. She wasn't sure what he meant; she had an inkling,
but surely, she thought, a man his age . . .

He broke one of the rear passenger windows of the Saab 900
sedan with a brick he wriggled loose from a wall around the lot.
He'd wrapped it in his coat, so it was surprisingly quiet. She
looked on in shock and embarrassed admiration as he fiddled
around beneath the steering column. A few moments later, the
engine came to life.

At about the same time, the hospital doors burst open. They'd
discovered he was gone. He pushed Jackie savagely in behind the
wheel. "Drive!" he barked as he wriggled over the gearshift to the
passenger seat.

It must have been a survival instinct kicking in, because she
had the feel of the car down almost instantaneously. She made
each curve with perfect precision, slowed before taking the speed
bumps by the lot exit, and then accelerated onto the main road.

Marlowe was pleased, but of course, would say nothing. He
kept his eyes on the mirrors. Jackie glanced over her shoulder and
saw a few men in white coats and black pants stumble onto the
sidewalk. They looked wildly around, but as they receded behind
her, they did not move to pursue.

When it was clear that no one was coming after them, Jackie
allowed herself to slump down in the seat a little. She eased back
on the accelerator and asked where they were going. Marlowe told
her—it was an address on the outskirts of town. Even though

there didn't appear to be anyone coming after them, she was to hurry all the same, because one could never be sure if the movements in the shadows were tree branches in the wind or something—else.

They went along in silence for a while, and Jackie had a chance to think—how strange it was, all of it. A couple of days ago, she had been a regular high school student with divorced parents and a brother who took care of her. Now, she was helping a murderer find his daughter in a town farther away than she'd ever been from home before.

Her eyes darted to the rearview mirror. Still nobody coming after them. How long would it be before the nurses called the police?

Then, her thoughts turned to Walker. She'd lost track of him in all the chaos, the accident. She wondered what had become of him. What if he had been pumping gas when someone like Thomas Marlowe came along? The thought made her stiffen up, and when Marlowe chuckled and said something about the weather, she replied only with a steely-eyed glare. He didn't seem to notice.

"Did you know my brother?" she asked.

"I don't know who the hell you are. How the hell should I know your brother? Stupid girl."

"Right." She closed her mouth and drove in silence.

The road snaked away from the town, up a shallow incline that mirrored the other side of the bowl in which the town lay. Trees began to poke up here and there in a strangely reversed pattern of the typical vegetation line. It was as though nothing living dared venture into the depression.

One or two houses dotted the rugged landscape—old ranches, farms. They reminded Jackie of some picture-book idealized image of home that had somewhere along the line gotten skewed. She couldn't imagine a pie cooling on any of these windowsills or a chicken roasting in any of their ovens. Most of them looked abandoned, and the few with lights on inside or cars in their driveways looked as though they were owned by people who seldom rose from their beds.

At the fourth or fifth one, Marlowe motioned for her to pull off. The Saab bounced onto the dirt road that took off from the paved highway. It was tilted, riddled with potholes, winding up to a darkened old villa with shuttered windows. She didn't like the look of it at all, but she swallowed her fear and got out when Marlowe told her to. *This is an adventure*, she told herself. *This is just what you always wanted.*

It had gotten cooler as they drove. The day had gone by quickly, and the sun, it seemed, was ducking early into bed.

Marlowe looked displeased as he hobbled out of the car and worked his way up to the front stoop. "Where are they?" he growled, as though asking the house itself.

"Where are who?"

"Them! Where is my daughter?" He waved the picture at her again. "Get them!"

Jackie dutifully climbed the stairs and pounded on the front door. There was no answer. It smelled like rotting wood, and the insects and evening birds were so noisy that she could scarcely hear the wind in the overgrown grass. Nobody had been here for days.

She knelt and pulled a small piece of paper from beneath the door.

"Well?" Marlowe demanded from the foot of the driveway.

"There's nobody here," she said. "But there's a note."

He read it over, then handed it to her. *I'm in back*, it said. It didn't look like a woman's handwriting.

She picked her way through the overgrown garden, weeds pulling at her bare arms and legs. At first, she thought the note must have been a joke from some of the local children. There was nowhere a person could be back here. It was not until she had looked more closely that she saw the shack nestled in among the weeds and overgrown tree stumps.

It looked abandoned, and it scared her. Jackie liked to think that she didn't scare easily, but this was the sort of place where abducted school children were butchered in front of a digital camera for their parents to see on the news. She didn't want to go inside, but she wanted even less to face Marlowe's wrath.

She glanced back at him a few steps into the thistles, and caught a look on his face that drove her toward the shack. It looked old, slapped together carelessly by some ranch hand or his father in the 1930s when money was scarce and times were hard. She imagined a family of impoverished children crowding into the shanty when the rain pelted the rotting wooden roof.

The door was hardly a door—more a collection of loosely-bound wooden shingles that hung together on a string of industrial bolts. She knocked timidly and waited while the cicadas filled the air with buzzing and the evening heat departed her. She was about to give up, to turn and shake her head at Marlowe, when there was a rustle from inside. It sounded more like an animal than a human, a skunk or a raccoon pawing through trash.

A shadow moved behind the door. Jackie stepped back, tensing up, unconsciously ready to turn and run when the beast within bared its face. And when he first stepped out into the muted sunlight, she thought he might have been an ape or a bear were it not for the massive, flabby arms, the neckless double-chins, the whale of a body. He was like a trundling lump of unleavened bread dough, skin pale as flour.

There was not a hair on his entire body. He looked at Jackie with frenzied eyes. "You're back!"

She didn't know what to say. He advanced on her, but now, she was too afraid to run, too afraid even to move. His breath assaulted her with thick, hot, malevolent waves of rot and decay. He smelled of vomit and sweaty, dirty orifices.

"Please," she managed. "Don't hurt me."

He halted in his tracks, hazel eyes narrowing. "You're not her." It was more the shaping of a breath than it was a statement with a voice.

"I don't know who you mean," she said, and then she heard footsteps in the undergrowth behind her.

Marlowe paused, a few steps away, and put a hand on her

shoulder. She looked back and could see by the distaste in his eyes that he would come no closer to the creature from the shack. "Ask him," Marlowe said, "where they've gone."

"I can hear you," the man snarled. "They've gone away. All of them."

"Thomas, who is this?" Jackie felt trapped between two animals facing off over the pride of their tribes. She didn't want to be here; this was their battle, not hers.

"Never mind that," Marlowe spat. Briefly, he looked the gigantic man in the eye, just long enough to determine that he wished to share the gaze no longer. "What have you done with them?"

"They had to leave. People came." The man sniffed. "People like you."

"What's he talking about?" Jackie asked.

"The people who were chasing us," Marlowe told her. "They came for my daughter."

"She's not your daughter!" the man exclaimed.

"Don't say that!"

"She's not! They said. They said she's not!"

"She's mine and that's the end of it!"

Jackie felt like crying. The men were both shouting at the top of their lungs, their rage mounting in near-tangible clouds that had begun to collide within her eardrums.

"He's a criminal!" the creature said. It took Jackie a few moments to realize he was talking to her.

"I . . ." She looked from the man to Marlowe, who looked angrier than she had ever seen him.

"He's insane!" Marlowe exclaimed, and then, to the man: "Where did they take her?"

The man spat at Marlowe's feet and started to turn back into the cabin. Marlowe shoved Jackie aside, strode up to the man, and grabbed him by one of the dangling shelves of loose flesh. The man let out an inhuman wail, but the strangest thing, the thing that stuck with Jackie more than anything else, was the familiarity of the move. These two men knew each other. However improbable of a pair they made, they'd met before.

"You'll tell me!" Marlowe hissed. "You'll tell me, or I'll make it hurt. I'll make everything hurt."

The giant man whimpered, wallowing in his own filth and shame. "I'll tell you," he growled. "She went to Egypt."

Chapter 14

Terry Young's dreams were strange and disturbing. The real world kept filtering into them, and when he awoke, he felt unrested and paranoid. The girl at the back of the bus had been talking about him; of that much, he was fairly certain.

He itched all over, and his mind was a conflicted mess of Shayla Hacker and Vicki Torres. He needed some way to focus. Through the legs of his jeans, he dug his fingernails into one of the scars—the longest, the oldest, the first. Vicki used to ask him about them, but somewhere along the way, they had stopped talking about that, too. His life was his life, though somewhere along the line, he'd started wishing it wasn't.

He felt his leg wet with blood, but it wasn't half as satisfying as with a knife. He caught one of the other riders watching him and stopped, unfulfilled. They already thought he was some kind of freak because of the way the girl was talking about him. The ironic part was, if they knew the truth, they'd probably be even more frightened.

The bus was delayed getting into the stopover in the city because of some kind of mess in one of the central intersections. Terry wasn't sure what it was all about. He craned his neck like all of the other passengers, trying to track the mesmerizing blue and red lights, the pieces of shattered glass and bent metal.

A policeman approached the driver and told him to take an alternate route. It led them away from the hotel where some of the others were getting off, and through a few back streets before they finally got to the fluorescent little oasis that was becoming so familiar to him. Another bus station.

When he got off, the driver told everyone that it would be a half-hour layover so that they could refuel and clean the seats. He stopped Terry on the way out. "Half an hour, sir," he said. "Thirty minutes. Would you like to borrow my watch?"

Terry couldn't tell if he was trying to be genuinely helpful or if he was just an asshole. He should call Vicki. They needed to talk. This was crazy, and he wasn't sure he could explain himself anymore, but she deserved to hear that at least he was thinking of her.

A uniformed officer stopped him before he made it to the phone. "Excuse me sir," the man said. "Could you please hold off on your personal business? There's been an accident here tonight, and the Lieutenant would just like to hear from everyone taking this route if they saw anything suspicious."

Terry shrank away from the officer. "Suspicious?" he said. "Like what?" *Like a strange man with a cabin who hangs about in a field beside a rest area?* His thigh was itching so badly it was almost more painful to avoid cutting it than it was to sink a knife into his flesh. He needed to get to a bathroom. Now.

"Strange cars, odd behavior on the highway. If you'll step this way, Lieutenant Keeler…"

Terry allowed himself to be corralled together with the other passengers, though he desperately wanted to be anywhere else. They stood in a sweaty throng while the sergeant in charge explained the same thing the officer had just told him. They would be taking the passengers aside one by one to have "a quick chat" with each of them. There was nothing to worry about, he assured them; this was merely part of a regular investigation into what was probably just an accident.

It was impossible to wait the ten minutes it took for them to get to him. They had cordoned off a small section of the bus

station, because the manager was on vacation and he had the keys
to the private rooms next to the security lab.

"Okay," the cop said—it was the same one who had spoken to
him earlier. "Sorry to keep you from your call, sir," he said. "Just a few
routine questions. Did you notice anyone following your bus tonight?"

Terry shook his head.

"Nobody at all? No other cars that you might have seen more
than once or twice behind you?"

"You can't see behind the bus," Terry said. "There's no rear
window. That's where the engine is."

The officer smiled. "Good point, sir."

"What's this all about?"

"Just routine—"

"Right." Terry looked around. "Well, if there's nothing else I
can help you with . . ."

The officer gave him a funny look. "Tell you what," he said.
"I'll let you in on a detail or two. You seem like the type who
might be able to put a few things together for yourself once you
have all the facts."

For a minute or two, Terry was puzzled, perhaps a little flat-
tered in spite of himself. *Do I really look that much more astute or
competent than the other passengers?* Then he figured it out. The cop
thought that Terry might know something.

"The accident was between a limousine and some kind of
truck. The driver of the limousine claimed that he'd seen someone
following him. At least, that's what one of the two passengers told
us. People in black cars. Did you see any black cars, Mister . . ."
he checked the ticket. "Mr. Young?"

Terry shook his head.

The policeman sighed. "Okay. If you think of anything, it
would only be helping us. Some people got hurt tonight. There
was a girl in the limousine, about sixteen, seventeen. It'd be nice
to tell her parents that we know why she's in the hospital."

Terry rose from the plastic chair they'd dragged over. He was
about to leave when the policeman snapped his fingers.

"Oh, one more thing." He pulled something out of his breast pocket and flashed it at Terry when he turned around. "Have you ever seen this woman?"

His reaction must have been obvious, because the policeman was suddenly staring at him with avid, predatorial attention. "You know her, don't you? Who is she?"

"She's . . . she's Shayla Hacker." Terry said. He leaned forward so that his nose was almost touching the Xeroxed photograph. It was the exact same picture as the one he had, the same one as the man in the rest area had had.

The policeman raised an eyebrow. "Who is Shayla Hacker?"

"Where'd you get the picture? Why are you asking me about her?"

"Are you sure you've told me everything you know?"

"Please, this is going to drive me crazy."

He considered, glancing at the picture himself before shaking his head. "What the hell," he muttered. "The guy in the back of the limo had it. We think he was looking for her."

A man in the limo? It couldn't possibly be the man from the rest area . . . could it? "I thought you said it was a girl in the limo. A seventeen year-old."

Another officer came up and tapped the policeman's shoulder. "Isaac says he wants you to finish this up and come down to the station. Says he brought in an old couple who might have found something when he ran across the accident. Wouldn't give details, but he said, and I quote, *it's fresh.* Whatever the hell that means."

The policeman grew suddenly clipped, urgent. "If you know anything, Mister . . . Mister Young, please do contact us. We're trying to bring criminals to justice here. That's all."

"Well, wait." Terry stood and followed him as he went to get the next person in line. "Can't you tell me anything more about her? Where does she live? Where was the guy in the limo going?"

"We don't know anything. I'm not at liberty to . . . look, if you can't tell us anything else, you're going to have to get out of the way and let us do our jobs. Please, sir, let me . . . get out of the way."

Terry kept darting in front of him. The policeman shot a quick glance back at the messenger—young and attractive, a woman who did well by her tight-fitting uniform. She swept in and took Terry gently but firmly by one arm. "You're going to have to come this way, sir. Buy yourself a soda. Get a candy bar. Stretch your legs, and don't miss your bus."

"But . . ." Terry protested, but the policeman was already moving on to the little girl from the back of the bus. He caught her eye as she was escorted over to the plastic chair. *Great*, Terry thought. *Who knows what she'll tell the police about me.*

But they must have been too pressed for time, because nobody came to talk to him again. They cycled the rest of the passengers through at double the pace they'd begun with, and started packing things up a full ten minutes before the bus was scheduled to leave.

Terry approached the policeman as he was about to get into his unmarked Ford sedan. "Hey," he called. The man turned around, registered who he was, and scowled.

"Look, buddy, I told you, if you don't know anything else . . ."

"Can you tell me where he was going? This is important." There must have been some measure of pathetic desperation in Terry's voice or face, because the policeman glanced at his watch, sighed, and then motioned for him to approach.

"Look," he said, "if you want more information, you can come talk to Lieutenant Keeler or Captain Hernandez down at the station. But you're going to miss your bus, and they only come through here every few days, so that's your call. I have to go. We're on something important right now."

"I'm coming."

It didn't take long for Terry to convince the driver that he needed his things from the compartments beneath the bus. To his credit, the man put up a halfhearted fight, warning Terry that he wasn't going to get refunded, that he'd probably be happier in the long run if he continued to his destination.

Terry didn't care. He was no longer interested in striking out on his own. Now he had a purpose. Nothing else mattered.

The police station was surprisingly active for a city this size at this time of night. It was no Podunk cow town, but it wasn't New York, either. He had expected a lonely desk sergeant with a mystery novel and a shaded desk lamp to keep her company through the night. That was what it was like back where he came from.

Instead, lights were on in most of the cubicles that spanned the space between the front desk and the offices across the back of the room, and even the interrogation chambers were occupied. The policeman handed him off to the receptionist.

"He's curious about something or other. Ask him. I've got to talk to Keeler." He jogged off through the labyrinth of desks and file cabinets toward an office in the corner.

Terry asked again who the man in the limousine was and what they knew about the girl in the photograph. They looked at him, two elderly women who sounded like they came from Brooklyn and wore New York fashion from the 1970s. "I don't think we give out that kind of information," one said.

"Is he even allowed to be asking those questions?"

Terry was eventually made to write his request on a slip of paper that was carried by courier to Captain Hernandez's desk. The Brooklyn Twins told him to wait on one of the small, stained sofas that faced each other in the foyer. He had to keep brushing the leaves of a dusty potted plant from his face, because there was some spittle-covered child's toy on the seat next to him he didn't want to get near.

The courier returned after almost an hour had passed. "He wasn't happy about this," he said, and then handed the same sheet of paper to the Brooklyn Twins. They looked it over, then summoned Terry back to their desk.

"He's escaped," the right one said. "The man from the car. He was in the hospital, but he's gotten away. Someone said they might have seen the girl at one of the farmhouses just out of town, though."

"We're really not supposed to be telling you this," the left one added. "I don't know why the Captain's making an exception in your case. Must be too busy to think about it, this time of night. Lots of business."

Terry was tempted to ask what was going on—why the irregular number of new cases at a time like this—but he sensed that he was already pushing his luck, and figured he should stop while he was ahead. "Can you tell me how to get there?" he asked on the way to the door.

"Northridge," the right one said, her tone suggesting she was telling him this only because she knew he would leave if she showed him how. "You want to go to Northridge. We're not sure which house." She looked over the piece of notebook paper again. "Captain says fifth or sixth one past the tavern, maybe? But I think that's just a guess."

"Thanks for everything," Terry said, and then he was back outside again.

He paced up and down the block a couple of times, and was about to go back inside and pester the Brooklyn Twins for a ride when he saw the cabbie station right across the street. A yellow light shone in the window, and he could just make out the silhouette of a lone, underpaid receptionist.

Ten minutes later, he had a ride. A fat man with more hair on his chest than his head beckoned Terry out to an old Chevy Caprice that smelled like incense. "Where you going this time of night?" he asked while fussing with the ignition.

"Northridge. Fifth or sixth house."

The man's smile faded. "Why you want to go there? All deserted and everything."

"I'm looking for someone."

"You're looking for the girl, aren't you?"

For the seventh or eighth time that night, Terry felt like shouting at the top of his lungs. Instead, he kept his voice level. "Why? Who is she?"

But the cabbie wouldn't say. All he told Terry was, in confidential undertones, "You want the fifth house."

~///~

Something seemed wrong. Flies were buzzing about the rotting wooden gate before the house, and parts of the grass had been trampled down, as though trodden by heavy feet sometime in the recent past.

"I thought you said this place was deserted," Terry said.

The cabbie shrugged. "Except for the people who stay out here."

Terry didn't ask. He just paid the fare and asked if the cabbie would wait a few minutes. He told Terry he'd wait five, then he was gone.

Terry checked his watch, nodded. He didn't want to be stranded out here. There was something about the place that filled his mind with bad thoughts.

Footprints riddled the pathway leading up to the porch, and they looked fresh. He brushed away a cloud of flies and knocked on the front door. There was no answer. He waited a couple of minutes, checked his watch, glanced at the taxi. The driver, bent, silhouetted over the steering wheel, was watching the clock.

Terry turned and was about to leave when he caught sight of a crumpled piece of paper wedged just beneath the door. There was writing on one side that looked as though it had been scrawled by an ape. *I'm in back.*

There was a small shed in the backyard, but that wasn't what caught Terry's attention. He couldn't take his eyes off of the puddle at the base of the rear stairs. He couldn't make out a color, saturated into the dirt as it was, but it was dark. He didn't touch it; judging from the flies, it was blood.

Only a minute left. Terry jogged back to the front to ask if the cabbie would wait another five minutes. He stopped at the head of the path and frowned. There was nobody sitting behind the steering wheel. Had the cabbie gotten out for a piss? Surely not. He'd been far too eager to get out of here for something so frivolous.

Terry approached the driver's window—he was probably lying down, or maybe he'd dropped something. The door was ajar, the seat empty.

"Hey!" Terry spun around, squinting into the dimness surrounding him. There was no sign of the driver.

He drew a pen from his pocket, and on the back of the note he'd picked up from the front porch, he wrote, *I'll be a few minutes longer. Please don't leave. Thanks.* He folded it onto the steering wheel and then he went back to the house. If the cabbie was still gone when he came back, then he'd start worrying.

The shack around back smelled bad, like rotting food and excrement. He ventured a few feet inside the door and decided not to go any farther. It was only one room, and he could see the back wall from where he was standing. There was a small cot, a rickety table, fragments of a few broken chairs. The floor was dirt; there was little else there.

Terry went back to the house and tried the door. It was locked, but something cracked in the hinges when he pushed a little harder, and it swung open with little resistance. There was dust on everything. All of the doors were shut, as though the house had been purposely compartmentalized. Footprints tracked across moldy carpet here and there.

"Hello?" Terry called. No answer. He hadn't expected one.

There was an elegant coffee table surrounded by a couple of chairs in what once must have been a parlor. He knelt beside it and began going through a few sheets of paper and old envelopes that had been stacked at one end. It was mail, postmarked almost twenty years ago. The only thing newer was a box on the floor.

He picked it up, and the lid came off in his hands. It was about the size of a shoebox, empty save for a few squares of wrapping paper. He squinted at the front. There was an address, a little town he'd never heard of in Indiana—Three Rooks.

He sifted through the rest of the box and found he'd been wrong; there was something else. At the very bottom, he found a fragment of a photograph. He knew before looking at it that it was Shayla Hacker.

Terry copied down the address and was about to venture farther into the old building when the sound of a car door outside
snapped his attention back to the front of the house. He leapt up
and ran for the door, half expecting to hear an engine a split-second later.

But the cab was still idling at the side of the road when Terry
reached it. The driver's door was shut, and there were fresh footprints leading away from it. Terry shivered. The grass around him
was rustling, and he could think of only one thing—*he was not
alone out here.*

He yanked open the cab door and tossed the note he'd written
out the window. Fuck the driver. He'd run off at the wrong time.
He locked the doors, threw the taxi into gear, and swung the wheel
around. The back of the car skidded across the dirt and gravel, the
wheels spinning in the rising dust.

He watched the house retreat in the rearview mirror and
couldn't stop shivering. *I came that close*, he thought. If he and the
cabbie had switched places, who knew where he would be
right now.

He was itching again. He scratched at himself furiously, and
when the pain wouldn't stop, he grabbed the spare key to the
trunk from beneath the driver's side sun visor and began digging
it into his flesh. He stopped when the blood gathered on the
leather seat beneath him. It felt good pooled up against his skin,
warm, comforting, but it was going to make a mess. No bandages, like at home. He clenched his teeth and tried to concentrate on
the road, but in the end, he couldn't help tearing a little deeper. It
just felt too damn good.

Three Rooks. What the hell?

Chapter 15

"Sorry for the wait. It's madness around here today." Lieutenant Isaac Keeler breezed into the office and shut the door behind him with his foot. He slipped into the chair behind the desk and took a deep breath. "Obviously, there are going to be a number of questions for you and your wife. This kind of thing, the body so fresh, it raises issues . . ."

Joseph Malloy raised an eyebrow. "How fresh? Nobody's told us anything."

Keeler hesitated. "I'm sorry, I can't discuss that with you."

"Come on, Lieutenant. I'm a detective."

"You're also a suspect."

He spent the next half-hour running through all of the same questions Joseph would have asked someone in his position. He didn't blame the man for it; he just wished they could be done. He could feel Jean's resentment mounting. They had tried to sleep a little while they waited for the Lieutenant to get done helping at the accident, but it was hard to get comfortable in the back of a police car.

There was nothing to tell Keeler, though. He repeated the story until the Lieutenant got tired of jotting it down. "Okay," he said. "I'd like to keep the two of you here for another night. It's not the Ritz, but we can plump up the pillows and add a few blankets."

Joseph leaned over and rubbed the back of Jean's neck with

one hand, and she shrugged away, bristling. On her behalf, he tried to talk Keeler out of it, but Keeler was having none of it. Joseph was too tired to argue with him any longer.

The cell was tiny. He could hardly move without touching Jean. She'd asked them to bring in a second cot. The sergeant looked at her a little strangely, but passed along the request, and fifteen minutes later, a uniformed young woman came in with a bedroll under her arm.

Jean squeezed her eyes shut and turned away from Joseph on her cot, but he didn't miss the lone tear that rolled down her cheek when the night watchman shut the cell door and turned the lock.

They weren't alone. There was a girl, a middle-aged woman, and another man as well, and they seemed to know each other. He listened in on their conversation for a while, but he felt guilty about it and tried to stop himself.

That night, he was to get little rest. It wasn't the body; he'd seen his fair share of those on the job. It was the woman that kept plaguing him, even in his dreams. Those eyes, that face—it was as though they were tattooed on the back of his eyelids. That and the trail of collapsed houses that followed her.

All of the others, save the man in the cell across from them, were gone when he woke up the next morning. Jean was standing by the window with her back to him. When she turned, her face was a mass of wrinkles and shadows. He knew that face—she hadn't slept much either.

"Joe," she said very quietly, "I think we need to talk." They were about to delve into a discussion he sincerely didn't want to have in his current state when Keeler came in with a stool.

He set it down in front of the cell, planted himself on it, and looked at both of them. "Okay," he said, when they stared in expectant silence. "A couple more questions. Then I can let you go, but we'll want you to stay around town, if you can."

"You haven't found any evidence, then."

"I beg your pardon?"

Joseph shrugged. "You can't hold us without evidence, so you must not have found any."

"Are you saying there's something to find?"

He shook his head. "I'm just curious about the investigation, Lieutenant, but you're right, it's none of my business. I'd like to make a call, if I may." Kelsey Robins, he was thinking. He should report back about everything that had happened. Also, Kelsey wasn't retired; his word would probably be worth more in Keeler's eyes.

"Yeah, a few questions first. Did you notice any cars on the highway?"

Joseph looked at him. "It's a highway."

"Conspicuous cars. Black. Seemed to be following other cars. Or a Greyhound. Did you see a Greyhound bus?"

Again, he shook his head. "What's this about?"

"One more thing." Keeler pulled a folded piece of paper from his pocket. "This is going to sound strange, but I've got to ask. Have you seen or do you know anything about this woman?"

Joseph sat heavily on the cot. Dimly, he heard Keeler asking him something—"Are you okay? What's wrong? Do you know her? Is she a friend?"

When he'd regained his composure, he told Keeler everything he knew, but the limited breadth of his knowledge only left the Lieutenant hungry for more.

"You're sure that's her?"

Joseph pulled out his copy of the photograph and slipped it through the bars. It was unmistakably the exact same picture. Jean watched it as Keeler looked it over, handed it back. "Why didn't you tell me about her?" she asked. "Why didn't you tell me that was why we were leaving town?"

"Would you have wanted to know?"

"Are you in love with her?"

Keeler cleared his throat, got up from the stool. He was clearly uncomfortable with being a part of such a personal conversation, but at the same time, Joseph knew Keeler wanted to stay on and hear if he let slip anything useful.

"Like I told the Lieutenant, I have no idea who she is. All I know is what Kelsey said."

"I'd like to call Detective Robins to check the story," Keeler said.

"That was the same call I was going to make myself."

Keeler let them out of the cell, brought them back to his office, and then went to talk to the Captain. Jean tried to start a conversation again, but Joseph deflected her questions and loaded comments. He was trying to listen to Keeler's voice as it rose and fell through the thin office walls.

"It's too much of a coincidence," he heard Keeler say. "And all of these questions about her. All of these people. Who the fuck is she?"

When he came back in, Joseph asked him point-blank what he meant by *all of these questions about her*. Keeler blinked, glanced over his shoulder. "Were you eavesdropping on my conversation?"

"Tell me, Lieutenant."

Keeler just handed him the phone. "Robins wants a word."

Kelsey bombarded him with questions. As briefly as he could, Joseph told Kelsey what had happened. "Christ," Kelsey said when he was done. "And what's all this about a murder out there?"

Joseph's eyes flitted to Keeler. That was the first time anyone had called it a murder. "I don't know anything. I'll call you later." He hung up the phone before Kelsey could protest or pester him with more questions, and then he asked Keeler again what he'd meant by all the interest in the woman.

"Another guy asked about her. Crazy guy from a tour bus. And rumors around town lately. Just stuff you hear on the streets, like everyone knows someone who's disappeared looking for this chick. The guy—Terry, I think was his name . . . he was talking to the receptionists last. They might be able to tell you where he went. I think he was looking for her, too."

After reminding them that he didn't want them leaving the town, Keeler let them go. Joseph went straight to the front desk. Two women were there. He asked if either of them had spoken to a man from a tour bus looking for a woman in a photograph, and they exchanged glances and laughed. "Yeah," the left-hand one said. "You could say we talked with him." Terry Young had been going to one of the addresses on Joseph's list.

In the RV, Jean sat him down and took the keys. "Joey, this isn't working."

Joey. She was calling him Joey again. That was progress. Then he really looked at her and his stomach turned. It wasn't progress. She was no longer angry, but instead, something much worse—she was defeated.

"I'm sorry," he said. Suddenly, he wanted to collapse and sleep for a week. "Sweetie, I know you hate this, but something's going on here. It seems—it's important."

"It's not your problem, Joey. Lieutenant Keeler, that detective back at home—it's their job now. You're retired. Someone knocked over our house. Let the police sort it out, and let's use the insurance money to start building a new life."

For a fleeting moment, he could see that life. Not caring. Letting it go. His skin crawled. Doing that would drive him crazy. Literally.

Jean was watching him. Deciding something. "It's never going to end with you, is it?"

"Jean . . ."

"I thought when you retired . . . I mean, Jesus, I know you, but I thought you'd be able to change. I thought I might be getting my husband back."

"But you have me. We're together. You've always had me."

She shook her head. "Joey, we haven't been together since you made detective. And I've been waiting so long to get you back. You don't know. The loneliness, the . . . it feels awful when you're just spinning your wheels, biding your time. I was stupid. I can see I made a mistake. I never really knew you at all."

"Jean," he began, but found he could barely talk.

She shook her head and put a single finger on his lips. "Don't," she said. "There's nothing you can say to change my mind right now. We need some time apart."

"I love you, Jean. I've always loved you."

She nodded. There was another tear. He couldn't take this. If she started crying, he was going to start crying, right here, right out in the police station parking lot. "I love you too, Joey. You know that." She put the keys on the dashboard and grabbed her purse where she'd set it down by the table in the back the night before. "And now I'm going to go."

"No!"

"You can call my mother. I'll let her know where I'm going to be."

"Be with me."

She smiled sadly at him and cupped his cheek with her hand, the way she hadn't done since they were young and foolish and passionately in love. And when she was gone, he thought, *Jesus, she's right.* He couldn't even remember how to be the kid who'd married her.

He ran out into the parking lot, but she was already gone. She had no phone, and he didn't know where she was going. There was nobody else around to tell him which way she went. After forty-eight years, he'd just split up with his wife.

Then he started crying.

He didn't know how long he sat there, trying to put everything in place. It could've been ten minutes, it could've been an hour.

It was mid-morning by the time he climbed into the driver's seat and turned on the diesel engine. He was running on automatic now. He pulled out the address list and the map. There was the footprint on the back. He should've shown it to Keeler. There would be time for that. He could come back here tonight. He didn't feel like driving to the next place yet, especially since he was fairly sure of what he'd find.

Propping the address on the gearshift, he hit the accelerator and pulled out of the lot. *What the hell*, he thought. Jean had been right about him: it wasn't going to be over. Not until he'd found the girl.

It wasn't until the lot came into sight that Joseph realized he should have known what to look for. The tall grass was trampled down, and there were tread marks in the soft earth surrounding what had once been a front stoop. There was still dust in the air, and when the RV's wheels bounced up onto the shoulder and Joseph climbed down the stepladder, he could smell diesel exhaust lingering where the bulldozer had sat. *It must have happened in the last hour,* he thought. *I'm getting closer.*

His first instinct was to jump right back behind the wheel and get to the next address before his pursuer made it there, but he decided to look around a little bit first. Fifteen minutes weren't going to make that big a difference, and if he could find something, any kind of clue leading to the person's identity, it would be well worth the time.

He looked all around the property, but it was the same story as everywhere else—pieces of furniture, a few intact fragments of someone else's past that had miraculously survived the collapse. There was something that might have been a tool shed in the backyard, but unlike before, this one hadn't been left standing.

It smelled bad. There were puddles of effluvia sitting among the grass, sunk deep into the dirt. With a glass from the RV's kitchen, he took samples of some of the stained soil. There were elements of red, some brown; he couldn't make out exactly what he was picking up, but he figured he'd probably be near an office that could examine it properly somewhere down the line.

He was on his way back to the road when something among the rubble caught his eye. It had once been white, and though fallout from the debris had colored it pale brown, it looked cleaner and newer than the rest of the building's remains.

Choosing his footing carefully, Joseph picked his way out to it, narrowly avoiding several sharp pieces of wood and metal bolting that protruded at sharp angles from the pile on the ground.

It was fabric of some kind, stiffer than an average shirt. He tugged at it, at last freeing it from the jaws of a splintered dresser. There were laces all up and down the front, and a few links of a chain tinkled to the ground as he extracted it. *Lord,* he thought, *I'm holding a straightjacket.*

It was unmistakable, the shape and design distinctive in their binding embrace. But it was unnaturally small. No man he knew could even fit his shoulders into the thing, let alone tie it up to encase his entire torso.

There was an inscription on the back, a stenciled logo and some text beneath it. Perhaps it would lead him to the source. He didn't have anything to copy it with, and the less time he spent standing alone with it, the better. He bundled it up, tucked it under his arm, and hurried back to the side of the RV.

On his way up the steps to the driver's seat, he trampled over a piece of crumpled paper he'd missed on the way out. He tossed the straightjacket into the passenger seat and knelt to pick it up. Smoothing it out on his leg, he read the hurriedly-scrawled note: *I'll be a few minutes longer. Please don't leave. Thanks.* It looked recent; the ink had not bled at all into the paper, and the indentations from the writer's pen were still fresh in the surface of the paper. On the reverse side, it said simply, *I'm in back.*

Who knew what it meant, to whom it had belonged. He shoved it in his pocket, hauled himself behind the wheel, and started the engine. There was nothing to see here, and there were many more addresses on his list.

As he drove, Joseph's gaze wandered to the empty seat beside him, where the night before his wife had sat. The piled straightjacket reminded him of a beehive, something elemental in its suggestion of disease.

Just this, he told himself. *Find the girl, and then everything will be different.*

He was right.

Chapter 16

Debbie Wendell could barely keep her eyes open. She held her head up with her hands, elbows propped on Captain Hernandez's desk. She'd been here all day. Jackie and Gregory Klein were both gone. At first, she couldn't have been happier. They just dragged her down, got into trouble, opened their mouths when they shouldn't have. But by the time she'd spent twelve hours being interrogated by policeman after policeman, it would've been nice to see a friendly face or two.

After another marathon in the Captain's office, they hauled her back to her cell. Her second night in jail was worse than the first. She actually slept this time, for a while, but when she awoke, she had a splitting headache, and she felt like she might be coming down with something.

Lieutenant Isaac Keeler woke her. It was barely light outside. "You're being transferred," he said. He looked almost as dragged-out as she felt.

He brought her up to his office to fill out some paperwork.

"What's going on?" she asked. "What's going to happen to me?"

"They're shipping you to Denver."

"Denver? What the hell?"

"It's the nearest place with the facilities they feel are appropriate for your . . . status."

"What's my status?"

He arranged a stack of papers into a manila file folder and fixed her with a stare she couldn't escape. "Ms. Wendell, you're a murder suspect, and you've also been tied to the disappearance of one of your fellow passengers on the flight you took in here. Your status is pretty serious. You wanted a lawyer? You're going to see your fair share of them now."

Debbie swallowed and said nothing. What was there to say? *Jesus,* she thought. In less than a week, her life had been transformed from drudgery to heaven to hell. She couldn't begin to imagine what was next.

She had an escort in the terminal this time. She watched the other passengers buy their coffees, their cinnamon buns, their celebrity magazines. Children played on the carpet at their feet, teenagers talked to faraway friends on their cellular phones. A week ago, Debbie thought, she'd been watching them from her usual post, as she brought another bundle of plywood or a few more sections of pipe to the new wing of the international concourse. Now, she was passing through in handcuffs.

She asked the cop when she was going to get her phone call.

"Yeah, in Denver," he said. "They'll handle all of that legal stuff when they book you. We don't do that out here. That's why you can't stay any longer."

She wanted to talk to her mother. "What if there's a medical situation I need to attend to?"

The kid looked at her. "Denver."

It struck her that there was nobody in the world who could help her. The only two witnesses who could possibly have attested to the fact that she'd been out of the hotel room when the murder took place had taken off to god knew where. Nobody trusted her, not after the stink she'd made with the airline, and the box she'd stolen from the airport back at home was off in someone else's hands.

Her mother was going to die alone.

By the time they loaded her onto her flight, though, self-pity had become something else, something stronger: Debbie Wendell was getting seriously pissed off. Whoever it was that lifted the box from the couch while she'd been outside had better watch their back. If it was worth killing a maid for, she wanted it more than ever.

And if it was Gregory Klein, so help her, she would paint the entire airport with his blood.

When the plane landed in Denver, Debbie was surprised to find not only her token escort of two uniformed police officers, but also an older man in a cheap suit and a beard that had begun to go white and fray around the edges. He didn't say anything as they ran through the security checkpoints and brought her out of the terminal, but she was very aware of his presence the entire time, the way his eyes never left the back of her head.

He stayed a few steps behind her to the parking lot, where they loaded her into an aging police van. She was even more surprised when he climbed in back with her. He waited until the officers had cuffed her to the metal security pole running across the baseboard, and then he leaned forward and offered a hand.

"I'm Doctor Lewis Yeager."

She raised an eyebrow, tugged against her restraints to shake with him.

"Debbie Wendell?" he asked, pulling out a manila folder.

She nodded, waiting for him to explain why they'd brought a doctor along to meet her, but he didn't. Instead, he sat back and watched her with piercing eyes as the van pulled out of the lot and began weaving its way through the airport traffic.

It was cold in Denver. She could see her breath even with all the windows shut and the heater blowing full blast. It didn't work very well; the engine must not have warmed up yet, she thought.

At the police station, they sent her to one of the sterile little interrogation rooms off of the main lobby. It was slightly larger than what she'd seen in the little village, far more high-tech. There was a one-way mirror on one side, all of the requisite recording equipment she'd seen in all the nighttime television.

They made her wait for almost an hour before Doctor Yeager came in, accompanied by a seasoned detective whom Yeager referred to as *Brunswick*.

"Ms. Wendell," Brunswick said gruffly. "You're aware of why you're here? You've been read your rights?"

"Am I under arrest?"

He and the doctor exchanged glances. "That's a matter currently under consideration."

"I don't understand. Don't you have to charge me for this kind of shit?"

"Perhaps, Detective, I could speak with her alone for a few minutes." Yeager pulled back a chair and plopped himself into it, directly across the scratched, metal table from Debbie.

Brunswick was obviously uncomfortable with the idea, but after a few moments' consideration, he relented. "You've got five minutes."

Yeager nodded. As soon as the detective had gone, he pushed away from the table and stood. "You want some coffee? A pastry or something? Probably didn't feed you too well on the plane."

Debbie rolled her eyes. Did they ever get tired of the Good Cop/Bad Cop routine? She'd thought they only did this sort of thing on TV. She could guess everything he was going to say to her. Something about how long a day it had been, all the stress she'd been under, and how inconsiderate policemen could be. Then he would try and catch her off guard with something like, "So did you lock the door after you murdered the maid?"

"Would you believe you're not the first person I've talked to about this?"

That she hadn't expected. "About what?"

"About the woman."

Debbie swallowed. "What woman? The maid? I wasn't even in the room."

"Not the maid. The girl. In the picture."

"What girl? What picture?"

"You had her box."

Suddenly, the blood in her veins went frigid. She had to force herself to relax. He didn't know anything. He'd heard a testimony from someone—the hotel receptionist, probably—and he was trying to pump her for information. This was how they worked. She'd seen enough TV to know that. She just had to keep a hold of herself. *Keep your cool and you can outwit them.*

"What box?" she asked with, perhaps, a little too steady a voice.

Yeager watched her for a few moments, then shook his head. He sat once more and stretched out across the table so that his hands were almost touching hers. He ran his fingers through his graying hair and then he fixed her with an intense stare. "I can help you, Debbie, but you have to help me."

"Did you study the teleplays for that line, or do you think you came up with it yourself?"

He snickered. "You know, I'd play hardball and tell you fine, go rot in jail for all I care, but that's not true. I do care." He stood, went to the mirror and reached for the camera hanging from the ceiling in the corner. In one quick move, he unplugged the power cable. The red light on the front, beneath the lens, winked out.

Now he had Debbie's attention. "Hey, what the hell is this?"

"What this is," Yeager said, "is personal. If Detective fucking Brunswick walks through that door, your window of opportunity has closed. Permanently. I'll deny this entire conversation, you'll get processed like all of the other murder suspects, and probably end up lost in the system for a few years before they slap you on the wrist and jam you in a cell. This is a chance to make a difference."

"What do you want?"

"The box, Debbie. What did you know about it? Where is it? What do you know about the woman?"

"What woman?" she bellowed.

He watched her a few moments longer. "You really don't know? What about the box?"

"I found it."

"Where?"

"In an airport. I was going to try and sell it. That's all. That's it."

"You didn't know about the woman."

She shook her head.

"You didn't know who the box belonged to? You weren't try-ing to find her?"

Again, she shook her head. "What's this about?"

The door came open. Brunswick crossed the room in three steps and reached for the camera power cord. "Smooth move, Doc," he growled. Heads, Debbie sensed, were going to roll for this. She only hoped hers wasn't going join them on the chopping block.

Yeager sighed, buttoned up his suit. He started for the door.

"Hey, wait," Debbie called to him. He shot her a severe look. "I'll deny this entire conversation," he'd said, and now, his eyes said that denial was going to start right now.

"I can help you," she told him.

Brunswick, who had bent to undo her cuffs and who already had a hand on her shoulder, paused in mid-motion and gave the doctor a dubious look. He obviously wanted her off his plate as soon as possible. She wondered how many times Yeager interrupt-ed his work with strange little requests like the one he must have made to see her today.

"I don't think so." A hand on the doorknob. But he wasn't out the door yet.

"I think I might know someone who has information you'd find . . . pertinent."

"I want you to appreciate how irregular this is." Yeager checked his rearview mirror before switching lanes, angling toward the exit that led into the suburbs. "If anyone higher up the food chain than Brunswick were to find out that I'm taking you out of cus-tody, there'd be hell to pay."

"Your idea, Doc," Debbie reminded him.

"You tell me everything you know tonight. I want to know where this Gregory Klein was going, everything you know about who he was looking for, every last detail you can remember."

"And then?"

"Then we'll see."

Debbie shook her head. "That doesn't work for me. I need a guarantee that you're not going to throw me to the wolves as soon as you have your prize."

Yeager threw a sidelong glance at her. She knew how to handle men like him. He thought he could manipulate her by maneuvering his way into a position of power and then holding it over her head. She met a hundred of them every year; the construction industry was full of them. All she had to do was show them she didn't give a shit about their big mouths and their bigger egos, and usually, they fell on their backs and whined for someone to help them up.

He hit the brakes so hard that she would have flown through the windshield if the seatbelt hadn't yanked her back into the seat. The car skidded. Yeager twisted the wheel, and they bounced onto the shoulder. A symphony of horns blared around them as furious drivers swerved to avoid rear-ending the doctor's Maxima.

She had barely caught her breath when he yanked on the parking brake and turned to face her. "Let's get one thing clear right now. You're a murder suspect. You should thank the stars that you're not sitting in a police station. You do what I say, when I say, and maybe you'll luck your way out of the pile of shit you've gotten into. You start putting up a fuss, you start whining and making demands, you'll be in the express lane back to the lockup." He let a charged beat fall before he leaned a fraction of an inch closer to her. "We speaking the same language?"

Doctor Yeager lived in a homely little bungalow at the far back corner of a gated community outside of Denver proper. It wasn't one of the ritzier places, certainly nothing like the wealthy estates the billboard at the front advertised.

She noticed the care with which he locked the Maxima before leading her to the front door.

Inside was the picture of a marriage that had started to deteriorate about six months ago and whose only medication was duct tape and cardboard boxes. Old newspapers sat piled in a plastic bag by the door, and while there was a coatrack nailed beneath a mirror in the entry hall, dirty jackets lay strewn across the kitchen chairs.

He got a few things out of the refrigerator, put on a pot of coffee. Then he sat down and demanded that she tell him all she knew.

"If I help you," she said, "will you get them to drop the murder case?"

"I don't care about the murder case. Tell me about the box."

"I think they're related. I think the killer thought the maid was me." She showed him the note she'd picked up on the couch. "There was a candle in the bathroom. Someone had been in my room. That's what I was going to tell the police when they . . ."

"Did you see him?"

"Who?"

"Anyone. The person who wrote the note—the person in your room—anyone."

She shook her head. "Unless it was Gregory Klein."

"Tell me about him. Where was he going?"

"He said he was looking for someone. A girl."

"What was her name? Was her name . . . ?" he stopped himself.

"Frida," she said after a thoughtful pause. "I think her name was Frida."

Some of the hope and excitement faded from the doctor's eyes. "Oh."

"Who were you hoping for?"

"Someone else. He didn't show you a picture, did he?"

"He had one, I think, but no, I didn't see it."

"And the box—what did it look like?"

Debbie shrugged. She started to describe it, but Yeager made a face and shook his head. He told her to wait a moment, that he might have a picture or a sketch. He went over beside the refrigerator to a door she'd thought had probably hid a pantry. Except that it was locked. She hadn't noticed that when she first followed him in.

And it wasn't just locked. It was double-locked. No, triple-locked. She watched with mounting curiosity as he dialed two combinations and jammed a key into a third deadbolt. The door came open with a groan. It was dark inside. He glanced back at her and then slipped through.

She got up from the table and poked her head into the narrow, half-sized doorway. At first, she could see very little, just shapes, things pinned to the wall. As her eyes adjusted, she saw that Yeager was rooting around among a stack of papers, sketches, documents, all kinds of bizarre informational detritus. There were maps with red circles on them, newspapers with certain paragraphs highlighted.

A shiver coursed through her body. *Jesus*, she thought. She was witnessing an obsession. This was a madman. She realized with a pang of fear that she really didn't know anything about Lewis Yeager at all. The police had let him take a murder suspect off of their hands, but all that told her was that he was probably able to hold his own. Suddenly, she wondered if she could get to the front door before he could.

"There's a photograph on the wall," Yeager said, snapping her attention back. "I don't want you to look at it."

She swallowed. "Okay."

"Don't worry," he said. "It's not kiddie porn or anything. But I think it's dangerous. I think it'll drive you crazy."

She sipped a cup of coffee and leafed through the sketchbook he'd handed her. She nodded—that was the box. There were a hundred different drawings derived from a single black-and-white photograph at the beginning. She got to the end and looked up at him.

He was peering at her with the eager, hopeful excitement of a schoolboy who was baring his soul. Suddenly, he wasn't so intimidating, but a thought struck her a moment after that one—was this even the same man who had almost gotten them killed on the freeway just to make a point? Did he have multiple personalities? That brought the fear flooding right back in.

"That's definitely it," she said.

"And you held it? You had it with you?"

She nodded.

"Incredible."

"Doctor Yeager, what the fuck is this about? What's in that box? Why is it worth killing a cleaning woman over, and why are you now willing to put your career on the line for it?"

"I don't know. Nobody knows. But it's fascinating, isn't it?"

"I'm going to need more than that."

He pushed back from the table, and, while he had his back to her, buttering some toast he had made without asking if she was hungry, he said, "I'm sick, you know."

She choked and almost spewed her coffee all over the tablecloth.

"I figured it out when my wife left me. Damndest thing. And I can't do anything about it." He chuckled and rounded on her, and there was a burning excitement swimming with the fatigue in his eyes. "But that being the case, I might as well indulge, right?" He sat down and began chewing the piece of toast without ever breaking eye contact with her. "I don't want you to get it too," he said, "but if that happens, at least you'll see it coming."

Chapter 17

It was chilly in the airport terminal when Gregory Klein walked off of the McDonnell-Douglas MD-80 and joined the stream of passengers moving toward the baggage claim. The flight attendant had come on the radio about ten minutes before they had landed and announced that for the first time this week, there wasn't going to be snow on the ground.

Gregory wasn't built for this kind of weather. In Los Angeles, everyone put on heavy coats and complained about the weather if the mercury dipped below sixty-five.

He went straight for the information desk and asked the young lady with the fake nails if there were any flights to Trenton any time soon. She raised an eyebrow at him. "Maybe a commuted shuttle," she said. "Prop plane. I can check, but you'd almost get there faster if you walked. It's about a two-hour drive."

"Oh." He hadn't studied any maps. He'd been in too big a hurry just to get out of the last city before the police decided they wanted to talk to him again after all. "Do you do one-way car rentals?"

An hour later, he pulled out of the parking lot in a brand new Chevy minivan. It was far too big for him, but it was all they'd had—the luxury cars always went fast with the businessmen, and with gas prices still so ludicrous, the compacts had been snapped up almost as quickly.

He followed the directions the information desk girl had given him, making a few turns here and there, staying on the freeway until he got to a small junction about an hour and a half into the trip.

The transition onto the smaller highway was rough and uneven. He got the impression few people ever took it. It was getting dark, and the first few droplets of what looked to be a monumental storm had begun to patter across the windshield. Gregory flipped on his lights and kept his eyes on the road.

It was nearly nine by the time he got into the little coastal village of Trenton. The trip had taken him three hours, and he hadn't stopped once. *Should have flown*, he thought. *Stupid of the airport to hire employees who dissuaded potential passengers from buying tickets.*

He slowed the minivan to a crawl and gazed out the windows at the passing facades. As far as small towns went, he had seen better. Here, there were nothing but grungy taverns and hotels that rented rooms by the hour.

The flickering neon slowly died away in the rearview mirror. Ahead, there was a string of street lamps and nothing but blackness beyond them. The road hit a T-junction. Gregory spun the wheel to the right and slowed to a halt. The rain had begun to spatter against the sides of the van in earnest now, and when he turned the engine off, it was so loud he could scarcely hear the radio.

Shielding his head with a rental brochure, he got out and jogged to the edge of the highway. On the other side of the T-junction, the ground dropped sharply away across jagged rocks. Spray bubbled up from the seething ocean beyond, exploding with white fireworks as it smashed against the coast.

In the distance, he could just make out the lonely beam of a lighthouse piercing the storm. Besides that, there was nothing.

The paper he was holding over his head had begun to turn to mush. He turned back toward the car and looked quickly up and down the road. The streetlamps appeared to strike out toward more wilderness in either direction. He was about to give up and turn back in search of another town when he caught sight of a small cluster of lights winking at him through the raindrops about a mile down the road. He couldn't make out what it was from here, but it was human life and it wasn't red neon, and already that set it above the rest of Trenton.

Gregory kept his eyes on it between the furious swipes of the windshield wipers. The cluster grew larger, fleshing out the dimmer stars that he hadn't been able to see from the ocean. It was not until he was very near to it that he saw the sign—*Sunrise Hotel.*

He let out a sigh of relief—this was just the sort of place he'd been looking for. Not a Motel 6, not a Best Western, and certainly not one of those roach-infested little hovels back in town. The hotel was built out of what appeared to be a converted Victorian mansion that had somehow been transplanted to the coast. A few additions had been slapped on here and there over the years, but none of them could have been newer than two decades old.

The parking lot was made of cobblestones, a feature he found so immediately endearing that he told himself right then that he would spend the night here regardless of the cost.

He left the minivan parked in an overgrown end of the lot, amid tangles of jasmine and other blossoming flowers he didn't recognize. It was a perfect little English bed and breakfast.

Inside, it was warm, if a bit musty. The air was filled with smoke from firewood, and orange flames licked at a pile of dry logs in the hearth. A young woman, pretty in a small-town sort of way, looked up from a book she was reading behind the reception desk. She smiled at Gregory.

Okay, she's cute. Not like the silicon, blonde *Playboy* bunnies that tooled around town in their Mercedes convertibles back at home, but cute in a way he'd almost forgotten existed. *Talk to her,* he told himself. *You can do this.* He smiled back and walked over.

"Let me guess," she said, closing her book. "Lost on the way to Bangor?"

Gregory shook his head. "I . . . this is where I'm going."

"Really?" Now she was interested. She took out a pen and the hotel registry, her eyes never leaving his face. "What's someone like you doing in Trenton?"

"Someone like me?"

She snickered. "You're not some skanky fisherman looking to room for two hours with his little fishnet whore. You look like a decent guy."

Gregory blushed. "Thanks. I . . . I'm looking for someone. I think she might be out here. In this town, I mean. Maybe."

The girl looked a little disappointed. "She your girlfriend? Wife?"

"No . . . I just . . . I'm not sure who she is. It's hard to explain. Her name's Frida. Well, I call her Frida. I'm not sure what her name is. But I'm worried for her. She sounded like she was in trouble or something."

The girl stopped halfway to the rack of keys propped up behind her chair and eyed him. Her hand slowly dropped to her side. Without another word, she ducked through a curtained doorway behind the counter, and then he heard her yell for someone, her mother, he thought. That was strange, because he hadn't thought she was *that* young. But then, he wasn't very good at judging ages.

He remembered how Jackie had assumed he was some kind of sexual predator when he mentioned Frida. He caught a glimpse of his reflection in a carved, full-length mirror propped by the hearth. Was there something creepy about his appearance? Was there a reason he seemed to strike people as an unsavory character?

There was movement behind the curtains. Muffled voices, one of them the girl's, rose and fell. Gregory leaned forward, trying to overhear anything they said. All he caught from their mumbled exchange was, "another one of them." Then the curtains parted and an elderly woman, at least in her early-seventies, stepped out. She sported curly gray hair, wire-rim glasses, and a pink blouse and skirt.

"Hi," she grunted.

"Hello. I'm sorry . . . have I said something . . . I mean, is there a . . . a problem?"

She looked him up and down, and some of the mistrust seemed to ease a bit. Or perhaps she was just deciding that he wasn't so much of a threat. He could see it in her eyes—she was thinking, *I could take him.* The shameful truth was, she probably could.

"Mandy says you're looking for someone."

He nodded. "That's right. Is there . . .I mean, is that a problem?"

"You got a picture of her?"

Gregory shook his head.

"Then it's not a problem. Fifty-three dollars a night, checkout is at ten o'clock sharp, and you get a free cup of coffee if you give up the room before nine. The maid likes to be done early."

As he went for his wallet, he asked, "Why would it be a problem if I had her picture?"

She fixed him with a steely glare. "I prefer exact change," she said. "We don't keep a lot of cash down here on account of the riffraff that comes through on a regular basis."

Try as he might, Gregory could coax no more information out of her. He took the rusted key she gave him and followed her directions up the winding central stairs to his room on the second-floor balcony. Light shone through the cracks around one or two other doors, and he thought he remembered seeing a few cars in the parking lot, but the hallways and the lobby were deserted.

The room was nice enough, a queen bed that smelled clean, in spite of the layer of dust on the top sheet. He pulled back the heavy curtains that covered the opposite wall and opened the French door onto a balcony. It overlooked the ocean, and even though it was still pelting rain outside, he stepped out and drew in several deep breaths. He liked the salt in the air; it reminded him of back in high school, when he used to go to the beach and draw the strangers that didn't look like they'd mind.

A knock sounded on his door. He came back inside and quickly ran a hand through his hair. Even in the minute or two he'd spent outside, it was a wet, disheveled mop. "Just a minute," he called, and pressed his eye against the peephole.

Mandy, the owner's daughter, stood outside, arms folded

primly across her chest. He did his best to straighten himself up
and then he pulled open the door. "Yes?" he said.

She stuck out a hand. "My name's Mandy."

"Gregory. Gregory Klein." He took her hand somewhat per-
plexedly and shook. "I thought I wrote it in the register—my
name."

"I came by to apologize for how I acted down there. I thought
you were someone else."

"It's no . . . I mean, no problem. But who? . . . Did you think
I was, I mean?"

She shrugged. "Come downstairs. Have a drink."

Mandy sank into the couch beside the hearth, and when Gregory
remained standing awkwardly on the other side of the coffee table
from her, she frowned and motioned for him to join her. He lowered himself onto the loveseat facing her and took a cautious sip
of Irish cream while she poured herself a matching glass.

"When you said you were looking for someone and that you
weren't from around here, I assumed you were just another one
looking for that girl. It's madness."

"Which girl?"

"There's this girl. Her picture's turned up in a few places.
Everyone thinks they're related to her, or a friend of a friend, blah,
blah, blah." She sighed, took a drink. Her expression clouded, and
she sat forward on the couch. "Funny thing is, most of them do
seem to know her, except they don't really know her, you know
what I mean? And see, you sounded like almost the exact same
thing, which is why I got so edgy right off."

"I'm not sure I'm following you," Gregory said. "What do you
mean? How many of them have there been?"

"Eh, five or six, I think. Not so many's we can call the cops or
anything, but enough to notice, you know? Mom's got this super-
stitious thing about them. She says they're all crazy or something.

I mean, they're all loners—again, just like you, that's why we thought—and they say they're just having problems or whatever, but Mom thinks it's something else. She doesn't want me to talk to them, and she won't let me look at the picture, or get involved or anything, you know?"

"So have you seen the picture?"

She shook her head. "I mean, I don't believe any of that shit, but I'm not going to go tempt fate either." She drained her glass and sucked up an ice cube to lick off the creamy residue. "You want some more?"

She got him another glass of the stuff just as the old woman pushed through the curtains. Her gaze darted around the lobby, settled on the two of them. "Mandy, what are you doing?"

"Talking to our guest, Mom," she said. "He's been on the road for a long time."

"You'd better not be telling him any stories." As quickly as she'd appeared, she darted away again.

Mandy made an expression of conspiratorial boredom toward Gregory. "She doesn't like me to talk about it," she whispered. "I think she's embarrassed because she knows how stupid it sounds."

"Don't keep him up late. And mind the counter," her mother called.

"It's right there, Mom. I can see it from here."

When the old woman's footsteps had moved upstairs, Gregory turned back to Mandy. "So where do these people go after they come here?"

"How do you mean?"

"Well…" He cast a meaningful gaze up at the deserted hallway. "I mean, they're not still here, right? Where'd they go?"

"Oh. They usually wander off to some other address, some other state, some other country. I don't blame Mom, they are sort of creepy. They're following clues or something. I don't know what they think they'll find. I don't even know if the girl exists." She emptied her glass again, and after a long pause, in which Gregory began to feel the cool warmth of the Irish cream liqueur puddle in his stomach, she asked, "So who's the girl you're looking for? You said you had an address?"

Gregory thought for a moment. He couldn't have forgotten. *Ninety-five sixty...eight? Four? No, seven.* He told her and the smile dropped from her face.

"You *are* one of them!" she yelped, and jumped up from the sofa. "You're one of *them!*"

Chapter 18

Jackie Savage felt six hungry pairs of eyes follow her into the cramped little room. The walls were hung with bamboo mats, the floors covered in thick Oriental carpeting. She would almost have thought she was in Japan if it weren't for the oppressive heat and the tinkling sound of the vendors in the street.

They closed in behind her, forming an impenetrable wall of hot, sweaty flesh. She tried not to think about them. Instead, she focused on the big man on the throne in front of her.

He looked like the classic Buddha—plump, dark-skinned, wrapped in a shawl that flowed about his considerable bulk with an odd air of grace. Except this Buddha was not laughing. He was watching her like a cat outside the bars of a birdcage.

When he started talking, it sounded like water burbling over rocks. His voice was so deep that she thought at first he might be coughing or heaving up blood. She didn't understand a word he spoke.

"I'm sorry," she said. "English? Do you speak English?"

His expression soured. "English," he said with a heavy accent. She nodded. "You are looking for the girl, I am told."

"My . . . my uncle is, yes."

"Tell your uncle he has come to the wrong place. He is not welcome here."

She swallowed. "Can you tell me where the girl has gone?"

"Leave."

Jackie wanted nothing more than to comply, but she knew that Marlowe would kill her if she came out of here with nothing to show for her efforts. "Please," she persisted. "Any kind of help . . . it's important."

"It is important to everyone."

Jackie frowned. "What do you mean? Are other people looking for her?"

"You are ignorant. You are but one of hundreds. Maybe thousands."

"But my uncle is her father. We really must find her."

His eyes narrowed. He stared at her for a period of maybe ten seconds that felt like ten years. She could sense the others closing in around her. They wanted to devour her like a pack of wolves. If he were not here, she thought, she would have five or six men covering her body with their massive hands. That made her skin crawl. She edged a little closer to the throne.

The move gave the man the wrong idea. He gave her a look of disgust and drew away from her. "I do not take gifts of little girls like you."

In spite of her revulsion, the other men in the room seemed disappointed.

"The girl you are looking for was here. We sent her away. She brought bad luck to all of us. For any more than what I have told you, go to the Zenith House on the border of the desert. There you will find any remaining information you seek. Now go."

"Thank you," Jackie said. She turned, hasty, more than ready to be gone from here. The other men looked to their superior and, with visible reluctance, parted to permit her escape.

Marlowe was sitting under the shade of a tattered umbrella on the other side of the street. Jackie started toward him but had to pause and flatten herself against the wall as a lumbering cart full of chickens and trinkets ground its way down the narrow avenue. Throngs of merchants parted for it like water, only to flow back into its wake.

It was miserably hot, and she couldn't cross the street without

touching a hundred other bodies. She was soaked with other people's sweat by the time she reached Marlowe. Even he, whom she
had decided was immune to most common human failings, had a
moist handkerchief he kept dabbing around his collar.

"She's not here," Jackie shouted over the din of the merchants,
the bustling crowds. "He said we have to go to a place called the
Zenith House for any more than that."

Marlowe heaved a sigh and then nodded, rose, and beckoned
for her to follow him.

They wove their way back through the labyrinth of miniature
streets, bounded on either side by three-story buildings and sand-
stone walls. Slowly, they moved back toward the modern end of
the city. It was like nothing Jackie had ever seen before.

Cairo was nothing like a sleepy Midwestern town.

She'd seen pictures in books and on TV, of course. She was
always reading up on strange, exotic places with the hopes that
someday, she would meet someone romantic to sweep her off
across the world. Marlowe wasn't quite what she'd had in mind.

Their hotel was just on the border between new and old. One
side looked out over the modern skyscrapers, the business districts,
the upscale restaurants and tourist traps. The other side, the back
alley, faced a completely different Cairo—one of tiny streets,
impoverished vendors, and vast oceans of sagging shanties. The
city's dichotomy fascinated her.

Marlowe showered and came through the connecting door to
her room as she was just finishing doing her hair. The hotel was
nice enough—there was a TV, the usual amenities, and most
importantly, there was air conditioning. Jackie had never been in
heat like this before. It consumed her whenever they walked out
the door, sapping the energy from her muscles, drawing the sweat
from her skin when she hadn't even known it was there. It always
sat on her shoulders when they walked around town like a heavy
troll with fiery hot breath.

"We're leaving shortly," he informed her. "I must run downstairs and consult with the concierge about this Zenith House."

She shrugged. She had gotten over resisting anything Marlowe told her. In many ways, he was becoming more and more like a father to her. At first, she had protested. When he declared that they were going to Egypt at once, she had told him she could not. She still had no idea where Walker was, or what had happened to her father. She called him once more, but again, she just got his answering machine.

When she'd gotten off the phone, determined that she was going to go to the police, going to forget the strange journey Marlowe had dragged her into, he was waiting with the picture. "Look how helpless she is," he'd said. And she had looked. And that was a mistake. Because he was right—she was just a little girl, possibly even younger than Jackie. And there was something about those eyes, both desperate and piercing. Like a creature trapped in foreign skin. When Jackie slept, she dreamt about them. They would be everywhere, on her brother, her father—even her mother, whose face she barely remembered.

The door clicked shut behind Marlowe, and Jackie was left lying on her bed. Sun streamed in the window. She went to it and peered out across the city. Her room was on the old side. Marlowe had grunted in disgust when he saw it and told her they'd get it changed, but she had insisted that it was all right. His, around the corner of the blocky high rise, had a view of a French restaurant and an expensive new mall, so he had relented, muttering that he didn't understand her.

To Jackie, it was a window to the past, to a mystical time and place, the likes of which she could scarcely have imagined back at home in her boring little classroom. How many days had she spent staring out the window at the schoolyard as rain pelted the grass and the swaying cornstalks? All of that seemed so far away now. It had been twenty-six hours since they'd left the only country she'd ever known, but already, that life felt like a distant dream.

With that thought, despite the delight she got from watching the merchants heckle the lost tourists and the locals, a wave of homesickness overtook her for the first time. She went back to the

bed and turned on the TV. Perhaps she could find MTV or the
Cartoon Network, something from home that would tide her over
and let her forget for a few minutes that she was about as far from
her little house and her big brother as she could possibly be.

The only English station was some international flavor of
CNN. The anchors were all worked up about some scandal with
the Pope. It was the same thing she'd been seeing on the news back
when she was at home, except now they'd taken it farther; he had-
n't only had sexual relations with some random woman, he might
also be concealing offspring. He was surely going to be removed,
the reporters speculated. He had brought disgrace to the entire
Catholic Church.

She tried to conjure up some interest for the story and to stick
it out until another one came along, but they kept harping on it,
and after a while, she just turned the TV off. Five minutes later,
Marlowe barged back in and said he had directions to the Zenith
House, and then they were off and running again.

They found a taxi service that would take them to the edge of town,
where another bus could take them all the way to the desert. It took
some considerable negotiating for Marlowe to convince the driver
to stop and let them off before they reached the sands and dunes.

"But there are hotels where I am taking you," the driver said
in broken English. "I have a brother who runs a very good hotel.
And a restaurant. You can eat and sleep good there. And cheap. I
tell him you are special customers."

Jackie shuffled to the middle of the bus and sank into a seat
that smelled of vomit. It didn't even bother her. She'd been assaulted
with a wider range of odors than she could even begin to describe
since they had arrived in Egypt, and this was nothing particularly
pungent or invasive.

She turned and peered out the window at the hazy streets that
zigzagged back into the tangled mess of Cairo. She would have

liked to have been here on her own, to be at liberty to lose herself in the tiny little backstreets and uncover the real treasures the city had to offer.

At length, Marlowe forced himself into the tiny seat next to her and put a sagging arm around her shoulders. "He will take us where we ask," he said.

The bus rolled away from the tiny depot. The engine ground, coughed, and sputtered. They weren't even climbing a hill. This was going to be a long trip. She watched the scenery meander by.

As soon as they left Cairo, it became flat, oblique, unchanging. The sun shimmered high in the sky, surrounded by nothing but clear, cloudless blue. The ground rose up to join it in golden-brown hillocks and dunes, punctuated here and there only by the occasional tuft of desert grass.

After a while, she tired of looking out, and so she turned to survey the other passengers. There was a little boy, maybe five- or six-years-old, sitting by himself at the back. When she twisted around in her seat and caught sight of him for the first time, he was already watching her. He had, she thought, been watching her for a long time. She smiled at him, but he did not smile back. He only stared.

She stuck out her hand. "Hi," she said, "my name is Jackie. What's yours?"

He didn't say anything. He probably didn't even speak English. Surely he was just fascinated with her foreign appearance: her pale white skin, her clothing, her long, unrestricted brown hair.

"Brother," he said in a high-pitched voice. Not even a trace of an accent.

"You're called Brother?"

The bus began to slow, and the driver called out to Marlowe that they were going to make his stop for him. "Jackie," Marlowe said. "It's time for us to go."

It was a pity, she thought. Talking to the boy probably would've made the trip go a lot faster. She was about to get up when he shook his head.

"Not my name. Your brother."

She smiled. "I'm Brother now?"

He shook his head again. "You look just like your brother."

Marlowe impatiently yanked her down the aisle and wrestled her off the narrow flight of stairs. Outside, she hit the sand hard, stumbled, struggled to stay on her feet, all the while twisting and pulling at his fingers. "Let go!" she snarled. "I have to talk to that boy!"

"You do what I say!"

She kept struggling until the bus was a few hundred feet away and it was clear that she'd never be able to catch it. The little boy came to the back and waved to her out the rear window, face pressed against the glass. She watched him depart and remained rooted to the ground until the roar of the engine had died away into the hot desert breeze.

Defeated, she allowed Marlowe to pull her away. "He'd seen Walker," she breathed. "He was out here."

"We're not looking for Walker," Marlowe said. "We're looking for my daughter."

She turned, for the first time taking in their surroundings. They were stopped at a tiny settlement at the edge of the desert, a caravan that had gotten bogged down in the sand and never managed to get moving again. A few hovels slapped together from clay and whatever planks of discarded wood the owners could find sat crouched close together. They looked like anemic beasts, trying to stay warm against the harsh desert nights by sharing body heat.

Beyond them, rising up against the purple evening sky, was a magnificent palace. The walls were covered in painted tiles, the windows masked with ornate wicker shutters, and the steps leading up to the front gate carved out of only the finest marble. It was such a stark contrast to the other little structures that it looked like a poorly-doctored photograph. Surely they could not both be in the same place.

"What is this?" Jackie wondered aloud.

"Zenith House," Marlowe said. "Perhaps we will find her in there."

No, Jackie thought. *Perhaps we will find Walker in there.*

Chapter 19

The road had become a blur to Terry Young. It had gotten dark, and the taxi's headlights did little against the all-devouring blackness. The car hadn't been maintained very well; it was all he could do just to keep it on the road. The steering was flaky, and every now and then the engine would hiccup, almost die, and then roar ahead as though he had just jammed his foot down on the accelerator.

His eyes kept darting across the winding highway. Ahead, lights from the village shimmered like the rippling confines of a mirage. He longed to be there, away from this pit of loneliness and despair.

He kept thinking he saw things on the road – small animals, people, other cars. And then there really was another car, and he had to swerve—fast—to avoid hitting it. Terry wrestled with the steering wheel, fighting it as the taxi swung toward the side of the road.

When he finally had it back under control, he glanced at the rearview mirror: pulsing blue and red light. Then headlights as the car turned around. He had almost played chicken with a highway trooper. Of all the luck.

It took the cop about thirty seconds to catch up with Terry. Terry pressed on for another half-mile, willing the guy to give up, and then, reluctantly, he eased up on the brakes and steered onto the shoulder.

The taxi idled hard when he put it in park. The engine coughed several times and then died altogether. The headlights dimmed. There was a knock on the window, and a spot of light from the officer's flashlight cut in through the glass, sweeping across the interior of the cab. Then he motioned for Terry to open up.

"Look, officer, I'm sorry about that back there." He stopped rolling the window down, leaving it at barely a crack. "I'm tired and there's so much on my mind . . ."

"Yuh-huh. Long night, sir? Little . . . partying?"

Terry had to laugh. Partying, he told the officer, was about the worst possible description of his life at this point. The policeman went to the back of the car and took down his license information, and then he asked to see Terry's cabbie permit. Terry swallowed. "I'm, uh, not on duty."

The policeman squinted at him. There was some kind of recognition in his stare. "Don't go anywhere." Then he went back to his car.

In the rearview mirror, Terry could see him talking to someone on his radio. The cop had the patrol car's dome light on, exposing his features in disconcerting orange shadows. He nodded, turned off the light, and trundled back over to the cab.

"Sir, step out of the vehicle, please."

Terry frowned. "I told you, I don't have any alcohol in the car. You can search. I'm giving you permission to search."

"Sir, if you don't comply, I'm going to have to call for backup and have you forcibly removed."

When he was out of the car, the man asked him to turn around, and then Terry felt handcuffs around his wrists. Suddenly, the policeman was reading him his rights. Cold fingers closed around Terry's heart. All he could think was that he'd never called Vicki, and now his only chance to talk to his new wife was going to be from prison. And he didn't even know what he'd done.

He thought he might have asked the man a couple of times what he was going in for. He wasn't quite sure. The entire evening was becoming a fog to him. The only thing he couldn't shake was that he had to get to Three Rooks, Indiana, as soon as he possibly could.

⌒〆〜

Lieutenant Isaac Keeler looked up when the patrolman knocked on his glass office door and quietly escorted Terry Young inside. Keeler looked surprised. "You found him? That was fast."

"Right where you said he'd be."

And then the other cop was gone, and Terry was left facing the Lieutenant. Keeler folded his arms and sat back in his chair. He had not offered to unlock Terry's handcuffs. "Do you know why you're here?" he asked at length.

Terry shook his head. "Am I under arrest?"

"Yes."

"What for?"

"For murder, Mr. Young. You're under arrest for murder."

Terry blinked at Keeler. It didn't make any sense. "Whose?" he asked. "I haven't killed anyone! I've barely talked to anyone!"

"Careful what you say, Mr. Young. You were read your Miranda rights, were you not?" He opened a manila file folder, went through a few documents, and then handed Terry a photograph. For one heart-stopping moment, Terry thought it was going to be another picture of Shayla Hacker. It would kill him if it was; that was too much. All of this was supposed to be freeing him, but it was turning out to be more of a trap than marrying Vicki could ever have been.

It was a picture of a tree. Just a tree. Something up in the branches had been circled with a thick, black Sharpie marker. He frowned at it, then back at the Lieutenant. "I don't understand," he said.

Keeler nodded, took the picture back, and replaced it with a second. This one was closer. He could see something in among the tree branches, but he wasn't quite sure what. It was something patterned, like a tablecloth. After a minute or two, the Lieutenant took that one away and gave him a picture of a slain body. The sleeves bore the same pattern as the tablecloth from the last snapshot.

"Someone was killed and shoved in a tree? I don't understand. Why would anyone do that? Why do you think *I* did that?"

Keeler picked up the photograph and handed it to Terry. Terry looked at it, then at the Lieutenant. "I've already seen it."

"I'm showing you something. Take it."

Terry did. He held it, looked it over, turned it upside down a couple of times, got bored with it, and gave it back to the Lieutenant. Keeler held it up to the light. He pointed to the shiny surface. "Fingerprints, you see? Photo paper is one of the best ways to pick them up."

Terry nodded blankly at him.

"Mr. Young, we found your fingerprints on a photograph this man was carrying."

Terry was almost certain he had never seen the man before in his life. He looked a little closer at the picture Keeler was still holding.

Now, he couldn't tell. The clothing did look slightly, vaguely familiar, but he had no idea where from. "I swear to you that I haven't done this," Terry said.

"Terry," Keeler told him, "you don't want to say things like that. You're under arrest. Be careful what comes out of your mouth. I'm going to have you booked and we'll deal with this in the morning."

"But surely one fingerprint . . . I mean, isn't that just circum-stantial evidence or something? You can't arrest me and charge me with murder just because you found something of mine on or around this body."

Keeler gave Terry a tired smile as he rapped on the glass door and beckoned to the police sergeant that looked up. "That's why it's good we had the testimony of a bus full of witnesses to confirm that you talked to this man earlier in the evening."

Terry blinked. That just didn't make sense. "What are you talking about?"

"Yeah, every last one of them. You know, they all remembered because you held them up and came running after them. They almost left you behind with him."

Time stopped in its tracks. Keeler couldn't possibly be talking about the man at the rest area. Terry had run for his life from that man. Surely the other passengers had all seen it.

"But that was just in a rest area," Terry protested. "We stopped to use the bathrooms and I talked to that guy for five minutes. That's all that happened."

Keeler nodded. "The body was found in a rest area, Mr. Young." The door opened and the sergeant walked in. "Take him to a cell and keep an eye on him. Make sure to get down anything he says."

Numbly, Terry let the officer lift him out of the chair and drag him through the door.

"Sweet dreams, Mr. Young," Keeler called after him.

Terry shivered. Suddenly, all he could think of was Shayla's face. *She killed that man*, he thought. *And slowly—slowly she's killing me, too.*

⚜

Terry spent much of the next day in interrogation rooms. Keeler came in again. He hadn't been there since the morning. He held a sheaf of papers in his hands: Xeroxed copies of all the notes the other officers had taken down while questioning him. He was shaking his head, as though already disappointed in the whole process. "Mr. Young, you've got to help us if you want us to try and help you. You have to tell us what happened."

Terry put his head in his hands. "I don't know what happened," he said, for what felt like the hundredth time that day. He'd barely slept the night before. He was starting to see things. This was right where they wanted him, because he was almost ready to confess to the murder just to make them stop with the incessant badgering. "I've told you or your men everything that happened. We talked, exchanged pictures . . ."

"And you're both looking for this woman, this . . . this . . ."

"Shayla Hacker. Yeah. I can't explain that."

"So what's so special about this girl?"

"I don't know."

"Damn it, Terry, tell me why everyone's so crazy about her."

Terry blinked. "What do you mean, *everyone?*"

"Everyone."

Suddenly he was alert, wide awake. "Who?"

"Tell me what happened."

"I have!"

"Again."

Impatiently, Terry went through their entire conversation again, from the start. "I ran when he kept telling me to come to his cabin."

Keeler's eyes jumped up from the paper he was reading. "What cabin?"

The string of headlights behind them looked like a cluster of lost fireflies, wandering through the darkness. Terry watched them rise and fall over the humps of the country road. One or two of them would occasionally flash their red and blue police lights just to make the oncoming traffic get out of the way. He became mesmerized by the image and almost didn't notice when they pulled into the rest area lot. This was like hunting with his father in South America—exciting, dangerous. Purposeful.

"Okay," Keeler said. "We're here. Where's the cabin?"

"He didn't say. He just said it was nearby."

Keeler gave him a weary look and then climbed out of the police car. When the other troopers had assembled, the Lieutenant briefed them on the situation. Terry felt a dozen pairs of hostile eyes trained on him. It was as though they blamed him for not knowing information he'd never been given. He alone was responsible for their presence out here in the cold when their husbands and wives were back at home with the children.

They fanned out and began picking their way through the woods. Keeler took Terry with him, and every now and then would glance over and ask if he was certain he didn't know where the cabin was. What was Terry to say?

They passed the cinderblock restrooms and ventured into the woods. He would have doubted if anyone would keep a property this close to a highway facility, but he didn't say so, because that would probably be misinterpreted as trying to direct their search.

Halfway through the night, when there was no longer any hint of light in the sky, Keeler called a break and the team reassembled at the very picnic bench where Terry had first seen his would-be victim. All of them were tired and cranky by this point. Under their breath, they muttered awful things about him. As time wore on and they got back to looking, they made less and less of an effort to speak quietly.

It wasn't until the light of dawn was just beginning to touch the clouds that Keeler's radio crackled to life and one of the officers reported that he might have found something. They were almost three miles from him, and it took them another forty minutes to get there.

He was standing in a particularly thick grove of trees, hands on his hips. He wiped his forehead and waved to them as they approached. "Can't seem to find anyone here. Might be the place."

Terry peered past him at the darkened structure hiding in the trees. His stomach turned. He had a bad feeling about the place. It was an old-fashioned log cabin, updated over the years with sealing windows, a couple of locks on the door. The entire structure stood on wooden stilts five or six feet off the ground. It looked like the woodland retreat of a paranoid schizophrenic.

Terry felt Keeler's eyes on him, searching for any recognition. He looked the Lieutenant right back in the face.

"Seen it before?" Keeler asked.

"Never."

Keeler sighed, grabbed Terry by the arm, and dragged him up the front steps. He knocked on the front door several times while the other officers skirted around the outside of the cabin. When they established it was empty, Keeler tried the knob. It was locked.

"We'll need paperwork to get in," one of the cops said, but then another gave a shout from the back: "Open window."

They gave the place a once-over, and then the other officers asked if they could go home. Keeler kept one of them on, a beefy man with a head as thick as his pelvis and arms that could snap tree trunks. "The rest of you can go. And thanks for sticking it out."

They nodded, too tired to even be angry with Terry anymore. They hiked away through the wilderness. Terry watched with growing unease until the lights from their torches had disappeared. What was it he was feeling? Something about the woods terrified him.

"Come on," Keeler said. "Time for the fine-toothed comb. Let's see if we find any of your fingerprints inside."

The beefy cop by the door kept leaning inside to clear his throat and look around. Terry felt sorry for him—almost. If he hadn't been falsely accused of murder earlier that same day, he might have had more compassion. As it was, the man's interruptions were starting to get annoying.

Keeler had Terry sit in the living room while he looked around the little cabin. It smelled of kerosene and incense inside. There was no electricity, but Keeler managed to light a small fire in the fireplace, and by the flickering light, he started to rifle through the stacks of papers and junk that sat in drifts and mountains on the floor.

After fifteen or twenty minutes, the Lieutenant took a break and sat down on the edge of the sofa where Terry was waiting. He rubbed his eyes with both his hands and then stared at the fire for several minutes without talking.

"Find anything useful?" Terry asked at length.

Keeler looked at him. "Why'd you do it, Terry?"

"I didn't. I told you."

The Lieutenant sighed. He got up and knelt in the far corner of the room again. Terry listened to him shuffle through more paper. Ten minutes later, he was back on the sofa again.

"It's worthless," he said. At first, Terry thought he was talking to himself, but when he looked over, he found Keeler watching him. "It's crazy stuff. This guy was some paranoid madman. Seriously, Terry, what did you want from him?"

Terry didn't bother to respond this time. Instead, he rose and went to the corner of the room where Keeler had been working. The Lieutenant followed, but said nothing to prevent him from sifting through some of the papers for himself. He was probably hoping Terry would turn up something that would expose a motive behind his supposed crime.

Keeler had been right, though—the cabin's owner had been stranger even than Terry had thought. He had half-feared, half-expected that he would find more pictures of Shayla Hacker somewhere up here. He was almost relieved when he found none. Instead, the photographs he uncovered—interspersed with old diary entries and sketches of places he didn't recognize—were mostly from the woods or around town.

There didn't seem to be any discernable pattern to them. There was one of a liquor store, another of an old tire swing that must have been somewhere nearby in the forest. A couple looked out at the highway from the picnic area where Terry had first run into the man. There were a few random people standing around the restrooms, a couple of cars in the lot—no clue at all as to why the snapshots had been taken.

Keeler stuck out his hand as Terry straightened, and he sighed and handed them to him. "These what made you do it?"

"Oh, shove off," Terry said. He went back to the couch and sat down.

Wood smoke was beginning to waft into the cabin. He coughed, waved it away from his face, but it wasn't entirely unwelcome. It reminded him of the first time he'd taken Vicki skiing. They'd stopped by a lodge for sandwiches and hot chocolate and sat by the fire, warming their red-tipped fingers and toes.

The chunky officer in the door coughed and then looked out at something. "Hey, Lieutenant," he called.

Keeler looked up from a small writing desk in another corner of the room. "We're not leaving yet," he said. "We haven't found anything."

"No, I just . . . did you hear something?"

Keeler frowned. "No." He looked accusingly at Terry.

"Don't ask me," Terry said. "I've been sitting here on the couch the whole time. And I didn't hear anything."

"I'll check it out," the large cop said. "Maybe one of the other guys took pity on us and brought some beers or something."

Keeler snorted. "That'd be nice. And maybe hell froze over while we were away, too."

The officer vanished from the door. Terry listened to his footsteps clop down the wooden porch steps and then crackle into the foliage outside. Then there was silence, nothing but crickets and the rustle of the wind in the tree branches.

"Check this out," Keeler said. He came over to the fire and sat down, thrusting an eight-by-ten photo at Terry.

Terry took it and held it up to the light and frowned. "It looks like a dump," he said.

"Ever seen it before?"

"Knock it off, Lieutenant. I told you, I didn't know the guy."

Keeler took the picture back and looked at it himself. "What do you think that is?"

"How would I know?"

"I said *think*. Take a guess."

"Why, so you can read something into it and lock me up with probable cause? I want a lawyer."

Keeler shook his head. "You're not fooling anyone. If you think you can get away with something like this just because you killed someone nobody will ever miss, you're wrong. Maybe that's how it goes in the city, but that's not how we work out here."

"I'm not from the city."

"Yeah, whatever." He snorted and set the picture down on the edge of the desk. "Myself, I think it looks like someone bulldozed a house and then took pictures for the insurance money or something. Seriously, the things people will do for a little cash . . ." He went back to the desk, paused, and turned. He eyed the empty doorway—the front door standing open. "He come back yet?"

Terry shook his head.

"Everyone's gotta go incompetent on the one night when I need people to just do their jobs." Keeler went to the door and peered out into the night, dropping the stack of photos he'd been looking at on the edge of the couch. "Lyman!" Keeler called. He let his voice die among the thick trees and then he cupped his hands around his mouth and yelled again.

Terry was getting antsy. He didn't like all this sitting around. He wanted to call Vicki. He wanted to figure out why there had been a box to a little town called Three Rooks, Indiana, in an abandoned farmhouse where Shayla Hacker had supposedly been staying. But he wasn't about to say any of that to Keeler. *Start blabbing*, he thought, *and the cops will make a mess of all of this.*

He rubbed his leg—the blood still sticky in his jeans. He wanted desperately to pick at it. That would bring everything into perspective. Right now, the world was like an astronomer's star chart, tiny little fragments of problems flying all around him, so numerous and so far apart that he hadn't a prayer of catching them all. If he could just focus everything... he needed a knife.

He began bouncing his leg up and down. It helped a little. The fabric of his pants rubbed the sore flesh. It was something he could concentrate on, anyway.

Terry reached over and picked up the stack of photographs Keeler had dropped. He flipped through them one at a time, and when he got back to the beginning, he did it again. Halfway through the second run through, he found the common element in all of them. Then he came to the sixth picture and he froze.

"Lyman!" Keeler called again. He took a few steps out onto the porch. "Where the hell are you? You think you're getting paid to go piss on the trees?"

"Keeler, get inside!" Terry barked.

Keeler frowned back over his shoulder. "That's *Lieutenant* to you, Young. And you're a suspect, so you just sit down, stay put, and try not to—"

Terry jumped up from the sofa, crossed the distance to the door in three strides, and yanked the Lieutenant through the door before he could resist or try to draw his gun. Terry reached out and slammed the door shut behind him.

"That does it!" Keeler was already going for his belt. "I'm handcuffing you to the kitchen sink, and when we get back to the station, it's going on your record that you—"

"Shut up! Someone's out there."

Keeler opened his mouth, closed it, and squinted back through the cabin windows at the early morning light filtering through the trees. "What are you talking about? What, you invite some of your friends along to finish off the job?"

Terry shook his head and jammed the pictures back into Keeler's hands. "Look real close at that top one," he said. "Look through the middle of the tire swing."

The Lieutenant frowned at him, stole a glance at the picture. Keeler's eyes focused. Terry knew exactly what he was looking at. On the other side of the tree with the rope and the tire, there was a black Ford sedan with tinted windows.

"So?" Keeler said. "I don't get it."

"Look at the next one now."

He flipped it over—the picture of the rest area. "Yeah, so? It's the rest area. Picnic benches. Must've frequented that place. That's how you knew where to find him, I'm guessing."

"Third parking space from the right," Terry said. He went to the window beside the door and flattened himself against the wall. Through the blinds, he tried to make out any sign of life in the forest beyond. He could see nothing from here, the sun not yet high enough, the battery-powered police flashlights dimming on the front stoop.

"It's the same car," Keeler said. "I still don't get it."

"Look at the other pictures. You'll find either that car or the people in it in every one."

"So?"

"Jesus, Keeler. He was being followed. He was being followed, and then he was murdered. And now we're in his house. Do I have to add it all up for you, or are you starting to get the picture?"

Keeler shook his head. "We're police. Don't worry about it. People respect the law around here. They recognize authority."

"We're in the middle of the wilderness, Lieutenant. People respect brute strength. There are two of us and god knows how many of them. And they probably have guns and a car. We're stuck in a fucking cabin all by ourselves."

"Three," the Lieutenant protested. "We have Lyman."

"Yeah? Where?"

Keeler went white. Terry felt sorry for him. He wasn't used to dealing with anything like this. The worst crimes he probably saw before this week were truancy and acts of teenage vandalism. He hadn't been trained to be hunted.

When he closed his eyes, Terry saw the jungle again. South America. "The hunt is on," his father would say. A sporting laugh, a pat on the back. "Go on, kiddo. The cotton-pickin' hunt is *on.*"

"I'll call for backup." Keeler's voice wasn't much more than a whisper.

Terry crawled beneath the window at the front of the cabin and reached up around the side to pull down the blinds. "How long will that take to get here?"

"Twenty minutes." He raised his belt radio to his mouth, then paused. "If they're prepped and ready to go at the station."

"But you sent them home for the night."

Keeler nodded.

"So what are we looking at?"

"Forty-five to an hour."

While Keeler called down to the station, Terry went around on hands and knees and locked all the doors and windows. He stopped by the back door. There was a dog flap cut into the wood.

He pulled the rubber back a few inches, and squinted out into the muted light. For a long while, he could see nothing. Then he thought he saw something move.

"I think they're here," he hissed.

Keeler joined him on the floor. "But I just called."

"Not the police."

"Oh. Shit."

"Do you have a gun?"

Keeler pulled the six-shooter from its holster. "Got three bullets," he said, holding it up to the firelight.

Terry made a grab for it, but the Lieutenant yanked it away. "You're still a suspect, Mr. Young."

"When was the last time you fired that thing?"

"Listen, I've got my training . . ."

"When was the last time?"

"What the hell do *you* know about guns?"

"This is life or death, Lieutenant. I swear to you I had nothing to do with that man's murder. I have no idea what's going on here, but I'm pretty sure we're being hunted, and if you're willing to bet your life on your marksmanship, that's good enough for me. If you're not, you'd better think twice about sticking to your principles on this."

Another long pause. Keeler was breathing hard.

"Look—Keeler, look at me. I don't know what's out there. I don't want to find out. Do you?"

After what seemed an eternity of hesitation, Keeler handed the gun over. He let out a relieved breath when Terry didn't immediately stick it in his face. Terry spun the carousel around until the first bullet was aligned with the firing chamber. It was natural, easy, just like riding a bike. *The cotton-pickin' hunt is on.*

He crawled back into the living room, pulled the carpet from beneath the sofa, and stifled the fire in the hearth.

Smoke filled the room. Keeler broke into a coughing fit, and Terry's eyes began to water. The two of them huddled on the floor in the kitchen until it had cleared. He was about to get to his feet

when something moved in front of the living room window. He
froze and stopped the Lieutenant from standing.

"Someone's out there," he whispered.

"What if it's Lyman?"

"Sneaking around without saying anything?" Terry cocked the
gun, crept a little closer to the door.

The knob shook. Terry jumped in spite of himself. All the
while, he had been concentrating on practicalities, telling himself
what must be done without considering the danger they were in.
But now, there was no avoiding it. Now, it was upon them.

It shook a little harder. The door rattled in its hinges. Still,
there was not a word from the other side. A part of him had been
hoping that Keeler was right, that it was just Lyman back from the
woods with a couple of beers from the boys down at the station.
Somehow, that didn't seem too likely.

Terry's eyes darted around the floor of the cabin and paused
on a nail sticking up near the kitchen. He nodded at Keeler and
motioned for him to go toward it. Keeler looked confused but did
as he was told.

Setting the revolver down, Terry began to pry at the floor-
board beneath it. A sharp *crack* from the front of the cabin
brought his attention back to the door. "You've got to finish this,"
he hissed at Keeler, scooping the revolver up in his hands again.

"What is it? What are you looking for?"

"A second exit. Take up as many boards as you can. *Silently.*"

Before the Lieutenant could protest or ask for more direction,
Terry rose to a crouched position and softly padded back into the
living room. There were now two shadows on the other side of the
door. One of them drew close to the living room window. Hands
cupped around a pair of eyes. Skin pressed against the windowpane.

It looked away, made some kind of silent signal, and then the
flashlights on the porch went out. Suddenly, Terry couldn't make
out anything in the darkness. He felt naked, exposed. He shrank
into a corner of the room and pointed the gun at the door. His

heart pounded, and right then and there, his resolve dropped out from beneath him.

All the while, he had been falling back on everything he'd learned as a child. In South America, he'd hunted and roughed it in the jungle until he was an experienced marksman and a solid survivor. He'd thought he could conquer anything. Somehow, when there was a human being on the other side of the muzzle, it was different.

He was trembling. He tried to steady his hands, but then his arms began to shake. They had to get out of here. He couldn't carry this on much longer.

Then the door smashed in, and Terry and Keeler were no longer alone in the cabin.

Terry's breath caught in his throat. All at once, the gun felt like dead weight in his hands. Who was he kidding? It had been years since he'd fired one, and he wasn't even sure if this one would work.

Footsteps sounded on the cabin floor. Behind him, he heard Keeler freeze. Then, everything stopped. For a moment, crickets alone filled the air.

A single nail dropped from the bundle of wood in Keeler's arms.

It clattered to the paneled floor and rolled for almost ten seconds before finally going silent.

The figure, a scant couple of feet from Terry, close enough that he could have reached out and grabbed its leg, took several steps forward, followed shortly thereafter by the second man.

They were both clothed completely in black. Terry couldn't see their faces from where he was crouching, but he thought they might have been wearing ski masks, anyway. They smelled of cigarette smoke and something else—an exotic cologne that reminded him of South America.

"Oh Jesus!" Keeler. They must have seen him.

They barged forward, fast, purposeful, zeroing in on him like machines. Terry leapt to his feet, stepped out behind them, and, without so much as blinking, leveled the pistol first at one, then the other, and pulled the trigger twice.

They dropped to the floor without uttering a sound, their collapsed skulls belching a mixture of blood and something thicker, chunkier. The crickets had gone, though Terry realized a moment later that it was not the surrounding sound that had vanished, but rather, his capacity to detect it.

"Keeler," he said, but knew he was speaking only by the vibrations in his throat. The Lieutenant wouldn't be able to hear him. He darted into the kitchen.

Keeler was crouched on the floor, eyes riveted on the two bodies piled in the entryway.

Terry grabbed the handful of wood from him and chucked it aside. No point in being quiet now. He ripped the last of the floorboards free and wriggled down through the opening.

It was a tight fit. Terry could feel splintered wood scraping furrows in his flesh. He grimaced, struggled to remain silent. The first thing he began to hear again was his own breathing, fast, labored. "Keeler," he hissed. "Come on."

The Lieutenant looked down at him, then back at the bodies. Terry reached up through the opening and grabbed him by the knee. Together, they squatted beneath the cabin. It was surprisingly warm down below, as though the heat of the day had been collected and funneled beneath the floorboards. It smelled of sand and closed-up rooms. Unused insulation sent up clouds of dust when he dropped to the ground. They were crouching in a network of wooden beams that made up the cabin's foundations.

"Where do we go?" Keeler hissed at him.

Terry put a finger to his lips. He was peering through the latticed skirting at the forest beyond. At first, he had not been able to see anything in the darkness, but with his eyes focused at the front of the cabin, he began to pick up tiny little motions here and there. Just the trees and bushes bowing in the breeze—or something else?

They were almost to the edge of the cabin when footsteps

made the floor creak overhead. The wooden slats, a few inches from their foreheads, bowed beneath a person's weight. Keeler went rigid. Terry could see the question on his face—*What if it's Lyman?*

Terry shook his head, then advanced to the edge of the foundation. Something glinted in the moonlight, off between the tree limbs. He pressed his face against one of the crossbeams, trying to get a better look. It was a car—black, American-made, a sedan. He'd lay even money it was the Ford from the pictures. There didn't appear to be anyone around it.

Terry grabbed Keeler by the shoulders and brought him up against the lattice skirt. "We're going for the car," he whispered. "I want you to follow my lead. Don't fall behind, okay?"

Keeler nodded.

Terry crawled to the gap in the skirting beside the front stairs and took one last moment to gather his strength and mentally prepare himself. If they got out there and found themselves surrounded, there was nowhere to run. He'd already killed two of them; he had no doubt that they would shoot him down on sight.

No time to think about it. More footsteps crossed the cabin floor. Gathering like a flock of carrion eaters. Terry nodded at Keeler and then he dove out into the open. He had feared that the snap of twigs and crackle of dry leaves beneath his shoes would attract too much attention, but he moved in near absolute silence. They had almost reached the edge of the clearing around the cabin when Keeler stumbled on a fallen tree branch and went sprawling in the bushes. He let out a sharp bark before he managed to restrain himself.

Terry froze, stricken. He whirled around just in time to see two dark shapes dart out of the cabin, somewhere on them the dull glint of pistol barrels.

"Keeler!" Terry hissed. He dove into the bushes, grabbed the Lieutenant, and hauled him to his feet.

"I can't!" Keeler said. "I . . . it hurts . . . something . . ."

Terry shook his head. "You must have twisted your ankle. We'll worry about it later. Bite the bullet and walk on it."

"No. I can feel it. It's worse."

Terry was losing patience for this. He gave the Lieutenant a yank, and the older man stumbled out of the bush, trailing something that looked like a metal shoe. A cold wave broke across Terry's skin. He knew before he bent to examine the device that Keeler had stepped in a trap of some kind. He was almost certain it hadn't been there a few hours ago when they first arrived.

"Shit." He swept the Lieutenant off his feet and half-dragged, half-carried him through the underbrush toward the car.

Luckily, it was unlocked. He yanked open the back door and jammed Keeler in, shoving at his bleeding ankle until he could get the door shut behind it. Keeler was moaning, and his face looked pale.

Terry slipped in behind the wheel and reached for the ignition. The keys were still inside. They were professionals, he thought, but they were also presumptuous. They had assumed nobody would get past them.

The car came to life and he threw it into gear.

There was a strange sound from somewhere in the back. Terry's eyes flicked to the rearview mirror, saw a tiny hole at the top of the rear windshield. It was a bullet hole, but he hadn't heard a shot. They had silencers.

The only way he'd know they were shooting at him was if they scored a hit.

No roads had made it this far into the wilderness, but there was a haphazard path of flattened vegetation where the Ford had first left the highway. Terry reversed into a small alcove of limp vines and creepers, swung around, and accelerated forward, retracing his stalkers' steps.

Sparks flew from the trunk; bullets were thudding into the car's frame like raindrops on an evening in the Northwest. He slammed on the brakes where the path diverged. Equal trails cut off to the right and left.

"Keeler!" he shouted. "Which way to the highway?"

The Lieutenant struggled to sit up in the back seat. "Right, I think."

Terry spun the wheel and the Ford bounced and skidded over

tree roots and mashed leaves. Ahead, the path widened. He could see orange light filtering through the branches. That had to be the highway. They were going to make it.

He allowed his foot to slip a few inches from the accelerator, and then, a moment later, something slammed into the back of the car. He hadn't been watching the rearview mirror. With its headlights off, the other car was next to invisible, hidden in the shadows of the trees.

It fell back a few feet from the impact and then accelerated and smashed into the trunk again, its own windshield shattering with the flash of a gun muzzle. For just a moment, Terry thought he glimpsed glowing eyes.

Suddenly, he had the heartbeat of a hummingbird. His feet fumbled over the pedals, searching for the gas. He found one, and slammed on—the brakes. The Ford jumped as the car behind them rammed them, full-on.

Kicking wildly, he finally found the accelerator and punched it as hard as he could. The engine growled and then they were rocketing forward so fast he could barely control it. They jarred left, right, through a thicket of bushes and a grove of small trees. Pinecones, nuts, and branches came pattering down across the roof of the car; thorns and vines slapped at the windshield.

Then, it was light and they were back on the highway, but the car was steering strangely, fishtailing everywhere.

"What the fuck?" Terry snarled.

"We've lost a tire." Keeler caught himself as they skidded again.

Behind them, the other car exploded out of the woods and looped onto the wrong side of the road. A few more gunshots flashed from the front and sides to thud into Terry's door. He ducked, clutching the steering wheel with white knuckles.

Sitting up in the backseat, Keeler was clutching his leg, face contorted with pain. He caught Terry's eye in the rearview mirror. "Broken," he said through clenched teeth. "At least the ankle. Fuck!" He glanced forward, caught sight of something dead ahead. "Jesus! Young, what's that?"

Terry looked back at the road and saw something large lying directly in their path. It looked like a bear or a deer—dressed in a policeman's uniform. "Oh shit!" Terry breathed. He swerved at the last moment to avoid bouncing over Lyman's body.

Behind them, the other car didn't see it soon enough. Terry flinched. One moment Lyman was there; the next he was gone. The other car skidded, turned sharply, bounced over an outcropping of rocks just off the shoulder of the road and launched into a fast sideways tumble—wheels, roof, wheels, roof. It landed in the bushes somewhere off the road in a pile of kicked-up dirt and darkness.

Terry didn't slow down until they were back in the outskirts of town and the mountain road was far behind them. Even then, he couldn't shake the image of Lyman's body from his head. The way it simply vanished.

Squeezing his eyes shut, he prayed he could get them back to the station before someone else came after them.

Chapter 20

Joseph Malloy spent the afternoon sitting at a soda fountain across from the library, waiting for the yellow Plymouth Duster to pull into the parking lot. Emily Willis didn't get to work until 3:15, and Joseph had been starving. By the time she appeared, he had downed two chocolate milkshakes and a piece of apple pie, and he felt ready to burst.

He watched her climb out of her car, retrieve her walker from the trunk, and then hobble down the narrow sidewalk to the front door. When she had disappeared through the automatic doors, he paid his bill, retrieved the straight jacket from the RV, and walked across the street.

The library was chilled to somewhere around sixty degrees. It felt like Antarctica to Joseph, but he didn't say anything, because the checker behind the desk seemed too hot and too impatient to deal with minor complaints.

Joseph made a beeline for the information desk. Nothing on it had moved since ten that morning, when he had pulled into town and asked if there was anyone who could help him identify a historical relic. Emily Willis, he had been told, was the resident expert on the past, and she didn't come in until after lunch. Apparently lunch had a way of creeping through the sun's zenith and well toward happy hour. She was given to playing pinochle with her friends, the high school girl who ran the desk in the mornings had told him. She had her little traditions, and she'd been working at the library so long, nobody liked to tell her how to do her job.

She was still settling in behind Information when he pressed the little bell on the counter. Her smile was halfhearted at best. "Be right with you."

He talked to her for a few minutes about the weather, local politics, things he knew nothing about. Then he showed her the jacket.

She frowned. "Where did you get this?"

"I found it. In someone's house."

"Whose?"

"Can you tell me where it came from?"

She fixed him with a suspicious stare. At last, reclining in her wooden rocking chair, she said, "Could be two places. They run an old asylum out of Brenner. There's the main office downtown and then a field office out away from everyone. That's where they keep the dangerous ones."

"Can you tell me how to get there?"

"They don't like visitors."

"It's important."

"Where did you say you got this from?"

She was wondering if it might belong to him—if he might have escaped from the asylum, himself. It was ridiculous, but he could see it, the mistrust, in her eyes. She was ready for him to go mad, start barking like a dog or jumping around the room.

At last he got her to Xerox a map out of an atlas and pencil in directions to the main building in Brenner. It was a couple of hours away. "And they won't be open late," she added. "They don't like visitors. Did I mention that?"

He followed the sun into the horizon, almost keeping up with the dying rays of light. The sky turned a stunning scarlet and at last surrendered the last clutches of life to the creeping violet shadow of the night.

He rolled into Brenner well after dark and parked at one of the local trucker motels. It was a seedy little place: neon lights, smoky rooms, and mildewed shower curtains. He didn't care; he just had to get out of the RV.

He spent the night sprawled, sweating, atop the covers, and then, first thing in the morning, he drove to the asylum.

It was nothing like what he had expected. He took a taxi because the receptionist in the hotel lobby told him there'd be nowhere to park the RV downtown. He saw that she was right.

Stepping out of the cab, he looked around. It was an odd mix of new and old here. There was a strip mall full of closed stores and a couple of hobby shops on one side. The bus stop out in front looked as though it had been abandoned for years. One or two poorly-dressed old men lingered around its benches, smoking or reading newspapers or just staring blankly into the sky.

On the other side of the street, a five-story high rise towered over the buildings around it. The few windows that looked out onto the avenue were tinted pale green and covered in a reflective coating that denied even a glimpse of the interior. The bottom floor was all glass, a couple of local shops—coffee, pizza, slushies and hot dogs.

The lighted sign at the edge of the street labeled it the Downtown Brenner Professional Building. Beneath the silver letters were the logos of the various restaurants inside, and at the very bottom, barely visible, there was a tiny square of white containing the lettering, *Brenner Psychiatric.*

Joseph pulled open the plastic bag he had taken from the hotel bathroom and peered in at the straightjacket. He'd be damned if it had come from anywhere so neat and immaculate.

Inside, the lobby was a complete culture shock. Joseph had

seldom gone to any of the bigger cities throughout the duration of his career, and even then, there had been a transition—a plane flight or a lengthy car ride. Here, there were sofas, wireless internet, suits on cell phones and flat-screen TVs. It was all so abrupt, so strangely out-of-place in the middle of a rundown village, that he felt as though he had been transported to some other dimension—to the Twilight Zone, he thought.

A glass-covered marble plaque was posted by a bank of brushed steel elevator doors. Brenner Psychiatric filled floors two through five. Reception, according to the directory, was in 201.

The second floor was even more sterile than the first. The carpet looked as though it had been shampooed and vacuumed that very morning. The walls were covered in single-tone wallpaper that must have been rolled on by a machine with no tolerance for error. Varnished wood ran around the baseboards of the corridor leading away from the elevator foyer, and spotless frames held to the wall abstract paintings by obscure artists.

A young woman with short blonde hair and perfectly straight teeth looked up when Joseph found his way to the reception room. She blinked impeccably-groomed eyelashes at him and asked in a voice made for radio if there was anything she could help him with.

He told her that he was hoping to speak to someone in charge. He had found an artifact from the institution, and he was wondering to whom it might have belonged. "I'm not entirely sure I'm in the right place, though," he said, looking around.

Two black leather couches sat side-by-side across from the reception desk. She told him to take a seat in one, and that one of the doctors would see him in just a few minutes. He sank into chemically-clean cushions that formed themselves to his body— the most oddly comfortable sofa he'd ever used.

On the glass coffee table sat a stack of neatly-arranged periodicals. Every one of them was current, either from this week or this morning. Only two sounds filled the room—the hiss of the ventilation system and the bubbling of a brushed-metal coffee machine on an oak sideboard by the door. Every now and then, the receptionist would click her computer's mouse. Even the machine itself had the manners to stay quiet.

After a time, Joseph got up, poured himself some coffee in a floral-printed paper cup, and went back to the sofa. He felt like a stain on the room's perfect symmetry, a blotch of the real world in this sterile little chamber of improbably straight lines and corners.

Prompted by nothing Joseph had observed, the receptionist suddenly looked up from her computer and said, "Doctor Sallimay apologizes for the wait. He is able to see you now in Room Two-oh-Seven." Each syllable emerged from her mouth a perfect work of art all its own.

Joseph thanked her and strolled down the hall until he found the right door. Doctor Sallimay was waiting in a conference room hung with plasma television screens that peered down over a spotless black table. A few pieces of abstract corporate art adorned the ochre walls.

He rose when Joseph entered and extended a handful of manicured fingers. "Good afternoon," he said, "I'm Doctor Emmett Sallimay. I'm told you have a question regarding our institution."

Joseph showed him the straightjacket. The doctor reacted as though Joseph had brought a fresh cow pie into his office.

"Oh, goodness," Sallimay said. He allowed himself a light chuckle. "We certainly don't use anything like that around here. So...vulgar."

"You're telling me this didn't come from this hospital?" Joseph got a degree of dark pleasure from shoving it at the man and watching the way he shied away, as if it were a hornet's nest of communicable diseases.

"Mr. Malloy, you have to understand, we pride ourselves in the best possible treatment available. We offer only the latest techniques and all of our facilities are kept in top—"

"I'm sorry, Doctor," Joseph interrupted. "But that wasn't my question." *Armani and a pricy stylist will get you nowhere with me, asshole.*

Sallimay looked a little taken-aback. He sank into a chair and made a steeple with his fingers. "My apologies. What was your question?"

"Where did this come from?"

"I don't know that I could say for certain. Would you like a cheese Danish?" He rolled from the table to a refrigerator beneath the plasma TV. From inside, he pulled out a whole platter of doughnuts, scones, croissants, and fresh fruit.

"What does the name Hacker mean to you?"

Sallimay had his back to the room, but even from here, Joseph could see his reaction. When he turned, Sallimay wore a false smile. "I'm sorry," he said, "you mean like the computer expert? That kind of hacker?"

"A girl. I've reason to believe she might have been here. I think she might have worn this straightjacket."

The doctor returned the platter to the refrigerator and removed a tall bottle of whole milk to go with the blueberry muffin he'd chosen. He brought them both to the conference table and spread a napkin in his lap. With perfect fingernails, he crumbled a piece of the muffin from the wrapper and deposited it in his mouth. Then he looked Joseph in the eye. "Mr. Malloy, I'm going to be very frank with you. I'm not at liberty to discuss our patients with you, and even if I were—"

"So she was a patient?"

"That's not what I said, Mr. Malloy. I'm quoting policy to you right now. That's what I'm doing."

"Detective," Joseph corrected. "You can call me Detective Malloy, *Doctor* Sallimay."

The false smile returned to Sallimay's face. He took a swig of the milk. "You didn't mention that you were with the police."

"Funny, I thought it might change the way you answered my questions. Can't imagine why."

"I'm going to need to see some identification, Detective." Gone was the air of over-accentuated politeness. Gone was the smooth, slippery demeanor of the salesman. Sallimay had figured out that Joseph wasn't some old dingbat looking to invest in the hospital or possibly commit a rich, ailing relative, and with that revelation, he had dropped any pretenses of enjoying himself.

While Joseph went for his wallet, Sallimay bundled the muffin up in a recycled paper napkin and tossed it in the trash. He put the lid back on the bottle of milk and rolled it on its side into the refrigerator.

They had collected Joseph's badge when he retired, but he'd kept one of his old ID cards for sentimental reasons. The design had changed several times over since then, but if the doctor didn't look at the date, he'd never know the difference. It was a bit of a chance, but Joseph fancied himself a decent judge of character.

Sallimay crossed the room in a few strides and glanced over the card without even reading it. Joseph smiled to himself. One of those men who assumed everyone was as forthright and impatient as he was.

"What do you want to know?" he asked.

"Was she a patient?"

"Yes."

"Is she still?"

"No."

"How long? When did she leave? What were the circumstances?"

"She was with us for three months. She left with members of her family. I believe it was about five weeks ago."

"Why was she here?"

"I don't know."

Joseph's narrowed his eyes. "I thought you were cooperating."

"I don't have that information, Detective. I didn't treat her. She wasn't even at this facility."

"How many are there?"

"Two."

Joseph frowned, and then he remembered what Emily Willis at the library had told him—one was for the clean, public, everyday treatments. The other hospital was for the violent ones they'd rather no one knew about. And he didn't have to wonder which one he was seeing now. Sallimay had inadvertently given him more information than he probably thought.

"Where's the other facility?"

"Two hours away."

"Why so far?"

"Hospital policy. I don't have a part in that. I'm a primary care provider, Detective. I don't worry about the political decisions, and I do *not* deal with that other—place."

"Shot in the dark, then."

The Doctor gave him a resentful look. "If I had to guess, I would say it was because the local citizens didn't much care for the idea of our extended programs taking up residence in their midst."

Extended programs. As sterile and surgical a term for it as the rest of this place, Joseph thought. "Who checked her out?"

"Members of her—"

"—family. Yes, you said. Who?"

"They would have that kind of information at the facility where she was treated." He pulled back his sleeve to reveal the face of a Rolex. "Detective, I'm willing to help you as much as you need, but I do have a schedule, patients to see. If you have more questions, perhaps you could direct them to someone else . . . ?"

Joseph rose and stuck out his hand. "I think I'm done here," he said. "You've been very cooperative."

Sallimay took his hand and shook it as briefly and coldly as etiquette would allow. Then he flashed the false smile, turned, and walked quickly toward the door. "I trust you can find your way out," he called over his shoulder.

Joseph nodded. "Doctor Sallimay," he called, just as the man was about to disappear into the corridor. Joseph held up the straightjacket. "All corporate sweet-talking bullshit aside, this is from here, isn't it?"

Sallimay grimaced, and gave a single silent nod. Then he was gone.

Now Joseph understood the unnaturally clean and upscale climate here. The higher-ups had designed this hospital to steal all the attention it possibly could from the real dirty work, two hours away. It was a combination museum and theme park to satiate the masses. They could come through here, satisfy themselves that their friends and relatives were receiving only the best modern treatment, and then go away never the wiser.

But the second facility was where the real action was. That was where he would find the answers he was looking for.

By two-thirty, he was beginning to think that the receptionist had given him bad directions. He wouldn't put it past her. He had an address, stenciled in gold on a small card with the clinic's logo, but he was unfamiliar with the area and had asked her the best way to get there. At first, she had told him she wasn't supposed to give out that information.

Joseph told her to talk to Sallimay. She tapped on her computer for a few minutes and then gruffly took the business card back and scrawled a few cryptic notes on the flip side. She didn't ask if they were clear enough for him to follow. Instead, she answered a phone that had conveniently rung the instant she was done writing.

The little town fell quickly out of the RV's mirrors, replaced by rolling hills and increasingly rustic surroundings. An occasional field of strawberries or spinach or corn punctuated what was becoming an ocean of golden-brown grass.

A couple of buildings rose up in the windshield ahead: a diner, a gas station, a few small shops. Joseph decided he would stop, grab a bite to eat, and ask one of the locals.

It was a friendly little place, but it made him shiver. The diner was virtually empty, save for a couple of locals who looked as though they never moved from their booths. The entire place had an air of stagnation. He wondered where these people lived, what they did each day between dawn and dusk.

The waitress greeted him with an unnaturally perky smile and when she brought the apple pie he had ordered, she gave him an extra scoop of ice cream on the house. He thanked her, and when he went up to the register to pay, he gave her a sizable tip.

"So what are you doing out here with such a big rig?" she asked him, nodding through the window at the RV. "One of those things, you could just travel forever, couldn't you? You all alone?"

"My wife . . ." he began, then stopped himself. "She's asleep. Drove through the night. We're seeing the country." He smiled at her. "But I'm also looking for someone, and I was wondering if you could help me."

As soon as he mentioned the asylum, the cheer vanished from her face. "Yeah, you came the right way. Missed the exit a mile or two back, point of fact. Hard to see. They don't like visitors."

"So I've heard."

"We don't much like visitors from there either."

"Okay."

She turned and left.

He thought she might be coming back, but she pushed through the swinging doors into the kitchen, and after a couple of minutes passed, Joseph shrugged and went back outside. He got into the RV, turned it around, and started retracing his steps.

Even watching as carefully as he could, Joseph almost missed the turnoff a second time. It was no wonder he hadn't seen it on the way in. It led off the highway at a sharp bend, through a stand of thick vegetation. It was a small gravel road, barely large enough for a sedan.

Joseph parked the RV on the shoulder a little way down the freeway and then hiked back to the trailhead. He wasn't sure this was even the right place; by the look of it, it might have been someone's private driveway, the entrance to one of the old ranches. He picked around the edges of the road until he found the sign. It was lying on its face in the dust a few feet from the stick that had once held it up. He turned it over, brushing the grime from the splintered wood: *Brenner County Asylum*. No "Psychiatric Clinic" here. This far from civilization, nobody needed to be alluring or politically-correct.

Tossing the sign aside, Joseph shaded his eyes and peered into the setting sun. The road rose and fell with the contour of the landscape until it vanished behind a shallow hill. He couldn't see beyond it, couldn't tell if the asylum was just on the other side or miles away. There was no indication of distance on the marker.

He went back to the RV, grabbed a bottle of water from the refrigerator, and then he started walking. Even though the light was quickly falling into dusk, Joseph found himself sweating after only a few hundred meters. It was moist here, the air a damp, oppressive hand weighing on his shoulders. The hill, which from the road had appeared to be just a few minutes away on foot, seemed to remain forever on the horizon. By the time he reached its base, Joseph was having trouble breathing.

Looking back, his spirits sank. The RV wasn't a tiny speck. The road looked no farther from here than the hill had from there—perhaps it was he who was faltering. It had been a long time since duty had required him to be in shape. At the office, they had started handing him cases that required only mental agility, deductive reasoning, the sort of thing he could do behind a desk in the comfort of the police station. He hadn't really noticed at the time, but now, he realized, it had all been carefully orchestrated. The galling part was, they had been right—they had known his physical limits more accurately than he had.

He took a short break and a few swigs of water before climbing up the gentle hill. Sun spilled over the top in warm, orange droplets of light. He squinted as he reached the crest, surveying the swaying grass fields before him.

There was the asylum. It sat nestled among the hills, almost invisible to the inattentive observer. The roof was rotting away, the walls tilted and bowed with the curves of the ground beneath them. It looked like a natural growth on the side of the earth.

Joseph crossed the remaining gap in about fifteen minutes, and found himself standing before the small, squat building. It had been built in a style unfamiliar to him—cinderblocks forming columns that held wooden slats between them beneath a tall, shingled roof.

Several other buildings joined the one he had seen from the hill, forming a small complex in among the rocks and the dust-blown trees. There were no barbed-wire fences surrounding them, no guard towers or much of any security at all.

Strange, Joseph thought. If this was supposed to be the place where they carted off the more volatile patients, why didn't they bother to secure them? Nobody out here would notice or care if a giant ugly stone wall were erected around the place. Nobody would hear if sniper shots were fired into the open fields. Why take the risk?

He walked past the first building, searching for anything that might suggest itself as an office. A few picnic tables were set up on a stone patio that had cracked from the weather or some kind of collision years before. A barbecue grill sat neglected in one corner, covered in hardened, fossilized shreds of rotten meat.

Still, no door clearly seemed the front one, no window designed for a receptionist to greet any visitors. At last, he circled back around to the front building and tugged at the first door he came to. It was metal, painted brown back in the '70s sometime. It didn't budge.

He tried several more until at last one gave. It was a random little opening on the side of the building. He had not been sure it could open; it looked as though it had been intended to connect to another building that had long since been removed by either architectural development or structural decay.

Beyond it was a narrow corridor, no sign of a lobby. He looked around and then stepped inside. It smelled of rubbing alcohol and cheap cleansers. The floor, gaudy plastic tile, was scratched and stained in so many places that he couldn't tell what color it had originally been. The walls, on the other hand, still hung heavily with a coat of muddy green paint that had never looked good, even when it was new.

Joseph walked to the end of the hallway and followed the cor-ner around to a cramped little waiting room. In an effort to seem either more inviting or intimidating—he could not tell which—a brown shag rug had been spread across the middle of the room. It reminded him of a puddle of vomit. There were a few folding chairs on one side, some dirty plastic lawn furniture that looked as though it had been excavated from someone's garage.

Behind a wall of tempered glass, an old woman sat slumped in a rolling office chair, her face pressed into the pages of a romance novel two decades old. She snored lightly. Beside her, the telephone sat disconnected, its cord wound about the receiver.

Joseph stepped up to the desk and tapped on the glass. The woman did not budge. He drummed a little harder, and when still she didn't respond, he made a fist and rapped on the window as hard as he could.

She jumped, looked wildly around, then focused on him with one eye. The other one drifted, aimless. She coughed and managed to wheeze, "Who are you?"

"A visitor," Joseph told her.

She shook her head. "We don't allow visitors here without appointments." Her eyes narrowed. "How did you find this building?"

He slipped his ID card through the small document hole at the bottom of the window. She stopped him from taking it right back and examined it with more thorough scrutiny than he had expected. She was going to see it was out of date, and then he would have some serious explaining to do.

But to his surprise, she didn't notice that. She handed it back and with an ambiguous smile said, "You're a long way from home."

Joseph nodded. "I'd like to ask you some questions about one of your former patients."

She lifted the coffee pot and raised her eyebrows at him. Joseph shook his head. It was like sour water. Something had gone dreadfully wrong in the stained Mr. Coffee machine.

He nursed the mug she had given him and looked around the tiny room. It was like a closet with a chalkboard; it reminded him of his second-grade classroom. There were no windows. A skylight overhead had been covered in fogged plastic that almost completely obscured any rays of natural light.

The walls were hung thick with posters and pictures pinned on corkboards. The only hint of any kind of serious work done on the premises was the stack of file cabinets against the far wall.

His eyes returned to the receptionist. Her hair fell across her forehead in a way that reminded him of Jean. Until now, he'd been forcing himself not to think about her.

He longed for her, ached for her beside him. This wasn't right; it was like sleeping on a new mattress. No—it was like sleeping on the same mattress in a bombed-out hotel on the border of a third-world country. He couldn't breathe. He couldn't make this work. He had to call her.

"Shayla Hacker. I wonder if she's managed to survive out there."

Joseph shook himself, tried to concentrate on what she was saying. This was more information than he'd been able to scare up in the entire last week, and here he was thinking about his wife. He had to be professional about this. If he'd learned one thing over the decades of work he'd done on the police force, it was that his personal life had no place on the job.

"What do you mean?"

She pursed her lips. Her name was even Jeanine—how could he not think of Jean? "You said you're with the police, right? So, you know, you'd tell me if it'd be wrong to tell you any of this. I mean, patient confidentiality and everything, right? I mean, I don't know anything about the law, but don't they have that thing, where if you know you're making me do something wrong . . ."

"I'm not going to throw you in prison for helping me, Jeanine," he assured her. But this woman was smart, he was thinking. She was doing her best to carry off the naïve country bumpkin façade, but beneath it, she was sharp as a tack. She was sharp enough to know that it could be profitable to appear daft.

"Well . . ." She flashed a lopsided smile. "That's a relief. I feared for that girl the whole time she was here."

Joseph leaned in close. "Why'd they commit her?"

"Beat the stuffing out of some old man and stole his car, and when they finally caught up with her, she was convinced she'd done nothing wrong."

Something was wrong—something about the sudden excitement and intensity in her voice. This was personal.

"Why'd she do that?"

Jeanine shrugged. "Cops said she was crazy. Jury agreed, and here she was."

"But you don't believe that."

"You're smart, Detective Malloy. You got a way of seeing through people."

Was she impressed, or was she just trying to flatter him off of his guard? It had been too long since he interrogated anyone; he had forgotten the procedures, the things to look out for. Some things were like second nature to him, and he had thought this would be one of them, but he was too preoccupied, too wound up in the case to be able to concentrate on the details and the protocol.

"Please," he said. "Anything you can tell me will help."

"She was convinced people were chasing her. And the thing is—the thing is, I think she was right."

"That people were after her."

"Y'huh."

"Why?"

"That depends on who or what you believe."

"I don't know what that means."

Jeanine leaned back, took another sip of her coffee, and then got up to get more. "She told the cops that there were these guys after her because of who she was. She thought she was some kind of celebrity or something. Now that part, I don't know that I buy." She filled her mug and came back to the table. "But I know there are plenty of creeps out there, and she's a good-looking girl."

"Celebrity?"

Jeanine waved him away. "No, that was the psychosis, I'm pretty sure. She was obsessed. You should see her room." She paused, arched an eyebrow. It would have been foxy if she were younger. "Do you want to see her room?"

The entire way across the small courtyard, Jeanine kept mumbling how she wasn't really supposed to be doing this, but if he was a policeman, he'd tell her if she was doing anything wrong, right? After a while, Joseph stopped listening.

They passed several other squat buildings, hiking up through the underbrush to a secluded structure he had seen but not registered when he first arrived. It overlooked the others, short, but positioned higher up on the hill. Small windows, obscured by metal grates and cut to be barely more than slits, looked out on the courtyard and the roofs of the other buildings.

Jeanine unlocked a metal door with several sets of keys and then pulled it open. It groaned, and she made a face about the noise. "Sorry," she said, "we haven't had a maintenance team out here for eight years."

It smelled like sleep inside—breath, sweat, body odor. It was so dark that Joseph had to stop and allow his eyes to adjust for a few moments before following her down the corridor to the old elevator at the end. The doors ground open grudgingly, and the floor shook beneath their combined weight when Joseph got in behind her.

She shoved a key into a small hole beneath the control panel and pressed the button for the third floor. Nothing happened. She smacked the panel with the back of her hand. The light behind the button flickered. Still, they didn't move.

"We could take the stairs," Joseph suggested.

The elevator swayed.

Jeanine shook her head, cast him a sidelong glance. "There aren't any. They built this building without them so that they could lock down the only exit."

"Isn't that a fire hazard?"

"What, I look like the fire marshal?"

The corridor cutting down the middle of the third floor was lit only by the window at the end. It cast long, barred shadows over the narrow floor. Joseph eyed the duplicate doors that faced each other on either side of the hallway, from one end to the other.

Jeanine led him to one particularly far from the elevator and tore away a shred of police tape that had been covering the lock. "Still there from the investigation," she said.

Joseph frowned, but bit back the question he longed to ask: *What investigation?*

"The police," she went on. "I know it seems like we're far from civilization, but they go nuts when someone breaks out of a place like this."

Joseph froze. *Breaks out?* "Doctor Sallimay said she left with some of her family."

"Is that what they're calling it now?" Jeanine snorted. "They'll say anything to keep their shining image. Suppose I should be glad."

"Why?"

"Because I helped her escape."

Chapter 21

Debbie Wendell awoke to the sound of fingers dancing on a keyboard. She hadn't slept well despite the expensive mattress and the ample climate control. The guest room Yeager had given her, thrust off one side of the house over a modest pool, was comfortable enough, if basic. She even had her own bathroom all to herself.

It was her mind that had kept her awake. At around three in the morning, she'd risen, walked to the banister in the hallway outside, and just stood there, staring down at the front door. Yeager had said he had locked it, that there was a security system that would go off if she tried to get out. She wasn't sure if he was telling the truth or if he was just hoping she was jumpy enough from her whole experience as a convict to be leery of calling his bluff.

She crept down the padded stairs and approached the door. There, she stood watching it, searching for any wires or tiny lights that might have betrayed a hidden detection system. She found none. After a while, she sat down, and then she lay back.

And then there were fingers on a keyboard. She awoke with a start, propped herself up, looked wildly around. Doctor Lewis Yeager was sitting on the stairs with a laptop computer perched on his knees. He smiled at her when she caught his eye. "I wondered if you might try to get out," he said. "You made the right decision."

"What are you doing?" She got to her feet, rubbing the kinks from her neck and joints. Sleeping on the floor. She hadn't done that since grad school.

"Booking a flight."

She paused. "To where? For who . . . whom?"

He smiled at the correction. "You're funny." Back to his screen. Debbie walked over to him and spun the laptop around before he could stop her. The map on the screen didn't make sense. "What the hell is this?" she snapped.

"The Amazon."

She allowed him a few moments to explain himself. Instead, he pulled the computer back onto his legs.

"Last night you wanted to find Gregory Klein. I thought you wanted the box, Lewis."

"I do."

"Good. So let's go back to *what—the hell—is this?*"

"Since when have we been on a first name basis?"

In spite of herself, she was embarrassed. She'd thought she'd detected something different in his demeanor this morning, and she had taken it as her cue to get a little closer, to drop some of the cold formality that had stood like a wall between them. Maybe she was moving too quickly. She just wanted a way out of his clutches, out of the arms of the law. She didn't know he was going to take it personally.

She was about to apologize when he broke into a disarming smile. "That's good. It's very good. I think it helps when doctors and patients have a casual relationship." He clicked once more on the laptop computer and then closed it. "I have to go pack now."

He looked eager, like a little kid about to set off on a summer road trip. He hadn't been lying the night before—there really was something wrong with him.

Sounds of frenzied packing drifted down from the second floor – rooting about in a closet, the collapse of stacked shoes and suitcases. She thought back to what he had said—how finding this woman had turned into some kind of mythical quest for him. The box was just a brick in the wall, a piece of the puzzle. He'd said there were others like him. He'd said there were dozens searching for her. It didn't make any sense. He'd told her she didn't understand because she hadn't seen the picture; the sickness began with Shayla Hacker's face. That was her name: Shayla Hacker. Debbie thought she sounded like some kind of World War II internment camp survivor.

Yeager came back down about ten minutes later toting a small black suitcase and another bag presumably containing his computer. "Are you ready?"

"To go to the Amazon? Doctor . . . Lewis, look, slow down for a second and tell me what's going on . . . Please?" she added, almost as an afterthought.

"Come on. I'll tell you on the way to the car." He flipped up a small metal plate by the door and entered a password into the security keypad beneath it. Catching her glance, he chuckled to himself. "No peeking. Come on, now, I have to trust you."

She followed him down the path to the Maxima, deciding not to point out that they would likely never come back here together.

They wound their way out of the sprawling suburban estate, Debbie watching the houses slip by.

"Last night you said something about a woman named Frida," he said as they turned out of the front gate and onto the main road, back toward the airport. "It reminded me of something. There's this art collector I know, Fanny or Franny or something . . . it's . . . that's just how my mind works. Anyway, I got to thinking, what would be the most likely thing for someone to do with the box if they got it from you. And I figured, they'd probably want to sell it, you know? Because there are a lot of stupid people out there who only see things for their monetary value, and they wouldn't think twice about pissing away a treasure like that at some flea market."

"Sure." Debbie kept her eyes on the road now. She decided not to tell him that that was precisely what she had been planning on doing as soon as she got to Florida. She hadn't been comfortable traveling with the amount of money she'd been certain it would fetch, and she'd wanted her mother to see the object that saved her life.

Would have owed her life, she mentally corrected herself. Now that she was working with Yeager, if they found it, he would never let her sell it. A pang of desperate longing squeezed at her heart. She had come that close. She had been within arm's reach of saving her mother, and now that chance was gone forever. Maybe if she just explained it to Yeager, he would understand.

"But then I thought," he was saying, "how you said someone had been willing to kill you for the box. They set you up in that hotel, right? And I mean, no ordinary criminal does that. It must've been someone who knew about it, but since they didn't try and ask you about the girl, they were probably after the box for its own sake. Which meant they might be trying to return it to its origin. Which I believe is in the Amazon."

He was looking at the road, but he wasn't seeing it. His eyes were burning, bright and eager, his mind a thousand miles away. He spoke a mile a minute, nothing like the Yeager she had met the night before behind the police van in the bitter cold Denver night. Perhaps he was just excited to finally have a companion in his deranged quest. *Or perhaps he's schizophrenic*, she thought.

As they approached the airport security checkpoint, Debbie leaned in close and whispered in Yeager's ear, "Won't you get in trouble for taking me out of the country?" He shot her a puzzled look. "I'm wanted for murder, Doctor Yeager."

"What happened to *Lewis*?" Off her look, he took her hand and massaged it like an overprotective husband. "Don't you worry. I've got everything covered. I have the authority to take you wherever I need you."

She didn't trust him; she was worried. But they passed through the checkpoint without incident, and it was only then that she began to wonder who he really was.

They sat in a row of chairs facing the window. Yeager dropped his bags at her feet, checked his watch, and looked over at the bank of fast food shops that stretched across the opposite wall. "I could use a coffee," he said. "You want a mocha or something?"

Debbie shook her head.

"Could you watch the bags?"

She told him that was fine and then, to her chagrin, he knelt and cuffed her ankle to the row of seats. "Sorry," he said as he rose. "But, I mean, the way you were watching that alarm code. I'm just thinking, this is—I can't take any chances. We've still got to get to know each other a bit better."

He returned almost twenty minutes later, after waiting through a line that stretched out and around the corner of the little coffee brewery. He had gotten her a mocha anyway. She took it from him without a word and sipped at it, dabbing the whipped cream off her upper lip.

They sat in silence for a while, watching the planes arrive and take off on the runway before them, and then, without prompting, Yeager said, "Tina just didn't understand how it was."

Debbie frowned at him. He had a faraway look again. She wondered how much time he actually spent in the present, and how much of his life he passed by in a daydream about another time or place.

His eyes flitted over to her. "She was my wife," he said. "She just . . . well, she was okay with my job, but you know, it got a little strained now and then. Normal work stress stuff. But that wasn't what drove us apart. It was in bed, you know? After I'd seen the picture of Shayla, I kept seeing her face—those eyes—when we were making love. And I couldn't do it. I couldn't fuck her."

"Stop." Debbie scooted away from him, as far as the cuffs would let her.

He looked at her and smiled again. She was cooling toward him. The night before, she had thought that he might be a decent guy, and even this morning, though certainly bizarre, she had convinced herself that she might come to trust him. But now . . .

Why did the charm always have to disappear so quickly?

"She left after the fourth time we couldn't do it. I felt bad, really. We'd set up this whole romantic night. You know the kind—flowers, the right music, candles everywhere. We went to this expensive Italian restaurant with a heated patio and we'd kissed over the penne, and I thought everything was going to be just like it used to be."

"I'm fucking serious-"

"Then when it didn't work, back at the house that night, I don't know what came over me. She was getting all pissy and I couldn't get it up, and somehow, before I knew it, I was just beating the shit out of her."

Debbie felt her throat seize up. Yeager was still smiling like a lunatic. He took a sip of his coffee, blew on it. "That's hot. I mean—no, ouch. Seriously."

"Where is she now?"

"Hell if I know. She threatened to call the cops that night, said it was all over, said she was going to end my career. So I beat her some more until I made her promise she wouldn't say a word about it. Didn't see her again after that." He checked his watch. "We should really get up there. On these international flights, if you're not up by the podium, they might give your seat away to some dickwad with a couple of young children who thinks he can muscle in on your flight because he's had a long day." He stood.

When he undid the cuffs around her ankle, he touched her foot with one hand, and she almost screamed right then and there. How was she going to spend hours sitting next to this man on a plane? How was she going to follow him across a foreign country? She looked wildly around for anyone she could go to. She needed the police. She wanted to go back to jail. She wanted to go on trial; anything to get away from Yeager.

She looked at him, thought of telling him that it was over, that the deal was off, that she wanted to go back to the cell. Then she imagined what he might do. He had beaten his wife because he'd been impotent. What would he do to a woman who denied him his bizarre, warped dream?

"What's that look on your face mean?" He touched her cheek. Debbie shivered, but before she could answer, his frenetic mind had moved on.

He handed her the laptop briefcase. "Could you carry that on for me?"

When the woman behind the airline desk asked for Debbie's passport, she felt a surge of hope.

"Sorry," Debbie said, "I don't have mine."

"Not to worry, dear." Yeager put an arm around her shoulders. "I've got it." She stared at him as he removed the little blue booklet from his luggage. He flipped it open and passed it to the receptionist, whose brow cleared as she checked the picture and then handed it back.

"Have a nice flight." Then she was moving on to the next people in line.

Debbie felt numb as Yeager escorted her down the ramp to the plane. When they were settled in their seats, he looked at her and grinned. "You're wondering where I got that."

"I don't even have a passport," she hissed. "What the hell, Doctor-"

"Lewis," he insisted. "Call me Lewis. I thought we were getting friendly here."

She swallowed the sour taste out of the back of her throat. "Where'd you get it, Lewis?"

"Made it. On my computer."

"Don't they have ways of detecting that?"

"I'm good."

"It's illegal."

"So is killing someone."

"I didn't kill anyone!"

Several people in the rows around them looked up, alarmed. She glared right back at them and dared them to say anything, and after a moment, they went back to their in-flight magazines and Sky Mall catalogs.

"Relax," he cooed, stroking her arm. "Everything's handled.

Everything's going to be fine. You've seen the box. You can help me identify it when we find it again. And we are going to find it again, Debbie."

She shivered and recoiled from him. "I don't want to do this."

"Relax," he said. "People would kill to be where you are. Even if you don't care about the box, have fun on the trip." He handed her a ticket stub. "How many people you know have been to Rio?"

It wasn't until they were off the ground that Debbie thought of Lloyd Kelson. She had been so preoccupied with Yeager and his psychosis that the memory hadn't surfaced. Even sitting there, staring out at the ocean of clouds beneath them, the entire episode had been out of her mind. Then, someone in the seat behind her asked if he could get out to use the restroom and it all came cascading back.

She squirmed around to peer through the crack between the cushions, half-convinced that it would be him. It wasn't, of course; that was impossible. Kelson, for all practical purposes, was just a figment of her imagination.

Debbie tapped Doctor Yeager on the shoulder. He was reading something scribbled in a little notebook—a journal, perhaps, or maybe just the mad ravings of an idle mind. "What would you say it means if someone disappears from an airplane in the middle of a flight?"

Yeager looked up and peered through his glasses at her long and hard. "I'd say that there must've been a parachute or a very flat corpse."

She shook her head. "No doors were ever opened. Except for the lavatory."

"What is this about?"

"You should read the case files of your prospective patients more closely, doctor."

He didn't seem to know what to make of that, and Debbie didn't feel like explaining.

For the rest of the flight—a good ten hours or so—Debbie and Yeager said little to each other. There were things she wanted to know about the box, about the quest, about his madness, but she didn't want to give him the obvious satisfaction of explaining them to her. He had beaten his wife, she had to keep reminding herself. He looked so unassuming as he picked apart his lasagna and unwrapped the cellophane around the dry little chocolate cookie from the cart. Could he really be capable of something so abhorrent?

Over a snack the flight attendants brought by a few hours after dinner, she finally cracked. "I want to ask you something," she said.

Again, Yeager looked up. This time, he had been absent-mindedly peeling at the little plastic container of ice cream with his spoon while continuing to read from his notebook.

"You're saying the box was made in Brazil."

"Correct."

"How'd this Shayla Hacker get a hold of it? What do the two have to do with each other?"

Yeager scooted a little closer to her and flipped a page in his book. "It's fascinating," he said. "This is speculation, of course, but I think you could definitely call it an educated guess." Hacker, he explained, had had the box commissioned for her. It had been built by an ancient tribe of spiritual people deep in the jungles of the Amazon Basin. Few knew of them, which supported another theory of his – "Shayla Hacker belonged to some kind of secret society."

Debbie frowned at him. "What, like the Harvard Skulls or something?"

He sighed impatiently. "More like the Freemasons or the Templars."

"I don't know what you're talking about."

"It's not important. I'm not even sure it's right. I just think she was part of something larger than herself." He looked as though he was going to say something more, but then he opted not to and went silent. After a time, his eyes returned to the page.

"Can I ask you another question?"

He didn't look quite as willing or excited this time.

"What do you see in her?"

"What do you mean?"

"You're traveling across the world at great expense, and you're not the first one I've met who's doing it. What do you see in her?"

Yeager's eyes narrowed, his face a mass of puzzled consternation. Then he snapped his fingers. "You haven't seen her picture yet. That's right. It all changes when you see her picture."

"What's in her picture?"

"Nothing. Just a girl. But once you see her, you've got to find her."

"I don't get it."

"I don't either."

She let a few moments' pause fall between them, and then she asked to see it.

"No."

"You have it, don't you?"

"You don't want to see it."

"Show it to me, Lewis."

"There's no cure. There's no antidote. It's an obsession, and you can't shake it. You don't want to start down that road. I . . . sometimes I wish I hadn't." He peered longingly out the window at the clouds beneath them. "Just trust me. I have to find her. Right now you don't. Enjoy the ride. Don't think about it."

She pushed him a little longer, but it was clear he wasn't going to budge. After a while, she gave up, sat back in her seat, and went back to watching the in-flight movie.

Something funny had happened with the time zones, and it was already mid-morning by the time they landed in Rio de Janeiro. As they climbed down the steps and walked across the runway toward the airport terminal, Debbie peered off across the sprawling valley to the lush green mountains around them. It was not like anything she'd ever seen in person before.

For the first time, possibly in her life, she felt grateful to a man —and Yeager of all people. It made her shudder. But he had taken her out of her little hole, out of the monotony of her life. She spent every day of every week fixing pipes, building walls, watching other people come and go from the country. She had seen businessmen who never appreciated their wealth and luck; she had seen bratty children dragged along to some of the most fantastic places on earth, and all they could think of was that they'd forgotten some plastic truck back in their suburban split-level. Never once had she been one of those people.

The air here was warm and wet. The sun had risen behind heavy clouds that cast a dull but strangely enchanting light over the fertile land.

When they got inside, she started toward the signs for the baggage claim and the airport exit, but Yeager grabbed her and shook his head. He led her to one of the desks, where he checked them into another flight. At first, she thought he might have changed his mind, that he was taking her back to America. It wouldn't have made any sense, but then, *he* didn't make much sense, and his mood swings had been rapid and intense enough to make her believe him capable of just about anything.

But no—it was a connecting flight he had arranged with a local airline that ran city-hopping trips around the country in planes small enough to carry just ten or twelve. The one they boarded forty-five minutes later reminded Debbie of the Learjets she had seen corporate CEOs climb into back at home.

It was surprisingly comfortable inside. The seats had plenty of room, and after they had made their somewhat rocky ascent, the flight attendant came through and served drinks to the entire cabin in about ten minutes.

Their fellow passengers were mostly dark-skinned, dressed for the swampy weather. They didn't say much, and they made no effort to strike up a conversation with Debbie or Yeager.

She could feel the doctor's excitement growing, and it was difficult to keep it down in her own stomach. She pressed her face against the window and watched the magnificent city surrender to the jungle. After only a few minutes in the air, there was nothing beneath them but untamed wilderness. The occasional glittering ribbon of water poked through here and there, untouched, beautiful.

As much as she resented it, she was beginning to do exactly as the doctor had said—she was starting to forget about his psychotic little obsession and to enjoy the trip for what it was. That frightened her. He had told her he was sick. He was good at getting women to lower their guards. She was not going to be his victim; she wouldn't let that happen.

They encountered some heavy turbulence that sent the plane jumping and rocking all over the sky. The First Officer opened the cockpit door and came out to apologize for the rough patch. Debbie didn't pay attention to him. She was watching, transfixed by the view through the canopy up front. It was like nothing she had ever seen before.

Get a hold of yourself, she thought. She was starting to become as giddy and immature as Yeager. She couldn't let him do this to her, couldn't let him drag her into his little world of secret societies and paranoia. She didn't care about his quest. All she wanted was to get her hands on a stack of money and take it straight to her mother.

The airport where they landed was more like a grass field with a few buildings set up around it than a hub to the rest of the world. The captain parked the plane wherever he felt like it, and the stairs they rolled up to the side were rickety, made of wood.

Yeager escorted her down and then they walked across the grass to a small, leaning hut at the edge of the field.

"Have you been here before?" she whispered to him.

He shook his head. "But I've read up. There are logs from people who searched for the box here. None of them could find it. Couldn't even find the people who made it. But I've collected a lot of evidence. And I have you. You've seen the box."

She shrugged. "I thought you said a lot of people knew what it looked like."

"There are details. If you can describe it accurately to the right person, it might get us somewhere."

Yeager approached a middle-aged man with leathery skin and conversed with him for a few minutes in Portuguese. Then Yeager beckoned for Debbie to follow him around to the other side of the hut. Parked up the narrow dirt road that led away from the airport was a line of five or six open-topped Land Rovers. They looked as though they had been through several wars.

Yeager led her to one and climbed into the driver's seat. Sitting next to him, she looked down at the rugged gears, the battered hood. "You know how to drive one of these things?"

"They're just cars," he said with a shrug. "It's a standard transmission, but my first car was an old Porsche that was finicky as all hell. I know what I'm doing."

I hope so, Debbie thought. She only nodded to him and braced herself against the glove compartment as he threw the truck into reverse and backed them out onto the road.

They climbed up into the hills for a long time. Now and then, when she got tired of the wind in her face, Debbie would turn around and peer back down the road the way they had come. The grassy airstrip became first a little clearing in the dense foliage surrounding it, and then nothing more than a dot of bright green in an ocean of darker hues.

The jungle itself grew thicker the farther they traveled. Vines began to hang low enough to catch on the top of the Land Rover's windshield, and every now and then, Debbie would feel something in her hair.

"Do you know where we're going?" she asked Yeager, when they had been traveling for nearly an hour and appeared no closer to any distinguishable landmarks than they had been when they began.

He nodded and glanced down at a hand-drawn map in the back of one of the books he'd been reading on the plane. There was a compass embedded in the dashboard where the radio should have been, but it moved about aimlessly even when Yeager wasn't steering, pointing to a North Pole first ahead, then behind, then a little to the left of them.

Debbie tried to swallow her unease. As much as she enjoyed the scenery, it was striking her more and more how far they were from any civilization. If either of them were bitten by something poisonous or if they broke a leg, who would be there to help them?

About two hours out from the airstrip, Yeager finally steered off of the dirt road. The Land Rover bumped over an outcropping of rocks and came to rest amid a stand of ferns and other vegetation. He let the engine die and flipped off the overhead floodlights he had been using to illuminate the road ahead of them as the evening sky had begun to darken.

Debbie looked at him. "What are you doing?"

"We're here."

She scanned the jungle around them—not even trace signs of shelter. The only proof she had that another human being had ever been out here was the road they were sitting on, and that could have been created by a herd of large beasts.

"We're where?" she said.

He chuckled and climbed out of the Land Rover, slipping a backpack onto his back. The laptop and the suitcase stayed in the truck. "You have to have a sense of adventure," he said with a wink.

Debbie closed her eyes. She was hungry, but she wouldn't tell him that in a thousand years. She wasn't going to be the weak little damsel in distress that slowed him down and kept asking where the bathroom was, where she could dry her hair and do her nails. She wouldn't give him the satisfaction.

Yeager hiked into the darkened folds of the jungle with the confidence of an experienced game poacher. He brushed the foliage away with one hand while holding the map with the other.

Debbie kept up, but her confidence was weakening with her limbs. After a time, she could hold it all back no longer. "Lewis, where are we going?"

"There's a village just up ahead."

"There's nothing up ahead."

"Trust me."

She stared at the back of his head. Why should she trust him? But then another, more alarming thought occurred to her—what choice did she have? Putting aside for the moment the extreme unlikelihood that he would allow her to leave him right now, if she did strike out on her own, where would she go? He had the keys to the car—and without the car, she was just a lone woman in the middle of the wilderness. They had driven far too far for her to hike back, and if she could, she didn't have any money, no way of getting back to Rio.

For the first time in her life, Debbie felt utterly helpless. It was like drowning. At first, she wanted to struggle against it, to thrash and squirm until she found a way of wrestling control back into her hands. But as she came to terms with it, hiking behind this strange, unbalanced man into a stranger, distant world, she began to feel peaceful. No control meant no responsibilities. No control meant nothing to worry about.

If she was going to starve out here, that was going to happen, and there wasn't a damn thing she could do about it. If Yeager was going to turn violent, she could resist him, but she couldn't stop him. Every fiber of her being wanted to fight it, but in the end, she had to concede that for the time being anyway, she had become the dependent little woman she had never wanted to be.

Yeager was right. Another fifteen minutes of hiking and lights began to flicker through the ropey vines and trees up ahead. A village came into view. It was small, simple, not much more than a couple of buildings huddled together in a tiny half-clearing in the jungle. But it was strangely cozy in that way.

A central fire pit united five or six little shanties that appeared to have been built out of whatever spare wood planks and stones the owners could gather. There was a well at one end and a clothesline that stretched between it and the fire pit. The settlement was alive with bustling activity, people rolling out dough, some kind of skinned beast roasting over the fire.

Debbie smiled to herself. It was like some child's fantasy, like discovering a little gem of excitement and adventure in a world she'd thought had long ago surrendered to an age of concrete and technology.

She tapped Yeager on the shoulder as they descended down the gentle basin into the edges of the village. "Is this them then?" she asked. "Is this the secret society? The tribe?"

He shook his head. "No, no," he said. "This is only the beginning."

Chapter 22

Mandy wasn't there when Gregory came down the next morning. He felt a little bit guilty, but honestly, he was more relieved than anything else. What would he have said to her? She had fled the night before, and he had gone to his room before her mother could come out and give him a piece of her mind.

Someone else was manning the reception desk now—another kid about Mandy's age, a boy, scarcely out of high school. He followed Gregory with a hardened stare. Apparently, Gregory's reputation had preceded him.

The parking lot had lost a few cars over the course of the night, and now the rental minivan was all alone among the trellises and winding vines behind the Sunrise Hotel. He drove out onto the highway, his eyes drawn to the gray sky reflected in the rolling waves on the ocean just beyond. It was beautiful in a muted, moody way that all of the beaches and beautiful sunsets in Los Angeles could never hope to fathom.

Gregory meandered back into town, keeping an eye open for Haverford Street. He didn't want to stop and ask if he could help it. From what Mandy had said, people around here weren't too friendly to strangers, and particularly not people headed to 9567.

He drove back and forth between a few stores, a pub, the small facades of a quaint little fishing village that had lost the *quaint* sometime in the eighties. When the locals began to stare, he moved on. It wasn't until about half an hour later that he found his way to the right place.

It was secluded from the main drag, nestled back among a grid of houses that had probably been developed after World War II to accommodate all of the returning Baby Boomers. They were unremarkable places, nice and inviting for the area but not overly opulent.

He watched the addresses climb, and when he got to the 9500 block, he pulled to the curb and got out of the van. The yards along here had become a little more overgrown. The paint was either dirty or peeling on most of the houses, and the cars that lingered in the driveways in this block were either cheap or immobile or both.

He spotted 9567 half a block away. He wasn't sure what it was about the property, but he knew he had found the right place. He stopped for a moment and just stared. Everything seemed to be happening too quickly now; he had expected another stumbling block, a wrong turn, a dead end. He had half-wondered if there would even be a West Haverford Street in Trenton, Maine, or if it was all part of some elaborate hoax that had dragged him across the entire country on a wild goose chase, hunting demons.

It was a modest little suburban tract house—nothing special. The windows were dark, and moss had taken root across one side of the roof. The lawn was badly in need of a mow, and the chain-link fence that enclosed the property had begun to sag along the front right corner. It looked like the sort of place a malingering grandmother would live out her days.

He didn't like it; it wasn't Frida. She belonged in something more majestic, or at least something a little less ordinary.

He walked up to the gate and nudged it open without taking his hands out of his jeans pockets. It was bitterly cold. He hadn't noticed it before, but now, with the van and its heater half a block away, he felt naked, unprotected from the elements. As he made his way up the front sidewalk, the threatening clouds began to spit half-frozen rain.

There was a red piece of paper tacked to the front door—an eviction notice. Gregory's heart sank. The sheet was dated sometime last week. The house was empty. He had known it couldn't be this simple.

He tried the knob, but the door was locked. Covering his head with a newspaper he found beside the fraying welcome mat, he tramped out through the mud alongside the house to try the back door. It was open.

It smelled like smoke inside, the ghost of badly-cooked meals left too long in the oven. He coughed, plugged his nose, and moved into the kitchen. Most of the furniture was gone, save for the few larger pieces the looters or the repo guys couldn't or hadn't bothered to get out the door. There was the stove, a rolling dish washer, a billiard table he could see through the open doorway of the living room. Everything else was gone.

There was trash strewn across the dining room floor and a few old blankets bundled up in one corner. A couple of Chinese fast food cartons lay in a pile by one door, and an empty whiskey bottle had rolled to the edge of the room. It was a shelter for squatters, he realized. He didn't blame them. Anyone who slept outside in a brutal place like this wouldn't last too many days.

He hunted around the rest of the house before finally giving in. There was nothing here. It didn't hit him until he had reached the back door that this was it—the end of his journey. He had gone after an empty voice at the other end of a telephone call, and it had led him here: a small, closed-up shell of a house in eastern Maine. There was nowhere else to go. He had no more clues to follow.

It was ludicrous how stupid he had been. He sat on one of the kitchen counters, staring blankly at the forlorn little power cord that had once been attached to a refrigerator. What had he actually expected to find? A soul mate? A young eager bride he could easily woo into his life? A companion even?

The reality of it all came crashing down on his shoulders as another painfully cold gust of ocean air drifted in through the cracks around the edges of the windows. He was on the other side of the

country, out over a thousand dollars in plane tickets and unthink-
ably behind on the databases he was supposed to be optimizing back
at work. His mother thought he was crazy, his boss would probably
have his head, and he had nothing at all to show for it.

He wasn't sure what had come over him. Looking back, it
seemed like madness. He got up. It was over—it had been a bizarre,
fleeting infatuation with the unknown, and now he could go home
and slip back into the monotony that was his everyday life.

Then he saw the basement door. It was cut directly into the
kitchen floor and tiled over in patterned plastic so that it appeared
nearly invisible. He would have thought it was just a square inden-
tation in the ground were it not for the tiny brass knob protruding from one side.

He went to it, knelt, brushed off the metal. There was a thin
layer of dust covering the entire thing. The squatters, whoever they
were, apparently hadn't looked around carefully enough to find it,
and the repo guys had either been in too much of a hurry or had
figured that whatever was down there would be a waste of time.

Gregory pulled at the door, found it heavier than he had
expected. When at last he got it open, he saw why. The underside
was crisscrossed with heavy metal beams. At first he thought they
had been added to strengthen it, so that something could be set on
top without fear of breaking the hinges, but then he noticed hooks
affixed to the bottom. They were heavy, drilled deep into the
metal. They looked as though they had been built to hold industrial machinery.

Beneath the door, a steep flight of wooden stairs descended
into the darkness. There was a light switch hanging from bare
wires on one of the wooden support columns halfway down the
stairs, but either there was no electricity or it wasn't attached to
anything.

A quick search of the house uncovered no flashlights, but
there was a half-exhausted book of matches jammed beneath the
pile of blankets by the rotting Chinese food. The cardboard
looked as though it had been wet—it smelled of beer and

something worse—and the first several matches he tried snapped in half before they ever gave a spark.

On the fourth or fifth, though, he got a tiny light going. He shielded it with his hand and climbed downstairs. It was freezing in the basement. The walls and floor were made of concrete, and it smelled like mildew and wet earth. More of the hooks ran in tracks across the rest of the ceiling.

The flickering light illuminated a pile of newspapers and a couple of magazines strewn across the floor. There was a small cot set up in one corner, a few paper plates dotted with grease stains, and an empty pizza box.

He could find no other clues to what he was seeing. The rest of the basement was empty, a vast portion of it drowned in a thin pool of water that had seeped in through a crack in the foundation. He was getting ready to go back upstairs when he saw something at the very end of the room. It looked like a fragment of confetti or colored paper.

Gregory went to it and knelt. He had misjudged the size—it was larger than confetti, closer to a Hallmark card. Most of the surface had been smeared with a muddy footprint. He turned it over. There was writing on the other side, letters fragmented by the signature distortions of a cheap copy machine. He tried holding the match up to it, but the paper was sopping wet, and one of the drips rolling off of it extinguished the light.

He pocketed it, turned to leave, and almost tripped on something. There was a cord running across the ground. Tugging at it with his hands, he followed it to the wall and a ragged end where it had been yanked free of something. It wound around in tight, synthetic braids; it was a telephone cord.

A chill shook him. This was where Frida had been when he called her. He wasn't sure how he knew; he just did. It was the same feeling he'd gotten when he first drove down West Haverford Street and caught sight of the little house from afar.

She had been kept like an animal down here. Even with the blankets on the cot, there was no way she could have been warm enough, no way she could have been comfortable. Who would do that? Had she been kidnapped? Who was she?

There were no more matches. He went back upstairs and spread the colored paper out on the stove. It was a flier, the kind people usually posted on telephone poles. Gregory squinted at it, trying to make out what it was. There was some kind of poorly-copied picture—it looked like a girl, but he couldn't be sure. Beneath it, in scrawled writing: *Who is Shayla Hacker?*

He felt a tickle on his arm. He'd broken out in gooseflesh. So that was her name—Frida: Shayla Hacker. And now that he had seen what she looked like, if even in a muddy little snapshot, he wanted more than ever to meet her in person. He knew something was wrong. The entire house reeked of a shady operation, a kidnapping or some kind of strange cultish ritual.

The magnitude of it all was starting to make him feel helpless. He stumbled out onto the front lawn, gasping in the fresh, crisp air. His roving gaze caught on the telephone pole at the corner of the sagging chain-link fence. It was papered with more of the fliers.

He went to it, ripped a couple of them from their staples and gathered them up in his hands. It was as though some other, hidden person within him had taken over now. He was acting on instinct and subconscious desire alone.

Before he knew what he was doing, he found himself pounding on the front door of the house next door. He could hear a television on inside, and after a minute, footsteps clomped up to the other side. A shadow fell across the peephole. "Who is it?" a surly voice asked from within. Gregory wasn't sure if it was a man's or a woman's.

"I need to ask you a question," he said. "Please, it's very urgent."

The door came open a few inches—a man, curly, unkempt hair. He was wrapped in an orange bathrobe, and he needed a good shower. He looked Gregory up and down. "What are you selling?"

Gregory caught sight of his reflection in the window beside the door: middle-aged man in casual but expensive attire, clutching colored fliers. The guy had every right to be suspicious. "I found these out there." He thrust a few of the fliers through the door. "Please, can you tell me who she is?"

The man's expression turned from vague disinterest to outright hostility. "Another one of you? I don't care who she is!"

"You've met others?"

"More'n I can count."

"But it's important. I think she might be in trouble."

"Yeah. That or she might be your aunt or your long lost love or God knows what else. I'm not interested. Sell it somewhere else." The door started to close, but halted a half-second before Gregory was going to thrust his foot inside and stop it. "But if you do find out, wouldn't hurt to come back and let me know."

"Soup's ready." The man crumpled up the plastic Ramen wrapper with one hand while he ladled the noodles into grubby little bowls with the other.

It was cheap, but Gregory had to admit that it smelled good. He took it and relished the warmth in his hands. He let the steam swoop up across his face. If he were wearing glasses, he thought, they would have been fogged opaque.

"So tell me about her," he said, sitting down on the living room couch off of the man's cue.

The man walked over from the kitchen, flipped off the afternoon football game on the television, and joined Gregory. "That's the thing," the man said. "I can't. Nobody can. You won't find one person who knows a thing about her. That's why everyone's curious. That's why everyone's looking for her."

"What, they just want to get to know her?"

"They just want to know what her deal is." He took a spoonful of the soup, started to put his lips around it and recoiled, blowing hard on the steam.

"But that's amazing. How come nobody talks about it?"

"They're embarrassed. An' scared."

"Scared?"

"It's—y'know—the *great unknown* or whatever. It's the same type of feeling you get looking at those missing children they always put on milk cartons. What happens to them? What happened to Shayla Hacker? Who is she? Nobody knows."

"So how'd everyone hear about her?"

"Have you seen her picture?"

Gregory started to shake his head. "No, wait, I have, sort of." He uncrumpled another of the neon pink fliers and spread it out on the couch pillow next to him.

"Naw, that's crap," the man said. "You can't see her eyes in that one. Once you see her eyes, you won't be able to stop looking for her. I'm telling you, not one person can resist." He set the bowl on the table in front of the sofa and got up. "I'll find you a snapshot. You've got to see it." As he began rooting around in a pile of unorganized papers on top of an old piano, he asked, "Why're you after her if you haven't seen this, then?"

"I told you, I think she's in trouble. She sounded worried on the phone—"

The man whirled around so fast that a stack of catalogs cascaded to the floor behind him. "You talked to her?"

For a man with such feigned disdain for Shayla's followers, Gregory thought, he was certainly fast to shed any pretense of casual disinterest. "I have," Gregory said. "By accident . . . sort of. It's complicated."

"How long ago?"

"About a week. A little more."

"Do you know where she is?"

"That's why I came. I thought she was here."

"Next door," the man nodded, sounding disappointed. "A lot of people think that. I'm not sure why. If she ever was, though, she isn't anymore." He went back to hunting for the picture.

"But I'm curious about this . . . this phenomenon. How many people are into this?"

He shrugged. "Everyone. Everyone wants to know who she is."

"But nobody talks about it."

"Strange as all hell, huh?"

Now what? Gregory thought. He looked down at the flier.

"Do you know who makes these?"

The man shrugged. "Old guy out on the beach, I think. But he stopped. People complained or something. Haven't heard from him for a while, but I saw him posting them sometime last week. Why?"

"I'd like to talk to him."

When Gregory turned off the minivan's engine, there was, for a few moments, only the sound of his own breathing and the crashing of the waves against the rocks. He savored those moments. Before coming out here, he had seldom heard silence like this. There were times when he had snuck out to the coast or up to a secluded spot in the Hollywood hills, but always there was the distant sigh of rubber on pavement, the eternal highway that was as essential to Los Angeles as a heartbeat.

The old house was perched on wooden stilts, hanging over the edge of the cliff. Back at home, it would have been a violation of earthquake codes, but Gregory doubted people worried much about that out here.

He got out of the van and shivered as the ocean breeze engulfed him. No amount of clothing could keep it out. Picking his steps carefully on the uneven ground, he climbed up to the front of the house. The windows were dark, and it looked abandoned. There were tire tracks in the gravel driveway, but the edges were windblown; they had to have been at least a week old.

Nevertheless, he knocked on the door and waited almost five minutes before trying the knob. It was open. Somehow, that didn't surprise him. It was the sort of place where nobody locked their doors. Nobody but Shayla Hacker.

It was cozy inside. The hardwood floors were draped with

rugs, and Venetian blinds hung in the windows. There was a couch in front of a TV, a couple of bookcases full of periodicals and some of the mainstream murder mysteries. It looked like a normal guy's house. What had driven this man to start searching for a strange girl from a photograph?

He slipped through a narrow corridor, and his breath caught in his throat as he emerged into the kitchen. It was a magnificent view. A small table sat in an alcove made of glass, hanging out over the edge of the cliff. Even the floor was studded with windowed tiles that allowed a view straight down to the bubbling foam that worked its way in and out of the rocks.

The sun was just beginning to glimmer across the water. Gregory just wanted to sit and stare at it until the last of the light died. He couldn't imagine how anyone could get any work done in this house. If he lived here, he would spend his entire life in awed observation of the world.

It wasn't until he finally forced himself to take his eyes from the windows that he saw the stack of unwashed dishes in the kitchen sink, the bags of garbage piled up by the door. The illusion was shattered—this was no longer the perfect retreat, but yet another temple to a girl none of them knew.

It was in the bedroom where he found the fliers. There was a computer set up on a desk beside the bed, and on the floor beneath it a printer full of pink paper. A couple of the fliers lay half beneath the mattress, waiting to be separated and stapled to a telephone pole. He picked one up, folded it in half, and tossed it away, careful not to look at Hacker's face.

It had been one thing when he was alone in the world, when he thought nobody would believe him if he told them he was chasing a stranger on the off chance that he might be able to help her. But now that he was part of some strange cult movement, everything had changed. He wanted to find her more than ever, but now, it was less out of concern for her well being and more out of curiosity. He wanted to ask her why she had started all of this, who the hell she thought she was.

Actually, he was angry with her. Angry for trivializing his concern, angry for stealing from him the one unique purpose he had ever developed in his life.

He began to take apart the bedroom with a ferocity that surprised even him. He searched the closet, full of polo shirts and plaid button-down cardigans. He emptied the dresser drawers. It didn't take long; most of the laundry was sitting, wrinkled, in hampers by the bedroom door or just draped across the nightstand by the light.

There were no clues to where the house's owner had gone. The man Gregory had met back on Haverford Street—Warren had been his name—had said the guy had just disappeared sometime the week before, it happened all the time. The owner had a summer house in New York somewhere, and he was given to lengthy retreats with little or no notice. Still, Gregory suspected that this time, something else was afoot. The timing was too perfect. Something had turned up. The owner of the house knew where she was, and it made Gregory jealous beyond rationality.

By evening, he was starting to feel the hopelessness creep back. Every time he hit a snag, he started to question everything he had been doing, and now was no exception. Maybe this was all just craziness.

Listlessly, Gregory wandered back out to the kitchen, stole some bread from the cabinet and a few slices of roast turkey and cheese from the refrigerator, and made himself a sandwich. The bread was stale, and the juice he got from a pitcher by the fruit drawer tasted as though it had been stored for a long time, but it helped to eat something. He had not been aware that he had been hungry; only that a headache had started to pinch at the back of his skull.

When he was done, he sat there and watched the waves lap in and out for a while, and then he decided he was going to go. He grabbed a notepad from the counter and stuffed a few dollar bills beneath the plate he'd used. He was about to leave a note for the owner, apologizing for breaking and entering, when he saw something.

Was he imagining it, or were there faint scratches in the

notepad? He held it up to the light, looking closer. Someone had scribbled something very hard on the top sheet and then torn it off, but the indentations remained. It was a word, maybe two, somewhat short.

He looked around in all the wastebaskets, flattened out a few crumpled pieces of paper. None of them matched the pattern on the notepad. Grabbing a pencil from the computer desk, he took a sheet of pink paper from the printer and gently shaded the top sheet on the notepad. The bumps beneath the tip of the carbon came into relief as he colored them in. When he was done, he held the notepad up. He was staring at two words: *Three Rooks.*

"Tell you the truth, I didn't expect to see you come back." Warren held open the front door, and Gregory slipped past him, into the house.

It was grimy and it still smelled like Top Ramen chicken soup, but there was something about the place Gregory found himself liking. Or perhaps it was the company—perhaps it was having a person he could talk to for more than the duration of a grocery store checkout line for the first time in longer than he could remember. There was his mother, but she usually cut him off or forced him to business after a minute or two of wasted long-distance charges. He hadn't had a friend, he realized, since before he'd moved out on his own.

"I found something," he told the man.

Warren raised an eyebrow. "You see the picture yet?"

"No. And I don't want to. But I was wondering if you knew what this meant." He pulled out the carbon copy he'd forged and handed it to Warren.

"Three Rooks?"

"Yeah. Some kind of code or password, you think?"

"What, like a computer thing?"

Gregory shook his head. "I checked his computer."

"Well, it could be anywhere . . . those computers can hide

things. They can be pretty complicated. I never feel quite at home using one . . ."

"Trust me," Gregory said. "Computers are my business. It's nothing on the computer."

Warren squinted at the note. "You know, it does sound vaguely familiar . . ."

". . .but you can't quite place it? Shit." It was just like the girl herself. She was *vaguely familiar* to everyone in the world, and intimate or certain to no one.

"I should think about it." He handed the note back.

Gregory followed Warren into the living room, where he switched on the TV and seemed to forget that he was supposed to be doing anything at all. Gregory was about to remind him, but then he started laughing at something on the show, and Gregory didn't have the heart to interrupt.

Besides, he told himself, when was the last time he had just hung out with a friend and shared a good laugh? Wasn't it at least as important as chasing some strange fantasy?

True, Shayla might be in trouble. *Might.* What if she was leading a hundred men in her wake as some kind of media stunt? It wouldn't be the first time people had done ludicrous things for attention. Out in Los Angeles, he'd seen it all, from an actress who arrived in divorce court with two untamed leopards on leashes to a soap star who had crashed his Aston Martin into a boutique hair salon just to up the ticket sales on his debut action extravaganza.

And Warren was here now. He glanced over at Gregory. "That was funny," he said. "You're not laughing. What's wrong with you?"

Sheepishly, Gregory sank onto the other side of the couch and tried to force his thoughts away from Shayla Hacker. He could worry about that tomorrow. For tonight, for one night only, he was just going to sit back and have fun.

An hour later, when the program ended, he got up. He couldn't take it any longer. He started pacing around the back of the living room while Warren channel-surfed. At first, Gregory had been afraid he was imposing, but if anything, Warren seemed gladder than he for the company. He kept stringing along conversations over ten, twenty minutes, reviving topics Gregory had assumed they'd exhausted just to keep up the dialogue between them.

At first, it had worked out well, but after a time, Gregory had found that he didn't have the attention span for network television. Not when he knew how superficial that world was. It was like getting a glimpse back into his old life, and he just wanted to close his eyes and turn away.

He surveyed Warren's bookshelf, looking for anything that might help him think. The shelves were stacked with old *Playboy* magazines. The only bound books were guides to NASCAR race statistics or diagrams of famous football plays.

"Do you have internet access out here?" Gregory asked.

Warren shook his head, not breaking eye contact with the TV. "I think maybe one company has it out here, but it's expensive and no one much uses it."

"Do they have it in the library?"

"The library? Why would they bring computers in with the books?"

"Right."

It took him almost forty-five minutes before he finally pulled the minivan into the parking lot of a small, squat cinderblock computer shop wedged between two dingy taverns. The windows were crisscrossed with metal grating, but behind them, Gregory could just make out a couple of glowing monitors.

The shop reeked of cigarette smoke. He felt as though he had smoked a pack himself after only five or ten minutes inside.

The man behind the counter was the picture of neglect. His thinning hair had been left in a wild swath across the top of his head. His ripped T-shirt, several sizes too small, couldn't quite cover the bulging belly that hung out over his sweatpants.

He sniffed back a runny nose and eyed Gregory through rimless glasses. "W'can I do for you?"

"The sign said you have internet access here."

"Yeah, sometimes. When it's working."

"Is it working tonight?"

"Yeah, sometimes."

Gregory sat down at the keyboard of a computer he could have bought at a flea market for fifty dollars. The mouse was sticky and smudged with more stains than he could count. He waited an interminable time while an hourglass remained planted in the middle of the screen and the machine seemed to be doing nothing.

When at last he managed to get on the internet, he went straight to a search engine and typed in *three rooks*. He waited while it consulted the database of online information and then came back with the results. There were hundreds, of course. The first five or ten were chess web sites, and apparently there was some kind of stone monument called Three Rocks somewhere that people constantly misspelled.

It wasn't until he clicked to the *Maps* section of the site that he found what he was looking for—Three Rooks, Indiana. A tiny town out in the middle of America's heartland, isolated from the nearest big city by a hundred or more miles of farm country.

Could that possibly be what the note had meant? He wrote it down, noting the zip code and the nearest urban center, and then he went back to the search engine. There were numerous other entries, but none of them made any sense. Indiana it would be.

Through an online travel agent, he booked a flight to the closest airport he could find. It was still going to leave him with an eighty-mile drive when he landed, and he wasn't sure about the rental facilities out there.

He was almost out the door when he had a thought and went back to the computer terminal. As it booted back up, he dialed Warren's number.

"You got work tomorrow?" he asked when Warren answered.

"If I get really lucky at the job bank."

"You like to travel?"

"I like to go to the grocery store on weekends."

"How about to Indiana?"

"I've never been out of the state."

"What do you say?"

"Did you find Shayla Hacker?"

"I found a lead. You want to come?"

"Are you kidding?"

With the click of a mouse, he had a second ticket and a traveling companion to the great unknown.

Chapter 23

Jackie and Marlowe were made to wait in a vast entrance hall while one of the servants ran off to find someone in charge. Despite the agony of knowing Walker could be somewhere nearby, of knowing that perhaps with every passing minute he was drawing farther away, she could not help but marvel at their surroundings.

They were standing in a room whose ceiling arched so high overhead that she could not make out all of the ornate, painted tiles that composed it. The walls were covered in gold carvings and elaborate etched stone, and the floor was made of pure marble. A man in a sash stood by the entrance, gently waving a massive palm frond to circulate the air. *Just like one of those 1930s adventure novels*, she thought. It was real. All of it. She had finally gotten her wish and walked into a fantasy. Somehow, it didn't feel quite right.

Footsteps echoed on the marble. Both of them looked up. An elderly man in a flowing purple robe was coming toward them. Light, filtered in through colored glass high overhead, reflected off of his bald pate. He was not looking at them, but rather at the statues he passed, as though paying his respects to his deceased ancestors on the way to some kind of ritual suicide.

When he reached them, he muttered something Jackie couldn't make out. She exchanged glances with Marlowe, who cocked an eyebrow at her. "I'm sorry?" she said.

The man in the robe blinked. "You are English?"

"Americans," Jackie said, nodding.

"And you are looking for the girl."

"Her, yes . . . and there was a boy, too . . ."

"The girl," Marlowe said sharply. "You know her? You've seen her?"

"Come with me." He turned as abruptly as he had arrived and strode off down the palace hallway, leaving them no choice but to follow.

The man led them up through a narrow spiral staircase whose narrow windows looked out on the glowing yellow desert sand beyond. In the distance, Jackie could see the pyramids rising up against the blue sky. It was strange to be in the presence of such magnificence, such age. There was nothing like this in America.

They emerged into a smaller room on the second floor that was covered from floor to ceiling in glimmering gold. It took Jackie's breath away. It was like walking into a cave full of treasure in an old pirate legend.

Between the stacks of fineries were leather-clad, overstuffed chairs, glass tables, silver platters bearing cups full of wine and other alluring morsels of food. Jackie hadn't realized it, but she was starving beyond measure. She glanced at the man in the purple robe, wondering if he was going to offer them a meal.

"You will wait here, please," he said, and retreated from the room.

She shuffled nervously toward Marlowe. "What do you think is going on?"

"Quiet," he hissed at her. "Patience."

She couldn't keep her eyes from the breads, the cheeses, the bowls of grapes overflowing onto scarlet napkins. They were sweating from the heat.

The man returned, flanked by two guards carrying machetes. He nodded to them and said something clipped, and then the guards turned on Jackie and Marlowe.

"Marlowe!" She darted behind him.

"Wait!" Marlowe said. "Wait, we are not here to cause trouble."

"You are looking for the girl," the man barked. "That is trouble enough."

"But she's my daughter!"

The man gave him a stricken look and then snarled another order to the guards. They halted, a few feet from Jackie. Close enough that she could hear the air humming across the tips of their blades.

The robed man padded toward them, stopping six inches from Marlowe. He leaned even closer, so that their noses were almost touching, and it was then that Jackie realized how disproportionately large he was. He towered over Marlowe as though he were standing next to a child. "What did you say?"

Marlowe did not flinch. "My daughter," he repeated. "We are looking for my daughter."

They sat on the floor while they ate. The table was low enough to make it comfortable, and a group of servants brought in pillows for them to lean against. Fueled by a mixture of intense hunger and anxiety, Jackie cleaned her plate in under ten minutes. It was replaced with a second one, heaped with all manner of rare delights whose taste she had scarcely noticed on the way down.

She listened to every word the men said, but whenever she tried to speak up, to add something about Walker, Marlowe interrupted her and gave her a disapproving glare. She could tell she was wearing down on his patience.

"She was here last week." The man in the purple robe—Aswad was his name—took a sip from his golden goblet. He had elected not to eat anything with them, and suddenly, with her immediate needs satisfied, Jackie began to wonder if that should worry her. After all, he had been quick with the hostilities once; would it not be like him to insure that he had a way of killing them again if he were not satisfied with their answers?

"Why was she here? What was she doing here? She was supposed to meet me in America."

"She was frightened. People were chasing her." His eyes narrowed. "People like you—*foreigners.*"

"What did they look like?"

"They were dressed in all black. They followed her everywhere."

Jackie stiffened. She thought back to the black cars she had seen right before they had gotten into the accident.

"Do you have a picture of her?" Aswad asked.

"I thought you knew what she looked like."

"I would like to know that you do. Since you are supposed to be her father, it is not an unreasonable expectation, no?"

Marlowe nodded. "Fair enough." He removed his wallet and pulled out the Xeroxed copy of the picture he had showed Jackie back in his own secluded desert plantation.

She was again drawn to the image, much as Aswad seemed to be. All three of them huddled together to stare at the girl's face, at her eyes. Jackie blinked, forced herself to turn away. There was something about looking at her that made her feel . . . what was it? Guilty? She had no idea why. All she wanted was to know who the girl was, what she was doing this far from home.

She shook herself—*No*, she thought. She had been searching for Walker, but as soon as she had seen the picture, she had forgotten all about him. What was it about the girl that made everything else seem suddenly trivial?

"I have seen that picture before." Even he sounded dreamy, as though he had just been somewhere very far away. "You are not the only one to have it, which means you do not have to be her father. Do you have another picture?"

Marlowe fixed him with a cold stare. "Where is she?"

"Until you show me more proof, I can say no more. You are welcome to stay here one night, if that is your wish, but you must leave on the next bus available." He stood from the table, gave a slight bow to the room at large, and left before either of them could stop him.

"Son of a bitch," Marlowe muttered, staring after him. "He knows something."

"He never denied that he did," Jackie pointed out. "I bet he knows something about Walker, too."

"Forget your damn brother! This is about her! This is about Shayla!"

She followed Marlowe back into the corridor, where another of the servants offered to show them to their rooms. Marlowe looked as though he was about to explode at the young man, but then, for some reason, he restrained himself. Marlowe nodded, and they made their way through a stunning atrium that looked out across the desert to another row of doors at the top of a balcony.

Their rooms—separate, but adjoining—were as glamorous and opulent as the rest of the palace. A giant bed lay beneath flowing sashes supported by four wooden posts. There was a huge mirror directly opposite the bed, and a dresser full of exotic garments that would have sold for a fortune in America.

Marlowe seemed to notice none of it. He shooed her away when she poked her head into his room. *Fine.* She'd only come to ask him what his plans were, but if he was going to snap at her, she was perfectly content to spend the evening on her own.

It was getting dark by now. The sky had become a bewitching shade of lavender, and as Jackie stepped out onto the balcony, she felt the chill in the evening breeze. She found it hard to collect her thoughts. Everything was so strange, so foreign here. A part of her wanted to just get caught up in the enchanting world, so far from home. But at the same time, she longed to know where Walker was. She wanted to talk to him, wanted someone who would listen, understand, sympathize.

She gazed up at the rising moon, and wondered what side of it hovered over Walker. It was strange—the same light touching both of their eyes, yet they were separated by a distance that felt incomprehensible.

She was so caught up in her thoughts that she almost didn't hear the whispered call from below. It sounded like little more than the wind toying with the sand, but when she finally rose and squinted down at the courtyard, she saw that one of the servants was waving up at her. His movements were furtive, purposely restrained. He kept glancing around, seeing if anyone was watching him.

Jackie got to her knees at the edge of the balcony and tried to thrust her head through the bars so she could get as close as possible to him. Even so, he was still a good twenty feet below.

"What is it?" she hissed back. "Who are you?"

The servant did not answer, but instead motioned with his hands for her to come downstairs.

She shook her head. "What do you want?" He gazed back at her, not comprehending. It was possible, she realized, that he might know something, but it was also possible that he was just a horny local kid who wanted to screw something exotic and liked the way she had looked passing through the palace. She knew her fair share of jerks back in high school, and this servant wasn't much older than they were.

"Why?" she mouthed at him.

He frowned, and then she saw comprehension dawn on his face. Cupping his hand around his mouth, he called back, very softly, "Walker."

She was on her feet in an instant, gone from the balcony before he had dropped his hands to his sides. Back in her room, though, she stopped just before grabbing the doorknob. Was she being stupid? He had merely noticed her attempts to interrupt the conversation at dinner or perhaps seen the longing in her eyes?

She decided that she didn't care. She could fend for herself. People didn't pick on her much in school, but she had turned away a few drunken jerks at the last dance, and she knew she had it in her to defend herself, if need be.

She crept down the winding spiral staircase. The palace had gone dark save for a few torches flickering in some of the larger rooms downstairs. Voices echoed out from the front chamber where they'd first been made to wait. It sounded like Aswad, but he was speaking in a language she didn't understand.

Out in the central corridor, she looked around. She wasn't quite sure which side of the house her room had been on, nor where to look for the servant. She started toward a swinging door and then leapt out of the way as it suddenly crashed open. Several servants barged noisily through, toting silver platters covered in drinks. Crouching in the shadows, she could smell the alcohol from there.

The sound of running water and the clatter of dishes eddied out from behind the door. *The kitchen*, Jackie thought. She wasn't sure if that meant she was going in the right direction or not. She was about to slink on through and take her chances evading the cooks when she heard a tapping on the window behind her.

She turned and caught sight of the servant's shape on the other side. It was fogged glass, and it was dark—it must not have looked out onto the desert. She searched the wall that held it for another door or any way in, but found nothing. The tapping drew her back and she tried to whisper her problems to the man on the other side.

He either didn't hear her or didn't understand her, but then she saw that he was trying to tell her something. He made a circular motion with his hands and then indicated downward. She looked behind her. A heavy wooden door stood ajar, and beyond it, she could just make out a staircase descending into the shadows.

Something about it bothered her; it reminded her of a tomb. *Someone could get caught down there*, she thought, and from beneath the desert, no voices were ever heard. Still, there was the window he was standing behind. If nothing else, they could break out that way.

The hinges squealed as she opened the door wide enough to squeeze through. She winced and stopped in her tracks, silencing even her breathing as she waited to see if anyone had heard. But there was no sign that she had attracted any attention from the people in the main room. If anything, their voices had grown louder. It sounded as though they were having some kind of party, it sounded like they were drunk.

The warmth of the day had not stayed in the stairwell, and as she descended, it grew even cooler, clammier. It clung to her skin like wet cellophane.

The corridor where she emerged was lit by a single torch at the other end. In the intervening space, there were more shadows than

she could count. She should have been scared. Perhaps it was
something about the servant's face, or perhaps, she admitted, it
was her own desperation for knowledge of Walker's whereabouts.

She started down the corridor and yelped when a shape moved
just two or three feet ahead.

"Do not fear," a young voice said in halting English.

Jackie struggled to slow her breathing. "Who are you? What
do you want?"

"Come." The shape turned and crept farther down the corridor.

Cautiously, Jackie followed. The light began to grow ahead of
them, and when they reached it, she found they were in a cramped
wine cellar, the walls stacked with barrels and racks of dusty bottles. At last, she got a good look at the servant's face.

Her estimate from the balcony had been giving him too much
credit—he was, if anything, younger than her, little more than a boy.

"You ask about Walker," he said. "I have seen him."

Her heart skipped a beat. "Where? When?"

The servant frowned. "Here. A few days ago."

"What was he doing here?"

"He was in love with the girl. They were together."

Jackie blinked. Walker had had his share of girlfriends throughout high school, most of them the type that Mom would have dis-
approved of, but to think that he had run off after this particular
girl, that he was in love with her . . . it didn't make any sense.

"Are you sure?" she asked.

The servant nodded. "Sure."

"Were they together? Did they leave here together?"

He nodded again.

"Where did they go?"

"Back to America."

Jackie's spirits sank. Though she had not admitted it to herself,
she had been secretly hoping he would take her to them now; that
they would be crouched in the basement somewhere, hiding out
until she could find them and ferry them back home. America was
a very, very long way from here.

"What part?"

He squinted at her, and she could tell her question hadn't gotten through.

"State," she prompted. Still nothing. "Region? What part of America?"

"Teepees."

"What?"

"They went to the teepees."

A sudden sound from somewhere overhead stole the question from the tip of her tongue. Off of the servant's terrified gaze, she glanced back over her shoulder, but she could see nothing beyond the shadowed corridor through which they had come. "Listen," she hissed, but he clamped a hand over her mouth.

Together, they crept back through the wine cellar to the bottom of the stairs. There, the servant paused and listened again. Footsteps moved back and forth overhead. Muffled voices found their way down through the heavy marble floor and the thick wooden planks that supported it.

"What's going on?" Jackie hissed.

"We must be quiet. We must not be discovered," the servant told her.

"Why not? Are you not allowed to talk to me?"

"He knows your friend is not her father."

Jackie gulped. She had surmised all along that there was something more to Marlowe than he wanted her to think. But she had followed him across the world, and now she was at his mercy. She didn't want to face the fact that he wasn't who he said he was.

The servant was slowly ascending the stairs. She caught up with him and grabbed his shoulder. "You have to tell me where they went," she hissed. "If anything happens, I have to know."

"America," he said with an irritated wave of a hand. "We must be quiet."

"Where in America?"

"Teepees."

"That's not a place!" She could feel the frustration mounting and tried to control it. She knew the geography of Egypt well enough, she thought. She had spent enough rainy days with her nose in a book from the library to feel at home in most parts of the world. And it had been painless; no, it had been fun. Couldn't she expect at least that much from anyone else she met? And American culture was so dominant anyway, didn't foreigners at least know the fifty states?

She yanked at the servant with a little more force, and he stumbled back, almost careening down the stairs. "Talk to me!" she snarled.

"Let go!"

"Tell me where they went." Her hands moved up the side of his shoulder to his neck. She didn't even realize it was happening until she felt him swallow and realized his Adam's apple was beneath her fingers. And then she froze. He was staring at her with a cold, unwavering gaze, his eyes accusing with their dispassionate disappointment.

"You are killing me," he said in a choked voice.

She released him with a little gasp. She would have strangled him if he hadn't said anything. What the hell was she doing?

The boy wheeled around and started climbing the stairs, but this time, she couldn't follow him. She had become a monster. And over what? A stranger who might or might not be her brother's lover. It was none of her business, and she hadn't even known Walker and Shayla Hacker had anything to do with each other when she began all of this.

Jackie squinted up at the young servant boy, squatting at the top of the stairs. He was holding out a hand to her, beckoning for her to follow. When she took it, all she could hear were the words he had spoken to her—"You are killing me."

"You've got to help me," she whispered to him.

"I told you. Teepees."

She shook her head. "That's not what I mean. I think I'm sick. You've got to help me."

"You must leave. Now."

Before she could protest, he charged forward, leading her

behind him by the hand. They did not go back to the doorway where she had entered. There were voices coming from there, and by the frightened look on the servant's face, Jackie supposed that his absence had probably been noticed. She wondered if they had also found her empty bedroom.

They came to a small hole in the stone wall, about three feet square. It was pitch black, cut out of the thick concrete blocks, winding back into the earth. She stood there staring at it until she again felt his eyes on her.

"You will go now," he told her, nodding toward the hole.

He had to be joking. She shook her head. "I'm not suicidal."

"What is this . . . suicidal?"

"I won't do it."

"You must."

As though on cue, the footsteps that had been thumping back and forth upstairs stopped short. There was another sound, a heavy creaking—the door. Light spilled into the chamber at the end of the corridor. The servant gave her a sharp shove.

"Go now!" There was panic in his voice. Whatever the consequences of her getting caught down here were, they would be worse for him.

"Where do I go?"

"America."

"Where?" She was frustrated enough to cry.

"Teepees. Three hooks . . . hooks? No . . . it was . . . there was *r*."

"What?"

He shook his head and pushed her. She stumbled against the wall, lost, dazed, reeling. The boy grabbed her legs and hoisted her from the ground. She fell forward, and with nowhere else to put her hands, she ended up in the tiny tunnel.

Hands touched her back. He was shoving her bodily into the hole. She snapped something indignant at him, but he wasn't listening anymore. Dimly beyond him, she could make out the flicker of approaching torches.

When she was all the way inside, he leaned his head through

the rectangular opening. "Stay quiet!" he whispered. It was a direct order, but there was a desperate, pleading tinge in his voice.

She tried to turn around and watch. The boy whirled, the other servants bursting in behind him. The passage was too small for her to twist back, and then the men were in the room. She froze.

Aswad was there. They were speaking harshly. She heard the servant boy start to say something in his defense and then Aswad cut him off. Someone else shuffled forward, and then there was the sound of flesh smacking against flesh. Jackie winced as she heard the boy cry out and stumble to his knees.

The servants—many of them now—were closing in. Jackie's heart pounded in her chest. She was breathing so fast she felt like she was going to run out of oxygen in the tiny passage. She had to get control of herself or she would pass out.

Images began flashing before her eyes. The boy at the service station, so far away now that it seemed nothing more than a dark, bitter dream. She saw the blood spatter against the back windshield, saw the chauffeur's stony face as he locked the trunk afterward. Worse, though, had been the look in Marlowe's eyes—empty, emotionless.

Jackie shivered.

Aswad gave the boy another kick, said something else, and then all of them laughed. His footsteps turned and disappeared back down the corridor. The other servants, jeering at the boy, filed out after their master.

In the silence that followed, all she could hear was her own breathing and the ragged whimpers of the kid. She crept backward, moving slowly enough to avoid making a sound with her shoes on the stone floor. "Are you okay?" she whispered.

He jerked, as though she had hit him again, and growled something she didn't understand. "Get out of here!" he added, when she didn't move.

"I'm sorry . . ."

"Leave!" The boy stood and swung at the black opening.

Jackie recoiled. "What will happen to you? Are you going to be okay?"

"Leave! Now!"

Before she could say another word, he shook his head and ran from the room.

Jackie felt awful. Who knew what would happen to him because of her? She wanted to run after him and apologize, comfort him, but she knew if they caught her down there with him after all of this, it would only make things worse. They might even kill him.

With a mounting sense of dread, she pulled herself into the passage and started crawling into its gaping mouth.

She lost track of time. There was no light anywhere, and the air grew warmer the farther in she got. It had begun to feel like she was crawling toward the center of the earth. And what if there was no exit? The thought had sent an electric bolt down her spine, and she forced herself to banish it from her mind. If she started panicking down here, she was sure to black out.

The passage narrowed. There was no longer any room to crawl, and so she had to shimmy along on her stomach. She couldn't turn around now even if she wanted to. It would take hours to retrace her steps like this. It had already taken several to get as far as she had.

Jackie Savage was going to die. As soon as the thought hit her, it stuck in her mind. The worst part was, she didn't even care that much anymore. She was so lost, so confused, that an end to it all almost seemed preferable. At least everything would be over, then.

Her mind numb, she kept moving through the night.

Jackie's body was covered in scrapes and bruises when she finally emerged into the light. The passage opened up through a small metal grate into the desert. She stumbled out into the sand and winced at the harshness of the light. The sun was already climbing toward the center of the sky, and the heat of the day was upon her.

Shading her eyes, she looked around. The tunnel burrowed into a sand dune. She could not see beyond it, but there was absolutely nothing on this side. She couldn't even see the pyramids from here. It was as though all human civilization had been wiped from the world save the one metal grate from which she had emerged.

She was too tired, too dazed to consider the implications—that in a few hours she would probably succumb to dehydration, that she could starve to death out here or have some kind of heat stroke. None of those possibilities occurred to her. Basic survival instincts had overridden her conscious thoughts.

She felt herself moving again and saw with a detached interest that she was climbing the dune. She registered a small cluster of buildings on the other side, people moving about. There were tire tracks in the sand. A part of her was making the necessary connections.

An old woman leaning over a water well looked up as Jackie stumbled into the small village. The woman's eyes went wide and she turned and shouted something to her young son and daughter, who were standing in the doorway of their little house.

Before Jackie knew it, she was being carried inside, and then she was in bed, and someone was splashing water on her forehead. It felt amazing. She smiled and lay back onto the mattress. Suddenly, she had the inexplicable sensation that she was precisely where she wanted to be—that she never wanted to leave this place. Ever.

The haze that had enveloped her head now began to clear. She blinked back the warm water the woman was pressing onto her temples and sat up.

The woman said something soft and gentle and tried to ease her back down.

"No, I'm fine," Jackie protested.

"English?" the woman said, sounding as though the very word left a foul taste in her mouth. She withdrew her moist towel and sat back as Jackie propped herself up.

"Where am I?"

"Not England."

Nice, Jackie thought—she had been picked up by the one woman in the desert who spoke English well enough to be sarcastic. There was something warm, something comforting about the little hut and the woman with her two little children.

Then she figured it out: this was a home. Not a house, not an apartment, but *home*. There was a mother here, kids. She was being taken care of. It was a pleasure so rare and so distant in her memory that it was like standing up after sitting in one spot for a decade.

But she had to find Walker. Walker—not Shayla Hacker. She had lost all enthusiasm for Marlowe's hunt. Looking back, her inherited interest in the quest seemed insane. She couldn't even remember the girl's picture, let alone why she had been so desperate to help him find her.

"I have to get to America," Jackie told the woman.

She snorted. "Very far away."

"I know. Where's the airport?"

"You have money? You have passport?"

"Oh, shit," Jackie thought.

Marlowe had paid for the tickets. Marlowe had forged a passport for her, and he had kept it with him after they had boarded the plane. For the first time, she began to realize just how much trouble she was in. This was how people ended up in places for the rest of their lives. People like her got trapped by misfortune and suddenly, all of their options dried up.

"But I have to!" she repeated, hearing the panic rise in her voice. "I *have* to!"

The woman shook her head. "In time, you will stop caring."

What if she's right?

Chapter 24

A young receptionist ducked into the interrogation room and whispered something to the police officer who had been standing guard by the door. He nodded, took out his keys, and went for Terry's handcuffs. "They'll see you now," he said, and hoisted Terry to his feet.

Lieutenant Keeler stood behind Captain Joel Hernandez's chair, looking tired and sweaty and uncomfortable. He didn't meet Terry's eye when he came in the door. *Bad news*, Terry thought. That meant they were probably going to accuse him of something, despite the fact that he had saved the Lieutenant's life.

"Sit down," the Captain said. He motioned toward one of the chairs in front of his desk.

"What's going on?" Terry demanded. "What's this all about?"

"Been a hell of a night."

"We have to find the girl. We're wasting time here."

Hernandez raised one of his large, bushy eyebrows. "I beg your pardon?"

Terry saw it now—none of them were ever going to understand. They were going to treat this as another in a string of mishaps that had defined this case, and they were going to overlook the common element of it all: Shayla Hacker. He had to get out of here.

For half an hour, he listened to the Captain search for

roundabout ways to tell him they were screwing him over. They put things delicately, made little insinuations and tried to goad him into admitting wrongdoing. "Awful strange, wasn't it?" Hernandez said, "that Sergeant Lyman would be just standing in the middle of the road."

"He was lying," Terry growled. "He was already dead."

"And you just ran him right over. Big man, Tom Lyman. Hard to miss."

"It was the other car."

"Right." Hernandez nodded, placating. "This—*other car.*" As though Terry had invented it completely.

Terry glanced at Keeler. He was sitting with his bandaged ankle up, staring at one of the Captain's award plaques. He hadn't said a damn thing in Terry's defense.

Terry felt the frustration mounting, the longer it went on. It was clear that the Captain wanted a confession so he could pin all of this on Terry and call it a day. They weren't going to let him out of the room until they got what they wanted.

At sometime in the middle of the morning, when they had all been up far too long and even the Captain seemed to be losing his focus, Terry asked to be excused. He couldn't take this any longer. If he had to recount one more time the way he had taken the Lieutenant's firearm and orchestrated their escape to such a skeptical audience, he was going to leap on the Captain's desk and start hitting people. And there was still Shayla. He couldn't force her from the back of his mind. Her face was always there, nagging, her eyes piercing his skull. He had to find her. He had to get to Three Rooks.

The guard waited outside the bathroom door. It was small, cramped, no windows. A fan rattled to life in the ceiling, but the passage behind it was the only possible means of escape, and that was a good ten feet over his head.

Terry jammed himself into one of the stalls and rooted around in his pockets for a few moments before he pulled out his keys.

Crouching on the toilet, he plunged the longest one on the ring—the house key—deep into the inside of his thigh. It stung, the pain sharp enough that he almost cried out. Then, the warmth—the sweet relief. He should have done this long ago—to have something to focus on, to have something to bring his mind back under control; it was better than any drug or addiction.

Then, Terry Young had a thought. They weren't going to let him go. He'd seen that in the Captain's eyes and heard it in his voice, and Keeler—Keeler was too afraid to even open his mouth.

The officer unlocked the door, and Terry nodded at him as he filed out of the washroom. Back in the Captain's office, he asked if he could speak with Keeler alone for a moment. They all exchanged glances.

"This isn't a private matter between you and Isaac," Hernandez said. "This is a criminal investigation. I've got a dead officer out there. Any details—"

"I understand that," Terry said. "I don't give a shit about your case. This is private."

With another hour of sleep the night before, with one extra ounce of energy, Hernandez might have resisted. Instead, he fixed Terry with a long, tired look, and then he pushed back from his desk and went to the door. "I'm gonna get a coffee," he said.

As soon as they were alone, Keeler let loose on Terry. He was sweating. "What do you want?"

He knows, Terry thought. *He knows he's been doing something wrong, and he knows that he should pay for it.*

"What do you want, Terry?"

It was the moment of truth. Terry could plop down into one of the chairs and try to strike a deal with a man who was probably willing to negotiate. Or he could do it. And before he knew what he was doing, his hands were in motion.

He slipped the keyring from behind his back, and in one quick, stealthy move, he ducked around to the other side of Keeler's chair and pressed the house key against his throat. "What do I want?" he breathed in Keeler's ear. "I want to get the hell out of here. And I think you might want to help me, but that's just conjecture. I don't know, Isaac. What do you think?"

Keeler swallowed against the sharp edge. "Terry. What are you doing?"

"You fucked me over. I need her. I need to see her and you just want to shove me back in jail because you're too ignorant to go searching for the real answers."

"This isn't a good idea, Terry. Let's talk about this."

"We've spent the whole morning talking. I can see where that's going. One-way ticket to jail. I'm not stupid."

"I didn't say you were stupid."

"Good. I'm glad we agree on something. Now get the keys to one of your police cars and take me out of here."

"You know I can't do that."

With a surge of rage, Terry squeezed harder. Keeler made a sound, and Terry felt something warm and sticky ooze onto his fingers. He was struck with a momentary pang of panic that turned to terror when he heard a *click* beside his temple.

Keeler had his gun out. With the twitch of a finger, he could cover the Captain's diplomas with Terry's head.

"What the hell were you thinking, Terry? This is a police station, for Christ's sake."

Terry released the Lieutenant and took a step back, his eyes fixed to the barrel of the gun. He'd fucked up. He'd fucked up, because he was no good at this. He had no idea what he was doing.

"You were there," Terry said, hoarse, desperate. "Keeler, you were there. You put me away, the guys who killed Lyman—they're still going to be out there. Is that really what you want?"

Keeler swallowed, glanced toward the door. Hernandez would be back any second. Then it would be over. Terry had attacked a cop in a police station. He'd never see the light of day again.

And then, Keeler's thumb moved. He uncocked the gun and replaced it in its holster.

"Okay."

⌐⫯⌐

Terry watched Keeler through the windows of the Captain's office. He was standing with his back to the door, leaning on crutches. Terry couldn't hear what he was saying, but from his posture, he could see the man was nervous. Maybe that meant he was actually going through with it.

When Keeler finally came back, he looked as pale as a sheet. "He's not buying it."

Terry's heart sank.

"So we're going anyway. He's taking ten minutes in the break room. Told him you pissed me off and I'm getting you into a cell. Follow me, Terry, and don't—for the love of god—*do not* say a word. To anyone."

On the highway, they drove until the sun began to fall from its zenith and glare into their eyes. Keeler remained on-edge, and Terry could sense in him a certain uneasy anxiousness, a longing to say something he couldn't quite get out. Terry was in no mood to finesse him, though.

"Can you tell me something?" Keeler asked when they pulled away from a gas station. "Can you tell me who she is?"

Of course. It wasn't only Lyman's death that had convinced the Lieutenant to put his career on the line.

Terry shook his head.

"I'm not asking for . . . I mean, I know you don't trust me and you don't like me. That's fair enough after what happened in there. But we're sort of in this together now, and I was just wondering if you could let me know . . . for myself, not for any kind of investigation."

Terry looked at him, and it was then that he saw Keeler for what he really was: not an asshole in a collared suit and a badge, but a human being with feelings and desires. Terry had been blinded with rage all morning, but now, thinking back, he could see the anguish on Keeler's face.

This was an ally.

"I can't tell you who she is," Terry said, "because I don't know."

Keeler sighed, tossed up his hands. "Whatever. Just curious."

"I'm telling you the truth."

"Sure. You're telling me that you traveled across the country, that you killed a man, for a woman you don't even know?"

"Yeah," Terry said. "That's what I'm telling you."

"Right. Why?"

"Have you seen her picture?"

The more they talked, the more it seemed clear they were never going to understand each other. Not too surprising. Terry wasn't sure he understood himself anymore. But he could feel that they were getting close. He didn't dare think that he might see Shayla Hacker in person, but he tantalized himself with the possibility that they could uncover more about her as soon as they got to Three Rooks.

Their conversation wandered. Soon, Keeler was telling Terry all about his family. He had divorced his wife of three years in the preceding autumn. He had wanted to have children and she had wanted to have a glamorous life of travel. They hadn't been able to find a middle ground.

"Couldn't even afford what she wanted on my salary," he said with a snort. "She was willing to get a job, maybe, but she didn't want anything that would interfere with the travel. I tried to tell her we'd have to save up before we saw the world, but she didn't want it that way. She was from Chicago." As though that explained it all.

But it did, Terry realized. She was from a different world. Most people from the coasts or the big cities didn't understand what it was like to live in a small town all their lives. He looked at Keeler and he could see what she had probably been thinking— she was going to come out to the heartland and marry herself a stocky country boy who would charm her with his accent and simple ways and show her how the other half lived. Except she hadn't wanted to actually live that way; she'd just wanted a glimpse. By the time they stopped for dinner, Terry felt as though he had known Keeler for years

"Hey, Keeler," he said as they stepped back out into the parking lot, his belly full of greasy diner food. "I'm . . ." He trailed off, eyes moving from Keeler's questioning face to the shadows behind him.

At the corner of the lot, there were a couple of cars parked together. It was too dark to see anything certain about the drivers, but the vehicles were definitely black—probably Fords.

"Oh, shit," Terry whispered.

Keeler started to turn, but Terry grabbed his shoulder. "Don't look. Don't let them know we've seen them."

"Who?" Keeler breathed.

Terry met his eye. "Who do you think?"

They made for the squad car, Terry helping Keeler along. Safe inside, Keeler squinted across the lot at the two cars. "Terry, let me call for backup."

"No."

"We need all the help we can get."

"They won't understand. They'll blame me for all of this. They'll say they're with me."

"I'll vouch for you."

"You just smuggled me out of your police station. How much do you think they'll trust you?"

Keeler sat back and closed his mouth.

Without flipping on the lights, Terry brought the squad car around and accelerated back onto the highway. It was dark out here; the streetlamps were sparse, and only half of them were lit due to some energy-saving measure they had just passed in the local government.

He felt the tension begin to ease. There was nothing in the rearview mirror. Perhaps he had been wrong. Perhaps it had been a pair of mortician brothers or just a couple of random strangers with similar taste.

He kept his eyes on the mirror as pools of orange light receded behind them. One, two, three—all empty. And then, in the fourth, as he was about to bring his eyes back to the road ahead, he caught a glint of metal. The car didn't have its lights on. Even morticians turned their lights on.

"Keeler?" He kept his voice soft, even. "What do they train you to do when you think you're being followed?"

The Lieutenant twisted around in his seat. "We're supposed to confront them. You know, show them our badges and figure out what the hell's going on."

"I don't think so." Terry pressed a little harder on the gas. The supercharged police engine roared beneath the hood, and they shot forward. Try as he might to power them out of harm's way, every time he looked back, he could just make out the dark shape in the rearview mirror.

And it was getting closer.

"Confront them," Keeler had said. The thought made Terry shiver. These people weren't interested in talking. Whoever they were, they were out for blood, and they'd do everything in their power to stop Terry and Keeler from getting to Indiana.

"Get your gun out," he told Keeler.

The Lieutenant asked him something, but Terry wasn't paying attention anymore. He eased back on the accelerator, his eyes still riveted to the mirror. The shape grew a little before the other driver realized what was happening, and braked to match his new speed.

"Hold on," Terry said, "this is going to get rough."

In the same split-second, he let up on the accelerator, yanked up the emergency brake, and spun the wheel to the right as sharply as he could. The police car veered off the road, spinning around in a near-perfect 180-degree turn. As they slid onto the shoulder, Terry flipped on the brights. The white beams cut across the black paint job of the car behind them. For a few instants, it was exposed in pure, naked light.

Then, the other driver turned as well. The black Ford skidded to the left, heading toward the opposite shoulder.

Terry gunned the engine, released the brake, and slammed on

the accelerator. The police car leapt forward, charging across the open highway to the other side just as the Ford was grinding to a halt.

The impact came before he'd been ready for it. He thought they had another good hundred feet or so, but the black Ford hadn't slowed as fast as he thought it was going to. There was a loud *crunch* from the front of the car, and the feeling of grinding metal shook beneath his feet throughout the entire frame. Then there was a poof of white and something soft was massaging his nose and cheeks.

And then they were stopped.

Terry struggled to get free of the airbag as it slowly deflated, spewing powder and dust all over his lap. Next to him, Keeler blinked, shook his head, coughed. "You okay?" Terry asked him.

The Lieutenant nodded weakly.

Terry scrambled out of the driver's seat and caught himself. He was dizzy. The ground seemed to be rising and falling like ocean waves beneath his feet, and the night sky was spinning over his head.

The black Ford lay on its side in the ditch beside the road. He hadn't realized they'd hit it with such force; they all must have been going faster than he had thought. The car was covered in dents and scratches, the windows shattered, the roof bent out of shape. He could see the outlines of two passengers lying slumped across each other inside.

Terry struggled with the passenger door and finally succeeded in wrenching open the one behind it. Someone in the cabin groaned.

"Get out!" Terry snapped. "Get out of the car."

A moan. It was two men, one of them large and stocky, the other one more average in size. The large one wasn't moving, and there was blood all over his face. *Shit*, Terry thought in a moment of clarity. *Vehicular homicide. I just killed someone.*

Keeler stumbled up behind him. "Terry?" he said weakly. "What's going on up there?"

With Keeler's help, Terry extricated the smaller man. He stuck his head back into the Ford through the shattered passenger window, but he could see that the larger man was a lost cause. The man wasn't breathing, his eyes open, staring blindly at the windshield.

They propped the smaller man against the rear bumper of the police car. He had short black hair, buzzed like a marine's, and he was wearing an expensive black suit with a black shirt and a black tie. In any other circumstances, he might have been funny, so ridiculously monochromatic. But there was something about him that frightened Terry. He looked like a member of the mafia—like he meant business.

There was a gold chain around his neck. Terry tugged at it, and it came loose from his collar to expose a cross. No help there. Probably plenty of religious people in the death industry.

The man stirred, and his eyelids began to flutter beneath the red glow of the taillights.

Terry gave his cheeks a few gentle slaps. "Hey," Terry said. "Wake up. Who the hell are you?"

It took them almost ten minutes to revive him enough to speak, and then he started babbling in some other language—something European, Terry thought. It wasn't Spanish, or at least, if it was, it was a different dialect from the one Terry had heard in South America. Not French either, by the sound of it—too harsh.

"What do you want from us?" Terry asked.

The man glared defiantly up at them and closed his mouth.

"Who's paying you to follow us?"

Without replying, the small man started to hoist himself to his feet. Terry grabbed him by the shoulders and forced him back down. The movement caused his suit jacket to shift, exposing another gold chain hanging from his vest, beneath the buttoned edges. Terry pulled at it and found himself holding another cross. This one was slightly different. It was more ornate, and there was writing on the back.

He showed it to Keeler, but neither of them knew what to make of it. So the man was part of some religious order? Some kind of cult? The more they learned, the less sense it all made.

Then Terry had a thought. He reached into his pocket and searched around until he found what he was looking for. He pulled the folded Xerox copy of Shayla Hacker's picture out and flattened it on his knee. The man squinted at it, curious, until recognition flooded over his face.

He squirmed and tried to look away.

"Yeah, you know her, don't you?" Terry said. "Shayla. Shayla Hacker."

"No!" the man exclaimed. He twisted and struggled and tried to turn away.

Terry shot a glance at Keeler, and the Lieutenant reached in to steady him. Under normal circumstances, the man could probably have taken them both. As large and loose as the black suit was, it could scarcely conceal his bulging muscles. But he was badly shaken from the accident, and Terry thought he might have had a broken leg.

"No!" He repeated. He said a couple of other things in what Terry thought was probably Italian. "Don't!" he managed. "I will tell to you."

Terry stopped with the picture, turned it away. "Tell," he said. "Who are you?"

"Antonio Furia."

"Why are you chasing us?"

"Because you are chasing her."

"And who is she? Who is Shayla Hacker?"

Furia shook his head. "That is why we chase you. You cannot know. Nobody can know."

"Why not? What is it about her?"

"She is a cursed child. She should not exist! We stand in the way of all who seek to find her."

"Why didn't you just kill her? Why track down everyone else who's seen her picture?"

Furia's eyes grew wide. "Because that would be the gravest of sins! We would all be consigned to hell."

"I don't understand. It's okay to kill us, but not to kill her?"

The small man nodded. "That is true."

"What is Three Rooks?"

"A town."

Terry tried struggled to stay patient. "I know that. What's the significance?"

"That was where she was born."

"And she's there now?"

"It is possible."

"I'm going to ask you one more time: Who is she?"

Furia shook his head. "You cannot do anything to me that would make me tell you such things."

He began to unfold the Xerox again. He felt Furia's breathing quicken beneath the hand he had on the man's chest, but still, he would not talk.

"Kill me!" Furia hissed. "I would rather you kill me than make me one of you!"

Terry paused. "What does that mean?"

"You are all mad. You see her picture and you want to find her. It is an insanity, a sickness. It began with her, but it spreads through the picture."

"That's the craziest thing I've ever heard," Keeler said, but there was a definite hint of doubt in his voice.

"There are dozens of you. Hundreds. She spreads like the plague. You all want to find her. None of you realize the effect she is having until it is too late." Furia averted his eyes. "Do not show me the picture. I have never seen her face, and I do not wish to now."

"Then tell me who she is."

Furia went silent. Terry shook his head and finished opening the page. He nodded at Keeler, who leaned in and grabbed the man's head with one hand, and one of his eyelids with the other. Furia cried out in Italian, and began thrashing like a harpooned whale. He worked his jaw as though chewing or biting at something, and then suddenly, as abruptly as he had begun, he stopped. His body went limp in Terry's arms, his eyes out of focus, his jaw slack.

"Shit," Keeler said. "He's dead. What the hell just happened?"

Terry had a sinking feeling he knew. He pulled open Furia's mouth. In the light from the police car's tail lamps, he could just make out the milky residue around the man's teeth and the back of his mouth. It was an old trick, something Terry thought they only did in the movies.

"Cyanide," he said, standing and refolding the paper. "He killed himself rather than look at her face." He tucked the picture gingerly back into his pocket.

What if Furia was right? Terry had noticed irregularities in his own behavior of late—the violence, the lies, the desperation.

Christ, he thought.

He was insane.

Keeler rose beside him. "Now what?"

"Now," Terry said, "we go to Three Rooks and finish this once and for all."

Chapter 25

The pictures that adorned the walls of Shayla Hacker's room in the asylum were going to give Joseph nightmares. Scribbled out in blunt colored pencil, they were like children's drawings gone horribly wrong. A family of three stood smiling together, linked by the hands, but behind them, dark shapes skulked in the shadows. Her rainbows were tainted with blacks and grays, her trees and flowers covered in mold or some other cancerous plague he could not identify.

"I felt sorry for her," Jeanine said, sitting on her bed. "See, they all thought she was crazy, paranoid, because she thought people were following her all the time. But she wasn't. I saw the people. Nobody else paid her any mind. I think in the end she was crazy, but it wasn't her fault. It was ours. We told her that reality was false, and what is that going to do to a girl?"

Joseph knelt and picked up what looked to be one of the older pictures, one of a chessboard with only three pieces left on it. None of them were kings. *Silly little child*, he thought. All castles. It was like a fairytale. He could imagine a kid building a whole world out of a chessboard, penciling in tiny, little knights and damsels to scurry around the feet of the massive horses, pawns, and bishops.

"They came around looking for her afterward," she went on. "The black men."

Joseph looked sharply back at her. "Who?"

"The guys in suits. Looked like mafia or government agents or something."

"Who were they?"

"Wouldn't say. Said she was needed in some kind of case. Police business, only they weren't policemen."

"How do you know?"

"I know."

Joseph raised an eyebrow.

"Do policemen show up out of uniform with gold crosses chained around their necks and waists?"

Gold crosses? Joseph frowned. What kind of people were these? "Do you know what any of these pictures mean?"

She shrugged. "Pretty obvious, right? I mean, they're people following her. Everywhere. I'm no doctor, but I can see that." She pointed to one of the drawings, the same happy family of three in a station wagon, and behind them a black sedan filled with people drawn in matching black. "Her parents never believed her either. Foster parents, I should say."

"You knew her parents?"

"I knew she was adopted or something. Shady business, all of that. She didn't have the proper paperwork, but there was nobody to call out on it. Parents were nowhere to be seen when she finally ended up here. They'd disappeared."

Joseph scanned the rest of the room and then his gaze returned to the picture he was holding. "So what about this one?" he asked, showing it to her. "Where are the men in black here?"

Jeanine squinted at it. "Beats me," she said. "Three castles. I don't know what that means. Some kind of chess move?"

Joseph shook his head. "You need kings for there to be a game." *Three castles.* Strange.

⚮

It was getting dark by the time Joseph emerged from the asylum and tilted his head back toward the evening sky. The trees in the courtyard stood utterly still in an airless night. It felt as though the world were holding its breath, waiting for something profound to interrupt the monotony of life.

Jeanine stopped him as he picked his way back through the tall grass toward the front of the complex. "It's late," she said. "Surely you're not leaving now . . . ?"

He shivered at the thought of spending the night out here and told her that he had come in an RV and that he had things to attend to. He wasn't sure what it was, but something about her lonely, cloying manner rubbed him wrong. She stroked the back of his neck as he passed her and he realized with a slight shock that she had been trying to seduce him all evening.

It was the first time in a very long time that anyone had taken that kind of interest in him. He and Jean had felt no passion in their marriage for some considerable number of years. It should have been nice, but instead, it gnawed at him, rubbing salt into a wound he hadn't realized he had been nursing.

He was lonely—achingly lonely. His marriage had fallen apart. Walking back to the RV, keys dangling from his fingers, it was the first time he fully accepted it. It would've been easy to blame it on something simple, the collapse of the house, but he knew in his heart that it was far more complicated than that. Their relationship had been deteriorating for longer than he could remember. He couldn't think of the last time they had lit a few candles, turned on some soft music, and waltzed slowly around the living room the way they had every Friday night right after they were married. He couldn't think of the last time they had been to a movie together on a Saturday afternoon. He couldn't even think of the last time they had shared a bottle of champagne.

After a couple of minutes, Joseph put the RV into gear and slowly pulled off of the dirt shoulder onto the highway again. He had no idea where he was going, knew only that he wanted to be away from the asylum after nightfall.

He had been planning to return the following day to search

for more clues, but the farther he got from the small cement com-
pound, the farther he wanted to be. Jeanine's face kept appearing
in his mind, her little half-smile, her eagerness, her pity for Shayla
Hacker. She was condemned to spend her life out here. The very
idea gave him gooseflesh.

⌒⫫⌒

An hour later, he rolled into a small town and stopped to top off
the gas tank and get a cup of coffee from a local diner. The waitress put him in a booth by the window that could have accommodated a party of sixteen. He felt small and very alone, wedged into
the curving leather bench seat.

Even the coffee cup looked forlorn. He sipped at it and peered
out the window at the fluorescent lights in the convenience store
across the road. It was some off-brand mini-mart, not even a 7-
Eleven, probably erected in a matter of weeks sometime in the
1980s. People were always sentimental about small-town America,
but they didn't know what they were talking about. The family-
owned fruit stands and single-room schoolhouses had long ago
vanished between folding blankets of corporate chains and white
trash suburban sprawl.

Over his second cup of coffee, he took out Shayla's drawing
and studied it, trying to think of any other meanings it might
have. The chessboard was drawn with little detail, but it looked as
though it had been constructed carefully, as though it were fash-
ioned after some particular design.

He started to fold it up as he got out his wallet when the waitress
smiled and nodded her head at it. "You from Indiana?" she asked.

He looked up at her. "Beg your pardon?"

"Three Rooks. That's their flag. My brother went to school
there, before the university closed. Smallest town in the world.
That's why I noticed. Never see anyone from those parts."

Joseph took the paper back out and showed it to her, just to
be sure. She nodded before he'd even spread it flat on the table.

"That's it," she said. "Yeah, wow, it's been ages since I've thought of that place. Used to hate it, but you know, it'd probably be a nice place to raise your children. So you're not from around there?"

On his way back out to the RV, Joseph chided himself. That was the first rule in detective work—question the locals. Their combined knowledge would dwarf any amount of studious police training and provide a wealth of details he couldn't even dream up on his own.

The waitress hadn't been entirely sure of how to get to Three Rooks, but she'd given Joseph a rough set of directions that took him from one small highway to another. "I don't remember for sure," she'd said, "but I think there are some stretches where you'll have to take a gravel road or two. Don't know how that'll go with your RV."

Joseph didn't know how well it would go either. He knew only one thing: that he had to find Shayla Hacker, and the sooner the better. She was destroying his life. The strange part was, the more clearly he saw it, the more he longed to find her, to finish this once and for all.

He was sick, but he could get help when this was over. It was no time to jump off of her trail just because he was afraid for his own sanity. He would have plenty of time to recuperate once he'd found her.

All traces of fatigue drained from his body. Maybe it was the two cups of coffee, or maybe the revelation that had arrived with them. Whatever it was, Joseph knew that he would get no sleep that night.

From dusk till dawn, he remained glued to the steering wheel. Three Rooks was only a matter of hours from where he was now.

Chapter 26

Debbie Wendell spent the most miserable night of her life beneath the stars and the dripping tropical vegetation. It had rained for more than three hours, and the rest of the time, it was so moist that she felt as though she were sleeping on a bath mat just outside the largest shower in the world.

Yeager had grown tight-lipped as soon as they had entered the village the night before, and he silenced her whenever she tried to ask a question or make some kind of visual contact with one of the locals.

The people here were all shockingly gaunt, but though they appeared impoverished, they seemed to go about their simple lives with an air of self-satisfaction that astounded her. She wondered who they were, tucked away out here among the ferns and the palm trees as they had been for longer than she could imagine.

Yeager shook her awake at sunrise the following morning. She thought at first that he wanted them to leave the village before anyone noticed their departure, but she saw as soon as they climbed over the rise and into the settlement that they were the last ones out of bed.

A roaring fire in the cooking pit already lapped at fresh meat that looked as though it had been speared that morning. Children were huddled around it, warming their wet skin before the flames and thrusting carved, wooden bowls at their mothers every time one of them walked past.

Debbie rubbed the sleep from her eyes and tried to catch up with Yeager as he descended into the shallow basin. She had finally gotten to sleep shortly before dawn, and she felt now as though she were living in a dream. She could scarcely recall the details of the day before—the airplane ride, the bouncing trip up the dirt road in the Land Rover. It all seemed so far away now, part of another life.

One of the mothers handed her a bowl full of warm broth, and after the children had been served, she found a small hunk of meat deposited among a few wilting vegetables and chunks of what she hoped was a potato. While she picked at her food, she tried to decipher some of what Yeager was saying. He struck up an energetic conversation with one of the elders as soon as they had arrived, and though they had not seemed to know each other, they quickly adopted an affable, friendly demeanor.

By the time he finished eating, Yeager was laughing and muttering to himself in Portuguese. He took Debbie firmly by the shoulders and guided her up away from the fire.

"What's going on?" she hissed, as soon as they were out of earshot. "Where are we going?"

He fixed her with a gaze that was part impatience, part general irritation. She didn't like that. His attitude seemed to have changed overnight. Perhaps it was the unforgiving conditions or perhaps it was something one of the villagers had told him, but he seemed, now more than ever, more inclined toward violence.

"They've directed me to the temple," he said.

"The temple?" He didn't bite. "Lewis, what fucking temple?"

"It's a cult," he said. "They have a temple."

Great, she thought. *I wonder if they perform ritual sacrifices, too.*

They hiked up through the wilderness, the ground a steep slope beneath them. She grew weary the longer they moved. She didn't realize how much elevation they had gained until she turned to survey their progress. Far below on the curving forest floor, she could just make out the spot of light that must have been the village. It looked small and rustic and insignificant, but strangely enough, it looked homey.

She couldn't explain the feeling. Perhaps it was just a desire for civilization of any kind. All she knew was that she wanted more than ever to turn back and wait for Yeager to finish his little crusade on his own. It was not until she thought of the box that she mustered the strength to pick up her pace. There was something about it that nagged her on a deeper level than the money it represented—deeper, even, than the prospect of saving her mother.

They reached a summit, and it was there that for the first time Debbie realized how beautiful it was here. They were perched on a saddle between two valleys. Lush green opulence stretched out on either side around them. It was like nothing she had ever seen before, like standing in an ocean of growth or on a carpet of life that stretched from wall to distant wall.

Yeager took her arm and pointed as she paused to catch her breath. "The temple," he said.

She looked where he was indicating, and then she saw it. She understood why she had missed it the first time; it blended almost seamlessly into the jungle around it. Only a few large stone blocks separated it from the foliage that crowded its borders, but what little she could see from here was breathtaking in its breadth and magnificent artistry alone.

Before she could ask a single question, he was charging ahead, hacking at the underbrush with a wooden spear one of the villagers had given him in exchange for his wristwatch.

They made fast progress across the adjoining valley, but even so, it was late afternoon by the time they began climbing the opposite side. Distances were so deceptive out here. She was used to the city, where mileage was either posted on a green highway sign or visible by blocks and intersections through the morning haze. Here, what appeared to be only a short stroll would turn out to be a day's hike or more. It was because you could see so far, she realized. Out here, a mile was only a tiny fold in the blanket of green growth that covered the whole world.

Then they were there. One moment there was nothing but trees and swaying leaves ahead of them, and the next, she was standing before a stone slab the size of a car.

Her jaw dropped. It was not a volcanic boulder or a granite deposit, but a head carved into a massive rock, carted here from god knew where. She stopped in her tracks and stared up at the empty eyes, the sloping forehead, the nose that protruded ten feet off the ground.

"It's incredible." She hated how weak and naïve she sounded, but at the same time, that hardly seemed to matter anymore. She must have looked like a schoolgirl, standing before the ocean for the first time in her life.

Yeager broke into a smile. "Beautiful, isn't it? And this is only the outside. Wait until we get in. I've seen paintings, and the villagers said it has been magnificently maintained."

"But how . . . where did this come from? Whose work are we looking at?"

He hiked back down to join her before the head. "Some say the Aztecs, maybe the Incas, although both of those were more concentrated in the North, in Mexico. Truth is, nobody knows for sure where these came from. There's something of a phenomenon. Again, most of them are in Mexico, but every now and then, a stray one will turn up here and there. They're art, we presume. That or some kind of spiritual statue designed to evoke the kind of reverence we feel when we walk into a church."

"It works."

"Just you wait."

They clambered up the steep stone steps to the foot of the temple itself. It was absolutely incredible. Shaped like a rough pyramid, though not as smooth as those in Egypt, it was studded with steps that ascended the broad sides in sturdy, carved magnificence. There was a small shelter at the very top that stood over a wide, flat table, and a few other columns and elements she couldn't quite see from down here.

Several other buildings, equally weathered by thousands of years' exposure, stood about the base of the pyramid.

"What is this place?" she breathed. There was something about the entire area that felt—*wrong*. It looked more like a sacrificial burial ground than a home for any civilized society.

"A spiritual factory," Yeager said. "They build things out here the likes of which nobody else on this Earth has seen for a thousand years. We should count ourselves lucky to be among the privileged few who ever have such an opportunity." He took a few faltering steps forward, and it was then that she saw the awed, glassy sheen in his eyes.

"Lewis, I don't like this."

"Come on." He turned back to her, all boyish excitement again. "We're almost there now."

"Something's wrong."

"Nothing's wrong. This is where we'll find our answers. You wanted answers, didn't you?"

"Lewis—"

It was too late. Before she could pry him away, she saw that they weren't alone any longer. Faces were peering out at them through tiny holes between the stone blocks. She hadn't noticed them at first, and she didn't know how long they had been there. Perhaps that was why she had felt uneasy—the sensation of being watched.

She edged closer to Yeager, who frowned at her before looking around, seeing them himself. "Be calm," he said. "No sudden moves. Don't give them any reason to become angry."

Now aware that they had been spotted, the natives edged out from behind the rock walls and columns. There were about a dozen of them. They were not what she had been expecting—no face paint, no loincloths, no tribal tattoos. They wore khaki shorts, some of them with grimy polo shirts. Most of them had sandals.

They closed in around Debbie and Yeager, forming a circle. She didn't like that; there was no escape from this. Yeager said something in Portuguese. The natives looked at each other. No recognition. He tried Spanish and a couple of other languages Debbie couldn't understand.

"What do they want?" she hissed at Yeager.

"What do *you* want?" The voice, deep and imposing, came from behind her.

Debbie whirled and scanned the faces of the men at her flank. All of them were dark, colored golden-brown by the sun. There was something strange about these people. Their skin was wrinkled and leathery, but there was a life in their eyes, a grace in the way they moved that suggested they were far younger than they appeared.

Her eyes stopped on one man who was raising his eyebrows at her. He was a good six inches taller than she was, with long brown hair tied back in a ponytail. If he shaved and put on a suit, she thought, he wouldn't have looked out of place on Wall Street or behind a desk at a recording studio. He had a square jaw, ruddy features—as though his face had been sculpted by hands too large and impatient to properly finish him.

"You speak English?" she asked. He nodded.

"Good," Yeager said, putting an arm around Debbie's shoulders. He was trying to look supportive, protective; in reality, she knew he was purposely holding her back. This was none of her business, he was saying. She should keep her mouth shut. "Perhaps you can help us."

"Why should we help you?"

"We're looking for information."

"You have not come to the right place."

"We're willing to compensate you."

The man raised an eyebrow. "Let us talk."

The man—when pressed, he identified himself only as Smith—led them and the group of natives past the looming temple pyramid to the cluster of ancient stone houses just beyond it. Debbie couldn't imagine anyone living here. It was more like a museum or an archaeological dig than any kind of home. She saw no place to sleep, nowhere to eat, and no decent shelter from the rain that began pattering through the treetops.

They crowded into one of the small huts, built of weathered stone and fortified with clay. It was uncomfortably close. Debbie felt like she could barely breathe.

Smith knelt and slid aside a wooden cover that had been concealing an opening beneath their feet. He removed from it a couple of wooden bowls and some sealed containers of something that looked like curry. He scooped it out, shooing away the flies and other insects that coursed toward the bowls like lapping waves on the ocean shore. Each of them received one.

Debbie raised the bowl to her nose and sniffed. It was curious—mangos and other spices she couldn't hope to identify. She took a bite. At first it was cool, refreshing, but after she swallowed, her mouth began to sting as though she had just bitten into a wasp's nest.

She threw a quick glance toward Yeager, but he was quietly devouring the contents of his bowl as if it were Shredded Wheat. Finishing, he set it down and looked levelly up at Smith.

Smith was impressed. "Now," he said, "what sort of offer do you have in mind?"

"You made a box here."

"We make lots of things."

"It was for a girl. Her name is Shayla Hacker. This was not too long ago. Within the last year or two."

There was a glimmer in Smith's eye. "Perhaps I know what you are talking about," he said. There was no *perhaps* about it. "What sort of compensation did you have in mind?"

"We will make it worth your while," Yeager said. "Anything you like. Just tell us what you know."

Debbie felt her stomach turn. Her mouth still on fire, she reached out, grabbed Yeager's arm and shook her head, but he wasn't paying attention to her. One thing she had learned the hard way through years and years of difficult business with difficult people: never promise anyone anything they like.

Smith smiled. "I think we can reach an agreement after all," he said.

He turned and as the natives cleared a path, he filed out of the little stone hut and into the courtyard. The rain had begun to patter on the leaves overhead, and Debbie saw the puddles come alive with rippling reflections and stirred up muck. Smith said nothing, heading toward the pyramid.

Yeager plowed after him, and Debbie had no choice but to follow suit. They reached the edge of the pyramid, and her uneasy feeling intensified. The temple seemed to be swimming with bad omens—with death. It had been the silent observer to hundreds of atrocities throughout a thousand years. This was not a place for people; this was a place for the silent generations to pass in solitude.

Smith climbed the steps, and Yeager and Debbie followed. The rain began to pelt harder, sheeting through the trees. Debbie peered up at the top of the temple, at the stone slab and the columns around it. Was Smith going to show them anything, or was he simply going to pitch them down the other side?

They never got to find out. Halfway up, Smith picked his way off of the staircase and onto one of the contoured platforms that wrapped around the outside of the pyramid. He proceeded toward one edge of the temple, his bare feet crossing stone after carved stone.

Debbie stared downward as they walked, trying to make out some of the inscriptions. All of the writing was in languages she could not understand, but the images that accompanied it were frightening enough in their own right. The ancient carvings depicted some kind of strange ritual. She couldn't make out many of the details, but it looked violent. The farther they walked, the more singular the carvings grew, until they dwelled obsessively on one woman and her infant child.

At last, they reached a stone that bore only the child's likeness. It reminded her of something she had seen on the side of the box. At the time, she had thought it was another studded gemstone or perhaps an artist's rendering of the sun or a distant continent, but she saw now, in the context of the other pictures, that it was a tiny baby, swathed in a cocoon-like bassinet.

Smith knelt. She watched his calloused fingertips trace the lines that bore into the edges of the stone before plunging into a tiny hole whose muddy filling had obscured it from view.

The sound of grinding stone echoed up from somewhere deep inside the temple. She could feel the vibrations through her feet. An opening formed before them as the door slid aside. Beyond was a blackness so pure and deep, it seemed almost palpable.

Smith stepped aside. "Go ahead," he said.

Yeager turned to Debbie. She shook her head. Every self-preserving voice inside her was screaming not to go inside. Yeager tried to pull her toward the opening, but she resisted. After a moment, he sighed and clambered into the lead.

Smith would not allow her to remain alone, and the other natives had stayed back in the stone hut at the temple's foot. Now, she wished she had stayed with them. But with Yeager ahead, at least she would have some kind of warning of what was to come.

She felt her heart beating hard in her chest as she climbed in after him. *This is just like work back at home*, she told herself. She could imagine that this was an air duct or a maintenance passageway, just another contract for her to fill by the end of the day.

At last, they emerged into a larger chamber. It was illuminated only by the dim rays of afternoon light from outside, but once Smith had entered, he lit a pair of torches by the door and took one for himself. In the flickering firelight, Debbie saw that the room was some kind of waiting chamber. There were a couple of stone benches, and attached to them, strange metal contraptions that had obviously been added years after the temple's construction. The walls were utterly bare. While outside, the architects had poured hours into the dazzling sculptures and carvings that adorned the temple, here, it was almost as though they had stopped caring about the building's image altogether. Why was that, she wondered? Wouldn't it make more sense to adorn the place with ever-greater beauty the farther into its heart one crawled?

"This way," Smith breathed, shuffling past them through a gaping maw of a doorway.

Debbie tried again to catch Yeager's eye, but he was like an enthralled young boy, captivated by everything around him.

Something in his gaze frightened Debbie. Irrationally, she thought of something he had said shortly after they had met, when he had just brought her back to his little suburban house. It was something about a picture that would drive her crazy. He hadn't let her look at it, but now she wondered what it had contained, because now he looked like a picture of a person—a picture that could easily drive her insane.

The next room gave her chills. In the center, there was a table made of a giant marble slab. Strange machinery—mostly made of stone with a few newer metal pieces added sometime many years after its initial construction—surrounded the table. Stone arms dropped from the ceiling and strange little metal instruments were strewn around the edges. The tabletop itself was shiny and black, but even so, Debbie could see that it had been stained with some kind of dark fluid. *Blood*, she thought. It was a gut feeling. Humans knew when they were near death.

"This is where we made it," Smith said.

"Yes." Yeager stopped in the doorway and stared at the tabletop, entranced. "This was where it happened."

"She came out of here a changed woman. Just like the prophecies."

Debbie blinked. She had thought they were talking about the box, but suddenly, she wasn't sure.

"We had been expecting her, of course. She was part of a legend we have cherished for many centuries."

"Yes."

"Her arrival was predicted down to the month. We were prepared on the first day, and waited three weeks until at last she was brought here to us."

"Yes."

It was as though Debbie had just drifted into some bizarre nightmare. "Wait," she said. "What the hell are you talking about? You're not making any sense."

Smith and Yeager looked at her.

"Who brought her here?" Debbie demanded.

"The escort."

"What escort?"

Smith slowly shook his head. "Nobody knows where they come from. It is not our place to ask. We only perform that which it was prescribed for us to perform."

"Describe them," she growled.

"They wore all black. They arrived from the sky."

Debbie rolled her eyes. *An airplane*, she thought. *Right?*

"They brought her here as they were supposed to. We had the box ready."

Debbie stiffened. "What was in it? What was so valuable that they had to fly this girl down here to pick up a box made in a fucking tomb?"

Smith looked at her, and it was not the indignant irritation in his eyes that frightened her, but rather the ill-concealed mirth. He was laughing at her for her naïveté. "Why," he said with the utmost care and delicacy, "her daughter."

Debbie's heart skipped a beat. "What do you mean?"

"She bore an abomination, a thread that could unravel everything."

Cold chills crept down Debbie's neck. "You put her daughter in that box?"

"We helped the daughter transcend, and the mother absorb. The box was merely for what remained of the physical vessel."

She tried to fight back the panic and rage that she could feel spinning in her head. "Why would you do such a thing?"

"It was written. I can show you the prophecy if you desire. We knew she was coming, and we knew what she could do. She is the last piece of a puzzle that began two thousand years ago."

"Where did she go?" Yeager spoke up. He was smiling, delighted by the gruesome story. "Once she had the box . . ."

". . . and the transformation," Smith interrupted. "It was visible in her eyes. That was how we knew we were successful. That was how we knew the revolution had begun."

"It wasn't a revolution. It was murder!" Debbie cried.

"She returned to America," Smith told Yeager. "She wanted to put her daughter to rest where she, herself, was born—Three Rooks, in the state of Indiana."

"Then that is where we must go!" Yeager exploded.

Debbie shook her head. "We have to call the police. We have to put an end to all of this."

"The police cannot do anything," Smith interrupted. "Nobody can. They are trying right now—the servants of the other faith. They will fail. So will you."

Debbie took a step back, turned toward the gaping door. Suddenly, she had to be out of the temple. She could feel the stale air inundating her, could feel the spirits of the dead perching on her shoulders. This place was going to swallow her whole if she let her guard down. "I'm leaving," she said.

Yeager caught her by one arm. "To Indiana," he said, more of a command than a question.

Debbie shook her head. She had followed Yeager on his silly little obsessive warpath for long enough. It wasn't worth it anymore. She had to see her mother. That was all that was important.

"You will wait," Smith bellowed after them as they started toward the exit. "We have not yet discussed," he said with a worrisome smile, "your compensation."

"What do you want?" Yeager asked him.

"What do you think?"

"I think you speak very good English."

"I think we need another box."

Debbie stared at him. What kind of place was this, where human sacrifice was bandied about like gold coins and credit cards? She felt as though she had stepped off of the last plane into the past, into a past that should never have been.

"One of you will not leave this place," Smith said. "I leave up to you who stays." He winked at Debbie. "Though I have a preference if you do not."

Debbie shrank toward the door. "Why? What possible purpose do you have?"

"Worship."

"Why would you worship the kind of God who requires pain and suffering for no reason?"

"Because He has never been wrong about anything in our lives, and He will not be wrong about this. He is hungry. He needs to be fed, and He likes the taste of the exotic."

Debbie leaned to Yeager. "Lewis," she whispered, "let's get the fuck out of here before this psychopath does something we're all going to regret."

Yeager looked at her over his shoulder, and for a moment, she thought perhaps she had broken the bizarre spell that had come over him. His eyes narrowed. "You cannot be serious," he said. "I will be the one." He turned back to Smith. "Me. Take me."

"You're sure?"

"Lewis!" Debbie screamed. "What the hell do you think you're doing?"

"I have spent half my life in search of that box. To end up in one myself is the greatest honor I can possibly conceive."

"You're insane! He said they made it less than a year ago. This isn't your life's work, Lewis; this is temporary madness. Come back home with me and we'll get you the help you need." She glared past him to Smith. "Far, far from this god-forsaken place."

Smith stepped forward and put an arm lewdly around Yeager's neck. "On the contrary," he said with a serpentine smile. "This is the closest you will ever come to God."

"Just promise me one thing, Debbie," Yeager said. "Promise me you'll find Shayla Hacker in Three Rooks. It is my dying wish."

Debbie turned and ran.

It was a blur to her. There was darkness, the cool, moist stone scraping against her shins as she struggled up through one identical passage after another, eyes searching only for the light. Then there was the heavy air, the rain, the dying sun, the eyes of the natives.

They stood in a silent cluster in one of the huts, watching her with dim, obedient, mindless eyes.

She bounded down the side of the temple, skipping steps, stumbling, barely keeping her balance. Mud splashed up her legs as she hit the ground, but she didn't even feel it. She darted into the jungle as fast as her legs would carry her, racing through the vines and leaves so fast that she might have been going the wrong direction, for all she knew.

A deeper, baser survival instinct pumped adrenaline through her veins, pressing her body to its limits, propelling her closer to the village and her single chance at escape.

Debbie ran until there was no more energy left. She tripped on a protruding stone and fell flat on her face in the mud. When she tried to rise again, she found she could not. Her muscles simply would not obey her any longer. She lay there, pathetic, worthless, watching as curious insects crawled toward her. *I'm going to die out here*, she thought. The jungle was going to swallow her whole, and then the natives would haul her corpse back to the temple to pack into a tiny box.

But try as she might, she could force herself to move no farther, and it was there among the ferns and stagnant water that she spent the duration of the night.

Debbie felt sick when she awoke. She wasn't sure if it was just a cold from passing another night in the rain, or if there was something more deeply wrong with her. All she knew was that she had restored little of the energy she had expended, and she still had a very long way to go.

Summoning all of her dwindling strength, she clambered to her feet and began limping through the underbrush. By the morning light, she saw that she had indeed been retracing the path they had taken to get out here. That was a good sign. If she got lost now, without a compass, without a map, and without any sense of where she was, there would be no chance of ever seeing civilization again.

Her heart leapt in her chest when she finally saw the village. It had seemed so small, so rustic and inhospitable when they had first crested the hill overlooking it, but now, it might as well have been a Hilton.

Then she heard the scream. It stopped her in her tracks, unmistakably Yeager's voice. She had no idea how far she was from the temple. She looked back across the second valley, and could just make out its stone summit protruding from the trees. A mile? Two?

It was an inhuman noise, remaining in her ears like an infection. The sound of an animal in the last agonizing moments of its life—a man realizing all of the mistakes he had made as his skin and muscle were stripped from his bones.

It was the sound of someone suddenly becoming very close to God.

"Find Shayla Hacker in Three Rooks," he had said. It was his dying request, and now Doctor Lewis Yeager was dead. Was she then bound to carry it out?

They hadn't covered the Land Rover, and now the seats were soaked. She clambered in behind the wheel and peered into the jungle up ahead. It felt good just to touch something plastic, something undeniably man-made, something from the twentieth century.

The road back down to the airstrip was longer and rougher than she remembered. The shoulders had loosened and caved in a little from all the rain, and several times, she almost slid into a ditch or a stand of trees. She wasn't used to driving a stick shift. Back at home, she always took a taxi or the bus. She didn't even have an active driver's license.

The men watched as she slammed on the brakes and skidded to a halt beside the grass field where she and Yeager had landed just a few days ago. In a way, she'd thought that she would never see this place again.

Debbie slept on the grass, and when the plane came in the next morning, she rose and boarded it without looking back at the hut. She could feel the leering gaze of the owner and shrank away when he touched her between her shoulder blades. Leaving this place, a part of her knew something had been irreparably changed, and that no matter what she did in the rest of her life, nothing was ever going to be quite the same again.

How had Shayla Hacker gone through all of this when she was scarcely more than a child? No wonder she had gone insane.

In Rio de Janeiro, Debbie locked herself in the airport bathroom. She was offended by her own reflection in the mirror. She looked weak, and she hated herself for that. Never in her life had she been weak. Not since she was a child. Not since her father had beat her into a quivering mess of bruises and broken bones.

The last time, she had vowed that she was never going to let any man use her again. He had fractured her skull. He wasn't a drunk. That was the problem with all of the support groups: they assumed you were grappling with alcohol. But it had been more complicated with Victor Wendell, or perhaps, she had sometimes thought, simpler. He had hated his family. It had nothing to do with drugs.

When she'd stepped between him and her mother, he had clocked her with the telephone, and the next thing she remembered, she was waking up in the hospital. The doctors told her she had been in a coma for a month. She was failing all of her classes in school, and she couldn't stand up without crutches.

The rest of the year, everyone looked at her with muted, tactful sympathy. People tried to help her do everything, and what was worse, she had needed them.

When Laura—her mother—had taken ill, she felt as though it was all starting again: the helplessness, the desperation. Better to be somewhere else.

Now, watching the tears roll through the mud caked on her face, she saw she had never really been in control at all. She had put on a convincing charade, but what she was doing now sounded like pure insanity.

She emerged from the bathroom and went to the ticket counter. Right now, at this point in her life, she needed to save Shayla Hacker. She needed to prove to herself that she was still capable of doing something right.

Chapter 27

It was only after they touched down in Indiana that Warren confessed he'd never been on a plane before in his life. Gregory had
known well before that. There had been the little signs, that look
of thrill in his eyes as they taxied to the runway, and the tight grip
and heaving breaths when they finally left the ground.

Once they had their bags, they went straight to the car rental
desks and Gregory got them a modest little sedan. Almost as an
afterthought, he asked the clerk where they might get directions to
Three Rooks.

"Is that a town?" she asked. "I'm sorry, I'm from Seattle. I just
moved here a few days ago." She told them to wait a few moments
and went to consult with her supervisor.

Five minutes later, she returned with an older man—in his
late-20s at most—in tow. There were shadows under his eyes.
"Three Rooks?" he said by way of introduction.

Gregory and Warren looked at each other and nodded.

The kid went to the computer and tapped in a few instructions.
"I've heard of the place. It's just that nobody ever asks about it."

Fifteen minutes and an extensive search later found them
climbing off a bus into the rental car parking lot. Gregory held the
folded computer printout the man had given them. It showed a
rough route on a winding highway through a series of mountains

and valleys that eventually would lead them close to the dot marked *Three Rooks* on the map.

"It's not exact," the clerk had warned, "but for some reason, the computer can't find a road straight into town. You'll have to either drive off-road or hike the last mile or so."

Gregory didn't buy it. It must have been some kind of computer glitch. There wasn't a place in this entire country that wasn't accessible by some kind of road.

"That's just what all you people on the coast think," Warren said. "You get out there and it's wall-to-wall people. I've seen TV even if I've never been there. Place like New York, you can't even see the Earth for all the people. It isn't like that everywhere."

They drove out of town and into the country. It looked a great deal like some of the landscape Gregory had traversed on his way to Trenton, except that the snow had given way to sultry fields of stagnant air and motionless rows of wheat and corn.

They had just settled into an amusing conversation about a TV show they had both happened to catch the week before when Gregory's phone chirped. He frowned and checked the caller ID. It wasn't a number he recognized. He flipped it open and turned it on, but there was no one at the other end. When checked the screen again, it was blank—no active call, no sign that there had ever been one.

"I didn't make that up, right?" He showed Warren the phone. "There was a call just then. Right?"

"I heard it make a noise," Warren said. "But I've never used a cell phone, so I wouldn't know what it meant."

He checked the *Received Calls* log. There was no record of anything today. When he got back to the main screen, he saw that the antenna registered no service. *What the hell?* he thought. *How could someone call when there's no signal from the satellite?*

The rest of the afternoon, Gregory couldn't stop thinking about it. What if that had been Frida—Shayla Hacker?

Warren tried to continue the conversation they had been having, and Gregory absent-mindedly contributed with stock responses, grunts, the occasional nod. His attention was now completely back on her.

The light had lost its afternoon edge by the time they drove up into the hills. This was taking far too long. He'd thought Three Rooks was only supposed to be an hour or so from the airport, but they had been driving for most of the day, and they were only now getting into the low-lying foothills that covered most of the computer printout.

They paused for a break at sundown. Gregory steered the Taurus onto the shoulder and they both got out. His legs were stiff and cramped, and even his hands had grown tired of holding the steering wheel.

Warren climbed up onto a massive rock and shielded his eyes as he stared into the setting sun. He told Gregory to join him and then pointed at something off to their left. It was far away, a good five or six miles. It looked like a cluster of buildings, though it might have just been oddly-shaped rocks huddled in the small valley.

Three Rooks. Gregory knew it in his heart. The map must have been wrong. After all, it was sketched out by a computer. It was very possible that the system had relied on old data, or perhaps had never had all the facts to begin with.

Back in the car, he tore up the map the clerk had given them and steered back onto the road. Warren seemed disconcerted by his sudden rush, but Gregory had grown past caring what Warren thought.

A couple of miles down the road, he began to fear that he'd made a mistake. There were no turnoffs to the left, and now the highway was getting narrower. The road fell into disrepair, and Gregory had to swerve across both lanes to avoid gaping potholes that could have swallowed whole tires.

Warren leaned over from the passenger seat and frowned at something on the instrument panel.

"What?" Gregory asked.

"You've got half a tank of gas."

"So?"

"It was full when we left."

"So?"

"There haven't been any gas stations since we left the city."

It took a moment for it to sink in: this was the point of no return. If they went on now, they wouldn't be able to get all the way back. "What," he snapped, "you want to turn around? You want to call the entire day a waste?"

"I didn't say that. I was just pointing out . . ."

"What do you want me to do?"

"I just thought you might want to know."

"What do you think we could possibly do about it?"

"We could go back and get more gas, come back out tomorrow or the day after. You know, bring some in a can."

"No!" He could probably convince Warren that they couldn't afford so much gasoline, but he himself would know that was skirting the issue. He couldn't spend another night dreaming that he'd found her.

Then he saw the road. Gregory slammed on the brakes. The Taurus skidded sideways across the highway and ground to a halt. Warren was clinging to the dashboard, breathing fast and hard.

Gregory twisted the steering wheel back and eased them onto the little dirt path that snaked away from the main road. It might have been forged by mountain goats. Wild bushes and brambles leaned in on either side, scraping the Taurus's paint and running thin, twiggy fingers across the windows.

It wound its way up the side of the mountain and around a couple of peaks before it petered out entirely. It had been shrinking and deteriorating for a while, but Gregory had managed to convince himself that it would pick up again around each corner. It was only when Warren let out a little whimper that he snapped out of his trance and realized where they were.

The Taurus was barely clinging to the road, almost sideways. One kick to the top of the car, and it would tumble down the cliff.

He peered out through Warren's window. There was nothing but steep rocky embankment and the occasional wild plant to cushion their fall.

"This isn't a road," Warren whimpered when he caught Gregory's eye.

Gregory looked back through the rearview mirror. It hadn't been a road for a long time, either. There was no way to go back. They would have to reverse the entire way, and even so, he wasn't sure that the Taurus could make the climb going backward. He'd had it in third or second gear the entire way up.

"Then we get out."

Warren shook his head. "There's nothing on this side of the car. I'll fall."

"Just be careful."

"Gregory, this is stupid."

Delicately, Gregory put the Taurus into Park, pulled on the emergency brake, and clambered out of the driver's seat.

It was warmer outside than he had expected. Warren had kept the air conditioner on the entire time, and it had been comfortable, so Gregory never adjusted it. It must still have been in the mid- to high-eighties, and the sun had already ducked below the mountain peaks.

He hiked up the embankment to the left of the car and peered out ahead of them. Then he saw it. They were very close. The town was just over the next rise. He galloped back down to the car, as giddy and excited as a child.

"Come on, Warren," he said. "We're almost there."

It had not been as close as it had looked. The sky was dark by the time they crested the final hill and began their weary descent down the side of the mountain into the valley that cradled Three Rooks.

The town had tantalized them, showing itself here and there behind rocks or through thickets of bushes numerous times, but then the trail they had forged would dive, and the entire valley would disappear behind an outcropping of rocks.

But now they really were almost there. He could make out individual buildings—a clock tower, a church, a few houses and shops. There was something strange about it all. He couldn't make out any details from here, but he got an odd feeling from the place. It was like a ghost town. He wasn't sure what made him think that, but it looked deserted.

"No lights," Warren said, and then Gregory knew he was right.

It wasn't pitch black just yet, and the moon was already rising on the far horizon to paint the entire landscape in pale grays and blues, but in a town this size, there should have been at least one or two lights burning.

As they were about to make their final descent, Gregory looked up just in time to catch the slightest of movements somewhere inside the village. It had been from the church, he thought, from the belfry. A moment later, the giant bell began to toll out the hour—ten o'clock. Its mournful voice echoed out through the valley, reverberating off of the distant stone walls to return to them a few moments later in all its warbling, distorted glory.

It should have been a good sign, he supposed, for even if the system were automated, this at least meant that the town had been inhabited recently enough to keep it running. But the noise brought with it an air of desperate finality.

They hurried down the final slope and came to a halt before a pair of stone columns supporting a carved block of marble: *Three Rooks, Indiana. Population: 103*. Not a one of those souls appeared to still be around.

Or—perhaps there was *one*.

"Stop!"

A man in a policeman's uniform, a brown moustache, and a thick stubble appeared. The man held a revolver out before him like a divining rod. It took Gregory a moment to recognize Lieutenant Isaac Keeler. It took Keeler half a moment less.

"Hey, I know you." He climbed out of the clump of bushes where he had been hiding. "I arrested you, didn't I? You were the one with the restraining order back in San Francisco or wherever that was, right?"

"Los Angeles." Gregory stuck out a hand. "Gregory Klein, if you recall."

Keeler didn't take it. "It's okay," he said over his shoulder. "It's not her, and he's not one of them."

Another man emerged from the bushes. Gregory thought he might look slightly familiar, too, but he didn't think he had ever talked to the man, and he doubted if he would be recognized.

"This is Terry Young," Keeler said. "We're working together on a case. What are you doing out here?"

"Looking for a girl."

Keeler stiffened.

"What's her name?" Terry asked. "Shayla Hacker?"

He said the two words at the same time as Gregory. They looked at each other. This was too much to be coincidence—which meant that they had to be on to something.

On their way into town, Young explained that they had encountered another man searching for Shayla Hacker—an older guy whom Keeler had also known from back in the city. He arrived in an RV, but he'd had to leave it out on the other side of the mountain.

As they walked, Gregory could scarcely take his eyes from the buildings they passed. Every one was either boarded-up or deserted, and they bore the sad, empty look of houses and shops that had been hastily left behind. He wondered what had happened here. It seemed like the ideal cradle for a perfect community, isolated from crime, violence, hatred.

But at the same time, there was something wrong about it. This place had been the victim of a plague he couldn't fathom.

Terry Young prattled on about the journey he had made beside Lieutenant Keeler, the barriers they had overcome together. He seemed to be avoiding the question that hovered, unspoken between all of them. When Gregory could stand it no longer, he stopped Young in the middle of the street.

"What about her?" he asked. "Have you seen her?"

"We just got here."

"You're talking about this place like you've been here for days."

Keeler shook his head. "Rolled in about fifteen minutes before you. Ran into Joseph Malloy on the way. We haven't thoroughly explored yet, but so far, there's no sign of anyone. No one at all."

Gregory's heart sank. Everything had pointed to Three Rooks.

Keeler motioned toward a building marked as a General Store. "That's where we've sort of plopped ourselves down. Seemed like the best place."

Warren and Gregory followed the two of them to the double-doors. Once, they had carried wide shop windows, painted with the specials of the day, but now they peered blindly out through thick boards nailed over the frames. Terry pushed one open and slipped inside.

It smelled of rancid meat and rotting vegetables. It was all Gregory could do to stop from gagging. He covered his mouth with a hand and noticed Warren doing the same.

"It's bad, I know," Terry said, "but there are still some cans and a few other non-perishables. Could come in handy."

Gregory looked at them, not understanding. "How long are you guys planning on being out here?"

Terry snorted. "How much gas did you bring?"

Gregory uneasily shook Joseph Malloy's hand. In Joseph's eyes, too, he saw the same frenzied obsession as with everyone else. Was Gregory just imagining things? Was it he who was going mad?

"What did you mean," Gregory said, "when you said I wasn't her and I wasn't one of them?"

Terry and Keeler exchanged glances. "You don't know about *them?*"

Black Fords, Gregory thought, *and black suits.* Aloud, he said, "Who?"

"They're following her." Joseph rolled a map out onto the big table in the middle of the store, brushing aside a few boxes of Ritz crackers and a plastic tub of peanut butter. "They've been tracking her longer than we have. But I think they might have tailed us into the valley. I don't think they knew about Three Rooks, but one thing's for sure: they're going to be here real soon."

Gregory swallowed. He went to the front of the store and tugged aside one of the rotting planks of wood covering the front window. A little of the dying light filtered in from outside. Stars were already twinkling through the evening haze overhead. It was dark, and he was trapped in the middle of a wasteland so large and expansive, he couldn't reach one end or the other in a week if he tried to go by foot. Suddenly, he felt very, very alone.

He turned back to the others. "What do they want? I've seen them following me from time to time."

"To kill her," Keeler said. "Least, that's what I think. I'm not sure why."

Gregory started to ask if Joseph had run into them when the church bell tolled again. The others went on talking, but something about the noise rubbed Gregory wrong. A moment later, he realized what it was: it hadn't been an hour since he and Warren had found the town. It hadn't even been twenty minutes.

"Hey," he said, interrupting Terry in the middle of a story he was telling Joseph. "who's over in the church?"

They all looked at him. It took a moment for the same thought to occur to each of them. A moment later, they were all racing out the front door, down the steps, sprinting down the asphalt of Main Street.

There was the faintest of lights in the bottom of the church. Young was the first to reach it. He bolted up the stone steps and thumped on the door with both fists. There was another half-toll from high overhead, and then silence. They waited, expectant, desperate, hungry. Nothing happened.

Terry turned back. "What do you think we should do?"

"We go in," Gregory said.

"We should call for help." Keeler caught Joseph Malloy with a pleading glance. "Right, Detective?"

"We don't have time for that," Joseph said. "There's no help out here."

A few steps into the darkened church, Gregory realized that *it* was catching. Just being around these people was turning him into one of them. What was he doing out here in the middle of nowhere, breaking into an abandoned house of God to hunt down some stranger who probably didn't want to be found?

The hunger gnawed at him. He had to know. He had to find her.

It was empty inside. The pews sat silhouetted against a single flickering light that illuminated the entire room in an uneven glow. Strange, unearthly shadows danced across a polished statue of Christ looming over them. The breeze from the open door toyed with the onionskin pages of a monolithic Bible on the pulpit.

"Hello?" Terry advanced before Gregory's eyes had adjusted. He was looking all around, searching up and down the barren benches for any signs of life.

"Shh!" Joseph caught him as he was about to mount the dais at the front of the room. They all froze and listened.

There was a whimpering sound coming from somewhere in the heart of the church. It sounded like a child separated from her mother. Distinctly feminine.

"Where?" Terry breathed.

"Upstairs," Joseph nodded toward a door at the side of the room. It was slightly smaller than the others, an attic or basement passage. Beyond it, Gregory could just make out the veiled shapes of stairs.

He started to follow them toward it when something caught his eye. It was one of the stained-glass windows that lined the central room. They were all beautiful, if somewhat unoriginal. Except for one. One above all the others seemed *alive*.

Gregory separated from them and moved to the edge of the room to place one hand on the dusty glass.

Warren noticed and lingered by the door as the others vanished through it. "What is it?" he asked. "What have you found?"

It was the Holy Father, his hand splayed across the forehead of an infant beside whom someone else was kneeling. The child's mother, Gregory thought. Was she crying, or was that just his imagination?

"It's glowing," Warren said.

Gregory squinted at the window. Warren was right. That was what had snagged his attention in the first place. The eyes of the Holy Father flickered as though lit by pinpoints of energy from another dimension, from beyond the gates of the spirit world.

He shivered in spite of himself. He'd never bought into religion too much, but in an abandoned church on the fringe of civilization, he suddenly felt closer than ever to the great beyond.

"Come on." Warren tugged at the back of his shirt. "They're going to be at the top before we even start climbing." As though on cue, footsteps sounded from somewhere high overhead.

Gregory turned and followed Warren through the shortened door, but he couldn't help stealing another look back at the window over his shoulder. The light was gone.

Then he was climbing. The stairs were steep, winding in revolving squares up the four corners of the bell tower. He could hear the clatter of the others, a couple of floors above them. Their voices echoed down in surges. Every now and then he would catch an excited word. Then he would hear the weeping girl, and his chest would seize up again.

He reached the top a few moments after they had.

"There's no one here," Terry announced.

"She's got to be somewhere." Joseph Malloy ran a hand through his graying hair and stepped around to the other side of the giant bell. It hung in the center of the belfry, tarnished and smudged with what looked to be the fingerprints of a child.

He of all people, Gregory thought, *should have the dignity and experience to put himself beyond this scavenger hunt.* But there was that same glow in his eyes. Youth. Passion. Greed.

"Hey, look." Warren pointed out across the darkened town to the hillside.

There were lights descending toward them, small, irregular,

but purposeful. That was what had been lighting the eyes of the Holy Father—not a message from the spirit world, but from the temporal one. A reminder that they were being hunted by a predator whose hunger had long ago overpowered its patience.

"They're coming," Terry said. "We've got to make ready."

"How do we *make ready?*" Gregory snarled. "For fuck's sake, we're in the middle of nowhere. We've got nothing but rotting beef on our side."

Terry fixed him with a cold, hard stare. "We'll figure something out."

Chapter 28

"Look at the picture again," the man said.

He shook Jackie until she opened her eyes, stopped even pretending to be asleep. At first, she had thought he was kind, that he was doing her a favor because he liked her. And she *had* recognized the girl in the picture. She hadn't lied to him. But he had grown annoying in his persistence. He seemed not to trust that she was telling the truth.

She shifted, rubbed her eyes, and took a sip of the ginger ale she'd bought from the stewardess. "Huh?"

"Look at it." His breath was hideous. It wafted out from beneath his waxed handlebar moustache, whistling through the measured gaps between his stained yellow teeth. He was a repugnant old man. She could see that now. She should never had said yes to his offer, but she had needed the ticket, had needed so badly to get out of Egypt, that she would have said yes to almost anything.

"It's her," she said after looking the picture over again. It was—the same girl Marlowe had been searching for. "I suppose she's your daughter, too?"

"My daughter?" His forehead wrinkled. He turned the photo around to look at it, then shook his head, his eyes lingering a few moments too long on the picture before he rolled it up and put it back in his red sweater. "I suppose you might call me her guardian," he said with a self-satisfied smile she didn't like in the least, "but we're certainly not related. You know where to find her, yes? You said you knew where to find her."

"What do you want with her?"

"I want to know she's okay."

"And then?"

"I want to tell someone she's okay."

"Who?"

"You wouldn't believe me."

"Try me."

He shook his head.

"Her father? Her real father?"

"Not quite."

The flight attendant came by again and collected their trash. When she left, the man leered at her, never taking his eyes from her ass. He looked back at Jackie with a hungry glint to his eyes. "A pity," he said, darting another look at the picture. "A pity she's so young. She's a cutie." He edged a little closer. "Pity you're so young, too. How old you say you were?"

Jackie shivered and recoiled from him. She looked desperately to the woman on the other side of her, but she had been out cold, her head against the window, since they had taxied onto the runway.

"Leave me alone," Jackie growled. "Or I'll make the stewardess relocate you."

"Oh," he said with a smile, "I can pull a vanishing act if I want to. The stewardess and I are old hands at that." He winked at her.

She didn't know what he meant, and she didn't want to. She looked away, trying to pretend that her mind was elsewhere. He tapped her on the shoulder so insistently that she had no choice but to look back.

"You just find her, sweetie," he said. "You walk and I'll watch."

When he was asleep, Jackie quietly got up and filed out to the aisle. She had to think. The man—he'd never given her a name, though when she'd pressed him, he'd said to call him Elk—had bought her the first ticket to the continent. They were flying into New York's Kennedy airport at around five in the afternoon. From there, it was up to her. All she'd had to promise was to take him with her.

She'd never been planning on doing it. She was from a small town, but she wasn't naïve. He was probably some pervert. At least, that was what she had thought at first. Then he'd taken out the picture, and she didn't know what to think. Was he an ally? Or was he stalking her?

One of the flight attendants put a hand on her shoulder. Jackie looked up, startled. She had wandered into First Class.

"I'm sorry, Ma'am," he said. "You're not allowed to be up here. If you're looking for the lavatory, you're going to have to use one at the back of the plane. We can't have people in the aft cabin coming up by the cockpit."

"Oh," she said weakly. When she turned and started back, her her eyes fell across the man's wrinkled face, and she shivered.

The flight attendant had moved to the first row of seats with an armful of purse-sized pillows, so Jackie slipped into an unoccupied chair on the end of the row. It was leather, roomy. She had never ridden in First Class before, but now, suddenly, she knew what all the hoopla was about. The seat cradled her, the armrests in just the right places. There was a crystal glass with a few drops of champagne left in it and a dog-eared paperback novel wedged into the seat beside her. It smelled of an older man's cologne.

The lady in the seat next to her opened her eyes and adjusted her glasses.

"I'm sorry," Jackie said, starting to stand. "I was just trying to get out of the steward's way."

"No, it's okay," the woman said. "Stay a minute." She smiled so kindly that Jackie felt compelled to do just that. "Loren loves to talk to the flight crew. He used to fly for the Air Force back in Korea. He gets a kick out of telling them all his stories. Poor little kids. They were just babies when it happened. Some of them weren't even born. Look at them."

Jackie looked. Loren, moustached, graying around the edges,

his hair tucked beneath a flat golfer's cap, was standing propped against the cabin door, a young flight attendant with a busty chest and long blond hair cornered in the alcove beside him.

Noting her dubious stare, the old woman sighed. "I'm not blind, my dear. I just know Loren doesn't have a chance with them. Somehow, that's reassuring. You're probably concerned with looking beautiful at your age, but trust me, when you get older, the greatest comfort in the world is knowing the both of you are ugly enough that you're the only ones who'd ever consider sleeping with either of you."

Jackie smiled at her and started to excuse herself.

"Oh, don't go yet, dear. It's nice up here. They'll give you some wine, if you want some." She reached for the flight attendant call button. "It's nice to have someone to talk to." When the steward came, he gave Jackie a dirty look. The woman ordered a glass of Chardonnay. He strutted off, and the woman giggled to herself and looked back at Jackie.

There was something about her Jackie liked. She wasn't sure what it was—perhaps just a gut feeling, though she'd never much bought into those. If there was one thing she had learned from all her reading and research, it was that science had an explanation for virtually everything.

"Loren and I have traveled across the country with each other," the woman went on, settling back into her seat. "Why, we've seen every state. I'd warrant we've seen most cities in them, too. Have you done much traveling?"

Jackie shook her head. "This is my first time out of the country."

Somewhere in the midst of the woman's cooing and story-telling and her own glass of wine, Jackie realized that she might have just sat down next to the one person on the plane who could help her. "Do you know where they have teepees?" she asked, when the woman—Gladys—was taking a breath for air and a sip of her dry martini.

Gladys gave her a funny look. "What, you mean Native Americans?"

She shrugged. "I guess so."

"Well, they're all over the country, of course. You have a lot of them in Wisconsin, some up in the Pacific Northwest, a lot throughout the middle of the country. I think you might even have some down in California and New Mexico, but it's not something Loren and I have particularly looked into. Are you interested in history?"

"I'm looking for someone."

"Who?"

Jackie tensed, but by now, she had dived too far into this to turn back. "A girl," she said. Absent in Gladys's eyes was the look of hunger that Jackie had seen in a dozen other people on her race across the world at Marlowe's side. "Her name's Hacker," she ventured, when the elderly woman said nothing.

Gladys nodded, as though waiting for more. No sign of recognition. That, Jackie realized, was what she liked about this woman. She was the one person she had come across in the last several weeks that had expressed no interest in finding the girl.

"And a boy," she went on. "Walker. Walker Savage. Do you know either of them?"

Gladys shook her head. "Sorry. Are they your friends?"

"Walker's my brother." It was such a relief to find someone so seemingly genuine that Jackie felt like opening up completely to her.

"Why do you think they're in teepees?" Gladys asked.

"It's not that. I'm just going off of something someone said. A kid—back in Cairo. And there was something about Hooks. Three of them, I think."

"Well, you see, you have to interpret sometimes. Even if they're trying to be helpful, you know, they don't always have the most complete command of the English language."

"What do you mean?"

"It's like a game." Gladys pulled a pen from the purse at her feet and folded down the tray table from the back of the seat in front of her. She slipped the napkin out from under Jackie's wine glass and opened it up, so that it covered most of the table. She wrote on it, *Teepees*. "Now," she said, "try to think like an Egyptian."

Jackie squinted at the napkin. Right now, she was finding it hard enough to try and think at all. She'd had a sip of beer once when Walker offered it to her, but she hadn't liked the taste, and she'd said no when he tried to pour her one of her own. That was the only alcohol she'd ever had.

"What's related to teepees?" Gladys pressed.

"I don't know," Jackie said. "Moccasins. Hunting. Bears."

Gladys wrote each of the words down, and then she circled them all and put, in parenthesis beside them, *Indians*. The old woman stared down at it for a moment, then smiled. "I think I have an idea," she said. "Do you have it yet?"

Jackie tried to focus, but everything seemed just a little too fuzzy around the edges, as though someone had sketched the entire airplane with a dull pencil and then rubbed a thumb across the page to give it a signature smudged look.

"Indiana, child," Gladys said. "Your friends are in Indiana. You said Three Hooks? Is it a town?"

"He said there was an *r*, too."

"Three Hookers?" Gladys chuckled to herself. "No, now that wouldn't be very proper of the county, would it?"

"It's *Rooks*." A man's voice, chillingly familiar.

Jackie and Gladys looked up together. There was Elk, gazing down at them with a smile that was more personal pleasure than it was pride in their deductive reasoning. "The town we're looking for is Three Rooks, Indiana. That was where Shayla Hacker was born."

Gladys smiled at him. "Why thank you so much, sir." She beamed at Jackie, who was staring at Elk with unmasked hostility. "Isn't that nice? You see, you never know who you're going to run into when you get on an airplane. That's why Loren and I like to travel so much."

Jackie rose, but the man who liked to be called Elk put a hand on her shoulder and pressed her back down into her leather First Class seat. "Don't you fret," he said. "Don't bother coming back to your seat. You've been very helpful, but that's all I needed you for."

He turned and departed down the aisle.

Jackie found Gladys watching her through confused eyes. Jackie, herself, felt as though the entire world was spinning.

"Who was that man?" Gladys asked.

"Oh my God." Somewhere in Jackie's reeling, poisoned mind, she had just made the connection. It was something the woman back at the town had said—Debbie. Debbie Wendell. Jackie wouldn't have remembered it except that Gregory had been going on and on about it at such length. She had been ferried in from the airport with a police escort because someone had disappeared on her plane after harassing her about something she'd had.

It wasn't Elk. How could she have been so stupid? That was ludicrous. Who wanted to be called *Elk*? It was *L.K.* Lloyd Kelson. And he had just manipulated out of her the one, most concrete clue she had toward both finding the girl and her brother before it was too late.

Jackie watched for Lloyd Kelson when she got off the plane at Kennedy, but she wasn't surprised when he didn't follow her into the terminal. She knew he could disappear, and he had said that he was done with her. Now she was on her own, and it was a race to see who could get to Indiana first.

Jackie approached four different families, pleading with them to help her out with a ticket or at least some money. No luck. She caught a glimpse of herself in a bathroom mirror and almost burst into tears. It had been days since she had even changed her clothes, longer since she'd had a decent shower. No wonder the flight attendant had tried to shoo her out of the First Class cabin.

Outside, it was muggy. New York was baking, mired in a late Indian summer. She stumbled out onto the main airport loop and shielded her eyes as she peered toward the setting sun. From the plane, she'd seen Manhattan, and a part of her had ached deep inside. She'd always wanted to see New York. She caught a glimpse of a tour bus as it pulled away from the curb. In the window was a placard that said it was going to Times Square. A couple of weeks ago, she might have dropped everything and run to join it on its journey to urban Eden.

She was different now. She had responsibilities, both to herself and to Walker. Stolidly, she made her way to the line of taxis and the crowd of people with heavy rolling luggage that stood, trying to flag them down.

Three cabs swerved around her as she wandered out onto the street, waving her hands at them. Horns blared. At last, one stopped. The driver, a skinny white guy who would have looked more at home behind a computer screen than a taxi wheel, waved at her to get inside.

His face was speckled with acne, and he wore about his neck a gold chain with a symbol she didn't recognize. "Where to, little lady?" he asked with a grin that made her want to curl up into a ball on the squalid back seat.

"I . . . I need to get out of New York."

"Jersey?"

"Indiana."

He laughed out loud. All the while, his hands busied themselves, pulling the car into gear, spinning the wheel, accelerating into traffic so dense she thought sure they were going to hit a half dozen cars on their way to the exit lane.

"You're something," he said. "Now where to?"

Jackie sighed. It was just a little noise, not much more than a whimper, but it must have carried a measure of pathetic authenticity, because then he looked at her—really looked at her—and the snide sarcasm left his voice. "Hey," he said, "you know that's against all kinds of regs, right? I mean, I'm not allowed to go more than ten or fifteen miles from Kennedy."

"Please—just take me as far as you can go." In barely more than a whisper, she added, "And I don't have any money."

She thought he'd be furious. She thought he was going to yell at her, kick her out at the next street corner or demand that she give him her wallet, her watch, anything of value she might have had on her person. But he didn't say anything. Instead, he only flashed her a self-satisfied smile in the rearview mirror. "We'll see what we can do."

Jackie wasn't sure she liked that at all, but she was too tired to protest or to think things through. The pleasant buzz that had bubbled around in her head on the plane had turned to a deep ache, and now all she wanted to do was sleep.

As she settled back into the seat, she peered out the rear window and caught sight of what she thought might be Lloyd Kelson's silhouette at the end of a long line before the ticket counter. There weren't any flights to Indiana until tomorrow morning. That, she had confirmed on the computer screens back in the terminal.

Perhaps, she thought, through some strange, unearned stroke of luck, she was going to beat him to Three Rooks after all.

It was pitch black. There was the sound of crickets outside the cab, and someone was touching her leg. She could feel sweaty fingers slipping up her thigh.

Jackie started awake and tried to recoil from the feeling, but then a hand grabbed her roughly on the back of the neck. Someone was crouching over her. She couldn't make out his features in the dark, but as her eyes adjusted, she recognized the wiry frame: the driver.

"Get off," she yelped.

He was breathing heavily. He took off his shirt, and his pale skin caught the starlight from outside the taxi.

"Get away from me!" She kicked, clawed.

"We're miles from New York," he said. "You owe me." He unsnapped the button of his jeans and kicked them off.

Jackie reached for the door handle, but he caught her fingers, folded them so quickly that she heard the joints crack, and pressed them against her heaving chest. "It'll be fast," he said with a strangely self-conscious snort. "Just let it happen."

In a single move, she gripped the bottom of the seat and kicked at him as hard as she could. He yelped and fell back, slamming against the door behind him. He hadn't shut it completely, and it fell open now, spilling him out onto the highway.

She leapt out, and bounded onto the road. The kid was scrambling away from her, looking wildly around. "Hey!" he said. "Hey, hey! Don't take it personally. Hey, I was just trying to see if you were okay! You'd been quiet for a while. Hey, get away!" He tried to clamber to his feet.

Jackie darted forward and kicked him in the chin. He fell back again, the skin of his shoulders slapping against the pavement. "Aw, come on, I was—hey, it's kinda a compliment, y'know?"

She seized him by the hair and dragged him over to the trunk. When she blinked, she saw the driver, Marlowe cackling, the splash of blood on the back window. And she saw herself, cowering in the seat next to Marlowe. She had been a helpless little child, nothing like the person she was now. Now, she was capable of showing the world she meant business.

Somewhere in the fray, she lost track of the blows and punches she dealt the kid. His yelps turned to whimpering, then groaning, and finally silence, punctuated only by the occasional sob. Jackie didn't let up. She no longer saw him or herself at all. She only saw the arms of the chauffeur, as though they were hers, the body of the gas station attendant. She wasn't responsible for any of this. It was happening on its own.

She unlocked the taxi's trunk, pulled out the tire iron, and broke the kid's ribs, then his spine, then his jaw. She watched as she beat the features from his face, beat the skin from his bones, beat the shape from his body.

When she was finished, he was unrecognizable. What lay on the ground looked more like the skin of a peeled peach or the discarded fat and gristle of a porterhouse steak.

Calmly, she knelt and rolled him into a ball of bleeding human flesh that she could kick off the side of the road. She watched as his remains tumbled down through the weeds beside the highway, rustling until they came to a halt somewhere just out of sight.

The road was empty out here. It would probably be some time before anyone discovered him, and when they did, there would be no way of linking all of this to her. Nobody was looking for her, and nobody would be looking for the kid.

Just like that, the adventure was over. Any shred of fun or excitement she'd felt in Cairo was now beyond gone. This was no picture book fairytale. Just then, she longed to be back home— longed to be reading about all of this in a novel while the rain hammered on the eaves outside.

She could never go back there, though. Not until she'd found Shayla Hacker.

She climbed back into the taxi, put it into gear, and pulled out onto the highway. She drove for another hour before she saw the blood on her brow in the rearview mirror and truly understood what she had done.

Through teary eyes, she glimpsed the turnoff. She hated that she was crying for him, but she told herself it wasn't like that; she was crying for herself, for the loss of innocence. She was no pure child anymore.

The suspension creaked and jittered as she maneuvered the taxi onto the gravel road. It was rough, looping up through the hills with sharp turns and abrupt drops, but fresh tire tracks had dug deep furrows in the pathway.

When she reached the top of the hill, she slammed on the brakes. There was another car ahead of her. It appeared abandoned, but there were footprints all around it.

Jackie turned the engine off, and it struck her right then that she had just driven a good hundred miles or so. She'd barely ever been behind the wheel of a car before now. Then again, she'd never killed anyone before either. Today was just a day for first times.

Had to happen sometime, she thought. *Might as well be for a cause.* But it felt . . . emptier than she had expected, being an adult. Making decisions that changed lives. For the first time, she began to wonder what exactly she had been hoping to find at the end of the highway, on the other side of the cornstalks.

At first, all was quiet outside. She stopped because her own footsteps sounded like an avalanche. That was when she heard the others. They were descending the steep slope just ahead of her; they couldn't have been more than half an hour ahead.

There were a few small lights in the village, too, and there was movement around the church steeple.

Jackie froze. She'd been expecting to be alone out here.

Then the footsteps came, not from a hundred feet away, not from a dozen feet away, but from right beside her. Jackie knew she'd been caught.

Someone touched her, and she screamed and started running.

Chapter 29

In Indianapolis, while she was waiting for her last connection, Debbie asked about Three Rooks. The younger kids in their starched white uniforms didn't know a thing about it, but there was an older man behind the counter with a hearing aid and a froth of white hair who perked up when she mentioned the name. The pin on his jacket read *Chuck*. Only people his age were actually named Chuck, she thought.

"They closed that place down a few years ago," he told her. "I think it had to do with some kind of environmental thing, but that's just hearsay. Ask someone at a gas station or a mini-mart when you get closer. I think they're really into local history around there. I seem to remember it was a thing when I was growing up."

She thanked him and went on her way.

At the last airport, she rented a Cadillac because nothing else was left, and then, with a folded map in hand, struck out on her own into rural Indiana. For the second time that week, she was amazed at the bleakness of the landscape. Debbie Wendell had never spent much time outside of the city before now, and it was odd to see so much rural landscape in such a short time. For years, she had lived as though nothing had existed beyond the coasts, and now, she could scarcely get away from the heartland.

She drove for most of the day. It never occurred to her to stop and sleep, to make up for the hours she had spent staring out airplane windows and the hapless night she had passed in Brazil. All of that was behind her now.

In the evening, as she sensed she was getting closer, she pulled off the two-lane highway and into a small turnout with a service station and a couple of old grain silos. The place was a converted farm, the triumph of industrial civilization over the idyllic simplicity of the past.

A wash of fluorescent light flickered over the lonely pumps and stacks of bald tires. The boy behind the counter looked up when she came in.

"Evening," she said.

He nodded at her. "Want me to fill her up?"

Debbie shook her head. "Actually still running strong. I just stopped in to ask for directions. I'm new around here and I'm a little lost."

"I can tell." When she raised an eyebrow, he motioned to the Cadillac. "Not many people come through her with fancy cars, and even fewer of them are brand new like that one."

"It's a rental."

"Yeah. What do you need?"

"I'm looking for someone—a girl. I'm looking for Three Rooks."

His face hardened. "Why? Who's the girl?"

Debbie shrugged. "I don't know. I'm just checking something out for a friend."

"Is she in Three Rooks?"

"That's what I heard."

"I don't think I can help you," he mumbled.

"Hey, wait. What's wrong with you?"

He caught her eye and his cheeks colored. He reached under the counter, pulled out a folded newspaper article, and spread it out on the glass. He turned it around so she could read the headline—*Station Attendant Slain by Unidentified Motorist.*

"Just disappeared," the boy said. "Wasn't around here, but that doesn't matter. Cops think it was done by a stranger. In a limo, they think, though they can't be sure. Don't see many people out here, not many people to hear me if I had to shout for help, you know?"

A limousine? Hadn't Jackie Savage, the little girl from the village, said she'd arrived in a limousine?

"Look," Debbie said, "this is urgent. You've got to tell me how to get to Three Rooks. A little girl's life depends on it."

It was just down the road, another forty miles or so. She'd see a cutoff to the left, up a windy road into the mountains. "They closed down the whole town a few years ago, though," he called after her.

She paused in the doorway. "Why'd they do that?"

"Some scandal." He shrugged. "Not sure what about."

⟨⟩

The Cadillac struggled up the road. Debbie didn't ease off the accelerator. She'd bought the rental insurance policy. If anything happened to the car, they vowed to take full responsibility in her name. As she crested the hill, the village came into view, and an odd mixture of both accomplishment and dread overtook her.

There were two cars parked on the slope ahead of her. They were hidden behind the summit, and she had to slam on the brakes to avoid running into the last one. She yanked on the emergency brake, pulled the keys out, and climbed out of the Cadillac. Debbie hiked over to the first car, a taxicab. The hood was still warm.

She looked around, peering down at the village, and that was when she saw the lights. They were dim, invisible when she'd first arrived, but now she saw they were everywhere, like fireflies flitting about the valley. There were a couple on the roof of the church, and a few, scattered down the mountain ahead of her.

That was when she knew that she had finally made it. Whatever she was about to find, she had reached her destination at last.

Chapter 30

While Gregory Klein was telling them all to cool their heels, to take things one step at a time, and Terry Young was barking orders to grab this, take that, be prepared for the approaching legions, Joseph Malloy vaulted the small wooden rail around the bell tower and walked out onto the roof. He'd seen something out there. He'd seen Shayla Hacker.

Clinging to a weathervane, arms wrapped around the rusting metal, was a girl in a white nightgown. She couldn't have been more than twenty or twenty-five years old, if that. He would have put her closer to her teens were it not for the muscles on her arms and the measured determination holding her rigidly fast. He couldn't take his eyes from her. Her skin was almost as pale as the thin fabric that clung to her.

She shied away from him as he approached. He had both arms outstretched to balance himself against the gentle breeze that grew fierce as it swept up across the church roof. He probably looked like a scarecrow. "Don't worry," he called to her. "I'm not going to hurt you. We're your friends. Those guys—they're the ones you want to watch." He nodded to the valley walls, the flickering lights.

She opened her mouth, and out poured sheer blackness, as if she was spitting ink.

Joseph stopped in his tracks. She shook her head at him, held up her hands when he again tried to advance. It had ceased to matter that there might be something wrong with her. It had ceased to matter that she might carry some disease. She was so close that he could almost feel her shirtsleeves on his fingertips.

"My dear," he said gently, "they're coming for you. They've wrecked a dozen houses, killed all who stood a chance of finding you. We're the only ones who made it this far. We're the only ones who can help you."

He reached for her, and that was when the figure leapt out of the darkness.

Joseph ducked out of the way as it swung a fist at him, but he was too old for this. "Please!" he barked. "We're your friends!"

"Then stay away from her." The figure sounded young, a boy frightened for the life of a lover.

Joseph frowned at him, trying to make out his face in the darkness of the night. "Who are you?"

Shayla Hacker shrank into the figure's grasp, intertwining her fingers with his. That was enough of an answer. It had been years since Joseph had felt such passion himself, but he still recognized it from the distant memories he harbored of Jean. They were lovers. This was Shayla's . . . her what? Husband? Boyfriend?

Something strange was happening to her fingers. They seemed almost liquid, flowing between the boy's like streams of sand.

"Malloy!" It was Keeler. He leaned out over the handrail, beckoning furiously at Joseph. "Get back here! They're coming!"

Joseph looked to the hills and saw that Keeler was right. The lights had reached the bottom and were surging down Main Street.

"If you care about her," the figure said, "you will stop trying to steal her away and go with your friends."

"Who are they?" Joseph asked.

"Sent by the church. They're here for the soul inside her."

"What?"

"Go!"

Joseph went, but he didn't go back to Keeler and Young and Klein and Warren. He ran toward the couple. "Come on!" He grabbed at the open window where the figure had appeared and yanked at the other man's shoulder.

It was dark and musty inside the church—the scent of a room that had stood unopened for many years.

"We have to keep moving!" the figure breathed.

"We're safe here."

"How do you know?"

"Because we're in a church, and you said they are from the church."

"So?"

"The religious don't defile their own temples."

Footsteps sounded on the roof outside the window. A moment later, Terry Young poked his head inside. "What the hell are you doing in here? Malloy, they're right downstairs! We need you!"

Joseph had known men like Terry Young throughout the course of his job; men who would destroy everything with their shortsightedness.

They could hear footsteps on the road outside now, moving not with any urgency, but rather with the self-assured regularity of wolves who knew their wounded prey had no hope of escape.

"I want to get out of here," the figure said. He grabbed Shayla's shoulders and the two of them bolted for the door.

Did her feet touch the ground when she walked? Malloy couldn't quite tell.

Something was happening on the roof of the church. As Jackie Savage clambered over rocks, through sprays of thickets and weeds, she caught a glimpse of something so white it almost glimmered in the pale starlight. Shayla Hacker. She knew it without even seeing the woman's face.

It was all she needed. She forgot about Walker. She forgot about the boy in the taxi and about Egypt and Marlowe, too. All she wanted was to look into Shayla Hacker's eyes.

The figure disappeared from the rooftop. Jackie hadn't seen

exactly where. She paused behind one of the larger boulders and
squinted into the night. Surely the girl would reappear. She *had* to
reappear. Jackie hadn't come this far only to have the end dangled
before her so briefly.

To Gregory Klein, the scene inside the church was enough to give
him nightmares. There was no blood, no Satanic symbols. The
way the others clustered around their quarry reminded him of a
cultish ceremony, centuries old. Their lives had lead up to this.

For his part, his interest in her had begun to wane. He was
beginning to feel just how rash and foolish he had been. He had
caught something. Flirted with a disease that had taken these
other people by force.

The kid looked young, scared, confused. A band of strangers were
shouting questions at him, firing them one after the other, as though
blaming the object of their obsession for its control over them.

Outside, the footsteps of their stalkers crunched around the
perimeter of the church in plodding, deliberate paces. Circling.
Lustful. Animals in heat. If they wanted in, Gregory thought, all
they had to do was break a window, smash a wall.

Unless there was something – *stronger* keeping them at bay.
Perhaps it wasn't a matter of *who* they were as much as *what* they were.

Terry Young needed to vomit. He squinted at Shayla Hacker and
the man beside her. A man beside her! Terry belonged there. "Who
the hell are you?" he shouted.

The kid looked around, from face to face, panic draining the
color from his features. He winced at a clatter from outside, the
stalkers starting their work on the front doors of the church.

"Savage," he breathed. "My name's Walker Savage. I'm her . .
. her boyfriend."

Terry snarled like a rabid dog. "Bullshit! You're one of them. You're chasing her just like they are, only when you found her, you were too big a coward to follow through with it. You were too stupid to kill her off, and now we've found you!"

"That's not true! I've been trying to protect her from them!"

"Who are they?" Joseph Malloy—steady, even.

Terry shot him a wild look. The lust, he realized, had affected each of them differently. For Malloy, it was a hypnosis. The same for Warren and Keeler. They stood dumb, enthralled.

Walker looked at Shayla as though asking her what she wanted. His arm snaked over her shoulder. Was Terry hallucinating, or did some of it come off in his fingers?

"Answer the question!" Terry barked.

A flash of fear appeared in Walker's eyes. Joseph stuck out a hand, grabbed his attention back, and it was only Terry who saw the look of resentment the detective shot him. *Whatever*, Terry thought. *So we'll be enemies.*

"It's okay," Joseph said. "We just want to know what we're up against."

"They're stalking her. They have been ever since the baby was born."

"Slow down. Tell us everything." He winced as another crash came somewhere downstairs.

How long would the old wooden doors hold?

"They're soldiers for the church," Walker said. He touched the top of Shayla's head with his chin. "She was raped. Her child belonged to the Pope."

"The Pope?" Terry blurted. "Are you mad?"

Joseph nodded, impassive. "Go on. Tell us everything."

"She was visiting the Vatican. She won't talk to me about it, about the time she spent trapped there. I think it's too frightening, too foul for her to think of. When she found out she was pregnant, she ran. They started chasing her. She came here first, so they shut down the village. Some people were told there were impurities in the water, an epidemic, whatever it took to get them to leave. Those who wouldn't cooperate disappeared.

"She couldn't run forever, though. They caught up. She was scared and she made a deal; she would help them cover everything up if they would stop chasing her and killing everyone she loved. She was told that they were arranging a foster family for the child—some guy called Marlowe. Used to be a Cardinal.

"But she knew—that they were up to something. She wooed the agent who caught her, convinced him to smuggle her away in the middle of the night. He promised to take her somewhere far away, somewhere where she would be safe. His name was Lloyd Kelson. He took her to Brazil."

Shayla hid her face in Walker's arms as he went on. "He told her that they had to escape all civilization, that the agents were using technology to track them and their only hope was to get as far from it as they could. He led her to an ancient tribe of savages in the jungle. They burned her baby, made her inhale the smoke, gave her the ashes in a box." Shayla began to sob. "It was in their legends—their religious texts. They were enemies of the church from a forgotten time and this was like their Judgment Day. Some kind of ancient ritual—the living soul of Rome imprisoned, tortured, walking dead."

Terry frowned. "And that's what those people—those—who've been following us . . . they're agents of the Vatican? Religious mafia, sent to kill her?"

Walker shrugged. "That depends on what you believe. I've never seen any person travel as fast as they do—knock down houses with the touch of a finger."

Terry thought of the glowing eyes in the windshield of the car that had chased him. But that was crazy—his imagination. Wasn't it?

"Lloyd Kelson had taken her picture. He spread it everywhere, looking for her. People are ashamed to admit it, but you will find that most everyone has heard of Shayla Hacker. Everyone has a brother or a friend who has gotten caught up in chasing her. Nobody knows who she is. They just know what she touches inside them. How she changes them. In certain places—once upon a time, she would've been worshipped. But now . . ." He looked at her and his face crumpled. "She is simply a question without an answer."

"Why you?" Terry barked. "Why you, why you, why you? Why did she pick you? Why are you the one who gets to hold her?"

Walker hugged her closer. "Because I was the first to love her. I saw her the night she had left her baby daughter's ashes in an airport. The burnt remains...they were still in Shayla's lungs, and when I ran into her, wandering the streets, alone, hopeless—I breathed her in. We became—part of each other. I had to help. We went to Cairo, but we were followed.

"When she told me the whole story, I suggested this place as a refuge—they had already looked here. What were the chances that they would come back?" He grimaced at them. "But then you came."

Little prick, Terry thought. *Accusing us of fucking everything up.* If Shayla was captured tonight, it would be on their shoulders. Never mind that Walker had been a worthless guardian. Never mind that he had forgotten to cover his tracks when he whisked her away. Never mind that it was his fault she had been so easy to find.

The church shuddered, and there was a crash from downstairs. This was it—now they had to make their final stand.

Debbie ran after Jackie. Within a few footfalls, she saw Jackie turn and yelp, try to run faster. But Debbie was upon her, and she grabbed the girl around the shoulders. The two of them staggered to the side of the road—Jackie wriggling, struggling to get away, Debbie grasping her with iron arms.

Jackie's features were the same, but the ember burning within her had flared up and now shone a strange color. She was like spoiled milk or tainted meat, a familiar personality that had somehow been skewed beyond all recognition.

"Remember me?" Debbie hissed. "Debbie Wendell."

The struggling began again. "You have to let me go! I've seen her! I've seen Shayla Hacker!"

"You're sick, Jackie. Please wait."

Jackie wrenched herself free, and staggered away.

Debbie squinted. Dark shapes were moving around the church. She wasn't sure if they were people or animals, and what was worse, they seemed intent on getting inside. But after what she had seen in Brazil, Debbie no longer faced fear with a veneer of pride. She faced it knowing she had seen the worst the world had to offer.

She saw Jackie slink into the shadows at one side of the church.

Debbie waited until one of the shapes came around the front again and threw its weight against the front door. "Hey!" Debbie shouted. The shape jumped. "Hey, asshole. Debbie Wendell. I want to talk to you, and I'm not going to take any of your bullshit."

Terry Young crouched at the edge of the stairs. Flickering light moved slowly toward the bottom step. In the air was the scent of other people, the nervous energy of occupied space. He shivered, glanced back at the others, and made a shooing motion.

That he had become the de facto leader of their coalition amused him. Perhaps it was the businesslike calm with which his parents had always charged into the South American jungles with elephant guns in search of their prey – perhaps that had been training him for this.

He had devised a scheme. Their first target had just begun to ascend the stairs. They moved into position, and then they waited.

The wood creaked. The agent was almost at the top when voices sounded somewhere on the ground floor. He paused.

Terry's breath caught in his throat. This wasn't going to work if he went back and fetched a horde of armed followers. They should take him now, but he wasn't high enough on the stairwell.

If he exposed himself, Terry would be facing the man alone.

Terry couldn't hear what anyone downstairs was saying, but

the agent appeared to be listening. He hesitated, glanced up at the darkness ahead of him, and then turned and scurried back down the steps.

Terry rose from behind the banister, but motioned for the others to remain in hiding. Someone would be back. It was only a matter of time.

"Jackie?" Debbie advanced between the rows of pews, scanning all of the shadows. She had to be there. Debbie had seen the girl slip through one of the open windows at the back of the church, and there weren't that many places for her to hide in here.

Debbie exchanged glances with the man she'd met outside. He shrugged.

He was nice. An older man, back when they had manners. She had liked him immediately. And he was sane. He'd brought a reasoned, balanced perspective on the whole situation. Now, if only she could find the others.

Jackie heard Debbie's voice from somewhere in the central room. She shrank away. She wanted to take this one step at a time, to suppress her natural instincts and think her way through this

She found the stairs. Shayla Hacker had been on the roof. That meant Jackie had to go up if she were ever going to find her.

Drawing in a deep breath, moving as silently as she could, Jackie advanced onto the stairs.

Terry strained, tried to see who was approaching. It didn't sound like one of the agents. Too hesitant, too light. He signaled the others to wait, but he had no way of knowing if they had seen him.

Then everything happened at once.

Jackie Savage reached the top step, and Warren leapt out at her, brandishing his pocket knife. Jackie shrieked and took a step backward. Joseph Malloy jumped out of the darkness and swung the broken slab of wood. She crumpled on the top step, overbalanced, and tumbled down the stairs.

When she hit the bottom, she lay in a still heap.

Debbie froze when she heard the scream. A moment later, after the crashing descent, she bolted into action. Marlowe did the same, running for the back room.

Bursting through the narrow door together, they found the girl at the bottom of a flight of stairs. She didn't look good.

Marlowe gasped, knelt, recoiled.

"What?" Debbie bellowed. "What's wrong with you?"

"I . . . I thought it was her. I shouldn't be relieved, but I am."

"We've got to help her!" Debbie was on her knees when she noticed the man she'd seen back at the police station in the village—Terry Young—on the stairs with three other men. Descending in front of them was Gregory Klein. He looked strong, as though he had grown since the last time they had met. He was no longer the awkward little geek from the big city apartment.

Then it clicked in her mind—he must have pushed Jackie.

Debbie threw her arms around the girl and tried to drag her away as Gregory reached her.

"Debbie?" he breathed. "What the hell are you doing here? How'd you get here? Where have you been?"

"Keep away! How could you do this?"

"I didn't! It was them! They're crazy!"

Terry could stand it no longer. The two of them were conspiring;

they were going to blame all of this on him. He raised his gun and fired a deafening shot into the ceiling. Everyone went silent.

"Enough!" He waved the gun at Debbie, Klein, and the agent. "The three of you will leave, and you'll tell your friends to go with you. We want you out of this town, now and forever. We want you to leave Shayla Hacker alone. You can tell the Pope whatever you want."

They exchanged glances.

"What's he talking about?" Debbie hissed.

Klein grimaced. "The girl they're all looking for—her boyfriend told them this story about the Pope and souls and demons. It sounds like bullshit."

The girl at the bottom of the stairs stirred. Debbie knelt by her. "Jackie," she whispered. "Are you okay?"

Terry advanced a couple of stairs and cocked the gun. "We want you out—*now*. You, the agents, everyone."

"There aren't any agents," Debbie growled. "What the hell is wrong with you people?"

"What do you call the man standing beside you?" Terry indicated Marlowe with the barrel of his gun.

The girl on the floor looked up at him and yelped. She started struggling to get away from him, but Debbie grabbed her.

"He's Shayla Hacker's father," Debbie said.

"No!" Jackie screamed. "He wants to be, but he's not! He just wants to find her like the rest of us. But we can't let him, because he's an awful man, and he led me to Egypt and he killed people!"

"Listen to yourself," Debbie interrupted. "Listen to what you've gone through." There was something about that sadness that struck a chord in Terry and made him cave just a little.

"Listen to everything you've sacrificed for a girl you don't even know."

"She's not just a girl!" Jackie said.

Debbie shook her head. "You're crazy. You've all gone mad. Think about what you've left behind for her. Think about everything you've been through. For what? For a pair of eyes." She nodded, advancing. "I've heard the stories, too. That's why I won't look at the picture. It sounds like bullshit to me, like science-fiction. If someone told me a month ago that you could go insane from looking at a snapshot of some crazy girl, I would have laughed in his face. But I've seen you people, and by God, that's proof enough for me."

Terry's gun slipped from his fingers, clattering to the floor. Everyone was looking at him, but he wasn't looking back anymore. He had heard Debbie Wendell, and in his mind, he had returned to the town, to the altar where he had abandoned Vicki Torres. It seemed like a lifetime ago, and what had he done since? What had he done that was worth leaving behind the woman he had loved? He had painted himself into a padded room with no doors or windows. He had been afraid of getting trapped, and he had made the world a prison.

He blinked, and when his eyes came open again, the man in the dark suit and black tie wasn't wearing a dark suit and black tie. It was a plaid, button-down shirt hanging from his shoulders.

Terry shivered.

"You've manufactured all of this," Debbie said. "These people—the 'agents.' They're just people. They're a search team. Some of them are police."

"That's not true!" It was Joseph Malloy.

"I'm a policeman," he told them. "My successor—Kelsey Robins – he's searching for Shayla, too. The way we are. He's not one of *them*. *They* knocked down my house!"

"Did they?" Debbie asked.

Did they? What the fuck kind of question was that? He thought of the rebuke in Jean's eyes, the way she had accused him of manufacturing reasons to keep his badge. Was it possible that he had knocked down his own house just to give the world a legitimate reason for his obsession with Shayla Hacker? To leave him with a period instead of a question mark?

Was it possible that for a time, obsession had even transformed him into *one of them*? Surely not. Surely.

It was sad more than anything else. They were beginning to see everything they had given up for no reason at all.

"Where is she?" Debbie asked the room at large.

"Who?" Terry sounded curt, indignant.

"Shayla Hacker. Where is Shayla Hacker?"

There was a rustle from the top of the stairs. One of the curtains billowed out, birthing a young man.

Jackie struggled to her feet. "Walker!"

When he saw her, the color drained from Walker's face. "Oh, Jesus," he said. "Jackie?"

The two of them ran for each other and met in the middle of the stairs, throwing themselves into a tight embrace.

When at last Jackie and Walker parted, they were both crying. "I'm sorry, Jackie. I'm so, so sorry I left you."

She gave him another hug, and then everyone looked to his side.

Marlowe approached. "Hey," he said. All of them could hear how hard he was trying to hold back the tears. "Hey, kid, it's me."

It was awful. Nobody moved. Even the air in the room seemed to freeze.

Debbie glanced about the room, searching for an ally or a kindred spirit. She locked eyes with Gregory Klein.

"Can't you even look at me?" Marlowe wept.

Debbie Wendell stepped forward and put a gentle hand on Marlowe's shoulder.

"He is looking at you," she hissed.

Everyone stared at her. Slowly, Marlowe craned his neck around until he met her gaze with pained eyes. "Not him," Marlowe said. "Not Walker. The girl."

Debbie shot a confused glance at Gregory Klein, who took a

faltering step toward her before stopping himself once more. "But there is no girl," Debbie said.

Terry watched as Marlowe got to his feet, turning his back on the girl. At his full height, Marlowe was an inch or two taller than Debbie Wendell. "You're mad," he said. "That or blind."

Debbie threw a glance in Gregory's direction—a pleading glance.

Were they in this together?

Terry blinked, trying to decipher it all. Suddenly, nothing made sense anymore.

Gregory swallowed. "She's right," he said softly. "We're the only ones here."

A tear rolled down Shayla Hacker's bony cheek, black as charcoal. It left a dark streak in its wake that looked like a bruise. Terry's stomach turned. For the first time, it occurred to him that something might actually be wrong with her.

"You're insane," Marlowe growled. "I can touch her with my own hands."

He spun around and reached out toward the girl. When their skin touched, something inside Terry's head snapped. It was like grinding teeth somewhere behind his temple. Like bone shearing against bone. He grabbed his head and yelled, but his ears heard nothing but ringing.

Terry lunged for her, collided with Joseph Malloy and Jackie Savage, who were also scrambling to reach the girl before something beyond their control pulled her away forever.

He was dimly aware of Debbie and Gregory backing away, their mouths open, their faces painted with matching expressions of perfect horror.

And then his fingers were wrapped about her arm. It was like velvet, liquid mercury.

Shayla Hacker threw back her head and bellowed. There was

no sound save a dull rattling in the depths of Terry's ears. Black smoke gushed out of her open mouth.

As though filtered through a glass jar, Terry heard what sounded like an infant crying in the distance. Was that a face in the cloud above Shayla's head?

Terry squeezed his eyes shut and with his free hand, dug his fingernails into his thigh until he felt sticky warmth in his palm.

It wasn't enough. Not anymore. Now, he needed to *feel*.

Gregory couldn't speak. Debbie bumped into him, backing away from the others, and he clutched her. She didn't shy away.

What unfolded before them was the strangest thing he had ever seen. Warren and Keeler hadn't moved since descending the steps. They stood off to one side, mouths open, just barely swaying. Jackie, Walker, Marlowe, Terry, and Joseph all grabbed at the air as though they were touching something much larger—as though they were touching God. They muttered inaudibly, like a chorus of corpses singing dirges to the living.

"There, there," Marlowe's voice stuck out. "It's okay, little one."

Debbie pressed against Gregory, unable to make herself look away.

For half a second, Gregory thought he heard the echo of a baby's scream.

Then, all five of them touched hands. Time seemed to stop. The air stood suspended.

It felt as though someone exhaled a breath across the surface of Gregory's brain. Pain. Blinding, insufferable pain.

"Goodbye." A girl's voice, sad but peaceful. He had never heard it before in his life, but he knew it belonged to Shayla Hacker.

The world spun. Gregory swayed, clutched at the air, and found himself leaning on Debbie, the two of them supporting each other.

He could see the loss in the others' faces, and for a brief moment, Gregory could feel a certain emptiness, too.

⟨※⟩

There was nobody outside the church when the nine of them stumbled through the weathered double-doors. They spent almost half an hour searching the town for their pursuers, but all they could find were some light footprints. Some of them—some of them almost looked like claws, strewn between the sweeping marks of long robes brushed through sand. Gone with the grace and expedience of angels—or something darker.

During the hike back up to the hills, none of them said anything to each other. It was not until she was seated in the back of the Taurus and they were out on the highway that Debbie Wendell could even find her voice.

"What happened back there?"

Gregory put a hand on her leg, threw her an affectionate glance.

"You really didn't see her?" It was Jackie. She was half-asleep, cuddled against the one person in the world she could still trust.

Debbie shook her head.

Jackie shrugged. "Then I don't understand either."

"She was carrying something that needed to leave." Debbie had thought Walker was dozing, but now he cracked one eye. "We helped her let it go."

"Her baby," Gregory said.

Walker nodded. "I could smell it on her breath—the little . . . what was inside her. The last time she told me she loved me, she said she had to go soon, or she might accidentally take me with her. She said it would happen to everyone. She said—she said I didn't need her anymore. None of us did."

"What does *that* mean?" Debbie said.

Jackie looked up at her brother. "We killed her, didn't we?"

Walker wiped his nose and stared pointedly out at the passing road. "What we killed was just an echo of something that had been gone for a very long time."

Gregory glanced over, checking his mirrors before changing

lanes. His eyes caught on Debbie's face, and for a moment, they stared at each other.

"So why didn't we see her?" Debbie asked into the silence.

"Because we didn't need what they needed," Gregory answered. "They needed her."

"And we needed *what?*"

Gregory just looked at her and squeezed her leg.

"I don't think you can measure it," Walker muttered, his voice now thick with sleep. "Just like I can't measure what I lost. I don't think that was the point."

Then she thought she did understand. This wasn't about Shayla Hacker. This was about Walker and Jackie, about Joseph, Terry, Keeler and Warren. About Gregory and about her.

But something had definitely happened in the church back there. She had felt it. There had been a presence in that room.

There had been a girl named Shayla Hacker. Perhaps, buried somewhere deep inside her, there still was.

Epilogue

When Debbie Wendell came out of the hospital room, her face was covered in tears. Gregory put his arms around her. He knew without asking what had happened. They'd called ahead before they got on the plane, and the doctors had told her that her mother probably wasn't going to live through the end of the week. If she'd had the money for an operation a little sooner, things might have turned out differently.

Gregory had offered to pay for one now, of course. He lived a comfortable life, and he had nothing to spend his money on. But it was too late. When he had explained his proposition to the doctor, the man had only shaken his head. It wouldn't do any good now. All they could do was enjoy the last of their time with her.

Slowly, they walked out of the hospital into the glaring sun. It was warm but pleasant, not moist and heavy the way it had been throughout the last few weeks. It reminded Gregory of Los Angeles.

A cool ocean breeze swept in from the beach, about a mile away. It smelled like salt, like the sea, like endless opportunity.

In spite of himself, he shivered, not for the cold, but because of what he feared was coming. He couldn't stand the thought of going back to his old life—not now.

For the past few weeks, for the first time in his life, he had

been a part of something larger than himself and his work. He had
been with people he could finally call *friends*.

Cautiously, he put an arm around Debbie as they walked.
That she didn't pull away was the greatest silent victory of his life.

Debbie turned to him as he fished out the keys. "Gregory,"
she said. "I have a confession to make."

He blinked, ready for anything at this point.

"I've been alone. All my life, I've been alone. And you know
what? I don't want that anymore."

"Okay," he said. "Neither do I."

Terry Young's heart leapt in his chest when he saw her. She hadn't
dolled herself up for this. She was just wearing jeans and a
T-shirt, and she had come with her father, but to him, she looked
incredible.

He rose, tossed the box of French fries into the trash, and went
to greet her. He opened his arms for a hug, but she didn't walk into
them. "Hi, Terry." She slipped past him to one of the diner booths
looking out on the open highway.

She and her father sat together, and when Terry slid onto the
bench across from them, he felt like he was facing a jury that had
already arrived at a verdict.

"This is going to sound like bullshit," Terry said. "Well, first
. . . I'm sorry, Vicki. Jesus God, I'm sorry."

"You're sorry."

"I was crazy, Vicki."

"Yeah, crazy about that girl from that picture you found."

"No. I was sick long before that. But I'm better now."

"Let's get something straight, Terry. I'm not here to patch up
our relationship. I'm here to give you your shit back and send you
on your way."

His stomach turned. "What?"

"It's too late for us, Terry."

"No, look—I went mad. I was mad, okay? But I'm better now."

"It's too late. I've met someone."

"What?"

She looked at her father, and he rose, allowing her to do the same. "Terry, I did love you. You broke my heart when you left, and some things can't ever be repaired."

"All I ever wanted was you."

"Sorry, Terry."

He cried in the attic for two hours that night, but he didn't touch the scars on his legs. Not once. There was enough pain without that. Really, there always had been. He'd just never been strong enough to let it out before.

Kelly Hoover wiped the mud from her hands and jumped to her feet. She bounded through the garden, in past the French doors to the kitchen sink. She rinsed herself, toweling off with a napkin just in time to grab the phone. "Hello?" she said, and then she listened for a few moments. "Just a minute."

She went back out to the garden. They had set up an umbrella with the picnic table, and Jean was still finishing off her lunch. She had offered to help, the way she always had all their lives, but Kelly had told her she had everything under control. She was just putting in a few rows of daffodils before it was too late in the season.

Jean took a sip from her lemonade and smiled as Kelly came back outside. "I love this," she said. "To me, this is paradise. It's a perfect temperature out here." She handed Kelly her own lemonade. "Who was that on the phone?"

"He's still on it," Kelly told her. "He wants to talk to you."

"Who?"

"Your husband."

Jean listened while Joseph tried to explain why he had abandoned her.

"Sweetie," he said, "it was just something I had to do. I think

I may have gone a little crazy for a while. I felt like it was the most important thing in my life, and I can see now just how wrong I was. Jean, I'm in love with you. Not the way we've sort of been in love since we got married, not in that stagnant bedside way. I'm madly in love with you. All over again. I have to see you, and if you tell me you won't take me back, I don't know what I'll do. I can't believe that I ever left your side. That should tell you just how crazy I was. But I'm better now. I'm better and I want to fix my life before it's too late. I know things haven't been great between us for a long time. I want to forget about all of that. I want it to be just like it was when we first got married. Can you do that, Jean?"

"No, Joseph. I can't do that."

There was a little sob on the other end of the line.

"I can't forget everything that happened."

"Please, Jean. I don't know what I'd do without you. Please take me back."

"Of course I'll take you back, you old fool. It can't be just like it was when we first got married, Joseph. It can be better."

And it was.

Rain hammered against the corrugated metal roofs of the school buildings. The other children darted from the covered walkways in front of the office to their parents' minivans or the steamy school buses waiting in a row beside the curb.

Jackie didn't run. She stood at the verge of the shelter, watching the droplets pound the sidewalks, splash up in the growing puddles.

For two weeks after her return, she had stayed after school every day of the week trying to catch up with all the work she had missed. Today was the first day she was allowed to go back to her old schedule.

From the outside, her life had changed little since she had gone searching for her brother that day. She was still the outcast of her class, still lost in thought more often than she was lost in a cloud of friends.

But Walker was there now. More *there* than he had really been for years. And Jackie was, too. She thought about Shayla Hacker every day of her life, but over time, she began to forget what her face looked like. One Saturday morning, she awoke and realized she couldn't remember it at all.

Jackie cried that morning. Then she got out of bed and forgot the girl ever existed. She was free at last to start a new life.

She just wasn't sure she wanted to anymore.